AN
IMMORTAL
SPY
NOVEL

THE
HANGED SPY

K. A. KRANTZ

The Hanged Spy; The Immortal Spy: Book 4
Copyright © 2018 by Kristine A. Krantz All rights reserved.
First Print Edition: November 2018

Cover and Formatting: Gene Mollica, LLC

Published 2018 by K.A. Krantz

www.KAKrantz.com

ISBN Print: 978-0-9862537-9-9
ISBN eBook: 978-0-9862537-8-2

Printed in the United States of America

Jenn
Woo, Woot, Wut, & Wine

CHAPTER 1

S hadowy dancers twirled on a continuous loop over crystalline walls courtesy of a self-winding music box. A towering cluster of glowing rose quartz provided gentle illumination. Incense of vanilla and star anise released lazy coils of smoky fragrance to coast through the partially collapsed tunnel within a dried-up cistern on the uninhabited Mid World of Vuornis.

Formerly uninhabited.

Now the population stood at one. Well, two if counting the quasi-sentient large metal Bi Xie with spiraling horns, massive wings, and a leonine body who guarded the tunnel. For all intents and purposes, Bix lived quite alone in this isolated haven. It was a fairly recent development, this new home of hers. Solitude wasn't ideal; she didn't like it one bit. However, it was necessary to protect her friends from the enemies who were hunting her. Enemies she couldn't recall due to missing two-thirds of her memories. Those forgotten chunks of her past included all knowledge of her family, her childhood, her first kiss, first job, first execution…hell, she couldn't even identify the potent magics baked into her essence. If it didn't happen in the last thirty years, she didn't have a clue, which was a huge problem when one happened to be a very old immortal.

For example, when, from whom, and why had she collected all the trinkets, totems, gewgaws, and doodads filling the cubbies that lined the tunnel? The fact the things were here was proof she'd brought them to her secret lair, but the brownouts she suffered whenever she reclaimed a portion of her displaced memories meant the actions didn't register in her conscious mind. She was still trying to figure out why her subconscious wanted these items and why now. Her best guess was they had something to do with the invading army trying to destroy the Mid Worlds.

The Mids were her home. Most of her friends lived among the greater collective, many of whom depended on the Mids for their continued survival. They couldn't leave to exist on some Other World like she could, and friends didn't abandon friends. Plus, she'd taken a vow to protect and defend the Mid Worlds from threats foreign and domestic. She was a girl of her word, so she stayed, doing her damnedest to figure out how to stop the bad guys while the leadership of the Mids got their acts together.

It was slow going.

All these thingamajigs she'd hoarded, and one of them, at least one of them had to be useful in this fight. She paced the tunnel, drumming a pair of carved batons against her thighs. She had no idea what the batons were. Hydra teething toy? Mermaid nunchucks? Frost giant toothpicks? The engravings in the porous glass-like material meant nothing to her. The pale turquoise color was pretty, and the batons stayed quite cool despite her touch. They radiated Upper World magic, which didn't clarify their purpose. Gods were the predominant inhabitants of the Uppers, and things that were trivial to a deity could be crucial to many other life-forms. So, knowing the batons' origin wasn't particularly helpful. The same could be said for each piece in her collection. They all emitted a magical signature hailing from Upper, Under, Mids, or Other Worlds. Museum placards with provenances and usage instructions would've been inordinately useful, but her subconscious wasn't a fan of writing things down. Alas.

Intense heat scorched her chest. The source? One of two

pendants she wore. Cursing, she hunched forward and balanced the burning pendant atop one of the batons. The pendant contained the Phoenix's dewclaw cupped by a shrunken angel wing and a dragon wing. On the surface, it looked like some new-age goth jewelry. In fact, it was a means of keeping a loose connection with the lone dragon-angel hybrid who was the living wellness gauge of all Mids' magic. In the food chain of Mids' indigenous peoples, Feng the Phoenix was at the top. Feng was also a literal pain.

"Feng, what the hell?" she groused to the owner of the dewclaw.

A cubby near the entrance to her humble abode flashed purple, then blue. A soft hum two octaves lower than that of the music box spilled from the shelf. Returning the batons to their proper place, she headed for the unexpected noise. A singing bowl with gemstone inlays in the shapes of flames glowed. As the sound of humming built, an image formed above the hollow of the bowl. Feathered red hair, cold aquamarine eyes, haughty angular features, and a thin Sir Francis Drake beard.

Behold, Feng the Phoenix.

"I have so many questions," she said to the hologram of a head.

"Bix? Where are you?" Feng scanned his surrounds. "Wherever it is, Mids' magic is feeble there. It's taken more than a little effort to locate you."

"Yet you achieved it," she noted drolly. Vuornis was her sanctuary. She had a lot of enemies, most of whom she couldn't remember but who remembered her quite clearly. They'd attacked her last home, and that was a godsdamned military base. Keeping her bolt-hole off everyone's radar was the entire objective. As much as she loved company, she tried to minimize the dangers of associating with her. She stayed in the Mids to be accessible, so her friends and allies could reach her, usually through the ley lines to which her smartwatch was connected. However, leave it to Feng to initiate a bowl call or whatever this was.

"Only because you're in possession of a chunk of the original

Phoenix's egg." Feng looked pointedly at the bowl in which he was floating. "That egg is as old as the first Mid World. It's believed all fragments were lost to time. Do you have any idea of its value to the Dragon Horde or the Angelic Host?"

"Religion isn't my thing. Neither are idols." She wagged the hot pendant. The closer she brought it to the bowl, erm, egg fragment, the clearer Feng's image and voice.

"That's because you've met the idols." His smile was fleeting. "Are you alone?"

Bix glanced at the Bi Xie sitting silent guard. It would animate only if she was threatened, but it probably heard everything, kind of like those voice-activated home assistants. Thankfully, it didn't spontaneously order bulk underwear or dollhouses. "Yep."

"As promised, I've been translating the ramblings of a dying man, searching for nuggets that'll help us combat the Devourers. A lot of it is useless paranoia; however, he frequently mentioned the Chimera's tracking system." Feng's inflections combined with his European polyglot accent made him sound quite the disapproving academic.

The Devourers were a foreign army of deities determined to consume every last bit of magic native to the Mids until all that was left were the toxic vapors of the anti-gods' existence. They were militaristic, hard to kill, and patient. They'd been creeping into the Mids for the last five years, entering below everyone's radar until very recently, when Bix and her team had stumbled upon a covert op in which the Devourers had been involved.

"I don't really have a system," Bix demurred, eyeing her stash of goodies and wondering if her subconscious did.

"Figured," Feng drawled. "I reached out to a few of my old contacts in the Consortium for any hints. There was a defense initiative, about thirty years ago, that never made it out of committee. It was a program intended to track you. They called it Project Resen."

The Consortium of four superpowers—the Fates, gods, dragons, and angels—who were *supposed* to be protecting the Mids were instead plagued by a traitorous faction tearing the organization apart from the inside. Time was running out for the good guys to mount any defense against the Devourers. The native armies of the Mids were helpless against the race of anti-gods who fed on the magic of these Worlds. Only gods could kill anti-gods, and the pantheons were part of the Consortium and its infighting. The superpowers were politically hamstringing each other while the enemy was advancing troops and setting up camps right under the Consortium's nose. Bix and her team were doing their best to save the Mids through information gathering and exposing secrets, the art of spycraft, but there was only so much they could do without the Consortium unifying behind the crisis.

"If Project Resen died in committee, why do we care?" She spoke to the hologram and to the doodads in the shelves to see if any of them reacted to the name. Names held power; though it was a long shot, it was something. Something that amounted to nothing. Okay, then.

"We care because Resen was conceived to track *any* entity that wasn't native to the Mids. That would mean Resen could track Devourers." Feng's holographic gaze followed her as she paced. "The pantheons put the official kibosh on it."

"Because it would track gods too. They hate anything that ruins their mystique." She snorted. "However, I do note your use of the term 'official.'"

"Exactly." He nodded. "The other superpowers quietly pursued the initiative off book, trying to keep it below the gods' radars. However, the pantheons weren't kidding when they said to drop it. They raze, smite, and annihilate any location and any individual that is so much as rumored to be associated with Resen's research."

Gods subsisted on the life experiences contained within a soul. Once a mortal life ended, that soul was hand-delivered to a hungry god. Any mortal anywhere in the R&D chain—including friends and family—could've exposed the entire operation to the pantheons.

"The gods don't mess around when they're united against something, which doesn't happen often." She knew of only one other time the pantheons had all been on the same page, and that was when they'd exiled her from the Mids a decade ago. The fact she was back irked a lot of them. "With the arrival of the Devourers, have the pantheons relented in their absolute stance against Resen?"

"There's hemming and hawing on the political front. Meanwhile, the pantheons' operatives continue scorched-earth protocols." Feng shook his hair from his face. "I've done a bit of snooping around—part of my therapy is to put myself in unfamiliar situations for varying durations—and the last two leads I had ended up vivisected. The entrails were warm when I found them, so I was clearly on to something."

For a time, Feng had been the Consortium's lead investigator, until he'd spent five years being horrifically tortured by some extremely disturbed individuals. While his body had mostly recovered, his PTSD kept him sidelined from being in the thick of the fight. That his therapists were encouraging him to reengage in moderation was a good thing. Sort of.

"Dude, I am thrilled you want to be in the field again, but don't go antagonizing gods on your own," she chided. "Yes, you can probably handle yourself with the lesser gods, but if they gang up or invite a midrange…I don't want you to backslide because you tried to go it alone. There's no shame in working with a team."

"On that we agree, which is why I'm bringing Resen to you now. I wanted to have more for you before turning it over, but…" He glanced down and away.

"But you can do research while my team and I do legwork," she supplied. "We live to get our hands dirty. You can be the analyst while we play operatives. Twinkie and knuckle draggers, an age-old partnership."

"As your *twinkie*," he said with mocking disdain, "I can tell you the Dragon Horde ceased all endeavors on Resen fifteen years ago. I confirmed that with the reigning queen. She will openly back any build efforts that survive the pantheons' sabotage. Until then, however, her resources are committed to ferreting out the traitors inside the Consortium."

"Okay, that leaves the Houses of Fate and the Angelic Host as potential R&D patrons."

He pulled a face somewhere between hesitation and constipation.

"What?"

"The Angelic Host is poised to move immediately on any build specs that come their way," Feng unloaded in a rush.

"The Houses of Fate are spitting in the eye of the pantheons? Wait, that's not a surprise. If anyone would, it's the Fates." She waved that aside. "Let's focus on the part where you want me to steal from the Houses, then hand over their research to you so you can deliver it to the angels, whom I despise."

"I'd never dream of denying you the opportunity to rub the Host's nose in the fact you got the goods they couldn't," he countered indignantly.

She grinned. "Why don't the Fates invite the angels over to dinner and give it to them?"

"Resen is intended to track *all* non-native entities," he reminded.

"And Fates evolve into Other World entities." She sighed. "They want to control the data without third-party interference. They want to control Resen to hide *their* movements while exposing mine and the gods. Tricky little shits."

"I realize Resen impinges on your ability to protect yourself. It exposes you and makes you quite vulnerable. I wouldn't mention this if there was some hint at an alternative." Feng had the grace to appear passably concerned.

"Yes, well, Resen's tracking *will* be a problem for me. However, the Devourers are a problem affecting all the Mids, so I'll deal with the consequences of Resen once it's up and running." She shrugged off his apology even as her mind was scrambling to find the exceptions and the loopholes. The Houses hadn't backed off researching Resen in thirty years despite the gods, which meant the Fates had something viable. It would be best for her to be in on the construction to learn how Resen tracked non-native entities. If she and her team got the build specs and reviewed them before handing them over to the Host, then maybe there'd be an opportunity to ensure she wasn't subject to tracking. Maybe. Bigger issue remained: save the Mids. If Resen could pinpoint where the Devourers were staged in the Mids, then the pantheons' strike teams could wipe them out instead of haranguing research facilities. Yes, it was a reactive defense, but it was way more than they had now.

"If—and it's a mighty big if—a Resen research facility still exists, and if their research is sufficiently advanced, then a team who can defy the gods needs to be the courier for the Host," Feng added. "There is only one such team. Yours."

Bix steepled her hands in front of her mouth. "We'd have to leak it. Whatever the intel is that the pantheons are trying to quash, it would have to go so wide that they can't erase it without erasing the Mids. That's the only way the Host will have the breathing room to build Resen. The Fates will try to gain control once it's built, but that's an issue for later."

"It's an issue for the Consortium to address, not us, in any event," he urged. "I can help with equitable dissemination if you'll let me. We can use the ley lines to store the specs. Deploy some type of genetic encryption to keep the data from going too wide, possibly limit access to just the superpowers depending on the information."

"Sounds like a good plan, and since it involves Mids' magic, I'll leave it with you." She pointed at the bowl. Mids' magic didn't like her. She couldn't wield it one whit. The best she could do was piss it off, which she did merely by existing. "I'll take the lead on finding out if there is an operational Resen research station and if they have any data worth stealing. If they do, then my team and I are on it."

Asserting she'd find a secret facility was pretty ballsy considering her best leads would alert the Houses of Fate to her interest. The Fates would retaliate with distractions and arrange for disastrous obstacles to pop up in her path. Those obstacles could be deadly for her team of current, former, and aspiring spies. While she was immortal, her teammates weren't. Trying to negotiate with the Houses on the up-and-up wasn't a good idea either. The Fates were contrarians to put it nicely, and compulsive liars to be frank. They were agents of chaos: grand, glorious, unexpected chaos. They had a better grasp on the future than most, but they made sure no one else did.

She could ask the Fates' chosen warriors what they knew about Resen, but she didn't want to tip her hand to the Houses. She could hack the Cross-World Intelligence Guild and see if they had any records of Resen. But, again, that would alert the Fates. There was really no place in the Mids the Fates hadn't woven their eyes and spies. If she got too inventive, the gods would notice and a whole other can of worms would open.

"Don't suppose you have a plan for how you're going to do this?"

"Short of shouting 'ready or not, here I come'?" Once again, she scanned her shelves of knickknacks for anything that looked promising. "This is going to have to be a game of misdirection. The Consortium, including the Houses and the Host, needs to think I'm after something else. Someone else, even. I'm better known for hunting people than data."

"Which person do you have in mind?"

"Um, hold that thought for a sec," she said with distraction as her attention kept returning to an ornately carved box of marbled red and black metals in the fourth row of cubbies from the floor. On the lid was her sacred symbol of the seven-sided pyramid. Her fingertips prickled as she retrieved the box. It was slightly larger than her hands. Heavy. Without an obvious lock, yet it was sealed.

A thirty-second GIF surfaced amid the mess of her memories from a forgotten lifetime. Hands she recognized as hers opened the box and removed a deck of cards. Tarot cards? Of a sort.

Better described as a precursor to Tarot. The emotions tied to the memory were smug anticipation. Her head throbbed as her mind sought the vocal track that belonged to the memory. Ah, there it was. Her voice, chilling and disdainful. The language, ancient Greek.

Ask the question. Let the cards decide life or death.

Hmm. Of the many allusions made to the original Chimera, no one had mentioned her affinity for prognostication. On the other hand, it wouldn't surprise her if the old Chimera had been screwing with the poor sod whom she was going to execute regardless of what card was pulled. High Executioner for All Worlds had been her cosmic duty back then. On the other-other hand, the execution orders had come from third parties, so maybe the cards had been a means for the accused to appeal to whoever had issued the order?

One way to find out.

The last time she'd encountered something of hers sealed without a lock, the pyramid had been the key. She pressed her thumb to the raised symbol. Tiny prongs popped from the metal and molded to her skin. With a hiss, the box top slid forward, releasing wisps of arcane magic.

Goose bumps rose along her arms, and her heart sped. Fear? No. Yes? Okay, a little bit of fear, but she recognized the resonance of the magic that was older than the gods and the titans. It wasn't her magical signature. It belonged to a faceless überentity with whom she'd recently struck a deal: the überentity would help her save the Mids from the Devourers in exchange for her springing it from some cosmic prison. Yes, there were all manner of bad things that would likely come from her living up to her end of said bargain, but these were desperate times…and she was desperate for a clue to Project Resen. If this was a way to communicate with the entity, it would explain why her subconscious had added the cards to her collection.

She pulled the deck of cards from the box, then returned the box to its shelf. The card stock was solid yet made from eternal night. The backs of the cards were a blackish teal that shimmered with the faintest hints of silver and gold. The fronts of the cards were…blank. Truly magical decks were always blank until the entity powering the deck answered the call of the inquisitor.

No answers without a question.

"Bix, you still there?" Feng prompted.

"Hang on. I'm going to try something." Possibly something stupid, but she didn't need to admit that to Feng.

During her early years as a spy for the Cross-World Intelligence Guild, she'd gone undercover as a fortune-teller in a circus filled with magical beings. Part of her training for the gig had been to learn cartomancy in all its many facets and forms, which included Tarot. Little did she know that the new Chimera and the old had shared an affinity for communications through cards.

Shuffling the deck released small tendrils of black smoke that wrapped around her hands like lacey gloves. The trick with imploring a greater entity was to push the request to the fore of one's mind, because greater entities liked to snoop through a supplicant's brain to get to the root of the issue. Also, they were nosy, wicked, and bored. Fiddling around in a lesser's mind gave the long-lived and immortal a fleeting moment of entertainment. Making the question the flashing neon sign in one's mind urged the greater entity to focus on that specific topic.

"Which person is most willing and able to lead me to Project Resen?" Bix asked aloud as she mentally repeated the question over and over while shuffling the cards. Crouching, she fanned the deck facedown in an arc on the floor and repeated the question.

A gust of primordial magic surged within the tunnel, scattering the cards, blacking out the quartz illumination, and silencing the music box.

"What the…?" Feng gasped.

The metallic screech of the Bi Xie awakening to defend Bix echoed throughout the cistern.

Shadows ripped from Bix's spine, slithering across the floor and walls, shielding her collection and her guardian. Darkness lived within Bix as part of the mist and midnight of which she was made. It responded to her needs in tangible or insubstantial states. It could act as anything, be it weapons, spare appendages, or as connections to the greater pool of limitless night. In this instance, her shadows merely waited, gauging the potential of an attack. Yes, she'd asked the überentity for assistance, but cosmic forces tended to misjudge the fragility of a World. Sort of like Godzilla loose in Tokyo. She wasn't at all sure the überentity could harness its might to just a Tarot card.

A red-and-gold glitter bomb exploded at the end of the tunnel, blinding her but not her shadows. Her darkness caged the burst, touching the displaced essence of the überentity. The entity didn't fear her darkness, nor was it susceptible to its fiercest attacks. In truth, it engaged with her like an old master and she was the whippersnapper. This contact, this connection of darkness to darkness was pure emotion, amused indulgence alongside rampant curiosity. There wasn't a lick of malice or spite.

It was being helpful, just as it had promised. Okay. Good. Good.

"Stand down," she called to the Bi Xie.

A whuff and a grumble answered.

"Bix, is everything all right?" Feng whispered, his voice fading. "Bix? Bix?"

"For the moment." She closed her hand around her hot pendant, giving as much physical reassurance as she could while the coruscation dimmed to form a very large 2D image in the space where the main tunnel ended in a cross tunnel that led to her bedroom. It was a card, stretching and straining as pixels painted a portrait.

The Hanged Man.

Specifically, a variation of the Tarot card of the Hanged Man, larger than life and in full-color animation. All Bix could think was *dislocated hips*. It was inevitably her first thought whenever she encountered someone suspended by their feet, which happened more frequently than gravity should allow. Gym rats with inversion boots hanging from a bar like some Dracula extra. Aerial acrobats in the silk ribbons like that fierce pop singer with the awesome hair. Then there was the braggadocious tyrant of the one-foot suspension, immortalized on some Tarot decks as the Hanged Man. Odin. Dangling from the branches of Yggdrasil, the Tree of Life, in his quest to become omniscient. Gods were really big on that whole all-knowing, all-seeing reputation, which was total malarkey. None of them were all-knowing, and the ones who could pull off all-seeing refused to do it because of the resulting migraines.

As for the meaning of the Tarot card of the Hanged Man, it encouraged viewing life in a new way. Reversing perspective, relinquishing deeply held opinions, and sacrificing self-interest. Sure, some folks interpreted the card as being ominous. Those folks resisted change, like say three of the four superpowers.

The man trapped in this card was absolutely being treated to a new perspective, along with a brain aneurysm and asphyxiation if someone didn't cut him down soon. His long braid of raven hair with streaks of gray swung with each wriggle and writhe. His ankles were bound with green rope, dangling him from something beyond the image's reference.

It was the Hanged Man's recognizable sneer that soured Bix's guts. That sneer caused a dimple next to the left nostril. The angrier the man, the deeper the dimple. Yes, the face was older, heavily lined, and profoundly scarred. The skin tone was ruddier due to the flush of being inverted. However, a younger version of this man held a place in her recent memories. He'd ridden her ass for months and not in the fun way. He'd been the number two in command of the first Dark Ops team to which Bix had been recruited. Forever up in her grill about dumb shit, he'd hated her for being Other World and for being a girl who enjoyed being a girl. She'd refused to conform to the man mold he believed every operative had to adopt to be an effective team member. If it hadn't been for their team leader, she'd have stranded this guy in the middle of a fae matriarchy every time he stepped outside his lane.

Then the day had come when he'd stepped on a Leshy land mine. Boom. Dead. Purportedly.

Waylon Nez.

A name she'd never forget. She'd personally delivered his remains to HQ. He had a star on the wall for fallen agents. So, twenty-five years later, why was she staring at an image of him alive? And why did a cosmic überentity know about her old teammate?

Bix ambled to the giant card and reached out a hesitant hand, half expecting to grab the Hanged Spy. The instant her skin brushed the foreign presence, the invading darkness vanished from the tunnel and with it, the überentity's resonance. The card shrank to the common size with a whisper of masculine laughter. Bix caught the card before it hit the floor. The back of the card was the dark teal of her deck. She headed for the dawning light of the quartz to closely examine the card and the man writhing within it. No, not within it. It was a reflection of some place. A closed window with a view. Curious. She studied the details of the background and invoked her gatekeeper magic to open a path to Nez.

Denied. Not enough detail in the card to identify the location. Without a clear image of the origin and the destination, she couldn't create a passageway. Well, so much for this being an easy mission. Probably should've rephrased her question to include the "where" along with the "who." She briefly contemplated asking the überentity for a clarification card but opted not to push her luck. The more powerful the entity, the more easily annoyed they were. Treating one like a glorified GPS wasn't in her best interest. There was bound to be a reason the überentity had given her a *picture* of Nez and not the man himself. Figuring it out was part of the message.

"Bix?" Feng's hologram beckoned. "Bix, are you okay?"

"Yeah." She used her darkness to collect the rest of her deck strewn around the tunnel from the überentity's arrival and departure. "I requested a clue, and the powers that be gave me one."

"The location of a Resen research site?" he asked with incredulity.

"Nope, an old Sage who may or may not have ascended to full Fate since last I saw him." Bix scratched her nail over the card's face. It didn't seem to affect the Hanged Spy.

"If the powers that be are lending a helping hand, then it looks like we have a mission green light to deliver the build specs for Project Resen to the Angelic Host." Feng tapped two fingers to his temple in a salute. "When you're ready to propagate the data, you know how to reach me."

His hologram faded and her pendant cooled, leaving her alone with the Tarot card of the Hanged Spy. A lot of emotions roiled through her, not a one of them a warm fuzzy. This op was starting off with a lot of maybes and one big ugly.

A spy who should be dead. A Fate-owned research station. A potential cross-World defense system that could ruin Bix's life. So. Much. Winning.

Gah.

What she needed was an objective point of view, like one from her original Dark Ops team leader. Her erstwhile boss and Nez's.

CHAPTER 2

A muffled masculine scream put Bix on alert as she stepped through gates into an unlit penthouse of white floors and pastel mosaic wall tiles in Rosslyn, Virginia, Primary Mid World. Linen sheers in long windows overlooking a snow-covered terrace diffused the city lights from surrounding high-rises and granted a warm contrast to the blizzard raging on this stormy February night.

Deep orange and red gel glowed around a leg wrapped from toes to high thigh in a compression boot riddled with pins. The demigod attached to said leg bowed his back and shouted into a fuzzy white pillow as the compression boot contracted. Blood dripped from the pins to a pile of towels carefully arranged between the coffee table and the aqua couch.

Bix froze. Her hands flew to her mouth, muting her cry as she watched her former boss and dear friend writhe in self-inflicted agony. Twice more, the boot drew blood. Twice more, Ashtad Ba'al howled into his pillow. His unseasonably tanned skin glistened with sweat, and his lightly scarred chest rapidly rose and fell.

"Impeccable timing as always, Bix," Ashtad gasped through the pillow covering his face.

Bix lowered her hands and cleared her throat. "At least this time, I arrived at your front door instead of dropping on the couch?"

"That would have been more of a surprise than either of us would've wanted." He gestured to his lap and to the low-cut briefs he was wearing…the only thing he was wearing other than a torture device.

"Never going to unsee that, man-kini," she teased as she took a seat at the white marble desk abutting the back of the couch.

"Like our second op together didn't require you to trail my naked ass around a kitsune bathhouse while I ingratiated myself with a weapons dealer." He lifted the pillow off his face and stared at her flatly. "I recall your commentary on the pattern of my leg hair provided the team months of amusement."

"What? The hair on the back of your left thigh swirls like mouse ears. Famous mice have famous theme songs. Sing-alongs are proven morale boosters." She pointed to the compression boot. "You want to tell me what's up with the iron maiden?"

"Not particularly." He tossed the pillow at her. "Put this in the laundry hamper, will you?"

"After you tell me what's going on with your leg," she insisted.

"Nothing you need to worry about." He winced as he pushed himself to sit straighter. He had a lean, ropy body with the slightest slope to his shoulders. The kind of build fashion designers loved, and he loved them in return. His closet was bigger than his bedroom, with a shoe collection that rivaled hers. Even at his most slovenly, he exuded modern elegance. Yet for all his pretty, he was faster and deadlier than a viper. At least, he had been. Whatever the deal was with his leg could change things.

"Try again." She poked the damp pillow. This thing had absorbed a lot of anguish. "We run missions together. I need to know if you're not a hundred percent."

"We didn't have a problem the last mission, so stop mothering," he snapped.

"That's funny coming from a supervisory special agent who

knows damn well why it's important I know your deal for both our sakes." She stood and rounded the couch, planting one hand on her hip and waving the pillow. "If you're worried I'm going to stop asking you for help, I'm not. If you're worried the only help I'll let you lend me is from the bench, again not going to happen. I'd never screw you out of the dangerous feats you need to ascend to full godhood, but you need to do me the courtesy of telling me what's going on so I can allow for this new...facet of you."

He glowered at her. She glared right back. With a groan and sigh, he unlocked the compression boot, revealing an expanse of thick white scars running from midcalf to midthigh. The scars had been gouged and torn by tiny maces attached to the pins that allowed his blood to drain. His leg looked like ground beef still on the cow.

"The scar tissue thickens to the point I lose flexibility and some muscle control. The nerves there are completely hosed and not coming back. If I don't thin it out, I can't bend my knee. That's what the boot does. It reinjures the tissues so I can have movement again." He carefully bent his knee, cringing. Streaks of electricity born of his innate magic shot from his fingertips and danced over his wounds, arresting the bleeding.

"Boon and bane of a demi's accelerated but not yet divine ability to heal." She nodded, clamping down all unwelcome emotions. Grim shit came with the job, so a tizzy over injuries merely served to piss off fellow operatives. "Okay. How long does this temporary relief last?"

"Two, three days. After that, I'm on the cane until I can get back to the boot."

"Don't fight the cane, Ashtad. There's a whole lot of sex appeal in a man who can blend dignity with vulnerability." She headed for his bathroom and the laundry basket therein. "If you get hurt on a mission, is the boot a new component of our first aid kit?"

"I keep it in the bottom drawer of the vanity in there," he called. "Get a good look at the case. Self-sterilizing."

Bix inspected the case, its placement in the vanity, and three spots he'd likely hide the case if it ever became necessary. As long as she had a clear image in her mind of the origin and destination points, she could open gates. Her proximity wasn't required.

"What do you want done with the bloody towels?" she asked as she returned to the great room.

"They're payment to the gnomes who built the boot." Ashtad rifled through a first aid kit on the cushion beside him. "House brownies deal with the delivery. You can leave the towels where they are."

Some Chwedlonol—the catch-all category of mortal magical races native to the Mids—believed that obtaining the blood of a demigod would compel that demi to grant them a favor once the demi ascended to full godhood. Ashtad had never made policing his blood an issue, so either there was no truth to that fable or Ashtad was banking on strangers demanding favors once he ascended. Gods granting favors always screwed over the requester. It was a favorite pastime of the divine; however, people who believed they were owed a favor were people who believed. Gods needed believers because gods needed to feed from their souls. Ashtad might subsist on standard human fare as a demi, but a smart demi planned for the future.

"You got a minute?" She perched on the coffee table to inspect the damage he'd inflicted on himself.

"A minute is about all I have. What's up?" He read the label on a bottle of iodine, then tucked it back in his kit.

She showed him the Tarot card of the Hanged Spy. "This guy look familiar?"

He reached for the card, then snatched his hand back with a yelp. "That's not meant to be touched by the likes of me. That is older than titans' magic there. What did you do, Bix?"

"I asked for a clue and got this. It's Waylon Nez." She dangled the card in front of him.

Ashtad paused with a roll of gauze half out of its sterile packet and grunted. Didn't say anything, just grunted.

"Your old number two? Not dead after all? Why don't you seem surprised by any of this?" She noted the laptop. The hour. The boot. The lack of reaction from her old boss. "Son of a... how long have you known he wasn't dead?"

"About two weeks after you'd been exiled, he made contact." Ashtad set about wrapping his leg. "Gibbering that we had to get you back, that you had to return to the Mids sooner rather than later. Sadly, he didn't have a plan for how to make that happen, so all I could do was concur. Never heard from him again."

"Nez, wanted to *help* me? Like that's not suspicious." Bix scoffed. "Does the CWIG know he's alive?"

While Bix had been disavowed by the Cross-World Intelligence Guild ten years ago, Ashtad was still an active covert agent. His mission was to find who inside the guild was leaking intel and getting operatives killed. Reporting to the director of the CWIG, Ashtad had a lot of access and a lot of leeway. That leeway allowed him the public-facing job of seneschal for the demigods working through their trials in the Mids. He was extremely well connected in the shady demi and shadier Chwedlonol communities, and his association with the infamous Chimera had boosted his reputation.

"There's always some conspiracy theorist or overly enthusiastic analyst who thinks they see old spooks around every corner. Yes, there are blurry photos supposedly of him that could've been anybody. Nothing concrete, nothing meriting opening a case. It's filed away with a hundred other cases of suspicious sightings of former or deceased agents." He made it down to his knee with the gauze before motioning for her to take over. "When he reached out all those years ago, he said he was deep under for the Consortium. Knowing we have a leak, I didn't say anything to management. I noticed he had more leaves, so I chalked up his faked death and promotion to his Fate-based trials and left it alone."

For each trial a Sage completed, a leaf was tattooed on his body. The health of the leaf reflected whether the Sage had passed, failed, or come out at a draw. The markings started at their arms and progressed along parts of their torsos, shoulders, and necks. For those who lived long enough to ascend to a Fate, they had a nice neck ring of autumnal foliage.

"Now you're prepping to go after him, hence the ground thigh?" Bix bandaged Ashtad's leg as she'd been taught in the CWIG academy. She'd done this for pretty much every member of her Dark Ops teams at one point or another. They would've done it for her too if she had skin that wasn't mostly invulnerable. "How'd he contact you this time? Dead drop?"

"Sent a Mayday. Didn't bother to encrypt the message." He gestured to his laptop. "His location is under attack. Gods, it seems. Breached the facility's outer security. Transmission ends with a door exploding off the hinges."

Gods attacking a site in the Mids. Where a Sage was undercover. Not just any Sage, but Waylon Nez. The call must have come from the last Resen facility. Hot damn.

"Who'd you pull for a team? Demis?"

"It needs to be a thread-free operation with no ties to the Consortium or the CWIG so we don't tip our hands to any Fates who might be working with the gods." Ashtad zipped up his first aid kit and tested his bandages, wincing slightly as he bent and straightened his leg. "Demis don't have threads, and they're not employed by either group. It's a mission tailor-made for us."

Threads of destiny were the domain of Fates. Every Chwed and human contained a soul provided by the gods. The dragons and angels created the body to house the soul. The Fates stitched the soul to the body. What body, what race, what destiny, what expiration date, and what kind of Mids' magic the individual could wield were all defined by a Cycle of Souls contract. Since each superpower derived sustenance from the beings produced by the contracts, those contracts had become the foundation of the Consortium. Being in breach of a contract was a very bad thing. Terminating a contract before its agreed-upon expiration date broke the contract, which was why gods going after Fate facilities staffed by Sages—who were technically human—was ample fuel for political pissery.

No wonder the Consortium couldn't get out of its own way to defend the Mids.

"A thread-free op, eh?" Bix sniffed, giddy on the inside. Nothing quite as affirming as hearing her own hesitance to alert the Fates echoed by her mentor. "I get that you don't want to blow Nez's cover. Where is he?"

"Nice try, but no. I can't let you in on the action." Ashtad stood with more effort than a man about to go on a mission should. "The demis and I have been the go-to group for ops that can't be linked back to anyone long before you came on scene. Your return hasn't changed that. It can't change that. You *can't* stop us from questing for godhood."

"Wow, sorry, didn't mean to push a button there." She held up her hands in peace and closed her eyes, not wanting the up-close view of his briefs. They'd always had a sibling-like relationship, which was why his junk near her face was never intentional on either of their parts. "You guys can have Nez. However, I need access to his facility before the gods raze it. He might've been working on something that could detect Devourers in the Mids."

"And gods want to destroy it? We thinking it's the faction inside the Consortium hitting his site?" Ashtad hobbled away, cursing as he bumped into the couch hard enough to make its legs scrape across the floor.

"Most likely it's legit sanctioned by the pantheons to keep the Fates from getting one over on the gods." She watched Ashtad's unsteady gait as he shambled toward his closet. "Which is all the more reason to let me tag along. Speed being of the essence. According to the image on this card, the gods have strung up Nez in the short time since he sent his Mayday. There's no one speedier than a gatekeeper when it comes to transportation."

"You used to beg like this when you were a probationary agent after I'd benched you for defying orders," he chided. "Remember the Houdini job?"

"I remember I nailed the prestige," she chuckled. "I also remember Nez was pissed at me because I left him in the tank longer than he wanted, even though I had to because he wasn't selling his panic to the audience. The ningyo drowned air breathers on the regular. They needed more convincing than his ego had planned to accommodate."

"It was *your* ego that needed to be reined in," Ashtad countered, grabbing his cane from its resting spot by his desk. "You'd put the mission over the team. That was the moment Nez stopped resenting you and started fearing you. He wasn't the only team member to have that response. Took me forever to break you of the mindset Hades had instilled while he was teaching you the basics of living."

"Relationships matter more than the task," she huffed, echoing Ashtad's routine chastisements. "Perfection is isolation. Flaws allow others to get close to you, for better and worse. If you're going to really live, you have to be imperfect and respect imperfections when you encounter them in others, blah blah blah."

"By the gods, you actually listened." He paused in the doorway to his closet and pointed at his laptop. A single shot of electricity woke it from its sleep state. "Put your smartwatch on the keyboard, then type: *Bix is a pain in my ass.*"

Curious, she did as he directed. His screen went red. Text in a huge font appeared.

Greetings, Bix. Copying Bug Protocol. Please stand by...

From the gap between the V and B keys, two thin black filaments emerged. Slightly thicker strings of black came next, followed by the thicker rubbery body of a literal technology bug. It crawled around the metallic bands of her smartwatch twice before inspecting the seams of the watch proper. It pushed itself around the projection lens in the side of her watch. A heartbeat later, her watch face lit up.

Greetings, Bix. What data shall we find today?

"Ashtad," she breathed with delight. "You saved my tech bug? I thought I'd lost it forever."

"I backed it up and set it to propagate in new hardware on command. All you have to do is send a text to me with that access code from anywhere in the Mids, and it will download a new tech bug to your device." He smiled and rolled his eyes. "Yes, you're welcome. I've seen the abuse you inflict on technology, and if data is critical to this mission, you're going to need your beloved bug."

"Thaaaaaank you." She reclaimed her watch and stroked it like a pet. "Does this mean I can join your demi team?"

"Nez's message is on my desktop. Take a look while I get dressed. If you want to be helpful without interfering in our challenge, set up a triage station for Nez and whatever survivors we can rescue. If there's anything left of the facility after we get the people out, I'll call you."

"I could be in the facility while your demi squad dukes it out with your fully evolved elders," she argued, hitting Play on the saved video message. It was Nez, all right. More leaves, but none that marked his ascension to full Fate. Dude was still a Sage. Yes, he had a lot of scars, some likely leftovers from the Leshy land mine. Twenty-five years had not been kind to his human body. Point zero zero one percent of humans were selected to run the gauntlet to Fatehood as Sages or Oracles. The rest of humanity didn't have a lick of magic; they grounded it, which prevented Worlds from being ripped apart by conflicting and disparate forces. Too bad for humanity, Nez had been chosen to be among those who decided the futures of lives yet to be contracted.

Strangely enough, absence had not made her thoughts of Waylon Nez any fonder.

"If the infamous Chimera, High Executioner for All Worlds, suddenly arrives on scene, you'll make the situation worse," Ashtad reasoned, his voice carrying from his humongous closet as she watched the video of Nez's Mayday message. "One god detects your presence and they'll call in reinforcements, especially if this is a sanctioned burn. We'll lose everything and everyone. We could lose the whole World, including the data. Stay away. Got it?"

"Got it, yes. Like it, no. Wait, Zamarad? Nez is on Zamarad?" She bolted up from her seat and pointed to the monitor. "The World where a single spore of pollen is bigger than a burger?"

"Based on the background in the cursed Tarot card you have, it would seem the gods have taken the prisoners outside where the flora fights back. With any luck, the environment of Zamarad has bought us a bit of time while the gods battle nature." Ashtad exited his closet, dressed in jungle camo and stuffing a respirator mask in his go-bag. His limp was slightly less than a few minutes ago but still noticeable. "But before you get too excited, you did notice that the facility proper was breached in that video, right? Any hardware is probably toast. Whomever we can drag out of there might be your best chance at recreating the data you've already lost."

She side-eyed his laptop. "The data is there. It's got to be. It's imperative we get it."

"Set up the triage. Standby for evac." He finger-combed his dark curls into a short ponytail. "If we all play our part, we all get what we need."

She slapped the Tarot card against her palm and grunted.

"Trust me. Trust my decisions. You used to be able to do that, remember?" He tugged his camo ball cap low over his brows. "How about you move me to the Rosslyn Metro station, eh? Got a team to rendezvous with."

"Don't you dare let anything happen to you on this quest, or I will end Worlds in my grief," she cautioned as she dropped him through gates. His soft guffaw lingered.

Alone in Ashtad's apartment, Bix closed his laptop and put it away in the hidden compartment in his desk. He never left it out. It held way too many secrets. Sure, they were encoded and encrypted out the wazoo, but he knew better than to leave temptation lying around. Leaving it out meant his mind wasn't firing on all cylinders. Whether he was worried about the op, about the scarring, or about the demis on whom he was relying, she didn't know. Whatever it was, she didn't have good feelings about it.

Standing between Ashtad and his pursuit of full godhood was something she'd never do, no matter her misgivings. He was well over three centuries old, hardly new to the game. As much as she wanted to prevent bad things from happening to him, she functioned on a grown-ass-man theory. Adults should know themselves better than anyone else, and if they didn't, they had to be allowed to make the mistakes that would teach them.

And as badly as she wanted the Resen specs, nothing was more important to her than Ashtad's friendship. He hadn't cut her out of the mission, he'd given her a role, and every role was important, even if it wasn't on the front line. Besides, the überentity might have shown her an image of Nez instead of the Zamarad facility because the physical records were already destroyed as Ashtad had said.

Nez might be the last hope for Project Resen.

That was a horrifying thought.

Right, then. Triage. Wounded mortals. One of whom was a Sage. She could wield a mean bandage, but more than that was beyond her. Good thing she knew a guy who knew a thing or two about battle injuries, Sages, and secret facilities.

CHAPTER 3

Golden sparks fell like rain and hopped along a concrete floor. The metallic tang of smelting rode the air inside a large commercial garage. A pair of wide rolling doors opened to the Chesapeake Bay lapping at the docks of Smith Island on the border of Maryland and Virginia, Primary Mid World. February's bitter chill combated the heat kicked up by the blast furnaces. An old box radio blared incomprehensible chatter from the top shelf of a banged-up toolbox. A '47 seafoam blue Indian motorcycle was parked on a pneumatic lift table. Deeper inside, a fine green haze of blended magic swirled around an iron pentagram set within a circle of sigils. The sculpture was large enough to mount a pair of angels with wings wide. A gas-driven welding engine roared against the winter tides.

The seven-foot blond controlling the arc and chipping the flux had his broad back to the water. Not even baggy overalls and welder's gear could make the man look bad. His wealth of hair was knotted in two buns, high and low, with the helmet's strap bisecting them. Tiny holes in his snug white T-shirt seemed to bait his muscles to go ahead, complete the rip, engage full stripper shredding. He wore a different prosthetic tonight, eschewing his usual rubber-coated robotic arm for a matte metallic contraption of claws and spikes that looked better suited to rip out an enemy's entrails than metalcraft.

Bix leaned against an overly tall, beat-to-hell workbench covered in tools and appreciated the view. There was something about a man so completely focused, so committed to his action, that a girl *had* to ogle the way his body met the demands of his mind to create a thing of beauty.

The pentagram looked nice too.

The welding engine slowed its growl and powered down. The stump of a welding rod joined the pile of steel midgets still casting faint wisps of green magic. The clamps securing the circuit were removed from the metal table. One thick glove came off. The helmet set atop it. One meaty hand unhooked the overall's straps, allowing the weight of the brass buckles to pull down the bib and back. Only the blond's wide stance kept the bottom half from ending up at his ankles.

Slowly. Ever. So. Slowly. He worked his T-shirt up his heavily tattooed torso, over his obscenely broad shoulders, off his frame, and tore it free from the prosthetic.

Sweaty cotton smacked Bix in the face.

"Tobek," she squawked, holding his damp, stinky shirt at arm's length.

"Sweetheart." He chuckled low and wickedly as he rehooked one strap over his shoulder, keeping his pants up as he sauntered to her. "To what do I owe the pleasure of your searing regard?"

"You know, there's a somewhat famous movie scene of a muscular sweaty dude getting his kink on while welding." She flung his shirt at him. "It's even got magic in the title."

"First, it was a grinder. That was the visual pun. Second, if you want to see an all-male review, the boys in the battalion put on one every year for charity. Third, I prefer an old-fashioned waltz." He stuffed his shirt in his back pocket. "You, however, are more than welcome to use that table as your stage in any manner you desire."

"With you as my captive audience? Do I get to tie you up too?" She stepped to him, purring in the back of her throat as she gently tugged his braided beard. She held his bright blue gaze, the vibrant color a result of his lifelong commission in the Mid World Army as a Berserker. Berserkers were the Fates' contribution to protecting the Mid Worlds, a tax imposed by the Consortium. Tobek was older than…well, she wasn't sure how old he really was, only that he'd outlived civilizations and probably a few Worlds. He was also the commander of the Berserker battalion and had spent assorted lifetimes as a doctor. If anyone could patch up a passel of researchers who might or might not be human, this smexy old fart fit the bill.

Tobek's laugh lines showed as he loomed above her, letting her play with his beard like a cat with a toy. "I am more than happy to take the detour to the gutter you're offering, but I don't think you're quite ready for how it will end."

"No screwing one's roommate, that's a rule, right?" She patted his chest.

"We don't live together anymore." He waggled his brows. "But you keep finding your way to my bed."

"When I'm *asleep*," she countered. Traveling while she slept was one part ingrained defense against things that had hunted her during her prolonged stay in the highly destructive ether that surrounded the Mids, and one part the result of her gatekeeper magic responding to her dreams. Where her mind went, her body followed. Her brain tussled with the inconsistencies about Tobek a lot, about who he really was, about her old relationship with him, about why she'd never freed him from the Fates. There was no denying they had a strong bond, an indescribable entanglement that was far more than the way his magic pushed and pulled at her whenever they were together. She carried an actual piece of him inside her, and he a piece of her. Their relationship was extremely complex and strange. Possibly par for the course when it came to immortals; however, she hated her ignorance of their entire shared history. Despised it. Loathed it with enough vitriol that it fed the thicket of malice living inside her.

Thing was, he couldn't tell her anything about their sitch. It wasn't a question of wouldn't; it was a matter of couldn't. She'd cursed him to silence way back in the days of having all her memories, way back when she knew all kinds of awesome and awful stuff, way back when she'd been the High Executioner for All Worlds.

Then the day had come when Devourers had staged their first assault on the Mids. She'd used all her magic to rebuff them, which had left her adrift in the ether as a hollow shell of an immortal entity. But, before she'd gone off to save the Worlds, she'd divvied up her memories among seven Mid World Guardians, gods whose magic was interwoven with the Mids. She'd reclaimed three of those seven memory segments. Once she reclaimed the other four, she'd know who was who and what was what. More importantly, she'd know how to destroy the faction of traitors inside the Consortium and the Devourers they were aiding. She might even know how to bypass Resen's tracking system.

Knowing what to do about and with Tobek would be a relief. Maybe. Hopefully. Thank the powers that be that he held to a personal code of ethics that allowed this flirtation without taking things further. As often as she crashed his bed, he could easily interpret that to be something it wasn't. She had way too much baggage when it came to intimate relationships. After seeing her last lover shredded into mincemeat, there were some mental blocks that would make being in a real relationship with her a great disservice to her partner. Tobek deserved better than that. For now, all he asked of her was to stop stealing his covers. Stealing his T-shirts was fine, though she preferred the laundered ones.

"I can sense an unwanted presence in the garage with us. Care to tell me what's going on?" He turned off the radio, silencing the chatter in languages she didn't understand. She'd reportedly forfeited her linguistic omniscience when she'd handed out her memories.

She tugged the Tarot card from her wide belt and held it up for his scrutiny.

One blond brow shot to his sweaty hairline. "Tarot? That damned entity is conversing with you via Tarot?"

The überentity had once taken an interest in Tobek, a let's-see-what-happens-when-I-make-you-scream-like-this interest, so Tobek's hostility was understandable.

"To defeat the Devourers, I'll take help from anywhere." She pointed to Nez writhing in his inverted state. "I need a clinic or a triage station for civilians caught in the divine versus semidivine crossfire. Urgently. Suggestions?"

"My resources are at your disposal." Tobek cleared a spot on the edge of the table and wiped it down with grimy rags. He motioned for her to sit. "What races are we dealing with?"

"I've got one elder Sage, and the rest I can't be sure." She tried hopping up on the table that'd been built for an extremely tall dude. Tried. "Safe to assume they're all magic aware."

The Consortium had a strict policy about keeping humans ignorant of the Chweds coexisting beside them. Humanity, as a race, had yet to mature enough to sit at the adults' table. Myths, legends, and religions were as much as humans were allowed to know unless those humans were Sages, Oracles, or Berserkers. Those three groups usually learned the truth after their souls were damned.

"Expected numbers?"

"No idea. At best, it's an entire research facility's worth. At worst, Ashtad and his demis snag one or two." She had to use gates to hoist her petard to the tabletop. "I wouldn't trust these guys near the coal plant. I'd treat them more like enemy troops. Necessary for the intel they hold but don't leave sharp objects nearby."

"Okay, that narrows the options quite a bit." He sported his easy grin. "Do you think the gods will be in pursuit of the survivors?"

"Abso—" Bix stopped speaking as red light streaked around the garage, flashing from the four corners without the normal accompanying siren. Tobek's brows furrowed.

"Excuse me. Emergency call from home." He rounded the worktable. His natural hand glowed green from his magic. He thrust that hand into a wall of toolboxes and cabinets. The illusion of rusty drawers dissipated, revealing a fifty-inch wall-mounted monitor. The MWA logo made two rotations on the screensaver before a familiar face appeared. Broad nose, bronze skin, head shaved save for a center stripe of black tied in a high ponytail. Xipil, Tobek's second-in-command of the Berserker battalion.

"Pardon the interruption, Chief," greeted Xipil in his usual reserved manner. "We have a code nine coming from station seventy-seven."

"Any system reboots?" Tobek detached his prosthetic and swapped it for his usual high-tech one. The medieval torture device went into a deep drawer that locked with a set of gore-stained fangs instead of a standard cam lock. Welcome to a high warlock's wall of weird.

"No, sir. No response from onsite security either. All communications have been severed. Station is dark." Xipil's gaze cut to the sides, most likely checking the screens surrounding his workstation. A flurry of activity accompanied glimpses of burly men rolling behind him in ergonomic office chairs. The call was coming from the operations center inside the renovated coal plant that served as the battalion's base in Old Town Alexandria, Virginia. For a short time, Bix had lived with Tobek and a third roommate in the basement of the plant. It'd been a twenty-four-seven testosterone fest, and she'd loved every moment of it.

Alas, she'd brought too much danger home one too many times, so for the safety of the guys who'd taken up arms in the name of her causes, she'd opted to move out. She was immortal. They were long-lived. She'd recover from whatever the baddies did. They might not.

"This is how the other ones started. Task the green team." Tobek toed off his work boots and dropped trou in front of Bix.

"Calling up the green team." Xipil tipped the boom of his headset into place. His muffled commands trickled through the garage's computer.

"Sweetheart, those untrustworthy civilians, where are they

right now?" Tobek hauled a mud-brown combat uniform from a locker in the wall of wonders.

"Zamarad." Bix looked away as Tobek changed. Ogling him while he was clothed was harmless fun. Doing it while he was near naked was one piece of temptation too far. It wasn't that she hadn't seen him in his long briefs before. It was about respecting that line they tried to hold until she had enough knowledge about their past to provide informed consent to any shenanigans in their future.

"Damn it," Tobek groused, slathering on deodorant. "Xipil, confirmed attack. It's the gods again. This time, there's a demi team trying to counter. There might be survivors for a change. Tell Gurp and Runjit to prepare for offsite triage. Let's wake up the Church of the Templars in Luz to prepare for survivors."

"Waking up the troop at Luz now." Xipil reached behind him, snapping his fingers. "Runjit, medics on deck. You're going to France to patch up Sages. Grab the goblin on your way."

Muffled commentary drifted across the connection.

"Will Bix be providing transportation, sir?" Xipil listed in his chair and raised a hand in greeting as he peered at the upper corner of his screen.

Bix waved back. Aw, man, she missed hanging with the guys. "I will if you send me all the necessary pictures of Zamarad, the facility, the church, and the town of Luz, please. And so I'm clear, that alert is for downed comms? Did it just come in?"

"Indeed, to both questions." Xipil was one of the oldest dudes in the battalion, but he looked like the young'un in the group. It amused the guys no end to watch him get carded buying booze at the local haunts.

"Code nine is a distress call that is automatically sent when any system is taken offline without proper authorization." Tobek zipped his tactical pants and stuffed his big feet into combat boots, using his magic to lace and knot them.

"Something's hinky." She checked her smartwatch as the alert for incoming images chirped. A tap on the small screen projected the pictures along her forearm. "The timing is off. Ashtad got the

Mayday from Nez over an hour ago. The end of the message is the facility being breached. Why didn't your alarm go off sooner?"

"Once upon a time, there were close to four hundred Fate-operated research stations across the Mids. Over the last thirty years, they've been systematically destroyed. Station seventy-seven is the last one. It's staffed by Sages and Oracles pretty far along in their trials." Tobek yanked on an olive-green Henley, covering the bulk of his ink and the prosthetic. "My guess is the folks there learned from the demise of the other sites and established appropriate protocols. Your friend on the card? He might have been on the forward line."

"The sacrifices." Bix swiped through the images Xipil had sent of the locations, starting with Zamarad. "Nez was trained to survive torture as part of his tenure with the CWIG. The gods are interrogating him and the rest of the front line while the others... what, escape? To where? To whom?"

"To us," Tobek answered as he pulled on his uniform jacket and zipped it. "The Mid World Army was tapped a little over a decade ago to aid the evacuations. Sadly, by the time we get the alarm and get on-site, there's nothing but smoldering embers."

"Well, now you've got a gatekeeper, so let's get your boys there spit-spot." She did a double take at him in uniform. It was the first time she'd seen him in anything denoting his name, rank, and battalion insignia. It was brown combat gear and not dress blues, but, ohai there.

"Green team is ready for Zamarad on the stage in the classroom." Xipil scanned his monitors. "Runjit and the medics are standing at the back of the classroom. Pushing preferred destination images now."

"See you on the other side, Xipil." Tobek hit a fat aluminum button, blacking out the screens and killing all the electricity in the shop. The bay doors rolled down their tracks and thudded into place. Lock bars snicked. Alarm lights dimmed. The only illumination in the shop came from the green mist still swirling around the pentagram sculpture.

"The pentagram's not done yet, so no absconding with it, yeah?" Tobek put on his gloves, strapped oxygen tanks to his back, and attached the supply tube to a full-face respirator mask before shutting his locker. "I'm sorry to cut short our visit. You know I enjoy spending all the time I can with you."

"I'm trying really hard not to interfere in Ashtad's demi challenge, but if *you* need me for more than relo, do not hesitate to tag me in. Okay?"

Tobek paused with his mask half on and cupped her cheek. "I love that you care so much and so deeply."

"Is that a 'yes, dear'?" She half smiled and leaned into his touch.

"Move the green team first, then me. I'll send an image when we're ready for exfil." He fit his respirator over his face. "Give Gurp five minutes to break the wards at the church before you start moving Sages and demis. The men at Luz will secure the patients. Runjit's team will provide medical support."

"Evasion noted." She checked her watch for the infil site at Zamarad and created gates connecting the classroom in the coal plant to the war zone. "Good luck, and watch out for the pollen."

She opened a gate in the garage and deposited Tobek with his team on Zamarad. The next round of gates transported the medical group from Virginia to France.

Since Tobek had killed the call with the coal plant, Bix tapped the silver cuff around her ear, triggering her comm. "Xipil, the boys are relocated, confirm?"

"Teams have left the building, safe to close the gates," Xipil answered. "We don't want any unfriendlies sneaking through."

"Closing gates." She lifted her hand to cut the connection but paused. "Hey, Xipil? It's good to see you again."

"Likewise, Bix. You've been missed." Xipil ended the call, leaving Bix in the eerie silence of the garage.

With Tobek's absence, the natural magic of the waterfront town settled. There was the batch of native and mixed magic collected around the pentagram Tobek had been working on when she'd arrived. Nothing else, though. She half expected a Fate to be lurking, or a god.

Gurp and Runjit needed a few minutes to get the pop-up clinic running, and she didn't need to be on-site to evacuate folks once Ashtad phoned it in. What she needed was the Resen data, and failing that, Waylon Nez alive and kicking.

She grabbed the Tarot card and studied Nez. If this was a live feed, her old teammate wasn't doing so well. Although an elder Sage, Nez was still human, which would put him in his early sixties. Being inverted and tortured for over an hour had to be straining his heart to near fatal levels. Plus, he wasn't wearing a respirator in that overly pollinated air. It would take time for Ashtad and the demis to get to him, time he probably didn't have.

Well, shit.

How to do this? How to ensure Nez survived without Ashtad or the gods realizing what she'd done? How to make sure Tobek and his guys didn't run afoul of the gods while trying to evacuate the other researchers? How to be a safety net without getting caught in her own webbing?

Overwatch. Yeah. That was it. She'd play overwatch. They'd never know she was there because she technically wouldn't be. Overwatch would allow her to see everything while being available to relocate the teams the moment the calls came. And if she had to extinguish a fire in or around the facility to protect the data, well, she'd blame it on the environment defending itself.

"Okay, Bug, show me three Worlds closest to Zamarad. Sort based on direct sight of the Fate facility."

Gathering data…

A slideshow of images painted her forearm. Gates opened.

CHAPTER 4

Being on Zamarad was akin to being a Lilliputian in the redwood forests of northern California, if the redwoods were fruit-bearing trees and shrubs shedding desiccated leaves heavy enough to crush a man's bones. Overripe fruit on the ground created impromptu gummy streams from the flowing juices and fed fungus that could dissolve an elephant in two hours. Maneuvering through the mulch and undergrowth was like scaling an unstable mountain range. Massive insects and arachnids were the primary means of transportation for anyone stupid enough to go on a nature walk.

It was all very icky and sticky, which made Bix extra happy not to *be* on Zamarad. She existed on a World adjacent, using viewing gates for remote reconnaissance of the fecund World. The hundreds of Mid Worlds fit together like florets on a head of broccoli. Ether existed as a highly destructive separator between Worlds and as a somewhat protective moat beyond. Bix had learned a long time ago how to sandwich a sliver of ether between gates to permit her to see a World in sepia tones where only potent magic registered in color.

The entire World of Zamarad emitted a curious pale bluish-purple aura, the likes of which Bix had never seen before. Nor had she ever encountered a basket weave of fine green lines radiating forty-odd miles around a structure bearing strong similarities to a huge Cylon centurion's helmet. Green magic usually denoted Fates, but individual Fates couldn't expend enough magic to cause the vibrancy of the weave at which she was looking. That had to be done by the Houses of Fate, as in multiple Houses, as in a coordinated effort. Unless…

Could the weave be a functional prototype of Resen? Had the researchers moved beyond the theoretical to the practical? Had switching it on alerted the gods to the facility's location? Gods were definitely on the ground. Little splotches of red pinpointed their locations. A baker's dozen, about five miles out from the station. From the looks of it, most were lesser gods, with one midlevel likely calling the shots. That was not going to be an easy win for Ashtad's team, but it would be a worthy challenge if the demis survived it.

"Bug, scan the mesh below and retain data. Identify interruptions and irregularities in the pattern. Try to identify the power source." Bix held her watch over the viewing gate. If she was looking at Resen in its nascent stage, no way was she going to skip gathering the intel left in plain sight.

Scanning… Analyzing… Two interruptions and thirteen irregularities identified. Power source unknown.

"Holy hell, they did it. They really did it," she cried under her breath. "Bug, show me the interruptions."

Bug projected the grid along her arm and circled two locations. She started with the site farthest from the facility. If she was right, the interruptions were gates: the one she'd used for Tobek's team, and the other used by Ashtad's team. Thirteen irregularities, thirteen gods, probably not coincidental. Gods didn't use gates to move around. The specifics of how they did it varied by deity, as did what and who they could take with them. She was willing to bet they'd come with little more than their innate magics to take out a bunch of mortals.

The weave had caught it all. Resen worked. At least in this little test area.

Verify. Definitely verify before jumping to conclusions.

Bix layered gates, pushing in on Zamarad with all the advantages of cosmic zoom. The most remote interruption spot was in a grove of ginormous pomegranate trees. Beautiful from a distance and up close. There were downed fruits spilling killer seeds aplenty, and an ant army conveying a dozen humanoids wearing camo. Gas masks obscured the faces of the riders, who were more than likely Ashtad's demigod team. Getting a whole ant army to be the cavalry had to involve a demi's power. They were heading at top speed toward the gods.

Site one verified.

Bix redirected to the second location seated amid an orchard of blueberries. Ding, ding. Just like the pictures Xipil had sent her. A swarm of beetles burst from the shrubby cover with big, burly dudes armed to the teeth along for the ride. She retreated swiftly. Didn't matter what gear Tobek had on, she could identify him purely by the way he carried himself, even when he was hell-bent on the back of a flying beetle. Tobek wouldn't detect her until she was on top of him thanks to the gates, but better to play it safe. No need to alert anyone to the fact she was almost-there.

Two sites verified.

"Congratulations to station seventy-seven. Applause all around. You've won a mass evac by the Mid World Army's finest. Go you," she cheered in her best announcer voice as she doubled back to the station and the nearby gods-versus-demis skirmish. It would suck to be this close to a defense against the Devourers and have a bunch of gods screw it up. "All right, Nez, wanted or not, I got your six."

A thicket of raspberries awaited her with thorns twice the size of grizzly bears. The prickly vines had, at one point, overtaken taller shrubs and shorter trees, winding around them as though they were trellises. Fat berry clusters resembled bloats of hippos, bouncing and swaying as gods applied their magics to torture the half-hundred hostages they'd suspended in all sorts of grotesque manners amid, over, or on the thorns. The gods held their forms to the size of minor giants, big enough to frighten the researchers but not so large as to squish them with unintentional movement. The gods stayed well below the canopy of the thicket; hiding themselves from anyone who might come looking, like, say, a choir of angels or a flight of dragons. The gods' appearances and their attire ran the gamut of pantheons. They were a blended team. Judging the frequent glances they cast toward the midlevel goddess in a long patterned mudcloth dress and matching headscarf, the goddess was the team leader.

Bix didn't recognize any of them.

The attention of the gods shifted from their helpless prey to the army of ants marching along the twists and tangles of the raspberries. The demis had split up, each traveling with their ants along different sections of vines. By all appearances, it seemed Ashtad's strategy was for half the demis to function as distraction while the other half rescued the fifty-odd humans who'd come from the research center. Alas, a cursory sweep revealed many of those researchers had died unpleasant deaths. A few were alive and twitching, but Ashtad would have to clear each body to know for sure. This whole rescue could've been so much easier for him if he'd allowed her to run transportation *and* overwatch. She could easily tell him the Oracle to which he was hastening had a thorn through the back of her skull. However, he was running lead on this, and she'd learned a long time ago the consequences of going rogue on a team op.

Speaking of teams, where was Waylon Nez?

Bix pressed closer, remote recon sparing her the struggles of navigating the hostile terrain. She moved through jumbles and barbs, unaffected by that which existed on Zamarad. Around her, the vines swayed, not the casual chaos caused by a breeze. No. They were untangling, straightening, creating a wall, a corral. Bix backed up, adjusting scale and searching for the cause.

A pair of camo-covered demis stood atop a hill of ants at either end of the thicket, mirroring coordinated dramatic gestures. Nature demis, vegetation, harvest, whatever they wanted to be called. Ashtad had drafted a pair of them to Zamarad. Brilliant. Their machinations made it so much easier for her to locate Nez dangling like a dying fish from a thorn midway up a stiffening vine.

Probably ought to make sure her old teammate was alive.

She opened a small gate and slapped Nez, hard. He jerked in his bindings, dropping a small silvery cube into the stream of raspberry juices cutting through the newly formed battle arena. Cactus-green eyes snapped wide. Yep. Alive. And the smack felt deeply satisfying. Maybe she had some unresolved issues with Ashtad's former number two, like that time Nez had summoned her back from leave on an urgent mission to record an illegal weapons deal slated to happen on a drow naval vessel. She'd grabbed the gear, set off solo for the mission, and while lying in wait for the meet to go down…the ship had gone down. As in exploded. As in he'd sent her to the scheduled sinking of a decommissioned ship. The look of fury on his face when she'd returned sodden but whole was hard to forget. That was the point she'd realized Nez hadn't merely wanted her off the team, he'd wanted her dead. He hadn't known she was immortal. Even if he had, it probably wouldn't have stopped him from trying to disprove it. The navy incident had been the start of many progressively violent attempts to kill her.

Leaving Nez in the tank during the Houdini job had been a dose of retribution, the first she'd done in full view of the team. That was what had scared Nez, the realization he was no longer safe in the presence of others. Whether Ashtad had known the extent of Nez's sabotage and had privately addressed it with his second, or whether he'd allowed it to push Bix into being a better agent, she couldn't say. All she'd known for sure was that narking on teammates was a quick way to get drummed out of Dark Ops. She'd wanted so desperately to belong that she'd held her tongue, endured, and studied Nez's go-to tricks.

The gotcha with Sages was that every one of them had a hardcore knowledge addiction in a very specific field. They hungered and craved in the truest sense of addiction, complete with suffering from overdoses and withdrawals. Nez's expertise was in behavior. Why people and powers did what they did, and how to get them to do what he wanted them to do without them realizing it. Oh, he was good, so good that even their teammates hadn't recognized when they were being played. Sometimes Ashtad had known and sometimes he hadn't. Bix had learned a lot from Nez during their escalating games of tit for tat. Then he'd stepped on the land mine.

That'd been twenty-five years ago, and she liked to think she'd matured a bit since then. A wee bit, at least. So she closed the gate and waited a World away at Nez's side while the demis engaged the ascended gods.

The sepia filter of ether prevented her from seeing the brutality in color, while the gates prevented the sound from coming through. Pops of red brightened as gods wielded their magic, trying to cut off the demis from the researchers. A few of the demis retaliated by aiming at the ground on which the gods stood. The demis might not be as powerful as the gods, and their magic didn't register through the filter, but the results were obvious in the few instances where their counterattacks landed. Each demi had some kind of magic at their disposal—the type of which was determined by their lineage and their trials.

Oh boy, was this a trial.

This skirmish had started out with potential, but it quickly favored the gods. Four demis perished in one coordinated attack by the gods, leaving only the harvest demis to provide cover for their peers trying to rescue the living Sages and Oracles. The goddess in the center of the arena placed her hands on her hips and leaned back, laughing. A wave of the goddess's hand, and the ants supporting the harvest demis turned on each other, biting off heads and ripping off legs. The harvest demis plummeted toward the fatally sticky stream.

Beetles tilting like X-wing fighters through the rigid vine walls caught the harvest demis before they hit the dangerous ground. Bix's heart grew three sizes as Berserkers paired off with the remaining demis, providing cover as the ants and their riders gathered survivors from their places of torture. The Berserkers wielded their weapons with enviable mastery to deflect divine attacks and to free researchers, swapping roles back and forth with the demis as needed. Tobek was the only Berserker possessing magic, a magic the god squad grossly underestimated.

He used it now.

Bix cheered as two gods took direct hits and poofed out of Zamarad. Gods couldn't die, but they could be grievously injured. Physical recuperation times varied, but their egos rarely recovered.

Wait. If the Berserkers were here, where were the researchers they were trying to evac while the sacrifices distracted the gods? Had Tobek's team stashed the survivors somewhere? The beetles weren't carrying spare passengers other than the harvest demis. She'd blame the lack of a call on testosterone but were there girl demis in that mix…who might not know a gatekeeper was waiting in the wings. Gah and grr.

"Bug, verify we're able to receive communication from Tobek and Ashtad," Bix asked of her smartwatch.

Verified. Open a connection?

"No, we'll wait for the boys to call. Just wondering why they haven't." Bix placed her hands on her hips and drummed her fingers against her leather skirt. "Tobek has an excuse. Ashtad doesn't."

Once a Berserker's battle lust was evoked, there was no pulling them back. Berserker rage made the guys faster, stronger, and unable to tire. It did not, however, make them invulnerable, and the gods took full advantage of that.

Berserkers fell along with demis, crashing to the ground. Some moved, some didn't, some wouldn't ever again. The instant the bodies separated from their flying destroyers, Bix moved them to the clinic in Luz. Relocating the monstrous beetles to France was no bueno on so many levels, so she couldn't grab them midflight. To hell with the fact Tobek and Ashtad hadn't tagged her in. Their teams didn't need to die when she was *right there*. She'd deal with whoever's ire later.

The goddess in the center of the melee snapped her head toward a gate as it winked shut. Her high-arched brows furrowed. She walked a slow circle, her eyes cutting right and left.

"Oopsie. Might have put that last gate a little too close to the shot caller," Bix mumbled to no one in particular.

One lone beetle spiraled up the vine from which Nez hung, chased by an ant. She recognized the hand movements of the demi on the ant as Ashtad calling forth a huge ball of electricity.

A flicker of color across the thicket caught her attention. Red grew bolder as the goddess in the center summoned her magic. A faint spot of green grew brighter in response. Tobek. Amping up. The goddess twisted toward Tobek and raised her hands...

Bix's hackles rose. No, not hackles, her gatekeeper magic. Someone was initiating a—

A flare of dark gray burst across the filter of ether. A heartbeat later, everything bleached white, the surge of great power obliterating her view.

The cuff on her ear crackled.

"Bix? Bix? Mayday, exfil, exfil," Ashtad shouted in her ear. "Devourers attacking. It's a godsdamned army of them. Mayday, exfil."

An image of the vine through the antennae of an ant painted her arm.

Gates opened.

CHAPTER 5

The intensity of color arrested Bix as she crossed fully into Zamarad. Not only was everything on this World bigger, it was more vibrant. The scents were overwhelming, cloying, and nauseating. Heart-wrenching sounds assailed her in an atonal symphony of pain as insects and plants alike wailed their agonies. Bolts of dark gray toxic magic cut through the wilds like lasers, destroying the native beauty. Scorching it. Rotting it. Filling the air with a thick miasma of poison.

Berserker, demigod, and god alike broke off their skirmish and faced the gigantic invaders of gunmetal-gray skin, long black hair woven through crowns of silver horns, and nipple-baring bronze uniforms. The anti-gods marched in columns of five through a portal of undulating liquid mercury at one end of the raspberry arena. A stable portal. Since when had Devourers mastered the programmable portals?

Fuck.

A scream from low and left jerked Bix's attention to the battle being waged as a demi took a bolt of Devourer magic square in the chest and melted in a puddle of bubbling crimson. Bix's stomach flipped. She located Ashtad clinging for dear life to the stem of a leaf. Nez hugged Ashtad's bad leg. Boiling body parts coated half of Nez. Their ant was nothing more than a smear along the trunk of the vine. Its head split in two, antennae still wagging. Bix could only guess that the Berserker covering Ashtad had met a similar end as the ant.

Gates moved Ashtad and Nez to Luz. Primary mission completed. The next round of gates transported any Sage, Oracle, demi, or Berserker showing any signs of life. The Berserkers astride the flying beetles she had to leave lest she unleash Mothra's cousin on the Primary Mid World.

"Bug, call Tobek," she demanded, expanding the relocations to the unconscious, the dead, and any body parts attached or unattached. "Force the connection if necessary."

A blast of gray magic sailed past her ear. More bolts followed as Devourers took note of her presence. She opened origin gates in the paths of their discharged magic and the destination gates within the ranks of the anti-gods, turning their magic against them. Devourers fell, but their comrades continued to march, high-stepping over the bodies of their wounded.

So much for no one left behind. Dayum.

"Sweetheart, I know you've been spying on us." Tobek's gruff voice came through crystal clear. "Wondered when young Ba'al would invite you to the show."

Ashtad would forever be "young Ba'al" to Tobek since Tobek and his battalion had taken in Ashtad when the young demi had first arrived in the Mids to begin his trials toward godhood. Tobek had a thing about names. He never used her given name. It was always "sweetheart," just as Ashtad was "young Ba'al."

"So much for you calling when you got the survivors, eh?" she snarked. "I can't move your guys while they're mounted unless you have a stable for monster beetles on another World and a picture you want to share with me."

"There are no survivors of the station beyond those the demis were able to save."

"What about the data servers? Did any of the hardware make it?"

"Sweetheart, priori—"

"They built a god-tracking system that works, Tobek. We *have* to get the data," she interjected.

"Roger that. We'll pull back to the station and check it for anything salvageable," he answered quickly. "The Devourers are headed straight for it. Defense is up to you now."

Alas, the Berserkers were just food to the anti-gods. Nothing the battalion could do would slow the Devourers. While the gods could've at least tried to kill the Devourers, they'd run like the cowards they really were. All except their leader. She stood to the side, watching the Devourer army march and not doing a damn thing.

"I'll give you cover, but no laggards. It's not going to be pretty out here once I shift to the offensive." Bix continued to dodge the Devourers' attacks, relocating herself often as she created circular gates to fell the enemy with their own weapons. "That includes you, Tobek. I mean it. Don't distract me by making me worry about you being caught in the crossfire."

"Take out their portal," Tobek said as the buzz of his beetle in motion confirmed he was moving somewhere. "Stop more of them from coming through."

"We need it to understand their science," she argued. "I'll move it someplace in the ether and let the gods have a run at it. The useful gods, that is, not this bunch of idjits."

"Destroy it," he insisted. "We can't risk the Devourers reclaiming it. Be smart. Be strategic. There's a time for intel and there's a time for action. Destroy the gate."

"If we can learn how to sabotage their means of accessing the Mids—"

"Swallowing a gate like that with another will create a vortex, a black hole," he interrupted in a tone that spoke of experience. "Fine if your goal is to blow this World and the neighboring ones."

"I could just move the station instead," she offered. "Then blow the World…and its neighbors?"

"Sweetheart," he drew out the word, lightly chiding. "The

native species of these Worlds deserve to live, not to suffer for your convenience."

"Nice way of making me the asshole." She scowled. "Are you clear yet? Can't have your eyes lighting up the darkness like floating targets."

"We're clear one mile from the station. Forward line of Devourers is at two miles." He sighed over a curse. "Mind the goddess. I know her, and she knows the old you."

Said goddess darted amid the ranks of the Devourers and threw out her hands. Devourers turned on each other, breaking formation. The goddess's laughter was rich until the first spatter of Devourer blood boiled her skin. She shrieked in horror as twice more she was caught in the trajectory of the infighting her magic had wrought. The goddess's dress and skin burned as if doused by sulfuric acid. Her oozing loamy eyes and bright red pupils found Bix amid the melee. Stark confusion twisted the goddess's melting features a heartbeat before she vanished.

"Yeah, that's what Devourer blood does to a god, ya ninny," Bix muttered to herself as she rolled her shoulders and took in the troops of Devourers still marching on Zamarad. "Good thing I'm not divine, but I *do* find divinity mighty tasty."

Tentacles of shadow and night slithered from Bix's spine, unraveling at rapid speeds to cover the arena and the surrounding five miles in total darkness. The Devourers' gateway shimmered like a mirror as more troops continued filing through, their numbers well over a hundred. The most Bix had ever taken down at once was a few dozen.

This was going to be a problem. A slightly more urgent problem than figuring out what had drawn the anti-gods to this World at this particular time. Was it Resen? Had the prototype enticed them in some way? Functioned as a beacon instead of a deterrent?

One issue at a time. Start with the gate. She sent tentacles through the Devourers' portal, sensing its origin. It wasn't the ether. It was a World. A Mid World. She focused on processing the sights, scents, and sounds being absorbed by her tentacles. Wherever the Mid World was, it bore strong resemblance to a hellscape from Hieronymus Bosch's fevered imagination.

The distraction cost her.

A sonic assault burst her eardrums, causing mist and midnight to trickle down her neck. Repeated blasts of toxic magic struck her in the chest. The force of impact sent her stumbling off the leaf of a raspberry. The Devourers' attacks followed her down, relentlessly pummeling her like large boxing gloves. They might not be able to break her skin, but she could still incur damage and feel pain. She landed hard in the sticky rotting roots of the thicket.

Oy, what pain.

What she needed was an oversized aspirin or an infusion of morphine. For an oddball Other World entity like her, there was no painkiller quite like the essence of a Devourer.

"You picked the wrong bitch," she groused as she regained her feet and sent her darkness into a dozen towering gray bodies. She drained their essence from them. With every long draught, a cloud of batting interrupted her pain receptors, muted her empathy, muffled her emotions, and freed the wild caprice of her instincts. She flipped her internal switch from taking to giving, force-feeding the Devourers the chaff of her expelled magic until they exploded from the excess of it. Utterly disgusting. Completely revolting. Remarkably entertaining.

Devourers' blood wasn't anywhere near as poisonous as their magic when it encountered Mid World magic. Toxic? Yes. She wouldn't recommend anyone eat Zamarad's fruit coated with their blood. Yes, the areas affected by it would decay faster. No, their blood didn't cause the instant chemical-like burn and boil of their magic. Only gods suffered horrifically from direct contact with the anti-gods' blood, and a god Bix was not. All the spatter did was ruin her god-created clothes and shoes. Messing with her shoes was more than sufficient to let her vindictive id run amok.

Peeved, she steadied herself against the prickly base of the vine and drained another dozen Devourers, then another, ending each batch with a smug grunt when they popped. Her veins blackened beneath her skin, then her skin followed suit as gluttony rode her, filling stores of magic beyond her corporeal self. Across her bosom, a variant of an Eternal Knot glowed green and silver, warm and reassuring. The piece of Tobek she carried within herself functioned as a lifeline to empathy, waiting for her to grab hold. She didn't need empathy right now, though. She needed to erase this blight from Zamarad.

Half the Devourer army still stood with more coming through the damn portal. Since she couldn't swallow their gate with one of her own, she infected it with a thousand tiny gates looping around each other like a Gordian knot. Inside each of those knots was another. The ripples of the molten mirror devolved to jittering pixels, pixels blurred and fractured, destabilizing the Devourers' gate until it blew. The concussive waves blasted forward and back, snatching up everything within its radius and shredding it all into confetti of death.

The World shook.

Bix waited for the tremors to abate before stumbling through the remains of the arena, swatting at the haze blanketing the once-lush thicket. The explosion had cleared an eight-mile radius, providing an unobstructed line of sight to the stupid station. The few Devourers that remained raced through the tarry black blood of their fallen peers for the single narrow door of the research facility guarded by a big bear of a blond Berserker. Green and silver magic sparked around his natural hand, while his prosthetic held a broadsword. The bright blue lights of Tobek's fully engaged Berserker's rage made him stand out like a neon sign in the shadows of the station.

Dumbass.

Bix threw open gates, placing herself between Tobek and the Devourers. More gates went up as a shield around the station, trapping Tobek on the inside as Devourers launched a second assault. She did not hesitate to lay waste to the remaining army.

When the last spray dampened her cheek, Bix dropped the

protective gates and turned on Tobek, the ire of her unregulated id barely contained.

"You arrogant shit," she cried. "You are *not* indestructible. I told y—"

Mist and midnight flooded her throat, choking her. Air refused to enter her lungs. Horror distorted Tobek's features. He hurled his sword end over end somewhere behind her, then lunged for her. Bix followed the path of his too bright gaze to two blue-and-white-marbled spears jutting from her chest, bathed in her blood.

Spears made of angel bones.

Confused, she pivoted to the side as Tobek caught her. A lone angel wept, his wrists and legs shackled. A collar of toxic gray magic ate at the angel's neck, and from its ghastly tether dangled a bleeding, severed Devourer hand. Tobek's sword glistened from the angel's gut. The angel's lips moved, but Bix couldn't hear anything over the ringing between her ears. The angel closed his eyes and curled his hands, grabbing air and twisting. The spears inside her rotated, inviting her to scream if only she could. Tobek seized a marbled tip with his prosthetic hand. Rubber and robotics instantly reduced to ash, a result of angel bones coming in contact with something made from Mids' magic. Tobek clutched her to him with this natural hand, the spears parallel to his bulk as he retreated to the station door. The angel stalked them, mouth still moving, tears still flowing, sword still impaling him.

The angel's head rolled across the ground.

The body crumpled, revealing a well-dressed gentleman in a three-piece suit and a bronze mask laced over choppy layers of dark hair. Amber eyes with red pupils gleamed from behind the mask. Bronze short swords dripped with crimson blood that turned to peonies as droplets hit the ground. The new arrival pushed up his mask, revealing the harsh pitiless features of Phobos, the Greek god of fear.

Spymaster for the Greek pantheon, Phobos was one of the few allies Bix had among the gods, though he was never pleased when her distress summoned him to her side, particularly when Devourers were involved…or angels, apparently.

Phobos strode to her as she convulsed in Tobek's arms. Without ceremony or apology, Phobos ripped the marbled spears from her chest and crushed them to dust, wiping his hands on his jacket.

Tobek pressed her head to his heart as the Greek god glowered at her.

Heal yourself, Chimera, Phobos commanded in her mind. *This weakness is unbecoming.*

CHAPTER 6

Bix listened to the song of her body repairing itself. It sounded like a microscopic orchestra guiding the mist of her blood and the midnight of her tissues into proper melodic and harmonic sequences. The more instruments playing, the more extensive her damage.

A whole opera was going on inside her.

Her eardrums restored themselves first, allowing her to hear Tobek's steady pulse echoing in the artery of his neck. He carried her as though she was a sleepy bride, her cheek resting on his shoulder while he paced the outdoor perimeter of station seventy-seven. His stride was measured, rocking her gently. He wore a different oxygen tank but the same respirator, which explained the tinny echo of his breathing.

She gingerly cupped her ribs. She no longer had holes in her chest, but she had a strong suspicion that if she weren't hopped up on Devourer-brand painkillers, she'd be pretty damn miserable.

"Don't rush it." Tobek pressed his face mask against her hair. "You've earned the respite."

Yes, yes, she had, as a matter of opinion, but she had too many questions to answer to dawdle in convalescence. She attempted a deep breath. Oh no, that was going to take a bit longer to do successfully. Shallow breaths. Those she could manage without the sensation of something ripping.

"You can put me down," she whispered against Tobek's neck and pointed at the ankle-deep rut he'd worn in the ground. "You've marched a moat around the building."

"I watched you be impaled. Right in front of me. Less than an arm's reach. By an angel I could've slain had I not lowered my guard. In my awe of you at your most radiant, I failed to protect you. I just got you back, and I almost lost you again." He huffed. "Forgive me. Forgive me for being so selfish that I need a moment longer with you close."

She smiled at his Neanderthaloid concern. Had her body been physically capable, there probably would've been a whole gaggle of warm fuzzies assailing her right now. Alas, having consumed that many Devourers would keep her fairly numb for a fairly long time. "Immortal, remember? I'll live. Who knows what would've happened to you had you been on the receiving end of angel-bone spears."

"Why use an angel? How were the Devourers controlling him? Why did he still attack after you'd removed the Devourers holding him hostage?" Phobos called from the site of the blown gateway. Gods lacked a need for proximity to hear or be heard. "Where were they keeping him? Angels can't exist beyond the Mids, so where did they stash him? Where is their base? Where are the damn plagues upon our existence?"

Bix patted Tobek's chest. "Please? Before he has apoplexy?"

With a mix of a sigh and a groan, her Berserker gently set her on her feet, carefully untangling his ruined prosthetic from the mess of her dress. His mulch-brown uniform was damp, and holes from Devourer-spatter transfer followed the shape of her body against his.

"I hurt you," she whispered. "I'm sorry."

"It's nothing. I've burned myself far worse frying chicken." His laugh lines creased, but the mirth didn't reach his eyes. Any attempt at a smile was hidden by his respirator. Probably just as well.

"Where are your men?" Bix asked Tobek, toeing off the tatters of her ruined shoes that were dissolving in the puddles of Devourer blood. The soaked ground squished between her toes, sending a shudder of revulsion up her spine even as her skin absorbed the Devourers' essence.

"Inside, searching for salvage as promised." Tobek walked with her to the beheaded corpse of the angel and retrieved his sword. "Thank you for getting the injured to Luz."

"Help me roll him?" She bit her lip and tasted the salt of Tobek's sweat as she crouched beside the angel. A bed of wilted peonies surrounded the headless body. The flowers had been poisoned by Devourer gunk before they could take root. Angel blood was the origin of all flora in the Mids. Evolution expanded upon their initial contributions, but any time an angel bled, it turned into plants. The type depended on the angel. "Did anyone we tried to rescue survive?"

"Too soon to say. Young Ba'al has requested an update on your recovery no less than every five minutes." Tobek used his lone functional hand to roll the angel's shoulders.

Bix reached for her ear cuff and grimaced. Gone. Likely a casualty of conflict. Her smartwatch was goo covered but intact. She'd deal with Ashtad and Nez after she figured out how a high-risk rescue had gone horribly wrong, starting with her angelic would-be assassin.

"The Chimera wouldn't have been injured if she'd been paying attention to her surrounds instead of overdosing on Devourers," Phobos derided as he prowled the tarry remains of the once-thorny thicket.

"Hey now," Tobek growled.

"It's okay, he's not wrong. I didn't see the angel, and I didn't sense him." Bix skimmed her fingers over the angel's collar pulsing with Devourer magic even though there wasn't a Devourer still standing.

"This is another regression in your skills brought about by feeding from the Devourers. You've been numb before, but it hasn't stopped you from hunting unseen prey. So, I repeat, regression," Phobos scolded. He'd been on her for a while about the unknown side effects of her indulging in Devourer essence. She was too busy trying to defeat the anti-gods to make notes and catalog any weirdness.

Tobek cursed under his breath. "Addicts ignore the side effects too until it's too late."

"Don't start with me about the addiction crap," she snapped. "I hurt. I took a painkiller. End of story."

"How many did you need to take to mute the pain versus how many you took because you lost control?" Tobek's blue eyes glowed faintly as he pointedly looked at her bare skin visible through the rips in her dress, skin that was blacker than her dress.

The downside of having someone give two shits about one's welfare was when that concern became patronizing. There was a fat line between being an asshole—like Phobos and most gods, frankly—and being a demeaning douche who took his concern and twisted it into a harness for control. That perversion of care was a real hot button for her.

"Let's worry less about how I took down an *army* and more about how the hell they knew angel bones are my weakness." Bix wiped away the blood, leaves, and dirt from the angel's naked chest. A combination of ink and scarifications covered one pec and shoulder. "These marks, Tobek, are this guy's choir and rank, right? Can you tell his archangel from this too?"

"What is it?" Phobos asked, instantly beside her. "I'm assuming you two are done canoodling? Are we moving past the saccharine-sweet show?"

"Archangel Michael," Tobek said, ignoring the god and tapping the intricate brand on the angel's pectoral. "This guy was one of the lessers. No one of consequence in the greater scheme."

"He absolutely is of consequence," Bix argued, working the severed Devourer hand free from the collar's tether. The pulsating gray collar shriveled to nothing more than a few strands of braided black hair affixed to a small bronze ring. The type of necklace one might pick up at a skater shop at the mall. "He spoke after he attacked me. I couldn't hear him due to the damage wrought by the sonic attacks of the Devourers. What did he say?"

"He was praying." Tobek unlocked his ruined prosthetic and slid it out of his sleeve. "'For my brothers and sisters, I must complete my task. In service to the Host, I am but a vessel. May the holy wisdom of pure native magic accept my sacrifice.'"

"Stooge," Phobos jeered.

"Every angel is a roving, independent, spare body part for their archangel. They are eyes, ears, arms, and hearts. Archangel Michael, poohbah of the war contingent for the Angelic Host, is sending his choir into the camps of Devourers to map the enemy locations knowing they'll be caught, knowing they'll be eaten alive if the gods don't rescue them in time." Bix angled herself toward the god and wagged the Devourer's severed hand at him. "Phobos, if the angels are identifying the camps, why was this guy left behind? Where are the gods to expunge the Devourers and free the angelic beacons?"

Phobos's lips thinned. His head tilted.

"You assholes," Bix gasped with horror. "The pantheons are leaving the Host exposed. They're not going to rescue the angels who've been taken prisoner."

"It's politics," the god of fear dismissed with a shrug.

"It's betrayal," she cried and winced as her lung objected to the full breath.

"It's extortion." Tobek hefted what remained of his detached prosthetic to his shoulder. It sparked and sizzled wherever metal hadn't melted from the contact with the angel-bone spears.

"The pantheons are in an extremely favorable position to extract certain concessions from the Angelic Host and the Dragon Horde." Phobos pulled the fob of a beating heart from his vest pocket and massaged the cover between his thumb and forefinger. "Call it what you will, but until the leadership of the pantheons get what they want from the rest of the Consortium, the pantheons' less than timely response to certain shared intel is the reality of the moment."

Gods were assholes. Always had been. Always would be.

Bix had the same opinion of angels too, but they were at least making an effort to save the Mids. No wonder the Host was desperate for any intel on Resen. They'd turned to their allies in the time of need and gotten the classic "the cost of our assistance has gone up." Of all the times and things to quibble over. It wasn't even the traitorous faction inside the Consortium exacerbating the situation; it was ordinary ego and greed.

Politics would be the death of the Mids.

Bix sat back on her haunches and stared up at the sky. Was the weave of Resen still active? Had the station recorded any of what had transpired today? The gates, the gods, the Devourers? Had the great minds of station seventy-seven figured out how to capture and put into plain, actionable terms what the threads of Fate had registered?

She eyed Tobek, then Phobos, then the sky, then Tobek.

"What?" Phobos prompted.

She debated telling Phobos about Resen. He probably already knew about the program, but he might not know how far the Sages and Oracles had gotten on Zamarad. He was one of her few allies among the pantheons. On the other hand, he was a god with an allegiance to the leadership of his pantheon.

"You are terrible at masking your emotions." Phobos sighed. "Say it."

"The Devourers have perfected stable gateways," she ventured instead. "The one they used to get here wasn't based in the ether where we've long assumed their forces are preparing for their full-out assault on the Mids."

Phobos swore in ancient Greek. "Whatever wiggle room the pantheons thought they had to extort the Consortium is running out. Where was the gate based?"

"In the Mids." Bix hooked the Devourer's limp finger into the wrist shackles imprisoning the angel. "I checked the other side before I destroyed the gate. It's a lot like Bosch's Hell. Red-orange skies, caricature buildings, teeming masses of all kinds of races, and none of them looking happy to be alive."

"I know the place. Some friends and I introduced Bosch to it." Phobos curled his lip. "Leave that political tango to me. You two should figure why the old foes came to this fungi-infested World in the first place."

"Probably has something to do with Project Resen," she said idly, though keenly attuned to his reaction.

"Resen? *Resen?* First the Fates want to use it against you; now they arrange for you to, what, salvage it? They love to jerk your chain and watch you dance."

Phobos's wry chuckle gave her more insight than his answer had. He'd known about Resen and wasn't surprised she finally did. It was as though he'd anticipated this happening, as if others had feared this moment and he'd picked up on it. Whether or not he was personally pleased and feigning professional irritation was hard to tell. Either way, he was stuck. She wanted Resen to go forward, and his bosses didn't. Sucked to be him.

"Is political clout the only reason the pantheons systematically sabotaged Project Resen, or is there something more to it?" She pressed the Devourer's thumb and forefinger against the seamless cuff and grunted with satisfaction when the cuff popped open. The poor angel's wrist was raw with the impression of teeth marks in the malformed muscle. Dude had been snacked on, shackled, then handed the bones of his brethren to carry in the middle of a marching army. For his sisters and brothers who were probably being held on Bosch World. The very idea made her stomach heave.

"You would do well to let Resen die along with anyone associated with it," Phobos cautioned. "You will lose what few allies you have among the pantheons if you champion that damn initiative."

"What is it, Phobos? What is it you guys don't want the rest of us to know?" Bix unlocked the other wrist cuff and draped the connecting chain across the palm of the severed hand. Toxic magic tickled her fingertips; active, even in death.

"It's power, plain and simple. Resen would knock the legs out from under the gods." Phobos slid the fob back in his vest pocket.

Tobek muttered something unintelligible behind his mask. Phobos glowered at him.

"No wonder the Fates wouldn't leave it alone, which could be why certain gods with an eye for the inevitable might take it upon themselves to *cleanse* Bosch World of its Devourer infection as a gesture of good faith before Resen forces all the pantheons to heel. As you said, time is running out." She took the hair necklace from the angel and looped the bronze ring over the Devourer's finger. The hair transformed back into the collar. Again, she looked up at the sky and the weave hiding in the atmosphere.

"Why would I volunteer for battle if I'm going to be dragged to your side because your regression in abilities has left you wide open to assault again?" Phobos challenged. "Can you even sense the presence of an angel anymore?"

"I can sense the spearhead you're hiding in your jacket's inner pocket." She bared her teeth. "Nice that you made it look like you destroyed the spears, but I know you well enough to pay attention to the sleight of hand."

Phobos inclined his head and retrieved the marbled point from his pocket. "Good but not good enough."

"How did the Devourers know her weakness?" Tobek asked. "What caused them to bring a prisoner armed with a specific set of weapons, today of all days, to this location? She wasn't supposed to be here."

"You needn't think too hard about who alerted the Devourers to her weakness. On one occasion, there were five gods present when she was wounded with an angel-bone arrowhead. If you believed they'd keep her secret, you failed to comprehend how deeply she is despised by the pantheons. Those gods ran home to share their great discovery with their leadership. That information spread quickly among the Consortium, no doubt including members of the traitorous faction."

Tobek let loose a long line of what sounded like multilingual invectives not even his respirator could disguise.

"The entire Consortium?" Bix hung her head as the weeds

of malice inside her stretched. "They all know? Including the Angelic Host?"

"Best worst-kept secret, second only to when we withheld your true identity from you." Phobos laughed cruelly. "I bet the angels will start cozying up to you. After all, if they can keep their body parts, you can keep from being injured. A logical alliance, wouldn't you say?"

"Awesome." She rolled her eyes. "So I should expect to be knifed, shot, impaled, or really whatever is most convenient for whichever enemy?"

"Or you could reclaim your lost memories, relearn how to wield your innate magics, erase all vulnerability, and once again be the terror that keeps us in line." Phobos raked her with haughty regard. "But not looking like an otter in an oil spill."

A snap of his fingers, and a whirl of navy smoke enveloped her, then quickly dissipated. In its wake, her battle-grungy body had been cleaned and her torn attire replaced with something more suitable for winter on the Primary Mid World. Her shoes he placed on Tobek's prosthetic, clear of the blood-soaked ground.

"I will do what I can to assist the Angelic Host on what you call Bosch World. In the meantime, watch your back, Chimera. Resen is an excuse your enemies will use to openly target you. And now that the Devourers are also armed to fell you, you are not as mighty as you were a few weeks ago." With that parting salvo, Phobos vanished in a cloud of navy and mulberry fog.

Bix stood and took her shoes from Tobek's sparking and sizzling prosthetic, which still rested on his shoulder. "You okay there?"

"It's just technology acting up." Tobek pinched the end of a smoking wire in the robotic arm. "Broken circuits, frayed wires, and live connections tend to be a little prickly."

"Do you need me to bandage it? Your amputation site?" She tucked her shoes under one arm and the Devourer trophies under the other, then set to rolling up Tobek's empty sleeve. "Or would you rather I send you to Runjit at Luz? I need to tidy up out here before I check in."

"Don't." He shook his head. "Don't clean up this mess. The MWA needs to see this, study it, record it, and learn from it. I, we, the MWA, we might not be able to kill Devourers, but we need to learn how to exist amid the aftermath of an attack. We need to know if the air is safe to breathe, the ground fit to walk on, the water safe to drink, how much toxicity per unit of measure has been introduced to the environment, etcetera. As bad as it was, this skirmish will help us prepare for our new reality of Devourers existing in the Mids."

"Okay, that's really depressing." She left an inch of heavily scarred skin peeking out from the fat cuff of fabric around his bicep.

"I'm going to stay on World, work with the team inside the station, and coordinate with the appropriate MWA forensics groups." He smoothed her hair behind her ear. "You should take a beat to finish recovering. I can tell by the cadence of your speech that you're still favoring your lungs."

"I'll go to Luz. Let's hope we have survivors who can stop us from reaching apocalypse mode. I'll leave you in the capable hands of your men here." She opened gates, taking her shoes and Devourer trophy in hand. "Thank you for keeping me safe while I suffered for my stupidity."

"Wait." He closed the space between them, his bright eyes searching hers. "Phobos and I disagree on a great many things, but was he right about you losing abilities. Are you decaying?"

"*Decaying?*" Bix echoed, aghast. "I'm not going to talk about that. I'm especially not going to explain what happens inside me when I feed from Devourers. You two can stuff it."

"Sweetheart, it might not be solely about the Devourers. It might be due to your singular source of balancing nourishment. You might need to find more gods to add to your diet." He winced and covered his pec with his hand as the curse of silence burned through his skin, shirt, and jacket in a variant pattern of an Eternal Knot.

Clearly, he knew more about the diet to which she was supposed to be adhering than she did.

She cringed, hating what the curse did to him. "One god has sufficed before."

"When you were barely tapping the surface of your abilities, when you weren't ingesting dozens of Devourers, right?" He hunkered over with a groan, dropping his prosthetic. Green mist glowed around his fingers. Tiny silver spears jutted from the cloud of his magic to pierce his uniform jacket and sink into his skin. "It has to be a balance. Balance is critical for you."

The confession sent him to his knees, screaming through clenched teeth.

"Stop, please, stop provoking it," she urged while he struggled to heal himself. "The next infusion of memories I reclaim from a god, I'll have to husk the god in the end. I'll make sure to feed from the unlucky deity first, okay?"

He sat back on his heels, panting. "It has to be more than that, and you *have* to stop taking so much from the Devourers. You may not like the word 'addiction,' but it doesn't change what it is."

"I'll stop right after you stop yielding to *your* addiction to pain, Mister Kettle." She knocked on the shield of his respirator with a knuckle. "I'll check in from Luz."

CHAPTER 7

Stepping through the gate into the Church of the Templars in Luz-Saint-Sauveur, France, Primary Mid World, was like walking onto a Hollywood movie set for the umpteenth reboot of Robin Hood. The triage clinic was below the twelfth-century stone church that had been fortified with twin towers and a polygonal defensive wall in the fourteenth century by the Templars. The clinic was in a massive circular chamber with all the dark and dank one would expect around the perimeter. The etchings in the stone floor reflected in the tung-oiled barrel ceiling. Fluted columns held cold torches in iron brackets of scrolled sigils. Three feet toward the center, all guise of history faded in the thousand-watt floodlights paired on bright yellow stands. Gurneys held more body bags than patients. Men in hospital scrubs and masks bent over rolling steel tables, their low murmurs underscoring the desperation and resolve hanging thick in the air.

Runjit stood out among the other medical staff what with his turban under his stretchy medical cap. He labored in the middle of a ring of machines and transfusion bags. The hairy ankles and feet of his patient twitched. Guess they'd run out of anesthetic.

"Pretty lady okay?" whispered a slightly phlegmy voice from behind a pallet of shrink-wrapped supplies.

"Aw, Gurp, I've missed you." Bix smiled at the squat, mottled brownish-green goblin peeking around the corner. The goblin was Tobek's majordomo, designer of her cistern sanctuary, and her erstwhile third roommate. No matter how crappy her day, seeing Gurp always cheered her up. Alas, he had a deep-seated fear of her in her I-ate-too-many-anti-gods condition. The original Chimera must've done something egregious while looking like she currently did, something he'd witnessed that had scarred him. He knew full well she wasn't who she'd been, so the distance he preferred to keep stung, but she respected him too much to push.

"You home with Chief. No miss then, yes?" He cut a sly grin as he slunk a little farther from his hiding spot. "We family again."

"As soon as we can confirm the boys at the coal plant aren't going to be endangered by my presence, I'll be home. Besides, we're always a family no matter where I'm living." She placed her shoes on the ground and double-checked the soles of her feet were clear of all Devourer-laced dirt before stepping into the sinister-snowmen pumps Phobos had manifested for her. Phobos was a grump on the surface, but he indulged her warped sense of humor.

"You bring things. Feel not right." Gurp rubbed his foot atop the other and eyed her trophies.

"These are from a Devourer." She held up the severed anti-god hand, the shackles, and the hair collar with its attached ring that she'd taken from the dead angel. No way, no how would she trust just anyone with these things, but Gurp maintained the inventory for the battalion and for all Tobek's super deadly wizard woo. While the MWA was on Zamarad collecting samples, she'd brought the worst bits for Gurp to study. "I didn't know if you'd had a chance to expand your…um, personal database with the newly available information. Devourer magic is toxic to all Worlds. Their blood is corrosive to gods and damaging to mortals if it gets in your bloodstream. I have no idea how any of that translates specifically to you, but I figured you deserved the opportunity to learn. I do need these back, but they're yours to inspect as you see fit."

His bulging eyes widened to saucers. The hairy wart at the

end of his bulbous nose waffled as he sniffed the severed hand, creeping closer to her. She looked away as he swiped a stubby finger across the bloody stump then took an experimental lick. Goblins ate everything. No exceptions. At least none from the Mids. Gurp's senses were better than any swanky laboratory at identifying unknown substances. His digestive system was a marvel and a wonder, an extremely gaseous wonder. While she was in awe of his abilities, she didn't need to witness the intricate details of how he did what he did.

"Blech." He spat and scratched his tongue. "I take? I box. I return later. Yes?"

"As long as these things aren't going to hurt you. It is *never* my intention to hurt you." She hesitantly gave her trophies to the goblin and waited to see if they burned his skin. When nothing bad happened, she released her pent-up breath. "If you can't resist putting on the necklace or the shackles, the hand unlocks them. They probably inflict additional cruelties upon the wearer beyond the obvious, so tread carefully."

"Gives us precious." He chortled, holding the bronze ring and collar up to the lights. "You go, see friends. They worry too."

"Yes, sir." She snapped her heels together, wondering at the plurality of "friends." Gurp wouldn't send her off to chat with the Berserkers without telling her which one wanted to see her. Waylon Nez would never consider her a friend, which left Ashtad as a singular "friend." She held a hand up against the glare of the bright lights as she walked the perimeter searching for Ashtad.

She bumped into a slight body standing eerily still in front of a column.

"Oh, jeez, excuse me," Bix apologized. Befuddled, it took her brain a minute to process the anomaly. Slight did not describe a single Berserker, yet slight accurately described the androgynous youth shying away from her. Light blue hair, lighter blue eyes, and damn near translucent skin. The hooks on the back of the left hand… Hooks on the hand equaled psychopomp. Soul escort.

Of course they'd be here. The victims of the god squad

hadn't been in good shape by the time the cavalry had arrived, and there was only so much modern medicine could do. The souls of Oracles and Sages near the end of their Fate-based trials were the ultimate delicacy to the god who owned that soul. It was the job of the psychopomp to deliver the right soul to the right god. Psychopomps came in various flavors, but the hooks on the left hand were common to all.

Bix gave the youth space and held up her hands in peace. "It's okay. I'm not going to give you grief. You're just doing your job."

The youth's expression remained stoic as the soul escort inclined their head. A loud clatter from the center of the chamber made Bix and the psychopomp flinch.

"Damn it," Runjit swore, discarding his surgical implements in a stainless-steel bowl held by one of the nurse-medics. "Calling it. Someone bring me a bag."

Sure enough, the bright soul of the Sage on Runjit's table separated from the fleshly body. It struggled to stay inside as its threads frayed, severing the soul's anchor to the Mid Worlds. A small woman of apple build with a pompadour strode away from the column three over from Bix. The psychopomp moved silently yet swiftly with preternatural speed to snare the newly freed soul. The soul tried to flee from her, but the hooks on her hand held it. With the slightest breeze, the psychopomp vanished, taking the soul to its final destination.

The Berserkers' shoulders slumped farther forward.

Bix glanced back at the youth waiting patiently for the soul they were to take as she progressed around the perimeter looking for Ashtad. This time, she made note of the other psychopomps cooling their heels in the darkness of the chamber perimeter. A half dozen remained. She chastised herself for not noticing them upon her arrival. At the very least, she should've sensed their magical resonance. Maybe Phobos and Tobek were right, maybe she was decaying. Ew. Issues for later.

Friends first. Data on Resen second. Delivery to the Host third. Decaying some point after that.

"Look, Sparky, the Mummy said their brains are all scrambled, so unless you can tell me what intel I'm digging for, I'm going to wait until Bixie gets here to brief me."

"Drew, we're running out of time. Trust me when I say *any* intel you can cull is important to her."

Bix followed the sound of bickering to a horseshoe of three gurneys set apart from the medical team. Ashtad's glossy sable curls caught the light, at least the curls that had been under his cap. The ends, much like his clothes, were coated in a thick paste of yellow and purple plant goo. He sat on the edge of his gurney, leaning against a safety rail while arguing with something on the floor. Angled into a mostly upright position on the parallel gurney was a heavily scarred shirtless man with tattooed leaves running from his wrist to his neck. One arm was completely bandaged up to his shoulder. A huge rectangle of gauze had been taped to his right cheek, from lip to mangled ear. His salt-streaked black braid had been wound into a topknot. Green eyes followed her approach as he adjusted his oxygen mask. A dimple beside his left nostril appeared.

Waylon Nez. Alive.

On the one hand, the satisfaction of a mission accomplished tickled Bix's brain. On the other hand, with her id mostly unfettered, there was a deep need to slap that dimple right off his face. Again. She fluttered her fingers at her sides, trying to resist the impulse as she rounded the half circle of gurneys to get a good look at the third person in the ring who sat with his back to her, head down, flannel sleeves rucked up past his elbows, fingers flying over a keyboard. A messenger bag and an army surplus field jacket lay in a heap beside him. An airline boarding pass stub peeked out of the chest pocket beside a rental car key fob.

"Cian?"

The youngest member of Bix's team, Cian Asariri was a Sage beginning his trials. A genius in applied mathematics and technology, he was seventeen and should've been back in Washington, DC, working on his thesis for grad school.

The kid looked up from his laptop and grinned. "Hey, Bix. Heard you kicked some Devourer ass. Looks like it too."

"Bix," Ashtad greeted with a sigh of relief, hopping off his gurney with a wince and enfolding her in a hug and a cloud of pollen. "Thank the gods."

"Let's not. They're part of the problem." She hugged him back despite the plant goo. Her attention dropped to the center of the gurney half ring, where a German shepherd waited, its tail wagging. "Hi, Drew."

"Hiya, Bixie. You eat the entire army or just overdo it on the self-tanner?" the dog teased, or rather the draugr inside the dog spoke via the dog. Drew was a body thief of sorts who normally preferred to wear human suits, more precisely dead humans since the soul had already vacated and the body didn't require maintenance. Drew *could* occupy the living and most often did so to read the life experiences contained within the soul. That handy skill made Drew a master interrogator, which was likely what Ashtad had been trying to convince Drew to do in the snippet of conversation Bix had overheard.

Her two best friends didn't get along. However, they were professionals, Ashtad more so than Drew, so they worked well together once they signed on to a shared mission. In the off time though, they wouldn't be caught anywhere near each other. The fact they were on the same continent inside the same supersecret and supersecure site raised a lot of questions. Most of which could probably be answered by the ginger boy madly typing on his laptop.

"Ci-annn," Bix drawled. "Did you hack my watch?"

"Don't need to. I built it, remember? The whole network we use for communications? All me. I even let Mr. Ba'al keep the backdoor he coded for himself." Cian glared at his screen as Ashtad snorted.

Ashtad could run loops around Cian in the tech arena, but only because Cian was new to the inclusion of magic and biologics in the tech preferred by Chweds...and because Ashtad mixed in Other World enhancements with any security protocols he developed. Ashtad made a good mentor for the kid in that field. A reluctant mentor, but a good one nonetheless.

"The herb nerd and I were picking up hotties in the park when you uploaded something that freaked him out." Drew scratched her ear with her foot. "I recognized a remote recon map of Zamarad involving too many gods. Since you didn't tell *us* what you were doing, we figured it was the boys in the battalion you were helping. The kid took the, um, technological initiative and here we are."

Ashtad rubbed his cheek with his hand and eyed Bix. "Remote recon?"

"What? You said I couldn't *be* there. I wasn't until you called," Bix defended. "How'd we do anyway? Survivors? Demis? Researchers?"

Ashtad shoved his hand in his hair. "Four from my team made it. Berserkers patched them up and sent them on their way. They were itching to get back to their havens for actual recovery. They send their gratitude to the Chimera."

"Coming face-to-face with Devourers in combat probably shook them to their cores," Drew noted.

"I'm so sorry for your loss, Ashtad," Bix murmured. "What about the researchers? Anyone survive beyond the guy who's supposed to have been dead for the last twenty-five years?"

"Looking like less than a quarter of the researchers will survive based on the psychopomps who've been in and out of here all night." Ashtad gestured to the soul escorts waiting in the shadows.

Nez pulled aside his oxygen mask. "Bix, I know you and I didn't end things on a good note, but trust me when I say none of this was planned. Not by us. Not by the Houses of Fate."

"Trust you? *Trust you?* The guy who decided I deserved to be dead more than I deserved my spot as a probationary agent? Fuck you." Maybe it was because her ego hadn't regained control over her id. Maybe she had deeper unresolved issues with the elder Sage than she realized. Maybe Waylon Nez was just a prick in need of a lesson.

Darkness shot from her spine and slammed the Sage into the ceiling.

The gurney caught his fall.

CHAPTER 8

"**W**hat?" Bix asked with artificial innocence as she recalled her shadows and smoothed her wide belt. A tiny dribble of rubble bouncing along the floor answered. The silence lasted another heartbeat before Nez succumbed to a fit of coughing. The Berserkers on guard duty unclenched their hands from their weapons and resumed their vigilance. The medics once again bent over their patients.

"It's been twenty-five years," Ashtad chided, retrieving the oxygen mask for Nez and placing it over the elder Sage's face.

"A guy who faked his own death demanded I trust him." She knocked debris from her shoulders. "I wanted to be clear that wasn't going to happen. Ever."

Their antagonistic history only added to the repugnance of now standing within arm's reach of a mortal whose limbs had exploded all over her. One moment, Nez had been dressing her down in front of half the team, the next click, boom, body parts. Looking at him in this moment, all she could see was a manipulative bastard singularly obsessed with death. Hers. An insecure, power-tripping liar, just like the Fates he aspired to be. To fake his death in the middle of an op? To subject the team to second-guessing their protocols and months of inquiries from management? Ashtad had had his ass dragged by the higher-ups for Nez's supposed demise. Losing an agent was bad. Losing a Sage? They were rare and valuable because they were walking data stores, and in the intel biz, that made them priceless. Nez was crafty enough he could've arranged for the inquiry to be buried after he'd bailed, but he was selfish enough he'd let the entire team hang. Thinking about everything that had happened in the aftermath of Nez's "death" pissed her off even more.

Now, here he was, saved by the teammates he'd screwed.

"I didn't fake my death, Bix," Nez gasped and wheezed through his mask. "It wasn't a one-up on the game you and I were playing behind Ba'al's back. I remember us on the op, having a chat. The next thing I knew, the life I'd led was officially over, and I'm being rebuilt and retasked."

"It wasn't a chat. I was ten steps behind you, listening to you berate me for my choice of footwear when you tripped that Leshy land mine. I dripped parts of you when I delivered your body to the CWIG infirmary. The team blamed me. Management blamed Ashtad. The fault was solely yours." She cut a scathing glance his way as dull pangs rippled through her stab wounds. Possibly what hate felt like. No. That wasn't true. Hate was violent and frustrated. This was disgust and disdain. "There is only one way you're alive, and it has everything to do with Project Resen."

"You're right, on all counts," Nez admitted without hesitation, pulling his mask aside. "An archangel fashioned this body, and that archangel patched me back together after the land mine incident. As soon as I could get around with minimal assistance, the Houses of Fate placed me at station seventy-seven."

"Where you fed intel to your archangel on Resen's progress with the blessings of the Fates," she finished for him as he sucked down more oxygen. "How did you get the message to the Host without running afoul of the gods?"

"Self-mutilation." Nez flipped aside the sheet covering his lower body, revealing the old scars up and down his legs from the land mine. There was a smooth five-inch hairless stripe on the inside of one calf. "I etch the message into my skin. The archangel perceives it and restores the smooth surface."

"Holy shit," Cian gasped, staring wide-eyed at Nez's messed-up legs.

"Kid, I got a second chance I didn't deserve." Nez tugged his sheet back in place. "I don't know if it means I'll ascend to a Fate, but I celebrated my sixty-first birthday last month when I should've died at thirty-six. A little discomfort now and then is worth getting older."

"Nez was about to bring us up to speed on Project Resen while we waited for you, Bixie," Drew supplied before Bix's snide comment made it out her mouth. "Are we correct in assuming the images you uploaded are related?"

"If you mean the green webbing over the station, yes." Bix planted her hands on her hips. "Nez, was the station recording the data when the gods arrived?"

"Yes, that's the only reason we had time to enact our security protocols." Nez winced as he adjusted his position in the gurney. "Unfortunately, we were unprepared for the assault of a goddess of discord. She turned us against each other without having to touch anyone or anything. The explosion you saw at the end of my message, Ba'al? That was done by an Oracle I had to kill with my bare hands."

"And the reason *you* aren't nuts right now?" Drew sniffed.

"I use an anger cube as part of my daily meditations. I had it on me when the attack went down." Nez huffed wryly and waved his bandaged hand at Ashtad. "Ba'al gave me one after I'd let Bix get under my skin too many times. I should've used it when I was her senior agent, but I sure as hell mastered it after I got to station seventy-seven. There's a reason Fates and those of us aspiring to become them don't congregate."

"What's an anger cube?" Cian asked.

"It's a cluster of microorganisms that leech the surfeit of certain emotions out of you." Nez flicked his torn ear. "It's usually worn as an earring with the stud entering your skull as sort of a straw for the organisms. The more the organisms eat, the more solid their state. Let's just say I had something harder than graphene."

That was the cube he'd dropped when Bix had slapped him. Oops.

"Since angels eat negative emotions, an anger cube is actual candy for them." Drew licked her paw. "They pay pretty well for that brand of dessert."

"The god squad hit four hundred other research facilities over the last three decades, and no one knew a goddess of discord was involved?" Bix cocked her head.

"There were never any survivors," Nez reminded.

"Yeah, let's go back to the part about 'detecting gods,'" Ashtad drawled. "I think I'm going to need a bit more detail on this Project Resen."

"Zamarad is home to a prototype for Project Resen, a blue-sky defense initiative to track Other World entities as they move in and around the Mids," the older Sage announced without preamble. "In theory, it is a lattice woven through the ley lines, a mesh, a sieve, that, when interrupted, scans and sends data to a series of redundant operation centers. If the entity is authorized, their presence or departure will be logged, but nothing more happens. If the entity is not authorized, then a Consortium security team will be dispatched to address the issue."

"It's border patrol for gods and Fates," Bix noted dryly. "Its original concept was couched in tracking me. Now, however, that Devourers are on scene, there's an urgency from all but one of the superpowers to have it built."

"So it tracks *anything* non-native to the Mids." Ashtad frowned. "And the Fates have been dedicated to figuring out how to build it? That's mighty suspicious."

"They knew the Devourers were coming to the Mids," Cian said, making no effort to hide his hostility for his kith. "That's the point of Oracles and the Fates who see the Future. They've known the invasion was coming and when."

"Time is hazy for those who get visions of the future. They use events to mark milestones and narrow possible outcomes." Nez patted the safety rail of his gurney. "Bix being exiled was the event that defined how long we had until the Devourers arrived."

"What about the Devourers today?" Ashtad bent and straightened is bum leg with a wince. "Who invited them to the party?"

Nez shook his head. "No idea. We never had contact with one."

"Well, we tripped somebody's booby trap," Ashtad groused, "and I don't think the pantheons' strike team saw it coming either. I can't shake the sense that something followed us out of there."

Nez's mouth opened, then shut, and he looked away.

"What?" Bix demanded. "What are you hiding, Nez?"

"Nothing," he blurted too quickly.

"Damn it, Nez," she snarled.

"It's painful memories, that's all," he insisted.

She didn't believe him, but she recognized this little ploy of his. As a behaviorist, he'd pull this poor-pitiful-victim routine to undermine a team leader, to make the leader appear too testy, too irritable, too emotionally unfit for the complete confidence of the team. The man hadn't changed. She had, though. She *had*. She knew how to deal with the likes of him. Hell, she could go toe to toe with a scheming god. An elder Sage had merely been good practice.

That was her story, and she was sticking to it.

"Did Resen catch the arrival of the Devourers?" Cian swiped his laptop screen, presumably reviewing the pictures of the grid Bug had uploaded. "They use gates to travel between Mid Worlds, so if Resen was running when they opened their gate, we might be able to compare that data against the gate Bix created and the gate Mr. Ba'al used to focus on inter-World travel. Maybe take it further and trace energy signatures to their origins."

"Ah, kid, kid, kid, I remember when I was like you." Nez sighed wistfully. "A young Sage, so sure that all the problems of the Worlds could be solved if I could just get my hands on the next piece of information."

Cian hung his head.

"Don't be ashamed of that feeling." Nez pointed to Cian's arm on which Cian's two leaves denoting his two trials were inked. One leaf was bright and full; the other wilted amid a crystalline fractal. "That certainty is what compels you to get up after failing a test. That certainty is what drives you to improve. That certainty is what the Fates will try to destroy. Don't let them. Never let them destroy your hunger."

Cian furtively peered at Nez's bandages. "Even when they do that to you?"

Nez laughed, a totally foreign sound. "Look at me. It's okay. Take a good look at me. Twenty-five years ago, I was a handsome guy. Strong jaw. Smooth skin. Hair that made the ladies go wild. I tromped on a land mine and came out looking like something scraped off the bottom of a peat bog."

"Man, that's not right," Cian offered weakly.

"It's cool, kid. I'm not pissed about it." Nez rested his bandaged arm on the bed rail and turned to better face Cian. "Our trials are designed to change us. Every Fate you will ever meet has some physical flaw. I'm not talking about extra toes, beauty marks, or bullet holes. I'm talking about disfigurement. The kind they can't help but see and have to compensate for every day for the rest of their lives. It's to remind them of every emotion a Fate is forced to confront when their bodies are forever changed. When they walk among the mortals whose paths they've woven, they must endure the reaction of those mortals to their flawed appearance. It is meant to be a taste of humility, an ego check so they are never too far removed from the lives they influence. The next time you see someone whose body is less than perfect, you look them in the eye and wink because that is a special brotherhood whose ranks you're going to join when the Fates are ready to do their worst to you."

Cian sat a little straighter, and his chin rose a little higher when he nodded.

Bix caught Ashtad's attention, pointedly looked at his leg, then back at his eyes and winked. Ashtad smirked and inclined his head. Sure, Ashtad was a demi not a Sage, but there was also a cadre of gods who'd come out of their trials noticeably maimed and who shared a bond of deformity despite their pantheonic rivalries. So, while Nez was a devious prick, his character flaw didn't mean he didn't know what he was talking about.

"What are the odds Resen's build specs and operational data survived the sabotage of a discord goddess?" Drew asked, bringing the conversation back to the pressing issue.

"Tobek is at the research station now with a Berserker team trying to salvage what hardware they can." Bix watched the youthful psychopomp whisk a soul out of the chamber and the morale of the Berserkers dip further.

"Well, that could be tricky for them," Nez hedged. "Guys, you have to remember this is a Fate-owned facility. Anything that looks like traditional hardware is purely for appearances."

"How's that?" Cian frowned.

"Sage servers," Ashtad said with a long groan of realization followed by an even longer string of colorful curses.

"There is no computer more powerful or efficient than the human body, so the Fates store their data in Sages who evolved not into Fates but into self-repairing servers," Nez disclosed. "These guys can't weave destinies. Their job is to be a living library and librarian all in one. What we need is stored on five servers."

"And we're down to you plus two survivors from the attack," Bix pointed out. "We failed. Damn it."

"Not yet," Nez hastened to say. "The station is as much a decoy as its contents. Resen HQ is well hidden. The servers are kept in their own suite with their own emergency protocols. The catch, of course, is that the gods used us to tear ourselves apart, so our own security team could be the servers' greatest threat right now."

"Right now? As in there's another facility on Zamarad?" Bix almost strangled Nez for holding out again. Almost. Instead, she opened tiny gates to the shelves of gewgaws at home, swapping out her befouled smartwatch for a new one, snagging a replacement earpiece…and a blank Tarot card.

It was a sad state of affairs that she trusted a faceless, unknown überentity more than a former Dark Ops teammate.

"Cian, patch us through to Tobek, would you? I need to refresh my tech," Bix asked the kid as she sent a text to Ashtad's virtual id with the access code to download a new bug to her hardware.

"Nez, why wait this long to mention a second station?" Ashtad crossed his arms. "We could've had Berserkers searching for additional survivors while Bix recovered."

"While Bix was out of commission, the Berserkers and the servers could've been hit by the gods," Nez countered. "Ba'al, no offense, but the Chimera has to be protective detail for these guys. There's way too much at risk."

"Kid? What is it?" Tobek's gruff rasp, distorted by his respirator, came through the speakers of the laptop.

"Boss wants to talk to you." Cian folded his monitor back and tented the laptop so it became a TV tablet. A TV with a close view of Tobek's furry face.

"Sweetheart?" Tobek grimaced, clearly hefting something heavy that the camera in his mask didn't record.

"There's a second facility," Bix said as her watch began its download. "I'm guessing that wasn't on the emergency evac plans the MWA had on file."

"It would explain the parade of psychopomps we've been tracking. They're headed underground." Tobek stomped on something, the sound faint through his comm. "The floor of this station is solid iron about four feet thick. It's going to take us a while to cut through it."

"I need an artist," Bix shouted to the room of Berserkers surrounding her.

"Me," Runjit answered, turning away from a gathering of beleaguered and defeated men. "Anything not to have to look at another mangled body. Gurp, pencils and paper, please."

The goblin hustled to retrieve the items.

Bix clapped Nez on his bare shoulder. "Nez, you're going to describe that server room in great detail to this lovely man until there's a picture I can use to create a destination gate, got it?"

"I…" Nez paused and shook his head. "As a frontline guy, I wasn't allowed to know what the server room looked like or how to access it."

Bix bit her tongue to keep *bullshit* from escaping. Being continually petty in front of her team would play into Nez's manipulations. She was better than that, even if taking the high road chapped her ass.

"You can't give up intel you don't have." Ashtad relaxed his stance. "It's understandable."

"The closest I can get you is the medical wing," Nez proposed instead. "The residences are farther away, but I can definitely describe my room if you'd rather enter there."

"Let's do medical since time is of the essence," Runjit suggested, joining their group as he opened a sketch pad. "Chief."

"Runjit," Tobek grunted, returning the greeting. "Gang, if there's a second facility, we've got a second chance at survivors. Sweetheart, you sure you're up for it?"

Ashtad and Drew stared at her with questions in their expressions.

"If you're following psychopomps, we should assume these researchers are hostile, victims of the goddess, which means she's returned to Zamarad," Bix cautioned, not acknowledging the concern. There were more critical issues than her aches and pains. "Warn your team and the nerds collecting Devourer samples that the goddess is on-site. If she thinks you have any intel on Resen, she'll pit your guys against each other."

"Understood." Tobek looked down. "Runjit, get your team in masks. Prepare to bulk subdue survivors as you receive them. Elder Sages and Oracles will take extra gas to knock them out."

"Yes, sir." Runjit paused his drawing and pointed a pencil at a nearby medic. "Ready the canisters, get everyone in masks, alert the guys outside."

The medic leapt to.

"Tobek, I'm going directly after the servers. I'm not going to move the researchers and risk drawing attention to my team. The data is my priority, and getting to it before the goddess is essential," Bix clarified as her bug lit up her watch face. Yes, leaving the researchers to their…fates was coldhearted, but choices had to be made. Researchers who *might* live and *might* know some part of the specs simply weren't as valuable as the living servers who had all the data to defend the Mids.

"Evacuating survivors is the MWA's job, so we'll own it." Tobek's face glowed green, likely the reflection of his magic as he used it to burn through the iron floor. "We've retasked a programmable gateway for the forensics team, and we'll use that to shuttle whatever survivors we find. You focus on your mission. We've got ours."

"We'll get you eyes inside the second facility as we go. Watch out for Devourers," she said in parting.

"You too," he articulated with too much emphasis. "Chief out."

Cian flipped his laptop to face him and looked at Bix expectantly. "What do you need me to do?"

"If I may?" Ashtad stepped forward, tightening their circle while Nez and Runjit worked on the drawing.

"Of course." Bix leaned in to hear him speak.

"Threadless and soulless." Ashtad gestured to himself, Drew, and Bix. "We run this threadless and soulless because Nez is in no condition and Cian, kid, I'm sorry, but we don't know the lingering effects of the Devourers and the gods on the World."

"That's cool. I'm good sitting here in a stone basement in a Pyrenees valley in France in the middle of February freezing my ass off," Cian snarked. "Why would I need something to keep me busy?"

"Actually, Cian, while we're doing this, I need you to prepare the tech side of things." Bix attempted to take a deep breath. Small sounds of tearing disrupted the music of her healing. There must've been a chip of the angel bone still inside her, preventing her from finishing the repairs. "We're going to need to copy the data from the servers and back up everything to multiple locations. Plan for those locations to be assailed. Let's make it hard on the gods who are going to try to destroy every reference to Resen. And we definitely want to review the data before we release it to anyone."

"Booyah," Cian cheered quietly. "Now we're talking. I'm going to need some equipment."

"I here," Gurp called, hurrying to their group. "I get. I help."

Cian and Gurp did a strange fist-bump-handshake combo and smiled. For a short while, Cian had been a resident of the coal plant, and Gurp would never have let a friendless kid be friendless for long. It looked like that camaraderie was still going strong.

"All right then, team. We need a plan." Bix held up the blank Tarot card and pushed her question to the forefront of her mind while speaking to her team and to the überentity. Yes, she was making a show of it because, yes, she wanted to throw Nez off his game. Whether he believed it was a Fate powering the card or something stronger didn't matter; what mattered was Nez witnessed something better than an elder Sage tweaking the strings of the future. "We know the goddess is on-site. We don't know if she's alone, so the less attention we can draw to ourselves, the less likely we are to bring home a divine tail who wants to kill us all. How do we make that happen?"

Arcane magic spiked in the chamber. A shadow streaked in red ripped the card from Bix's hand and spun it atop the pillow on Ashtad's gurney, forcing the card to stretch and grow as it rendered life-size imagery. Gurp whimpered and hid behind Bix. Runjit didn't even pause sketching, unperturbed, as though his tenure with Tobek had inured him to random occurrences of showy magic. Ashtad shoved his hands in his pockets and backed away. Drew leapt up to Cian's gurney and growled. Cian stared slack-jawed at the card, while Nez eyed it with all the caution it deserved.

"Glad my head wasn't there." Ashtad jerked his chin at the card spinning atop his pillow.

The card slowed its revolutions until it halted facing Bix. The Seven of Swords. Ugh. The Don't Get Cocky card. While it meant a careful strategy was necessary to achieve one's goals, it always came with the caution against overconfidence. An initial success might not be a lasting one. A little more planning, a little more thought, and the next time around might turn out better. The card traditionally showed a thief absconding with five swords from an enemy camp while leaving two behind as the enemy returned home enraged. In this version of the card, the swords were men wrapped in green lattices of zeroes and ones. The enemy camp resembled a cryoprison from a sci-fi movie. The enemy themselves, naught but evil eyes of red and green—gods and Fates. The thief in the card stood with arms wide behind the men and sparks flowing from his fingertips. There was no mistaking the thief as anyone but Ashtad. The überentity had even included the gold streaks in Ashtad's curls.

"Think the message is for you, Ba'al," Nez wheezed through his mask.

Ashtad sidled closer and rubbed his jaw. "Nothing quite like being called out by a cosmic entity. That background usable for you, Bix?"

She tried to open a gate to the cryoprison depicted in the image. Nothing. She shook her head.

"Then I hope you guys didn't get claustrophobic since last we ran an op together." Nez tapped the sketch pad as Runjit showed Bix a picture of a rather ordinary subway-tiled public restroom with an amazing aquatic view out the lone window. "Resen HQ is in the middle of an aquifer a mile underground."

CHAPTER 9

S ingle-stall, unisex bathrooms for when you've got to go…
and infiltrate a secure facility. Nez had verbally walked Runjit
through the medical biome, and Runjit—being a large guy who
attracted notice yet had to occasionally sneak through buildings—
had recommended the infamous Chimera and her team enter
Resen HQ via the bathroom. Last place hostiles tended to double-
check once the fighting started. Runjit had had a point, so here
Bix, Ashtad, and Drew were, loitering in a public bathroom in the
medical biome of Resen HQ, watching stringy roots sway beyond
the window on the water's current.

When Nez had said Resen HQ was underground, Bix had
imagined concrete bunkers or reinforced mining tunnels. Connected
biome islands in groundwater aquifers hadn't crossed her mind. A
mile underground was hella far down, unless one happened to
be on Zamarad where nature was ginormous. The islands were
anchored to select root systems of plants that provided clean
air and energy for the biomes while the plants' bioluminescence
provided ambient lighting for the entire aquifer. The layout bore
strong similarities to the Palm Islands of Dubai, only submerged.
The place was beautiful and sprawling. The aboveground station
seventy-seven could have fit on a single frond. As it was, the flora

damage from the Devourer's blown gate had blacked out only a small section of Resen HQ.

"Now you see why remote recon wouldn't work," Nez said all too smugly in Bix's earpiece.

"Remember, Fates aren't gatekeepers, Nez. Even if you ascend, you'll never know the wonders I can see," Bix taunted. She'd left the two Sages with Runjit's team at Luz. Nez was running overwatch while Gurp and Cian mapped out some newfangled, hybrid tech system to deal with the data transfer for which Ashtad had made a few suggestions. Only after her team had a chance to review Resen's build specs and make some modifications would she call Feng and have him prepare for secure dissemination along the ley lines.

"At the moment, I care more about the wonders Ba'al can see," Nez countered dryly. "Adjusting camera for low-light optimization."

Ashtad balanced the eyeglasses with the baked-in cameras on the bridge of his nose. "You two going to bicker the entire op?"

"It'd be like old times." Nez guffawed.

Back then, Bix's greatest concern had been proving to her team that she wouldn't let them down. Nez's campaign against her had required her to work smarter to thwart him while excelling at her job. She'd gotten good at dealing with those distractions while keeping her focus where it needed to be for the mission. These days, the game was the same but the stakes higher. She and her team weren't subverting upper-caste Chweds or Mid World local governments; they were tangling with superpowers and anti-gods. The enemy could create entire races and extinguish them at a whim. Yes, Bix could go toe to toe with the big bads, but at what point was she asking too much of her friends? At what point would her decision to tag them in equate to handing them a death sentence? The body count from the debacle of the surface rescue was proof of too much rope, too much danger, and too much time waiting to intercede.

Was she really giving her friends opportunities to grow, or was she just being selfish for not wanting to run missions alone? The more she stepped into the shoes of the infamous Chimera, the more it felt like she was being forced into isolation for the safety of those around her. She wasn't sure how to deal with that.

"My offer to take over the old Sage's body still stands." Drew pulled back her upper lip in a caricature of a canine smile.

"This body wouldn't get you far, draugr." Nez chuckled. "Oh, and I'm on the cusp of ascension, so I doubt you're strong enough to extinguish my soul. That, and I'm not dumb enough to let you inside to attempt it."

Nez would've been justified in his bravado if Drew had been a common draugr, but she wasn't. Over the last few months, Drew had occupied lesser gods and Devourers. Nez didn't stand a chance. If Drew really wanted in, she'd get in. The only thing holding Drew back was the minor issue of Nez's body being a walking supercomputer and Drew being an Other World entity of volatile energy. There could be system damage for both parties that might sideline the mission's success.

"Nez, what's with Mids' magic around here? Fates are Other World. Sages and Oracles are human, therefore grounding entities. How is it we're in the middle of a native magic hotspot?" Bix rolled her shoulders and stomped her feet as Mids' magic batted at her like a clowder of cats and she was their mouse toy. This much native magic didn't bode well for her. It screwed with her senses while excess Devourer essence dulled her mind. Plus, the angel-bone chip in her lung complicated her breathing. So, no, she wasn't exactly up to par. The mission and her team needed her to be, especially when they were trying to thwart a midlevel goddess who also happened to be the leader of an elite wet works unit.

"We're uncommonly close to a ley line." Ashtad held up his hands, and electricity sparked around them like loofah mitts. "The potency is phenomenal. If I had to guess, it's what's powering Resen."

Bix couldn't recall a ley line being this… puissant, but she'd seen the unusual aura of Zamarad during remote recon. Now she knew what it was. The freakishly high concentration of pure native magic tried hard to expel her from its presence. It hadn't been as strong when she was in the raspberry thicket. Despite the Devourers, she would've noticed it…unless it was another side effect of that decaying problem. Ugh.

"The station aboveground is probably an antenna." Ashtad pried the faceplate off the light switch and wired in a remote transmitter. "Cian, you should have access to the closed system now."

"Breaking through the firewalls," the kid chirped. "I need ninety seconds."

"Ninety seconds to shop for a new body, Drew. You ready?" Bix asked her four-footed companion.

"Make sure you deliver this suit to Aspen Hill Pet Cemetery. Only the best for this good dog, okay?" Drew shook her thick coat from nose to tail. "I'll need a count of five to compensate for the new perspective once I change suits."

Bix scratched Drew's ear. Bix loved dogs, didn't matter their origin, their World, or their size. She had a huge soft spot for furry beasts. Alas, she didn't have a lifestyle that allowed her to keep one. She did have shadows, though, shadows that emerged from her spine and slithered under the bathroom door. Bix shut her eyes and let her darkness feed her the sights, sounds, and scents of the medical biome.

Barroom brawling.

There was no patching up happening out there. Pure fisticuffs. Blood streaked the frosted walls. Unconscious bodies slumped against the baseboards. One woman held her side from which a switchblade protruded, hobbling after a guy crawling toward a scalpel. There was a three-way slugfest in a surgical suite. Everywhere Bix's shadows went, chaos reigned.

"It's Thunderdome throughout the medical wing." Bix stifled a curse. "The goddess of discord has definitely been here."

"Probably tortured the location from one of Nez's peers on the front line or pieced together the information from the souls she consumed," Ashtad murmured. "We've got to hurry. If she gets to the servers…"

"Remember, you want an Oracle to guide you," Nez urged. "Oracles are security. Sages are data drones."

Oracles were women; Sages were men. The Houses of Fate had very clear gender roles for their trainees. Bix's darkness scanned the women already on the ground, checking for breathing. For this mission, a dead Oracle was less preferable than a healthy one. An injured Oracle would be ideal. It'd be faster for Drew to dominate, thus allowing Drew to coexist without releasing the soul. If Drew unleashed the soul, that soul would be delivered to a god. The op would be blown before it got started.

"Tick tock, Bixie," Drew nudged. "Odds are high at least one of those Oracles knows we're coming or is right this moment getting a vision of our plan."

Bix chose an olive-skinned woman with an undercut, a peat-green uniform, and a weapon's belt of uncommon weapons. The goose egg on her arm spoke of a broken bone, and the way she favored one leg indicated a shot knee. The fat lip and bloodied knuckles sealed the deal. The Oracle took two steps toward the brawl in the surgery room and one more through the gates connecting to the restroom.

"What the—" the Oracle gasped.

Ashtad jabbed the Oracle in the throat, then knocked her off her feet with a leg sweep. Drew pounced on the woman and sniffed the mouth gasping for air. A stream of crackling pale blue transferred from the muzzle of the dog to the lips of the Oracle.

The Oracle sat upright, wheezing and clawing at her neck as the dog slumped atop her. Ashtad placed a firm hand over the Oracle's mouth, quieting her. While Drew fought for control of the new body, Bix used gates to discreetly deliver the deceased dog to the doorstep of the pet cemetery in Maryland, Primary Mid World.

The Oracle switched from clutching Ashtad's hand to patting it twice.

"It's all kinds of crazy cakes down here. They're not fighting to escape, they're fighting for the sake of screwing over everyone else." Drew gained her new feet and popped her broken bone back into place. Drew experienced everything secondhand through the suit she wore, so pain, smells, flavors, etcetera were muted. "This woman knows her actions are wrong, but resentment and envy are overwhelming her self-preservation and self-control. For an Oracle of the Present, the widespread pandemonium is really fucking with her."

"The effects of the goddess of discord," Ashtad said, retrieving Drew's comm from a pocket. "Emotion gods can't build on what's not there, so your Oracle has always been envious of her peers."

"Yep, and now she's operating at a personally self-destructive level." Drew took her earpiece from Ashtad and studied her face in the mirror. "The good news is our girl here has access to the server room. The better news is she has access to the security station that has a view of the server room, so we can get Bixie a nice picture of the room and bypass their lockdown. No artists required."

"Good, that'll save us critical time. Has she seen any of the gods roaming these halls?" Ashtad pressed his ear to the bathroom door.

Drew squatted a few times, testing her bad leg. "Suspects she passed one but is unsure because the woman was in a security uniform but the face and hands are blistered. Still, wasn't someone she immediately recognized."

"Discord, definitely, post-Devourer encounter. She's a midlevel goddess, and they take time to heal from blood burns. Probably manifested the security uniform or simply took one off a victim." Bix splayed her fingers at her sides as urgency to get to the servers quickened her heartbeat. "Cian, how you doing? Time is a factor."

"Almost there," the kid answered.

"If discord is here in the biomes, then it's smarter for Bix and me to go incognito." Ashtad straightened and adjusted his glasses again. "We don't want to tip off the goddess to our presence and waste time with whatever she throws our way."

"As long as I don't open a gate too close to her, Ashtad and

I should be fine in the shadows. We'll do our best to avoid the brawlers too." Bix swept her hair over her shoulder and prayed to the powers that be discord hadn't restaffed the god squad in the interim; otherwise, this rescue would go from fraught to fugly. Drew could escape by jumping from corpse to corpse, but Ashtad…One well-timed attack from a god Bix couldn't detect and that'd be the end of her friend.

"Okay, guys, I'm in," Cian said. "It's Fight Club everywhere. You're not going to be able to avoid it."

"You are on hot mics and cameras the minute you exit," Nez reminded. "Anyone monitoring the security feeds will find you."

"If I cut them, they'll know something's up," Cian cautioned.

"Leave them as is. I've got the map of this place and the path of least resistance." Drew stared at her reflection and at the smattering of moons in many phases marking her neck. The moons denoted her suit's Oracular trials. "This suit was about ten years away from ascension. At fifty-five, she's one of the youngest Oracles here."

"Odd staffing choices." Ashtad double-checked his pocket flaps, resecuring them so an accidental rip of Velcro wouldn't alert anyone to his location.

"Don't let the gray hairs fool you." Drew ran her hands along her buzz-cut sides. "Oracles of this age are true experts in hand-to-hand combat. The women take up arms while the men take down history."

"We do more than that, you know," Nez objected over the comms.

"Not from her point of view," Drew quipped, turning to face Bix and Ashtad. "You two ready to waltz with darkness?"

Ashtad extended his hand to Bix. "May I have the honor?"

"It would be my pleasure." Despite the pressure of the op, Bix smiled as she set her hand in Ashtad's and stepped into his embrace. Ashtad had taught her to dance for a specific assignment, and it had quickly become their go-to blend-in activity for many subsequent missions. She loved to dance and would take any excuse to do it, even if it was for purely logistical reasons. Her tentacles wrapped around them, enveloping them in shadows.

"Mmm-hmm, don't let a certain Berserker commander catch you two like that." Drew flicked off the bathroom light and opened the door into the Wild West. She barged into the hall and grabbed the nearest pair of Oracles and sucker punched them. "That's for nominating Lin Bai to the front line, bitches."

A lesser operative would have tried to slink through the throng. Not Drew. One advantage of reading a soul was that Drew knew all the coworkers, all the locations, all the on-dit, all the everythings the Oracle she occupied knew. Drew could more than act the part of the suit she wore, and watching her do it with such finesse was better than primetime TV.

Drew took off at a long lope, dodging blows and occasionally pausing to flip a raving researcher over her shoulder or deliver a staggering left hook to another Oracle. Bix used gates to move from one pocket of shadows to another, tailing Drew like an insubstantial pinball. Sometimes Bix would move ahead and wait for Drew to pass. Sometimes Drew veered off and Bix had to backtrack. When Drew ripped the driver out of a golf cart and sped off across a narrow tunnel connecting one biome to the next, the grand chase began.

Bix hid her grin in Ashtad's shoulder, recalling the many, many ops she and Drew had run like this. Only back then, Bix hadn't had the cover of darkness. She hadn't known about her shadows. No, she'd hopped from spot to spot, relying on costumes to help her pass unnoticed. The thrill of knowing she could be caught had made her smile every damn time. And the times she had gotten caught? Thank the powers that be for the safety net of a team.

She chuckled noiselessly against Ashtad as the risk of exposure increased.

"Cameras are going dark along the route to the security biome," Nez whispered in the comms. "Got to be the goddess. She's two pods ahead of you and moving fast."

"Picking up speed," Drew confirmed.

Ashtad thumped their clasped hands against his chest, minimizing the space they occupied as they navigated brightly lit and bustling biomes with minimal pockets of shadows. His other hand rested in the small of her back, unfazed by the darkness coiling around it. His steady heartbeat told her of the complete trust he held in her. Moving this quickly, this frequently through gates would make anyone with the slightest doubt in her sick. It boiled down to their essence resisting the threat she embodied. She vividly recalled the mission in which Ashtad had given up his last bit of fear toward her. For a memory-broken girl feral beneath a façade, who'd desperately wanted to belong to a community that embraced the gray, his complete acceptance had meant—still meant—more than the whole of the Mids to her.

"Seven sixty-two," Ashtad breathed in her hair as she moved them, his thoughts dovetailing with hers. Seven hundred and sixty-two had been the number of gates they'd traveled on that total trust mission to round up a cross-World child-trafficking ring. For thirteen straight hours, Ashtad had personally cuffed every member, no matter how insignificant. Management had released a few of those reprobates back into the wild, eyes and spies for related projects and networks. Ashtad kept tabs on all of them to this day; though, the list had gotten significantly shorter over the years.

A loud crack and protracted thunderous rumbling refocused Bix on the chaotic halls of Resen HQ. Large etched slabs rolled across the corridors and thudded into place, sealing off the exits from the biome and trapping Bix and her team. Drew slammed on her brakes; the golf cart's tires screeched as the bumper crumpled against one of the slabs. Oracles, battered and limping, stood on the other side of each slab. With broken knives and bloodied hands, the Oracles pried scanners out of the walls and smashed the screens with their boots.

"Shit," Drew muttered into her comm. "They've cut us off from the security biome and from the servers."

CHAPTER 10

Slipping into the shadows cast by the broken-down golf cart, Bix and Ashtad waited while Drew made a beeline for the nearest palm scanner embedded in a wall.

"Let me see if the locks work on this side." Drew used her sleeve to wipe blood spatter off the scanner.

"Berserkers have breached the facility," Cian updated. "They're coming from the residences."

"The goddess has one more biome until she reaches security," Nez said over a sigh.

"One? How the… Preternatural speed is cheating, I hope she knows that." Drew laid her hand on the scanner's screen. The archway glowed orange, flashed three times, then nothing. Again, Drew tried to open the lock. Again, nothing.

The Oracle on the other side of the etched slab blocking off the corridor stuck out her tongue and flipped Drew the bird.

"I can rewire it, but it'll take time we don't have," Ashtad offered.

"Then we ditch the subtlety and keep going," Bix answered. "We've got to beat the goddess to the servers."

"We're six biomes away from the security center." Drew backed away from the scanner and sneered at the Oracle taunting her on the other side. "Let's do long jumps. Let me be the only one seen. I want to know if there's someone alive in security to intercept us. If I get tangled up, you guys move on."

"No time for you to have a go at your tormentor there, Drew," Bix half joked. Drew had a vengeful bent, a deeply twisted one that was married to her impulsive streak.

"It's all good. That gal is an Oracle of the Future. Watching me vanish right in front of her will freak her the hell out, which would make the owner of this suit extremely happy." Drew hooked her thumbs in her belt and marched purposefully toward the sealed tunnel and the tormentor.

Bix used gates to move her team as far as she could see down the tunnel. Time was not on their side, and the Mids couldn't afford failure.

The indignant squawk of Drew's tormentor was barely perceptible as Drew kept walking and Bix kept deploying gates. The process repeated again and again with Drew the only visible element. If anyone was watching a camera, it'd look like the feeds had been spliced. Drew kept her stride even and uninterrupted as she strode through gate after gate with a shadow keeping its distance.

They passed psychopomps in each biome. The halls teemed with soul escorts in pursuit of wily souls freed from their bodies, freed from their threads, and freed from the grueling quest for full Fatehood.

Bix didn't pause, neither did Drew as Nez and Cian kept the updates running in their ears. Ashtad held Bix tighter as they moved into the sixth biome, the security center. Drew led the team down a dim corridor awash in the yellow-green of monitors.

"At least breaking in isn't going to be a problem." Drew high-stepped over a corpse collapsed across the threshold of the security center.

The hydraulic door locks clicked an eerie dirge, caught in a loop of sensors registering the body in the doorway. Inside, five more bodies sprawled on the floor of the overpacked room, two more lay wedged in their chairs, trapped by a large electronics console that better suited a spaceship than a monitoring station.

"Normally, when you snap a human neck, the heads don't stay backward." Drew crouched amid the cluster of dead Oracles and rolled the nearest one over. "No other damage, not even to the knuckles. I don't think these ladies saw their attacker coming."

Bix recalled her darkness, unmasking herself and Ashtad.

"The goddess is getting her hands dirty? What changed?" Ashtad checked one of the corpses in a chair. "Still warm. No rigor. Discord was just here."

"She must have seen Drew on the monitors." Bix motioned to the bank of screens on one wall. "She spotted one of my gates when the Devourers struck and probably put two and two together."

"You guys going to conduct an official autopsy right now, or are you going to continue with the actual mission before the goddess gets to the servers?" Nez prodded over the comms.

"He's right." Bix scanned the room, looking for a clue to where discord was headed. "The only thing to slow her down is the lock on the servers' room. I need the image of the room if we're going to pull off this rescue."

"MWA reinforcements following the Berserkers inside, widening the sweep," Cian said. "Chief is eight biomes away. The Berserkers are gassing the researchers and letting the MWA haul the bodies."

"Bixie, you've got to get that goddess before she picks up on the arrival of the MWA or they're dead meat," Drew urged.

"Data. Data is the priority," Bix asserted, even as her brain screamed objections. People mattered more than the mission, but if this mission failed, more people than were on Zamarad would suffer the consequences. Then again, the last time she'd let the Berserkers contend with a divine threat, they'd lost men. But she couldn't not let the soldiers do their job. Smothering them would only build resentment. She had to trust they could handle it. Trust that Tobek would call if he needed her. Trust. It was hard to do, but she had to do it. "Tobek knows his people and knows the threat."

He also knew the goddess, but there was no point in bringing it up to the team. If Tobek had wanted her to know something critical, he'd have told her. He hadn't even bothered to tell her the goddess's name. That alone spoke volumes.

"Let's get the servers and get out." Ashtad punched buttons on the panel. "What booby traps are we looking at, Drew?"

"The kind that'll take off body parts." Drew shouldered Ashtad aside and keyed in a string. The front wall of the monitoring room dropped, revealing an idyllic conservatory. Instead of walls lined with color-coded bundled cables, lines of blinking lights, and cooling pads covering the floor; it was a garden, an outdoor vignette kept indoors. These weren't the monstrous variants of flora that existed aboveground, these were more akin to the formal gardens surrounding a human palace. Except for the sculptures—those were a bit odd what with being vertical frosted pods containing people. Men, specifically, in track pants, T-shirts, and leaf tattoos.

Great. Pod-people. That should've made it easier to move them. Should've. Except they weren't really people-people. They were Sage servers that belonged to the Houses of Fate, and Fates loved deceptions, obvious and otherwise.

"We aren't lucky enough for those pods to be glorified takeout containers, are we?" Bix asked Drew, leaning over the console and trying to get a better look at the oddly designed floor of the pods. "Like, could I just pluck them and go?"

"I wish." Drew pointed at the garden. "Can't take the men without separating them from the pods. Can't take the pods without blowing up the biome. Because all the biomes are linked, blowing this one starts a chain reaction that destroys the World. To make it extra complicated, check out the lower legs of the guys inside the pods. See how they're cuffed into the pod? It's a physical connection. It's like their legs are plugs, and the pod floor is a huge socket. If the servers don't key in a code to eject themselves from the sockets, they lose their legs. They lose their legs—"

"We lose data since their entire bodies are storage devices." Ashtad whistled low and jerked his thumb at the garden. "I can cause a power surge. The electrical disruption ought to force the system controlling the pods to reset and potentially eject the servers in the process."

"That could work." Bix nodded. "How fast can you do it?"

"This close to a ley line? Pretty damn fast." Ashtad tucked an errant curl behind his ear. "I need to be down there with them, though."

"Anyone want to recall the caution card we got before we started this op? Seven of Swords? The *This Deception Could Go Poorly for You, Sparky* card?" Drew wagged a finger at Ashtad.

"Not going to lie, it is a risk." Ashtad cracked his knuckles. "Electricity, plus servers, plus combustibles. But we don't have time to play this safe. The goddess is here somewhere."

"Why hasn't she already done it? Why hasn't she blown the pods? Destroyed the data? What is she waiting for?" Bix's guts warned this was a trap. Too many things weren't adding up, but the faster she got her friends and the servers away from the goddess, the faster she could yank discord out of the greater game. Except, what did the Fates have up their sleeves? She hated not knowing which trick they were playing. "Nez, why would the Fates blow up the servers? If the point is to preserve the data, why would they build a self-destruct? Nez? Nez?"

"Nez blacked out," Cian answered instead. "Medics are working on him."

"Shit. We're too deep to bail now." Bix grimaced, making the call that went against her better sense. "Drew, eyes on the monitors. You watch for the goddess. Cian, warn Runjit I'm delivering Sage servers who might have just had their legs amputated. I'll drop them in the center of the chamber, so move gurneys and lay tarps. Ashtad, you're up."

Gates to the garden of servers opened.

CHAPTER 11

Lilacs and forget-me-nots blended with the citrusy scents of lemons and oranges riding above the earthy aroma of healthy soil. The artificial breeze flowed with enough strength to ruffle a few hairs but not lift away locks. The occasional chime of tiny bells decorating herbal plots disrupted the white noise of burbling fountains. The absence of insects made it an incredibly pleasant prison, as far as prisons went.

Bix suffered no illusion that this was anything less than a prison. These Sage servers weren't free to roam around the biome much less Resen HQ. She really, really hoped there were bathrooms and bedrooms hidden behind the walls of the garden. Otherwise, those servers were nowhere near human anymore, which would make fixing them super problematic if anything went awry.

"Five pods. Five guys. Five," Ashtad murmured to himself, holding out his arms and moving them like the sweeping hands of a clock as electricity built within him, sending pricks and tickles over Bix's skin wherever she touched Ashtad. "Bix, the metal wind chimes, can you place a set at the top of each pod, please?"

Bix put her back to Ashtad's and did as he asked while scanning the room with every sense she had for the goddess of discord. The goddess had been ahead of them the whole run; she was bound to be here now. What was she waiting for? To kill Ashtad because he wanted Resen? To eavesdrop on comms to see if she could learn the location of the survivors?

"Bixie, back of the third pod to your right," Drew whispered.

"Hello, Auntie," the goddess sang as she rolled around the lime-green outer casing of the pod. Her words were slurred, mangled by the damage to her face. She looked every bit the victim of an acid attack after three months of recovery. Yet, in the uniform of the station's security team, she also looked as fierce as any Senegalese soldier.

"Auntie?" Bix tilted her head. "We're not related, are we?"

It was possible. Maybe. It wasn't as if Bix remembered her family.

"In the greater sense? Of course, we are all descendants of the Chaos, the feminine eternal." The goddess's distorted laughter still held that rich tone from the surface battle. "But in this case, auntie is an honorific for an older woman. And you, dear Auntie, are older than all of us in this chamber combined."

"You speak like you know me," Bix challenged, keeping the goddess's attention. Tobek had mentioned the goddess knew the original Chimera, and this time was as good as any to find out in what way. Meanwhile, she pressed her shoulder blade against Ashtad's to get him to pivot so she was the one fully facing the goddess of discord.

"I know you better than most, though there are six others who could claim the same." The goddess chuckled as her eyes darted low. "I am I, and I am what you gave me."

"You're a Mid World guardian. That's why I can't detect you. The excess of Mids' magic is hiding you from me." Bix cursed under her breath as her skin turned clammy and her heart sped. The original Chimera had divested sections of her memories to seven Mid World guardians. Her memories had driven those guardians insane, to the point they were feared by their pantheons. Bix had reclaimed three segments. Four remained. Discord was apparently one of the four. Shit.

"Of all the times," Drew quietly shrieked. "No, no, no. Not now, not now, not now. Bixie, not now. Finish the mission. Do not finish off the goddess."

The disadvantage of assimilating a chunk of memories was the downtime required to recover from it. Each merge took longer than the last to find its matching puzzle pieces within her mind. The third assimilation had taken weeks of her being utterly unaware of what she was doing, to whom, and where. She wasn't the only one affected by it, either. Her team, her friends, they suffered consequences too. Drew was right—now was not the time. After Resen was delivered to the Host. After Tobek and the Berserkers weren't at risk from a divine cleaner. After her team was as safe as she could make them.

Alas, two gods had been eager to keep the memories she'd given them. One had been desperate to be rid of them. All had hunted her in one fashion or another. This goddess seemed neither eager nor desperate.

"Your name, memory keeper. What is your name?" Bix demanded.

"I am Musso-Koroni." The goddess inclined her head. "Forsaken by my pantheon and embraced by the Consortium. I am here on their business, Chimera. You should be pleased with their decision. For the Mid Worlds to have the knowledge required to build Project Resen would destroy the balance. You uphold the balance. Resen must be terminated along with all who know about it. That includes the storm god's son, whatever is inside the Oracle, and the soldiers swarming this World."

"As a Mid World guardian, you have a duty to your divine essence to protect the Mids," Bix countered as Ashtad tapped his heel against hers, then clenched his butt repeatedly. It was a code they'd used on many an op when words could not be spoken. The number of cheek clenches equaled the number of seconds until action. The heel tap opened and closed the phrasing. He'd repeat the tactile message three times: the first to get her attention, the second to deliver the message, the third for action. Bix kept speaking to the goddess, holding discord's attention. "If you allow the Devourers to destroy the Mids, you will sacrifice yourself in the process. You will weaken until you become a husk. Your believers gone. The souls on which you feed, taken by gods whose powers are not interlaced with the Mids. Destroying Resen destroys the Mids, which destroys you. Why care what the Chimera thinks?"

"I went to the Chimera centuries ago, begging for release from this continuous life, and she said to me, 'Abide a little longer. Be my protector. Keep safe my secrets until I can come for them again. If you do this for me, I will set you free without pain, without suffering, without the weight of time wearing you down.'" Musso-Koroni smiled, or rather attempted to. "Tell me, Auntie, when you were floating in the ether, hollow as a husk, were you aware of time? Does time exist in the ether? Or did you awaken after your prolonged rest oblivious to the idea, to its very construct?"

"Don't romanticize the reset a husking inflicts," Bix ridiculed. "You awaken in agony and it is chased by confusion and fear. You don't know *what* you are. The concept of *where* is ages in coming. As for time itself? Glacially slow in the ether compared to the Mids."

"I think I will enjoy it anyway," the goddess dismissed, skimming her fingers over a pod. "Will you take me now, Auntie, or will you insist on us playing our parts in this game directed by fickle powers?"

"Who set you on Resen?" Bix refused to examine the goddess's baiting as anything more than a ploy to sow conflict and doubt within Drew and Ashtad. "The name of your handler inside the Consortium, who is it?"

"There is no one member," Musso-Koroni derided. "Quashing Project Resen was a consensus decision of the committee. My team deploys at the behest of the committee, not a single member."

There were so many things wrong with that statement, but Ashtad tapped Bix's heel for the third time, and the final countdown began. The electricity in the room flared, sizzling over her skin, lifting her hair, arcing across the metals she wore. Her comm went down with a piercing whine. The control panel in the security room blew. Amid the shower of sparks, Bix removed Drew from Zamarad.

"Always for others, never for yourself," the goddess shouted over the din of electric destruction and threw out her hands. "All who know about Resen must die. The Oracle you have denied me will now die slowly at the hands of the demigod cowering behind you."

The bells atop the pods exploded like fireworks. The pods cracked, high-tech eggs splintered, ejecting Sage servers like cassettes from an old tape player. Bix caught the Sages midair and moved them along with Ashtad to safety. More gates went up as layered walls, trapping the server garden. Bix dropped to a crouch, slapping her hands against the floor to move the biome and just this biome without any tethered systems, connections, or sections.

Gates to the highly destructive ether opened.

CHAPTER 12

Nothing. No exploding biome. No attacking goddess. Nothing but the swift corrosion of the garden as the electrical storm petered out. Created by Mids' magic, the security biome could not withstand the voracious appetite of the ether. Walls vanished, plants disintegrated, pods dissolved to less than dust, until all that was left was the goddess of discord.

Bix's pulse thundered as she surveyed the unexpected calm enforced by the ether.

"Thank you, Chimera." Musso-Koroni swept a grand bow. "The Fates' servers were safe from me inside their shells. I couldn't have destroyed their minds without your help."

"You didn't have time to throw your magic," Bix argued as she straightened. The song of nothingness in motion played around them. Darkness so oppressive hindered all light save for the glow of divinity the goddess exuded.

"A show. A distraction." The goddess flicked her wrists and shrugged. "Believers want to see magic in action. They want to see it start and stop. We both know what is innate requires no gesticulations, no showmanship. It exists because we exist. My magic filled that chamber with every breath I took."

Bix looked up at the goddess through the fall of her teal bangs and curled a lip. "That's why you waited for us to arrive in the garden. That was the trap."

"The storm god's son has been exposed to me twice now." Musso-Koroni drummed her fingertips together. "I am curious to know if he is still the steadfast ally you believe him to be."

"If you've harmed him…" Bix snarled.

"You'll what? Husk me? Take back that which is yours and leave me adrift out here to be captured by the Devourers?" The goddess turned her blistered cheek toward Bix, a cheek that continued to heal with the swiftness of a midlevel god. "Removing me would be inconvenient for you, yes? Yes. I heard the Oracle."

Bix didn't answer that. There was a game afoot with the goddess, and Bix didn't have a good feeling about it. These days, if a god attacked her, she'd husk them in a heartbeat, but not this goddess. She wasn't exactly sure what she *could* do to Musso-Koroni that wouldn't end with Bix in recovery for a month or more and the mission completely fubared.

"There are things I know about you, Chimera, things I have pieced together from your countless snapshots of moments alongside unmatched emotions and sounds." The goddess tapped her temple. "I also know the old Berserker you keep at your side. I've known him since we arrived in the Mids together for our demigod trials. Of the many things I learned about you from him, I learned you are a patient entity. Therefore, I will be patient too."

"Does that mean you'll stop trying to destroy Resen?" Bix asked, unsure of what a goddess of discord considered "patience."

"Of course not," Musso-Koroni scoffed. "You have your mission, and I have mine. I mean only that I will be patiently waiting for you to fulfill your promise to *me*. The Chimera, regardless of her age and form, has always been an entity of her word."

"Meanwhile you continue to hunt my friends and allies? That's not patience, that's a threat," Bix retorted.

"If I wanted to threaten you, I'd take your Berserker. He is your heart, after all." Musso-Koroni hooked her thumbs in her belt. "You fight so hard for him and don't understand why. He does. He knows it with every breath he takes. He's just waiting for you to remember."

Her *heart*? Did that mean Tobek had been her lover? Her consort? Or was that some dig at Tobek being the means by which the original Chimera had managed her emotions? The latter was easier to believe. Dude had a long list of redeemable qualities, no doubt, but he and the Chimera version 1.0 had had a serious power imbalance that couldn't have made for a healthy relationship if they'd been lovers.

"Tobek said he knew you. Didn't say if you two were friendly, though."

"You two didn't start off friendly. In fact, he despised you for millennia before you were even aware of his existence. You are the reason he is indentured to the Fates. You are the reason he failed his god trials. You are the reason his original pantheon abandoned him, and you remain the reason every pantheon he has since fathered has denied him and forced him out. To this day, he continues to be rejected by those he raised up to be mightier than their forefathers."

Bix didn't want to listen to the lies of a goddess of discord, but Musso-Koroni had told her more about Tobek in one minute than Bix had been able to learn in months of living with the man. She knew better than to listen to a deity doling out bits of personal history. She knew firsthand how easy it was to get addicted to the tidbits. She knew, and yet...

"Did I tell the Fates to bind him, to deny him his ability to ascend?" Bix asked despite her better sense.

Musso-Koroni stared at her, then broke up laughing. "No, no, no. You were not aware of him at the time. He thought he knew you, though, which made him a fool. He failed to understand the cyclical dance of the fire and the night."

"The Phoenix and the Chimera," Bix translated. "When the Phoenix burns every five hundred years, he razes the Mids until I come along and extinguish his fire and his life."

Bix's relationship with Feng was complex, but at least they

both knew how this iteration of it had started and how it would end. The middle, however, was filled with surprises, like the two of them becoming allies against the Devourers. Who'd have thunk it?

The same could not be said for her relationship with Tobek. He knew how it had started. She didn't. They were both immortal, so their relationship *couldn't* end. Meanwhile, the middle was proving to be fucked the hell up.

"In our time, fire meant warmth, warmth meant health, health meant survival that became prosperity." Musso-Koroni raised her unmarred brow. "He struck a deal with the Fates to protect his people from the darkness, to spare them the creep of unending night."

Bix laid a hand over her stomach as her guts knotted. "The Fates didn't correct him. They let him damn his people."

"The Phoenix made his last stand in the heart of that village, reducing every living thing to ash, everything except the demigod who'd traded his divinity to save his people." Musso-Koroni grunted with disgust. "Too headstrong. Too prideful. Too full of the masculine weaknesses. That is how he ended up as the original Berserker. The Fates' first chosen warrior."

The who what now? *Original* Berserker? First one? Hot off the press? Holy shit.

"Rage was Tobek's initial reaction, wasn't it? That's why a Berserker's power is rooted in their rage." Bix's heart wept for Tobek's folly, for the horrific deaths he was not allowed to forget. Her hand rested over the Eternal Knot warming beneath her skin, his response to her distress. "What was Tobek going to become that his pantheon feared so much? A god of war?"

"A god of so much more, and that was way back then. Imagine what he'd become now if the Fates were to cut the ties that bind him." Musso-Koroni tilted her head, advancing on Bix.

Bix backed away as her mind reeled from the revelations. Part of her was overjoyed that she wasn't the one who'd damned Tobek, but the knowledge opened a dozen cans of worms as to the what and why of their relationship. After all, the first time *she'd* met *him* was in her role as executioner. She'd been ordered to kill him by someone she couldn't remember. But, why would a goddess of discord tell her the story of his hubris now? What was Musso-Koroni's game? What did she get from this? Bix to distrust Tobek? A part of her always had, instinctually. A small part. Like ten percent. Maybe fifteen. It had a lot to do with not knowing their past. Musso-Koroni's story caused Bix to trust Tobek a little more, not less.

Then again, the goddess could be lying, as all gods were wont to do.

"If you knew him as a young godling, then tell me his name. The one he had when you two began your trials," Bix demanded.

"That name is dead and powerless." Musso-Koroni seized Bix's arm, causing a frisson of energy to skitter along Bix's skin as foreign magic assailed her. "He has been known by many names over the course of his endless damnation, each with their own stigma. The only name of value is the one he accepts, the honorific given to him by his men, the ones who have never deserted him. You, on the other hand, number among those who fled from him in his greatest hour of despair. You now call him by a name no other has used. A name that holds no power, no meaning, no privilege. You are a poison to him."

Bix shuddered with the panic rising within her. "Tobek…"

"He is in great peril." Musso-Koroni flashed a brilliant smile in a beautifully restored face. "Did you really think the Houses of Fate would build a secret facility and not incorporate a defense against the gods they're trying to keep at bay? My team and I only stunned the beasts. I imagine they're waking up right about now, quite hungry. He is the closest thing to a god on that accursed World."

Bix leaned back as her brain tried to pick apart the meaning. "They?"

"Nabaziix," the goddess chuckled, releasing Bix. "The god hunters. We may not be able to die, but being eaten alive is no great pleasure."

"Tobek. No, not Tobek. Not Tobek." Bix reached for her tech...tech created by Mid World magic, tech destroyed by the ether. Dread washed over her in great glacial waves as she threw open gates.

Musso-Koroni's laughter followed Bix back to the Mids.

CHAPTER 13

"Tobek?" Bix screamed as her shadows coursed through the biomes of Resen HQ, filling every corridor, closet, and room, turning the entire station pitch-black. "Tobek? Tobek?"

Her darkness transmitted her voice beyond her immediate surrounds and returned images of soldiers carrying unconscious Sages and Oracles. Not a one of those soldiers was a Berserker.

"Tobek!" She struggled to hold on to her sanity as visions of Tobek being dismembered in a dozen different ways in a dozen different cosmic locations threatened to trigger her gatekeeper magic. "Tobek?"

The Eternal Knot on her chest warmed, glowing soft shades of green and silver. Tobek. Her nails clawed at her skin, at the knot. "Tobek, damn it, where are you?"

She wanted to shout at him to beware, beware the Nabaziix, but if the MWA didn't know Tobek was a demigod, she didn't want to be the one to out him. He certainly didn't talk about his origins, and all the other Berserkers were human. Desperation made people do stupid. She couldn't be desperate.

She wasn't desperate. She was terrified. Uncommonly, uncharacteristically terrified.

A strong arm wrapped around her waist and hauled her

against a soggy, solid chest. The blessedly familiar push and pull of blended magic calmed her panic.

"I'm here," Tobek soothed. "I'm right here, sweetheart. I'm right here."

She spun around and gripped him in a tight hug. Her shadows retreated from the biomes and coiled around him, locking him against her. His great big chest vibrated under her head. He didn't try to escape. He let her hold him while the tremors of terror racked her.

"Nabaziix," she whispered. She'd encountered a Nabaziix once. It'd tried to swallow her whole. Fortunately, she was a gatekeeper, or she might have gained firsthand knowledge of the creature's digestive system.

"A nest of them, yes. We found them." Tobek stroked her hair, the rhythm reassuring.

She closed her eyes and cursed herself for being so stupid. Of course he'd handled the Nabaziix. He had a team of Berserkers at his side. She'd been silly to be worried. Why had she been *so* worried? She glanced at her hands clutching Tobek's jacket as if her life depended on it. No, like *his* life depended on it. Her skin still showed the tint of surplus Devourer essence. She shouldn't have been able to experience that level of fear, but she had.

The goddess. Must have been. How, though? Musso-Koroni was a goddess of discord. Bix had seen proof of the goddess's influence in these very halls. But Bix didn't feel hostility or resentment or envy or anything more than fear, fear for Tobek and only Tobek. Not the rest of her team. Not her friends. Not the mission. Tobek. A man she knew beyond a doubt was more than capable of taking care of himself.

Nothing made sense. What the hell was wrong with her?

"Is that why you're wet?" she asked, loosening her hold and recalling her shadows into her body. "Am I hugging Nabaziix drool?"

This time, his laughter was audible.

"It's water from the aquifer." He gently tugged her hair.

"*Somebody* removed a biome as we were crossing the connector. Sent us for a swim."

"Thought the passages were sealed," she offered sheepishly.

"It's good you did. It led us to what the Devourers were after." He tipped his head from side to side. "And the Nabaziix."

"They're in the water? Outside the biomes? And *you* had to reconnoiter? Isn't there an entire branch of the army who aren't Berserkers up there investigating the Devourer aftermath who are better equipped to run a naval mission?" Bix narrowed her eyes at him.

"I'm going to pretend you didn't imply Berserkers don't know how to conduct amphibious maneuvers." Tobek thumped the tip of her nose with his knuckle.

Bix gasped and slapped her hands over her mouth. "Don't tell me you have a secret submarine stowed at the coal plant. Is that why you guys are on the waterfront? Is there an underground dry dock beneath the parking garage?"

Despite the sodden uniform, the respirator, and the oxygen tank, Tobek managed to covey unholy mirth in his expression. "If you are cracking jokes, then you must be feeling better."

She hung her head and gave him a bit of breathing room. "Um, yeah. Sorry about that."

"Hey, no, no." He caught her hand in his. "Never apologize for caring. No. Not to me, not for me, not ever. Okay?"

"It must be the excess Mids' magic that's making me loopy." She huffed and introduced more space between them. "I'm not entirely sure what's going on with me, to be truthful."

He let go of her hand, allowing her the distance. "Want to talk about it?"

"Not in the middle of an op."

No how, no way did she want to divulge the depths of her crazy right now, and she sure as shit wasn't going to download the conversation she'd had with Musso-Koroni about *him*. This was not the time. This was not the place. And this was not her right mind.

"All right." He straightened and adjusted his oxygen tank.

"Grab a new watch and let me show you what the guys found in the bedrock below the aquifer."

"Below the aquifer? Just how much oxygen are you toting?" She opened tiny gates to home and fetched another smartwatch and earpiece. At this rate, Cian was going to have to triple the production of her tech. Gah. Cian. Cameras. Hot mics. She keyed in the update code for her bug and bit her lip. Her team was going to razz her so badly about her little freak-out. She totally deserved it too.

"It's not the quantity, it's the quality of the refill spell," Tobek objected with mock affront.

"That's what she said," Bix teased as her watch flashed its welcome.

Greetings, Bix. What data shall we find today?

"I've warned you about those gutter comments." Tobek took her hand in his and bent over it, bringing it to the shield of his mask. "Bug, switch channels to coal plant forty-one, authorization seven-seven-two."

Bix's smartwatch lit up. *Greetings, Herr Schmidt. Awaiting authorization from: Bix.*

"You co-opted my bug, Herr Schmidt?" Bix asked indignantly, calling him by the code name he used when shit was hitting the fan. "Switch channels, Bug."

Switching channels.

The murmur of men not in the biome with her tickled her ear.

"Cian and I have certain understandings." Tobek put his hand to his ear. "Xipil, send the last image green team uploaded to her phone, would you?"

Bix's watch face changed colors. *Incoming image from: Coal Plant.*

"Display," Bix said to her bug.

An image of a cavern hewn in bedrock blasted along her sleeve.

"Ready to see what's been driving you crazy?" Tobek ran his gloved hand down her arm and tweaked her fingers.

"He's standing next to me." She stuck out her tongue as gates opened.

The picture on her watch had failed to convey the mystical beauty of the cavern. Landing on its uneven and sloping floor, Bix gawped at the light show playing along the walls. It was like standing inside a black opal lit from its core. Watery blues and midnight plums twirled with sultry golds and forest greens. The air flowed like gentle tides lapping against a wintry beach, crisp and clean. The massiveness of the space obliterated the claustrophobia of being miles underground.

Alas, for all its beauty, it did not like Bix, not one bit. She clung to Tobek's amputated arm, steadying herself against the swells of strong native magic attempting to evict her Other World self from its heart.

"You sure you're well enough for this?" Tobek asked, turning to her. "You still haven't recovered from earlier, have you? That's not good."

"It's like I'm trapped in a dragon queen's belly while she's running a marathon," Bix wheezed, rubbing her ribs. "There is definitely a pure source of Mids' magic down here. I'm not a fan, and it is mutual."

"This is too much for you. Head back to Luz," he urged. "You can check this out once you're balanced."

"Bite me," she groused. "I'm here. I've got my frilly big-girl panties on. Let's do this."

"If you can endure it, I believe you will find it quite rewarding. A once-in-a-lifetime sort of thing." Tobek smoothed her hair over her shoulder.

"Once in a lifetime, eh?" She gave him the side-eye. "Since you probably know how old I really am, that's saying something."

"Sticking it out, then?" he cajoled.

"Why not? It's not like it's going to kill me." She took a painful shallow breath and kicked her own magic up a notch, digging into the surrounding native magic with enough force to make her grateful she'd pigged out on Devourer essence earlier. The pendant containing Feng's dewclaw warmed as the Phoenix aided her from afar. "Besides, I'm not leaving any of you guys down here. This has got to be the magical equivalent of radiation poisoning. Let's get through this *tout de suite*."

"*Noswaith dda,* my lady of darkness," greeted a joyfully familiar Berserker. Angel hunter, proud Welshman, and Runjit's freewheeling battle buddy Hywl bowed as he exited the mouth of a tunnel, as sodden as his commander.

"Hywl." Bix smiled and pointed to the Welshman's squishing combat boots. "I am so sorry about that surprise bath."

"I got to ride a Nabaziix for the first time." Hywl rocked up on his toes. "Popped a cherry I didn't know I had, it did. That says something, I assure you. Oy, Chief, we found some of these while you were topside."

Hywl gestured to two of his men who presented Tobek with broken clay tiles.

Tobek inspected the chunks. "Wards. These are shattered wards that would've kept the angels and dragons at bay. Whoever did that exposed a back door to the biomes."

"It wasn't the god squad." Bix examined the tiles over Tobek's shoulder. "The last thing they wanted was for more people to discover what was happening on this World."

"There are multiple strike marks." Tobek brushed his thumb over the divots. "Shallow. The perpetrators weren't particularly strong, so they're unlikely to have been one of the superpowers."

"Perhaps researchers with chisels?" Bix had one researcher in mind, the same researcher who regularly carved messages for an archangel into his leg. Maybe Nez had been planning something with the angels? Setting up a dead drop below the aquifer?

"It's possible." Tobek chucked the useless tiles aside. "Hywl, why don't you show us what the Devourers were after?"

Seven men from Hywl's team went first into the narrow tunnel. Another seven plus Tobek brought up the rear, leaving Bix as the stuffing in a man sandwich. Drew would be cackling with delight if she were in Bix's pumps. Bix would've been too had it not been for every step bringing her closer to the source of potent Mids' magic and the source of rhythmic shushes and sloshing.

Bright light turned the black opal pale, forcing Bix to shield her eyes as they emerged from the tunnel into a cavern smaller than the first but no less awesome. Dozens of tunnels dotted the walls, each hollow gleaming with its own jeweled light. The Berserkers fanned out along a narrow ring of rock surrounding an undulating pool of a substance constantly morphing from liquid to solid to energy. Its colors flared in continuous change. It gave off no scent beyond clean. The temperature fluctuated through extremes with alterations of state.

Bix's instinct was to suffocate it right out of existence. Her darkness rippled up and down her spine, eager to oblige. Yet her heart ached with pangs of bittersweet recognition. Amid her broken memories, there was a thirty-second GIF of a similar entity surrounded by starlight and space. There was no hostility tied to the memory, just wonder. That same wonder suppressed her instincts now.

"It's—it's struggling," she whispered, looking to Tobek.

"Yes, it is." Tobek put his arm across her shoulders and tugged her to his side. "That is a newly born ley line. It is striving to adapt, to exist."

"Ley lines are born?" She rested her head against him, fascinated by the cycle of swells growing into towers and softening into limbs, then scattering as sparks to fall as rain.

"Ley lines are akin to the circulatory system of the Mids. Mids' magic is constantly evolving. As new Worlds are added to the collective, native magic must grow to accommodate them. Proper development includes..." He paused to gasp and chuckle as one of the ephemeral arms stretched above them, then brushed the top of his head.

"Proper circulation," she finished for him as the substance in the pit tentatively reached out to each Berserker. The men stood still, not flinching. A few laughed, Hywl among them.

When the substance extended toward her, her shadows

responded unbidden. Tentacles fanned from her back. The substance jerked aside, then divided, mimicking the shape and sway of her darkness. Weird.

Bix stepped away from Tobek as the substance cycled through its states, continuing to mirror her darkness.

"I think it's trying to dance with you, sweetheart," Tobek whispered through the comms.

"You know that's another way of saying it's picking a fight," she countered drolly.

"It's curious. You're different. It's learning," Tobek chided lightly. "Weren't you in a similar position not that long ago?"

Sure, back when she'd crawled out of the ether knowing nothing but hunger, wrath, and the acute determination to live. Her curiosity had held a violent edge. Feral, to put it mildly. This baby ley line seemed quite the opposite, so Bix bid her darkness to be gentle.

Seven tentacles of night slowly extended around her, then waited. The ley line adopted seven different states and hesitantly bumped against her darkness. The feathering touch caused painful longing to explode inside Bix with such force that she doubled over with a cry.

"Sweetheart." Tobek lunged for her. She held up a staying hand as tears trickled down her cheek. A tendril of the ley line captured them.

The swells of the greater line changed tempo, surging in asynchronous time, pitching higher, clashing together, growing volatile. The colors darkened. The cavern trembled. The ground heaved, throwing Bix and Berserkers against walls and shunting them off through the sieve of tunnels.

CHAPTER 14

B ix's darkness formed a protective ball around her as she bounced off walls and floors before slamming into a crevice and coming to a stop. Groaning, she cradled her head in her hands while her senses unscrambled. Alas, the din she heard was not her own screaming.

Monstrous keening ricocheted around the shuddering tunnel.

"Great. What are the odds the monsters are not as overgrown as the plant life here on Zamarad?" Bix muttered to herself and to anyone who might be listening. She checked her watch. Undamaged. Thankfully. Her earpiece emitted static with a side of crackling. "Guys? Anyone still linked?"

"Aye, m'lady," answered one low moan. Other barely coherent grunts checked in too. Some confirmed the visual presence of their peers, others isolation.

"Tobek?" Bix struggled to her feet, wincing as her body bemoaned the damage of being a racquetball. Her ankle twisted as her heel snapped off her pumps. Mumbling nothing kind, she took off her shoes. "Tobek? You out there?"

Silence.

"Anybody have eyes on Chief?" Hywl's rasp came through the comm. A round of negatives came in response.

"Okay, boys, if you can send me a location pic, do so. Those who can't, sound off." Bix tugged her dress into place and waited as Bug stacked the queue of fish-eye images and associated names. She had no idea where the guys had the external cameras fitted to their gear, but she was relieved they all did. Gates sent the bulk of the team to an outer chamber at Luz where the air was clean, the magic nontoxic, and orders could be coordinated with the coal plant.

She kept Hywl with her at his insistence. Frankly, she was grateful for his company. Whether it was the aftermath of touching the baby ley line or the tumble through bedrock, her senses were all out of whack and she had a sinking feeling in her gut.

"Base, turn on the locator beacon for Chief. Enable the two of us to track him." Hywl ripped off a flapping tatter of his uniform jacket and stuffed it in his pocket.

Bug projected a blinking silver light on her sleeve. As the bedrock of Zamarad was unmapped, the beacon didn't do a whole lot of good.

"Bug, what can we do about making that ping useful?"

Searching… Unable to identify reference points.

"Shit," Bix groaned.

"Don't worry, we'll find him," Hywl assured Bix, running a finger along the deep crack in his respirator mask. "If we have to play Hot and Cold, we'll do it."

"Aw, Hywl, I love your optimism, because you're absolutely right." Bix patted his arm. "Tobek can't hide from me. Not even when he actually tries. I'm more worried about what's going to get to him before we do."

As if sensing her challenge, fetid breath blasted past them on rank hot air. A jeweled eyeball pressed against the opening of the tunnel in which they stood.

Hywl drew his combat knife and stepped between her and the opening. It was his instinct to protect, and it was so damn charming, she didn't have the heart to burst his testosterone bubble. At least not until a long snout rammed the opening, widening it with each determined blow. A large nostril sniffed the opening. With a whine of disappointment, it turned away, giving Bix enough of a view to know the exact type of company they had. A bigger, meaner, and singularly focused cousin of the basilisk…who drooled…a lot.

"That is your buddy the Nabaziix, and that is how we're going to find your fearless leader." She looped her arm around Hywl's and smiled up at him. Gates moved them in pursuit of the beast tracking its prey. She gave it as wide a berth as the terrain allowed, sometimes going ahead, then falling behind, or switching to adjacent as it tromped through the labyrinth of tunnels.

"Fair to say we kept away from its head on the ride through the aquifer. Think I'll buy it some breath mints." Hywl wagged his blade at the reptilian mash-up of a sea serpent and a polacanthus dinosaur with eight feet. Its spikes screeched along the bedrock, making it rain rubble. Every time its barbed tail smashed a wall, the entire area quaked.

"This isn't the first time the Fates have used Nabaziix as watchdogs. My guess is our friend here guards more than the research station. A baby ley line that has yet to connect to the greater grid of the Mids would be a temptation for an entire class of gods, even without Resen." She braced for the wave of fear to overwhelm her as it had in the ether and hoped Hywl wouldn't panic in the face of her darkness. Of all Tobek's men, Hywl seemed the most at ease around her, but then he was that way around most people. An outwardly affable guy until he encountered an angel, then he was all lethal hate. She and he had that in common.

"We found the nest of these beasties farther in, and Chief put them back to sleep. The ley line explosion must've awakened them." Hywl squeezed their linked arms against his side. "I do get why they would hunt Chief, my lady. He doesn't talk about it, but those of us who need to know, know."

"Thank you. I didn't want to assume." She sighed with relief. Make that double the relief, because that terror from the ether had yet to attack. It must have been caused by Musso-Koroni and not the excess of Mids' magic. Phobos exacerbating her fear she could understand; that was his emotion to twist and enhance. However, Musso-Koroni was a goddess of discord. What did Bix's need to protect Tobek have to do with discord?

The silver beacon on Bix's sleeve flashed bigger and brighter. *Herr Schmidt in 300 feet.*

Bix stretched her senses, searching for the telltale push and pull of Tobek's magic with hers. As had happened in the biome, she couldn't sense him. Just as she hadn't been able to detect the angel before he had impaled her. Just as she hadn't been able to feel Musso-Koroni inside the server room.

Ley line or decay, which was it?

Herr Schmidt in 200 feet.

"I'm sorry, my big slobbering friend," Bix said to the Nabaziix. "We need to relocate you and steal your prize. Thanks for all your help, though."

Gates returned the Nabaziix back to where they'd encountered it. Its indignant cry was distant enough that they should have plenty of time to get Tobek out of whatever pickle had him incommunicado.

"My lady, this is the path to the ley line." Hywl tapped the visor light in his mask. Though the face shield was fractured, the light still worked. It shone on a set of broken wards.

"Shouldn't the tunnel be brighter, then?" Bix picked up the tiles and skimmed her fingers over the gouges. They weren't made by a chisel as she'd originally thought; the slope of the fractures was too even, too consistent to have been formed by the repetitive strike of a tool. No, the damage looked more like claw marks, which ruled out Nez as the vandal. None of the gods on Musso-Koroni's team had been animal gods, and the scratches were far too small to belong to the Nabaziix. What the hell else was down here?

"Should be." Hywl moved ahead of her again, ever the vigilant protector.

Herr Schmidt in 100 feet.

"Tobek?" Bix called, carrying the tiles with her.

Herr Schmidt in 50 feet.

"I don't like this," Hywl grumbled, raising his arm, his blade fisted like a man who knew how to brandish it as an extension of his body rather than a s'mores stick. "Something's off."

Bix could no longer tell what was off, normal, or decay. The inability to apply her most basic survival skill was infuriating. Anger was a comfortable emotion for her. It kept her focused. So focused, she bumped into Hywl standing stock-still in the mouth of the tunnel.

"By all the unholy…" The Welshman crept forward, allowing Bix a view of the cavern.

Herr Schmidt has arrived.

"No, Bug, Herr Schmidt hasn't gone anywhere. Terminate beacon." Bix walked to the broken ledge surrounding the baby ley line. What had once been bright and joyful now pulsed in darker hues. A whirlpool of magic existed as a moat around a continuously exploding tower of energy. Suspended in its center and encased in the bright green radiance of his own magic hung Tobek, back arched, eyes bright, mouth wide. Buck naked.

His Eternal Knot glowed teal and midnight, her brand upon his chest, the piece of her he held by his heart. The knot inflicted untold pain whenever he dared speak of their past. Was it hurting him now, protecting him, both?

Darkness shot from Bix and pierced the ley line. Sorrow crushed her in its grasp.

"Keep your grief, you little brat," she snarled as the cool solace of rage rallied to her defense. The thicket of malice inside her grew thorns and burrs, adding to the brambles striving to smother her compassion. "Give me back my Berserker."

Fire raked across her chest. Flames formed a wall in front of the ley line, forcing her darkness to retreat.

"Bix, no," commanded the fire. The blaze coalesced into massive wings and a fiery whipping tail framing the shape of a man as tall as Tobek with a swimmer's broad shoulders and lean frame. Arresting aquamarine eyes opened and stared at Bix. "Bix, it is protecting him. Trust me when I say if you attack it, you attack him. You will be the cause of his suffering."

"Feng, move," Bix demanded quietly of the Phoenix as her darkness flooded the cavern and raced beyond. It pushed into every cranny of the bedrock, then moved up to swallow the aquifer.

"Bix, think, come on, you know he is uncommonly connected to native magic. You and I feel it in his presence." Feng calmed his fire, looking more like a man and less like a firebird. "Logic, Bix. Logic over emotion. You cannot win a battle of emotion with an infant. It lacks the ability to comprehend."

"Feng…" she cautioned again.

"I can get him out of there," Feng insisted, not budging. "But you have to stop scaring the ley line and every living thing on this World. That includes the Mid World Army that is on Zamarad to gain an understanding of the effects the Devourers have on the Mids. Remember the Devourers? The real enemy we're up against?"

"I wouldn't harm the MWA," she argued as her darkness learned the rhythm of the changes of the ley line, moving with it, mirroring it.

"You wouldn't hesitate to rip them to shreds if they threatened him or any of your confidants," he corrected. "You've already caused the very branch you strive to protect to sustain injuries, haven't you? Unintentional though it was, Berserkers still got hurt. Consequences, Bix. We are apex entities; there are always negative consequences to our actions no matter our noblest intentions."

"I can only do my best," she whispered as his arguments wormed their way into her rational mind.

"Then don't be a bully." Feng turned and stood beside her. "This ley line, this infant raw magic, this pure and curious essence of the Mids, is acting on instinct. You are more evolved. Be the adult."

"You're sure Tobek's not in pain?" She glanced up at Feng, at a man who'd been horrifically tortured, who knew pain physical and psychological.

"Do you know that when a ley line is born, so too are an archangel and a dragon queen?" Feng slid his hands in the pockets of his camel tweed slacks. "Born of pure magic isn't a pretty euphemism. They all hatch from the same source and are eternally linked to each other. I'm not lucky enough to have kids of my own, but you don't have to be a parent to wonder where those other infants are right now."

That shorted out Bix's temper. She'd long wondered if, somewhere out there, she had a kid. A child she couldn't remember. A child who wondered why it was alone, why she'd abandoned it. It sickened her to dwell on the notion, so she didn't. However, Feng was right—one didn't have to be a parent to know that a child needed others, attachment, connection, touch. Hell, those were the things she'd craved as an adult in exile. Continued to crave, as a matter of fact. From those seeds sprang relationships, and nurturing those relationships motivated her to fight for the Mids.

She looked down at the broken wards in her hands, then back to the ley line and to the old demigod trapped within. Saying nothing, she handed the broken clay to Feng. His well-manicured fingers traced the gouges along the break in the ward.

"The researchers." Feng tutted with disappointment. "Made by them. I can detect the magic they used."

"Do you think they used those wards to confine the infants down here?" She studied Tobek, still trapped but not struggling. He was like a scorpion in aspic. "Because it looks like small claws broke those wards, claws that could belong to a young dragon who was protected by a ley line."

"I don't know," Feng murmured, and, with a wave of his hand, reduced the clay to dust. "Humans are capable of great atrocities and great kindness. Hard to say which was at work before the jailbreak."

"There's a nest of Nabaziix keeping watch." Bix pulled her darkness from the recesses of Zamarad until only the chamber remained bathed in her shadows. The curious roars of the beasts chased the retreat. "They wouldn't eat the kids, would they?"

"Doubtful." He smirked. "I imagine they're more like the

family mastiff. The Houses of Fate know the long-term value of a new dragon queen and archangel. They'd choose guardians who could protect all three newborns."

"So how do we convince the baby ley line to let go of its father figure?"

Feng angled toward her as his red brows arched.

"What?" Bix gestured to the ley line. "That's what children do when they're frightened. They cling to their parents."

"Well, Mommy puts away her shadows and relocates the Berserker burning a hole in my back with his glare." Feng turned fully and faced Hywl, whose glowing Berserker-blue gaze was trained on Feng's heart.

"I'm not leaving my lady alone with you," Hywl growled.

"Hywl, it's all right," Bix assured. Throughout the history of the Mids, the cyclical battles between the Phoenix and the Chimera were legendary. She and Feng were supposed to be vicious nemeses, but the truth of the present was they were both broken versions of their previous incarnations. Those flaws, as much as the current circumstances, allowed them to be allies.

"No, it's not." Hywl adjusted his grip on the knife he still held at the ready. "I failed you before. I'm not doing it again."

"Hywl, you've never failed me." Bix shook her head as she further shrank the footprint of her shadows, leaving only a ring around the whirlpool protecting the ley line as a catcher's mitt in case it dropped Tobek during a change of state. "You've been my favorite angel hunter from the get-go."

"Begging your pardon, my lady, you don't remember it, but I can't forget." Hywl held his own as Feng ambled over to him.

"Feng, that wasn't an invitation." Bix sighed. When it came to pissing contests, Feng could smite Hywl with the bat of an eye. In the Mids, where innate power defined one's place in the caste structure, Feng outranked a dragon queen and an archangel.

She didn't know whether to hug Hywl for his stalwart support or to slap the stupid out of him. She did, however, make a mental note to interrogate him about their history when this mission was over. Unlike his commander, Hywl wasn't cursed to silence. Probably. Maybe.

"Hywl y Gresynus," Feng drawled, looming over the Welshman by a head. "What a curious moniker. Hywl the wretched, the reprehensible."

"Feng, don't be a dick," Bix scolded.

"I'm not. It's the name on his soul contract." The Phoenix smiled. "I'm checking his reset clause to know whether he can survive the side effects of freeing his boss from the ley line."

"And?" Hywl and Bix prompted in unison.

"The dragon who made and remakes his body must have loved the idea of a Berserker haranguing the Angelic Host for a very, very long time. As long as his dragon maker lives, so will he, if he can keep his head. He'll suffer the injury and the human lag time of recovery, but he will recover. The Fate who recruited him completely screwed him on the recovery time, though. The god who owns his soul insisted on the head lopping." Feng clapped Hywl on the shoulder. "I, however, remember you were part of the team who came to my rescue, so despite your opinion of me, I wish you no ill. You have my gratitude."

Bix wasn't sure who was more surprised by which part of Feng's revelation.

"Still not leaving her," Hywl groused.

"You will suffer horrifically, your flesh peeled down to the bone. You will take years to physically recover." Feng ran his finger down the crack of Hywl's face mask, mending the fracture. "I am unqualified to estimate a mental recovery."

"Hywl, I can't let you go through that for me. I wouldn't let Tobek do it. I certainly will not let you. I need you at Luz to give Runjit a ration of gas because he's getting grumpy contending with all those elder Sages and Oracles." Bix smiled empathetically.

"He does tend to get a little uptight when I'm not around," Hywl conceded.

"If it's any consolation, she's more likely to hurt me during this process than I am to harm her." Feng stepped away from Hywl.

"Oh, take these." Bix removed her watch and ear cuff, handing them to Hywl. "They'll probably melt during this. You can tell the gang at Luz what's happening."

Hywl flipped his blade back in its sheath and took her tech. "As you wish, my lady."

She sent her faithful angel hunter to Luz and faced Feng. "Well, how bad is it really going to be?"

"Much worse than I said." Feng ignited, full blazing glory. "Put away the last of your shadows. I have to convince a giant baby to let go of its woobie."

CHAPTER 15

The sun shone brightly over the Church of the Templars. Dense snow blanketed homes and streets, reflecting the cheerful rays. Wind whipped through the drifts in the crenelated stone wall surrounding the church where Berserkers kept watch. The scent of baked goods and merry fires filled the crisp air. The faint sound of chatter followed a smattering of tourists hustling to shops and restaurants outside the wall. Overlooking everything, on the roof of one of the two towers flanking the church, Bix and Feng stood across from each other, staring at Tobek, the levitating demigod pater.

Freed from the ley line, Tobek remained immobile and encased in a capsule of his own radiant green magic. Tiny slivers of silver sparked around him like lightning in a bottle. At Feng's insistence, Bix had moved the three of them far from Zamarad and the ley line trying to cling to Tobek. Knowing how wrecked up Tobek usually got after overdosing on magic, Bix had transferred them to Luz, where Runjit and his team could assume care as soon as she drained Tobek of the excess.

"You sure you want to stick around for this part, Feng?" Bix asked as she curled her bare toes in the clean snow. Cold didn't bother her, and the distance from the ley line made her feel downright good. Sure, one lung still plagued her, the pangs noticeable now that her standoff with the ley line had sapped much of the Devourer painkiller. Her veins retained the telltale black tint, but the rest of her had faded to normal. Mentally, she was in control of her senses, and her impulses had been brought to heel by her discipline. "I haven't done this with witnesses before. I don't know how it'll impact you."

"It'll be interesting to see it firsthand rather than experience it through the pendant you wear." Feng ran his fingers through his hair, shaking out the bits of rubble that had fallen during the ley line's tantrum as he'd pried Tobek from its tempestuous hold. "Besides, you need me to anchor you to this World while you drain him, and it will likely be safer for those in the area if I remain to counteract whatever surprises may come from this."

"Whatever happens, don't touch either of us. We're not exactly our normal selves."

Feng took three long steps back, leaning against a merlon. "Pretend I'm not here."

"There will be no gates to protect anyone because I might lose control of the sizes depending on what happens. This will be very public, I'm afraid." She skimmed her fingers over the bubble holding Tobek. His magic felt both familiar and different, as if something was changing him or changing within him.

"I'll worry about the mortals. You take care of your Berserker," Feng assured.

The last time she'd done this, Tobek had had containment spells in place that had keyed off his unique blend of magic. She hoped that between her instinct and Feng's mastery, they could limit the side effects. The location of a tourist town in the Primary Mid World added the advantage of the humans' neutralizing presence. She'd taken all the precautions she could without exposing anyone to greater dangers.

This was as safe as it was going to get.

Bix waded into the bubble. Tobek's magic flowed over her, the push stronger than the pull, though, the pull was scrambling to catch up, to balance. His silver lightning glided over her skin, featherlight, a fleeting caress. She took his hand in hers. Her gaze fixed on his face, not on his naked body still arched, still motionless.

"I'm sorry for this," she whispered. One long tentacle of shadow shot from her and pierced Tobek's Eternal Knot glistening amid his sea of ink. He sucked in a loud, long breath. His body curled forward, fetal position, then arced back violently. Six times the convulsion repeated, and on the seventh, Bix's darkness dove past his physical form, past the storm of his wild magic, past the curious mixture of his origins, into the miasma where the abscesses of his solitude and anguish festered. She took nothing. Instead, she gave what he consistently offered her: comfort and reassurance.

His Berserker's bright eyes snapped to her. Recognition dawned in their depths as his body straightened and aligned with hers, toe to toe, chest to breast. His smile wasn't his usual easy grin. There was no hint of casual, no spice of wicked. It was the welcome of an intimate friend, the pleasure of a reunion long past due, the succor of home. He held their clasped hands to his lips, then drew them along his furry cheek.

A burble of laughter crept up her throat. Her heart ached with joy, stretched full of contentment. She placed his hand over the swells of her breasts, over the part of him hidden within her. The silver lightning within the bubble concentrated around his hand, then dove into her flesh, outlining the knot brightening under his warm touch. Every emotion held in his smile poured through those tiny blades and sank deep within her body. Tenderness tickled her cells and surged with the mist through her veins. Her darkness pumped those sentiments back into his body.

He gasped. His lashes fluttered. His chest trembled with the low rumble of his mirth.

His amputated arm shimmered as the silver of his magic sprouted from his scars, forming engraved bands articulating on brass rivets. Section by section, cuff by cuff, detail by detail his silver arm grew from elbow to wrist to fingertips. Those cool metal fingers folded around hers.

Her vision turned hazy from tears of happiness. She pushed up to her tippy toes and brushed her lips across his. His lips were warm, soft, and irresistible, so she lingered a bit in that moment. He pressed, ever so gently. She pressed a little less gently. Neither was enough. She laced her hands behind his neck and tugged him closer, her mouth demanding more.

He hesitated.

A tortured groan warned of his restraint slipping. He cradled the back of her head with his silver hand, fingers tangling in her hair as he took control of the kiss. She let him own it for a while, then reclaimed it as their magics cycled through each other. Her darkness through his bright. Her omnipresence through his might. Silver to starlight.

When something rather rigid and insistent popped up between them, they broke from the kiss and shared a quiet laugh of mutual frustration. He rested his brow against her crown.

"I do not have on pants," he noted with a fraught rasp.

"You do not," she confirmed, breathing in his scent of nutmeg, cedar, sandalwood, and musk with a hint of wintergreen.

"I am having difficulty manifesting clothes. I apologize."

"Is that a new difficulty?"

"Yes." He slid his metal hand from her hair and danced his fingers through the darkness that now surrounded them before resting his hand on her hip. "It was one of the first things I learned to make with Mids' magic. Now my basic skills are overwhelmed. Where once I carried a shipping crate, I now shoulder the entire ship. I am Atlas on his knees."

Tobek *was* different. Deep within his composition, her darkness cataloged the changes percolating within him, hard kernels planted eons ago trembling on the brink of bursting. Into what? No idea. He teetered on a cusp, though. It couldn't be to godhood. His pantheon, the one that had abandoned him here in the Mids, would have to hoist him the final distance for him to ascend. They wouldn't do that now; he'd be too powerful. Perhaps titans had to do the lifting at this point. If he ascended to a titan, he'd be too mighty for the Mids, yet it was the ley line that had incubated this pending evolution. Mids' magic instead of Other World. Tobek was a scrumptious testosterone cluster of contradictions.

"Will Atlas allow me to help him stand?" she asked, keeping to his analogy.

"Give me time to inspect and understand my new circumstance. The ley line…" He traced his fingers of flesh through the forest-green glow of the Eternal Knot on her chest. "I'm changing, aren't I?"

"You don't exude the Slimer shade of ectoplasm you once did. The woodsy hue becomes you, though." She wiggled her hips. "And you have two arms right now. Two. How long is the shiny one going to stick around?"

"I can only be whole when you are whole."

"Don't set me up to ask a bunch of questions I know you can't answer. You're in no condition to bait the curse of silence right now."

"I am going to hug you very closely, then I am going to let go," he said firmly, as if trying to convince himself, "because beyond this frame of quiet night, we have altered something. Every cell of my body is perceiving things I am unable to identify."

"Probably caffeine deficiency. It's been a while since you've had any." She giggled as Tobek crushed her in a bear hug, then took two long steps back. With the distance, his silver arm faded away. He cleared his throat and poked his Eternal Knot and the shadows still connecting her to him. Pouting, she withdrew and recalled the thousands of strands of night that had woven around them during their embrace.

Fire burned brightly atop the opposite tower amid the hard night holding the village of Luz. Streams of deep green sigils flowed down the towers, covered the circular church, and painted the ramparts.

Bix steepled her fingers against her lips and choked back laughter. "That's you, Tobek. That's all you."

"That is you." Tobek pointed at the sky, then at the clock tower not far from the church. "It's one in the afternoon."

"That's Feng." Bix mimicked Tobek's pose yet pointed at the conflagration on the other tower. "He's been watching over us, trying to minimize our havoc."

"Phoenix," Tobek harrumphed in salutation, not raising his voice.

The fire on the other tower went out. Mids' magic spiked beside Bix, and Feng appeared, quite flushed and unwilling to look at Bix.

"You okay?" she asked quietly.

"This has been an enlightening experience," Feng mumbled. With a snap of his fingers, he re-dressed Tobek in a Berserker mud-brown uniform. "You might be able to do that for yourself now, Chief. I can teach you, if you'd like."

"Thank you." Tobek tugged his jacket collar, declining to correct Feng's assumption. "I'll think about it."

"Good, then I suggest we head inside, where your combined teams have been working overtime on Project Resen." Feng twitched his barbed tail. "Once you end the light show, that is."

Tobek sauntered to the nearest merlon and inspected the magic pouring over its boxed edges. "It took thirty-one of us to cast these protection spells nearly two thousand years ago. Long before the church or the fortifications were built. I'm surprised the spells encompass the newer construction."

"They didn't," Feng refuted. "You did that. Today. Bix kept your magic contained to the church compound, but you raised the wards. Lowered them too—you've included the aquifer under the town as well. Well water drawn within church grounds will be quite pure."

"What are the wards blocking?" Bix eyed the premature night sky. That wasn't her doing. Her darkness was snugly contained within her form. The stars watching from its canopy were red and in clusters of three. The longer she stared at them, the more winked out of existence.

"All superpowers of mid and lesser caste along with most Chweds. Correct me if I'm wrong, but this is intended to be a human sanctuary." Feng arched a disapproving red brow. "He'd block the upper-caste superpowers too if he could, but he hasn't harnessed that magic. Yet."

"War is cruelest to those who are nothing but fuel and fertilizer," Tobek said without apology, walking the perimeter of the tower roof. He let loose a four-toned whistle. Answering whistles floated up from the ramparts. "Site is secure. No one harmed."

"I am capable of doing my job," Feng objected.

Tobek paused beside Feng and looked the Phoenix up and down. The men were of a comparable height, but Tobek had the bulkier build. "I've known your predecessors. Capable was never a question."

"Whether I am trustworthy is." Feng grunted. "For now, Chief. For this war and for now."

Tobek nodded and sniffed, then slammed his palm against Feng's chest. Green and silver magic dug into Feng, igniting his fire. Flames burned red, then gold then dark green. The streams of spells flooding the church grounds vanished into the stones, imperceptible to the eye and the touch. Tobek dropped his hand, and Feng's fire went out. The Phoenix staggered back with his hands over his heart. Confusion twisted his features.

"If you were trustworthy, you wouldn't have tried to modify my spells and expose this compound to hostile forces." Tobek's expression was cold, his tone implacable. "Next time, pay closer attention to your translations of the dead languages used to write these spells. Feather is a feminine noun."

Feng thrust his jaw to the side and inclined his head. "I'm part of the team, aren't I? The old spells excluded me."

"Feng, you told me the top players could still get in, that Tobek didn't have the juice to block your caste." Bix moved toward her Berserker as darkness rippled under her skin.

"He can't block us." Feng narrowed his eyes at Tobek. "But he can make our attendance unpleasant."

"She is your passkey. If she's not with you, you're going to be in a lot of pain." Tobek held out his hand to Bix, and she took it without quibble.

"Feathers, Feng? *Feathers?*" She pursed her lips. "Did you extend an invitation to the Host to this location?"

"Streamlining the delivery of the build specs," he countered. "We've already seen the lengths to which the gods will go to stop this. They summoned Devourers, for Pete's sake."

The god squad hadn't, in fact. She didn't know if Resen itself had attracted the Devourers' attention, the ley line, or if the faction inside the Consortium had their own version of Nez. There were a lot of options, none of which were her priority at the moment.

"We don't know if we were successful in getting the specs," Bix disclosed calmly. "I exposed the servers to the goddess of discord. I have no idea if I screwed the pooch. On the off chance the data is intact, I'm not releasing any part of it until my team reviews it."

"Never trust anything that comes from the Fates," Tobek tutted. "There's always a catch, and they play for the long game."

Feng sighed and slid his hands in his pockets. "You're right, of course. My eagerness to be useful has clouded my judgment. My mistake and my apologies. I'll notify the Host to stand down."

"Hey." Bix caught Feng's gaze. "We'll get there. We just have to be smart. Apex entities and consequences, right?"

Feng inclined his head. "Indeed."

With one last look at the entity in the sky, Bix opened gates to the clinic beneath the church.

CHAPTER 16

Industrial fans whirred and roared inside the underground chamber at the Church of the Templars, pushing air toward box vacuums with small colorful parachutes billowing out their back. Air quality sensors bobbed in the continual breeze, transferring data to laptops set on rolling carts. The people on their feet wore gas masks. The people lined up in neat rows on gurneys were barefaced and out cold. Not a single psychopomp stood in attendance. Yay for small favors.

Feng cast a quizzical look at Bix. "A hospital?"

"Gassed the researchers en masse to keep them from harming themselves and others."

"Now they're cleaning the air? That I can do for them." Feng flared his wings and beat them thrice, sending powerful gusts sweeping through the chamber. All activity paused. The air sensors chirped and flashed green. Large green check marks appeared on the computer screens.

"Sir?" a medic called. "All clear here."

The all clear echoed from the other sensor stations.

"All right, team, masks off," Runjit ordered, removing his own mask as a cheer went up from the Berserkers manning the clinic.

"Thanks," Bix murmured to Feng as she set off for the wall

of Chwed tech that had overtaken the opposite side of the round chamber. Three wrought iron chairs that looked as if they'd been purloined from a summer-season bistro were set in front of the main computing stations. Cian and Ashtad sat at either end, furiously typing, while Gurp used his chair as a step stool to hook another Merkaba energy-star server into the four others floating against the cove of the barrel ceiling.

Tobek strode to the goblin's aid, hoisting the chair along with the goblin. Gurp shrieked with delight upon seeing Tobek and launched into rapid banter that Bix didn't understand. The unguarded smiles on both her former roommates' faces warmed Bix through and through. She missed those moments, the chittering and rumbling of the two of them debating endless topics over meals and modifications to their home. It was the soundtrack to the happy, low-key days.

"A *goblin*," Feng noted with quiet surprise.

"Don't be racist," Bix warned.

Feng huffed with affront. "Goblins have helped me out of more sticky wickets than I care to admit. I have nothing but respect for them. I am simply surprised one has bonded with Chief. They usually attach themselves to women who have been discarded by family and society. Honestly, I'd expect the goblin to be your familiar rather than his."

"Familiar like in a Mid World magic way?" She grinned as Gurp demanded Tobek's hand, sniffing and inspecting it for all the changes Gurp doubtlessly sensed in his buddy.

"As in what Chief is to you." Feng chuckled.

That got her attention. "Excuse me?"

"Your familiar," Feng repeated as he angled to face her. "You didn't…? What happened on the rooftop today? Oh, I see you didn't. I… I'm sorry. I know your memories… I assumed he would've mentioned…"

"Assume I know nothing."

"You are an apex entity." He raised his brows and waited for her to nod. "The Mids reject you because you are too powerful to exist here without damaging native magic. At some point you knew this, so you claimed a vessel to harness and convert the excesses of your might while you are here. Chief is that vessel. He is your conduit as much as he is your guide and your companion. He is also what shields the core of native magic from you. That is why the ley line took him. To protect itself from you."

"Holy hell," she whispered, scratching her inert Eternal Knot. "Proxy punching bag explains why the superpowers are keen to thrash him but the Fates can't let him die."

"The give and take of magic that happened on the roof, that circular processing between you two, it should only go one way. He should only take from you and convert it into something that safely encourages the evolution of Mids' magic." Feng rubbed his chin. "Apparently, the side effect of being your familiar forces *him* to evolve as well."

She'd suspected the evolution; she'd been hazy on the details and clueless to the familiar. "Evolve into what?"

"I have no idea." Feng pivoted to study Tobek with blatant curiosity. "But I believe the Fates' role in his preservation has shifted from saviors to inhibitors. His contract as a Berserker is holding him back."

Bix couldn't wholly blame the Fates for that. While mortals had threads of Fate within them, securing the soul to the body, Tobek had threads of Fate woven around him that bound him. It was a detail Musso-Koroni had failed to share during the tale of Tobek's hubris, but a detail Bix had figured out a while ago. She was fairly sure she could sever those tethers; however, the original Chimera could've done it too and hadn't. If the reason was because Tobek being restrained allowed her to stay in the Mids, then, selfishly, she could understand why version 1.0 hadn't freed him. But he'd been in the Mids too long now for freedom to equate to a return to demigodhood. He had no pantheon to welcome him, so he couldn't complete that final demigod trial to become a god. She didn't know what would happen if he shed his bonds or what he'd become. Pretty sure he wouldn't stay a

Berserker. Why Tobek didn't resent her for keeping him fettered was super weird no matter which way she looked at it.

"Sweetheart?" Tobek called from the computing wall. "When you're ready?"

"Time to own up to my sins." She clasped her hands together as her team and Tobek's seconds gathered around the computers. She paused for a double take as Drew, still in the body of the Oracle, rolled Nez to the group. Rolled. As in pushed Nez in a wheelchair with an oxygen tank attached.

Drew leaned into Bix as the draugr applied the brakes on the chair. "This isn't new for him. The guy hasn't walked since the Leshy land mine."

That made Bix feel a teensy bit like a dick for slamming him into the ceiling earlier. Just a skosh. Dude would always be an ass. Maybe. And maybe she was the one who needed to let go of old anger and get a new perspective.

"So, how screwed are we?" Bix asked as the gang formed a circle.

"We've fed the Chwed and human news that the unexpected solar eclipse we are currently experiencing was foretold by the Templars in an archive recently discovered by the church." Cian jerked his thumb at a monitor. "The light show was a tribute to the history of Luz and the Templars, and proof of the arcane power of the holy defenders. This place will be crawling with tourists and woo hunters for a few decades."

"I think she meant the Sage servers, kid." Drew winked.

"Now, now, Cian has a bright future in propaganda," Ashtad defended. "He even convinced Hywl to forge the ancient text."

"I spent a lot of time in the church illuminating manuscripts back in the day." Hywl waggled his ink-stained fingers. "A bit of 'day is night when God's judgment casts the holy ghost across the land' is like reciting the alphabet. I'll need a hand aging the paper and ink, though, eh, Chief?"

"No problem. Thank you both for covering up our very public transgression." Tobek bowed from the shoulders to Cian then to Hywl.

"Oh, I almost forgot. For you, my lady." Hywl fished her watch and earpiece from his pocket and handed them to her.

"Thank you." Bix smiled, then turned slightly to address Ashtad and Drew. "The pods were protecting the servers from the gods. I exposed them to discord's magic when I moved them. Did any of them survive?"

"Mmm, we've had more successful missions," Drew hedged. "Probably should've paid more attention to that caution card from the Tarot delivery service."

Bix shook her head. "Nothing, then? Resen's over? Destroyed? The gods won?"

"Not nothing," Ashtad sighed. "But it's not good either. On the pro side, we got all five servers out alive with legs attached."

"But?" Feng prompted.

"They've got brain damage," Runjit said flatly.

"The electricity I used to short out their pods flowed through them," Ashtad admitted.

"We knew the risk." Bix grimaced and massaged her ribs. "Can we get *anything* from them?"

"Bix, they're not human." Runjit shrugged. "They're less than full Fates but more evolved than an elder Sage. I don't know how to repair something that's not flesh and blood."

"Let me look at them," Feng offered. "If there's anything left of Mids' magic in their composition, then I might be able to help."

"Yes, by all means, follow me." Runjit waved the Phoenix to join him. "You're welcome to examine our other patients while you're here."

"What about the other survivors? Are there enough of them that we could piece together the research since the servers are fried?" Bix watched Feng lay hands upon the men in track pants set apart from the researchers. They woke and clutched him, whatever parts they could reach. Feng stiffened, his eyes a little too wide. She wasn't worried he'd intentionally hurt them. Her concern was for Feng being in the midst of all this aftermath, all these damaged and dead bodies. She wasn't sure how or if that would trigger his PTSD.

"Depends. Do we have thirty years to recreate it?" Nez asked, lifting his oxygen mask. "We'll have to bring in new researchers who are younger, therefore less knowledgeable, because most of us are at the age of ascension or death. If we're lucky, we'll have time to uptrain the new team before we expire."

"In thirty years, there won't be a place in the Mids that isn't infested with Devourers." Drew crossed her arms. "If Project Resen is going to be useful at all, it's got to go live in months, not decades."

"The reason the Fates use humans as servers is because they're self-repairing, right?" Cian ventured, turning to Ashtad. "If the hardware is sound, then that leaves the glitch in the coding."

"If the Phoenix can heal the fried cells, then sure, we could consider the hardware sound." Ashtad tipped his head. "What are you thinking, kid?"

"I'm thinking any place that employs self-repairing hardware also has a protocol for patching software. It's just good Net Ops." Cian scratched the leaf encased in a fractal on his arm. "We need to find whoever runs their NOC and get these guys hooked up to see what can be salvaged."

"Their network operations center would be the Grove of Sages," Nez volunteered. "You'd have to get these guys to the Grove without the gods interfering."

The elusive, mysterious, and top-secret Grove of Sages, where men who'd almost made it to Fatehood found themselves stuck as long-lived supercomputers hosting the history of the Mids, countless other Worlds, and numerous other races. The Grove was wholly owned and operated by the Houses of Fate. That could be good or bad depending on the caprice of the Houses.

"That's why I'm here." Bix gestured to herself. "Transportation with a sidecar of security. The faster we get these guys to the Grove, the less time the pantheons have to restaff the cleaning team."

"There's the risk that even after a patch there will be segments of data that can't be retrieved, but Cian's idea is better than the alternatives." Ashtad perched on the back of his chair. "How do we find the Grove?"

The Berserkers in the circle stared at the ground.

"The Grove is a mash-up of *Brigadoon* and *Hotel California*." Nez took a long draught of oxygen. "You're going to have access issues even a gatekeeper could find problematic."

Hywl leaned over to Cian. "*Brigadoon* is a musical based on an old Scots legend about—"

"My man, I work in a leather bar with a drag show every Tuesday night. We have our very own Cyd Cherries." Cian did a little soft-shoe improv that ended with a wink. "And my thesis advisor fronts an Eagles cover band. I got the references."

"So when is Brigadoon supposed to appear next?" Bix asked, making a mental note to attend a drag show starring Cyd, especially if Cyd could dance like her namesake.

Everyone looked at Nez. Nez shrugged. "No clue."

"The Grove can be summoned," Tobek rasped, still staring at his boots.

Hywl winced.

"Awesome," Bix said slowly. "What's the catch?"

"You can't trust what they tell you." Tobek sniffed. "Best case? You get these servers up and running, and they have the complete data. The catch is they'll only give you a fraction of what you need to know."

"They'll spin their answers in a way to manipulate you into doing what the Fates want, at great personal cost." Hywl rubbed his thick black muttonchops. "Thing is, my lady, every soldier in here has quested for the Grove at some point. Not a one of us has come out the better for it."

She knew the Fates had tricked Tobek into his military commission, but was deceit how all the Berserkers had been recruited? Was the Grove the entrée to the army, or had the guys sought the Grove after signing their lives over to the MWA?

"The Grove should be destroyed," Tobek rumbled. His eyes adopted the faint glow of waking rage. A chorus of grumbling "Hear, hear" echoed from the Berserkers in the chamber.

"*You'd* destroy the Grove? You?" Bix challenged. Regardless of how he'd gotten into the defender-of-Worlds role, Tobek had an artifact and tome collection that would make any historian from any century weep. "The guy who prides himself on continual education would destroy a living library? Just because the librarians are assholes?"

"The Grove is bait for the unwitting. Propaganda dressed up as revelations. The Houses have priceless information. They hoard it, they twist it, and they ruin lives with it." He stared at her, his jaw thrust to the side, eyes brightening. "I understand the importance of Project Resen, but you all must understand that information from the Grove comes replete with viruses."

"But they want Resen built. Why screw us on that?" Cian asked.

"We probably aren't going to know in what manner they screwed us until after Resen is launched," Feng posited, returning to the group with Runjit. "The bodies of the servers are as hale as I can make them, but there is much to them that is no longer of the Mids. They're mute, though for no physical reason I can discern."

"Psychological trauma or programming glitch?" Bix massaged her temple. "Either way, we're not acquiring anything truthful or otherwise from them unless we get them to the Grove."

"Why don't you, um, entreat the cartomancy guide?" Nez winced as he adjusted his position in his wheelchair. "You clearly have more faith in whatever is answering your questions through the cards than you have in the Fates. What's the harm in appealing to a higher power who's taken a fancy to you?"

Feng raised his brows as he regarded her. Ashtad and Tobek looked like they'd swallowed rotten limes whole. Hywl and Runjit swapped bemused glances, while Gurp sidled closer to Tobek with a whimper.

"The old nerd has a point." Drew dropped her head on Bix's shoulder. "Do it. Do it. Do it."

"Might as well. It's obvious the Fates need our help, but is it in support of Resen or some other game we don't know about yet?" Bix reached through gates to retrieve a blank card from her collection. Holding the card up to her circle of collaborators, she closed her eyes. A question formed in her mind before she gave it voice. "Will calling on the Grove of Sages provide honest and useful guidance to build Project Resen?"

Primeval energy filled the chamber with red sparks and tugged the card from Bix's hand. Tobek and Feng looked up and around, suddenly alert and at attention. The tension trickled out to the Berserkers in the room. Hands went to weapons. Ashtad sat very still, his eyes darting left and right. His lips thinned as his focus settled on the card spinning in the center of the circle.

As it had with each prior request, the card grew as the überentity painted the answer to her question. The card balanced on a bottom corner and slowed its rotation so everyone could see.

The Seven of Cups. The card of confusion, an abundance of choices, and surprising options. Cups usually dealt with interpersonal issues. Relationships with the self and with others. Normally the card had seven chalices, each brimming with a lure of wealth, power, fame, knowledge, stability, companionship, or enlightenment. This card had seven tattooed men in a circle with their hands cupped. Within six of the hands were reflections of the four superpowers, the Phoenix, and Tobek. Six of the tattooed men stared at their hands. The seventh man looked out from the card as the reflection of darkness dribbled from his hands, changing to starlight that was swallowed by the inky blackness of the background.

"That isn't a card of clarity, my lady." Hywl stuffed his hand in his pockets as the front of the card pivoted his direction.

"We're going to get the answers to Resen," Bix corrected. "They're just going to be buried in a lot of other data."

The appearance of Tobek and Feng on the card—both

intimately and uncommonly connected to Mids' magic as father figure and child—said that a pure source of native magic would be the key to deciphering the secrets received from the Grove. The darkness, well, that was her, only she couldn't tell if she was bleeding for Resen or controlling the distribution of its intel. Regardless, she kept that bit of interpretation to herself. If anyone else in the room picked up on it, no one mentioned it.

"Those are seven Sages in a circle." Drew lifted her head from Bix's shoulder and wagged a finger at the card. "Either they're the Grove or they're how we summon the Grove."

"Both." Tobek kneaded the back of his neck. "The Grove is fragmented into seven parts, protected by the original seven Houses of Fate. The Grove unifies every seven months in the time of Houses, which is not the time of the Mids. It is much slower. You need seven Sages to call upon the seven Houses to request a meeting with the Grove. The Houses decide if there will be a meeting, when, where, and at what price."

"You sound like you've done this a lot." Nez chuckled. His humor tanked in the face of Tobek's flat stare.

"Tobek, if you and your guys want out of this venture, now's the time," Bix suggested quietly. "No harm, no foul."

"I promised you my full support, not support that only suits my pleasure." He pushed off the chair. "We'll need the five Sage servers, this one in the wheelchair, and you, Cian, to ensure the Houses are crystal clear on what's at risk if they refuse to play ball."

"M-me?" Cian stammered and pointed to the fractal on his arm caused by a disease for which there was no cure. "If it requires me to be a magical conduit, I've got to pass, Chief. I'm allergic to it now, remember?"

"Not a conduit, kid. You're a hostage. You're going to bleed for Project Resen." Tobek raised his voice to the chamber. "Let's clear the center. Use those on the gurneys to make a frame. Buddy up with a patient in case the Fates answer our call through one of the unconscious."

The Berserkers complied with all haste.

"Sweetheart, I need you to relocate that card. Its presence will skew the spell." Tobek unbuttoned his uniform jacket and handed it to Gurp. "Then I need you to stand on the point marked north and the Phoenix on southeast. Precisely on point, not a step off."

Only once the gurneys and equipment were removed from the center of the chamber did the engraving of a compass with cardinal and ordinal points become apparent. Laid atop the compass was a pentagram.

Bix sauntered to the huge card still spinning in the chamber. At her touch, the card shrank, then settled in her palm. The presence of the überentity departed with a breeze that playfully ruffled her hair. Nez had posited the überentity had taken a fancy to her, but it was far more likely the entity could taste freedom with every ask she made of it. She didn't know what it had done to be imprisoned, and she really needed to figure that out before she had to pay her end of the bargain.

Alas, she didn't have time for that right now.

She took her position and opened tiny gates to add the Seven of Cups to the other cards on the shelf beside the red-and-black metal box at home.

"This should be interesting," Feng muttered, taking his spot in the position of fire at the southeastern point of the pentagram.

"You going to be okay with this?" Bix asked quietly, knowing he could hear her despite their distance. Of all the things that might trigger his battle rattle, being an ingredient in a spell had to rank high on the list.

"We're about to find out, I think." Feng puffed out his cheeks. "Be ready to move me, just in case, yeah?"

"Got a preferred destination?"

"Anywhere nonflammable," he joked, sort of.

"Seven Sages, in the center, inside the circle, please. Let's get them positioned." Tobek followed Gurp to one of the pallets, disappearing behind the pile of supplies for a heartbeat, then returning with a gnarly athame. The green handle could've come from a horn or a jawbone. With Tobek's magic, it was hard to know.

The Berserkers aided six of the Sages to their places on the floor inside the center circle. Cian got there on his own, his sleeves pulled over his hands and his shoulders hunched.

"Cian," Bix beckoned in a loud whisper.

The kid looked her way, wide-eyed, as he took a seat in the circle, facing her.

"If it gets to be too much, you give me a sign, okay?" she urged.

"Since when does Bix the Gatekeeper coddle anyone?" Nez snarked as Hywl set him on the ground next to the Sage servers and across from Cian. "Man up, kid. You're jumping way ahead in your Sage quest. Most of us don't try to connect with the Grove until we're in our forties."

"Most of you aren't friends with the Chimera," the kid shot back, lifting his chin. "Emphasis on *friends*."

Bix beamed and gave Cian two thumbs-up.

"Anudrengr, you get east." Tobek gestured to the spot with the athame. "Since you're inside a living Oracle, you should expect her threads to grow stronger or sever depending on the pleasures of the Fates who answer our summons."

Drew hated her ancient name but tolerated Tobek's use of it. They had a history neither of them ever mentioned, no matter how nicely Bix had posed the questions. Drew skipped to the eastern point of the compass and the pentagram.

"This is like spin the bottle." Drew rubbed her hands together and shimmied, leering. "Can you make it stop on my cuddlemuffin, my Runjit? Pwetty pweeze?"

Runjit rolled his eyes and Hywl sniggered as they took their places beside occupied gurneys on the perimeter.

"Gurp, southwest is yours." Tobek spun his blade, slapped the hilt into Ashtad's hand, and held it there. "Young Ba'al, you will be placing the call. You haven't summoned the Grove before, have you?"

Ashtad shook his head.

"Good. They love fresh meat. Nice and gullible." Tobek clapped Ashtad on the shoulder and jostled him. "Breathe. You're not slitting the Sages' throats. You just need to nick a leaf deeply enough for it to run. Try not to hit an artery. You do remember your knife training, right?"

"Aye, Chief." Ashtad took his place in the center of the circle. "Sit or stand?"

"They'll yank you up by your short hairs, regardless," Runjit quipped, and the soldiers guffawed.

"Ashtad, you control the negotiation," Bix reminded. "We're doing the Houses a favor, and the Seven of Cups confirmed they damn well know it. If they're dumb enough to impose a price, refuse it. If they're slow in their response or assembly, feel free to remind them you are far from alone."

"I've negotiated with a superpower once or twice," Ashtad countered indignantly as his expression softened. "But thank you for giving me permission to play the bogeyman card."

"All right, then, let's knock on the doors of the Houses of Fate." Tobek took his place on the western tip, the place of water. "Start with the servers, end with Cian."

CHAPTER 17

The blended magic of Mids and Other World swirled through the chamber under the Church of the Templars as Ashtad slid the athame through the lone healthy leaf on Cian's arm. Cian's diseased blood dribbled on the stone floor, then was pulled into the etchings of the pentagram to mix with the freshly drawn blood of his kith. The blood of the Sages beaded and bounced, skipping over one another like a game of jacks, leaving dots and streaks in the thin trenches as they connected the five points of the star. When the last droplet settled, the blood changed from red to green, sending up multihued streams framing the spaces between the elemental points.

Other World power blasted over Bix, tickling. Drew and Gurp giggled. Feng glowered. Tobek opted for stoic as the sheen of the Fates' magic reflected off bits of the netting the Houses had used to bind him as their first warrior. Either Bix's eyes were playing tricks on her, or Tobek's restraints were fraying. Was that what the ley line had done to him? Tried to break his contract with the Houses? Holy hell.

"You guys didn't have to use a battering ram. The grunts in the back would've sufficed to anchor the spell," groused a familiar feminine voice as a hologram took shape in the space between

Bix and Drew. A black mohawk reached for the ceiling. Tattooed Oracular moons in various stages of luminescence marked the woman's neck and wreathed her ears. Heavy black eyeliner framed grass-green eyes sweeping the chamber. A rolled blunt balanced on her burgundy lips. The smoke coiling around her head formed the shapes of runic symbols. Skuld. One of the Norn and a Fate of the Future. The Fate with whom Bix was most well acquainted. "We've been expecting the call."

Six additional holograms appeared in the gaps subdividing the ordinal compass points, leaving the north-northwest spot empty. Five women, two men. The Houses of Fate definitely had a feminine majority, possibly because the men were more useful as supercomputers.

"We are pleased to see the Phoenix and the Chimera collaborating again," one of the male Fates intoned. "Though we question the current state of the original Berserker."

So the Fates noticed it too, the fraying netting. Had to be.

Tobek didn't respond to the jibe. His rage-bright eyes were locked on the Sages in the center of the star. The Sages sat with spines straight, transfixed on something not in the chamber. As long as Cian kept breathing, Bix would leave him be and allow the spell to continue.

"A death walker and a caretaker," one of the female Fates cooed. "Interesting balance."

Drew and Gurp waggled their brows at each other.

"And then there is you, Ashtad Ba'al, seneschal of the demigods, aspirant Chair of the Consortium," a third woman mused. "You are the supplicant. You wish to be the recipient of the data to build Project Resen."

"In light of the current threats facing the Houses, I am the body most capable of receiving and transferring the data into usable form." Ashtad bowed. "Once the servers are patched, of course."

"In light of the current threats, we are disinclined to assemble the Grove and further jeopardize the histories of the Worlds." Second Fate dude had to be the pissant.

"The Angelic Host is prepared to secure whatever site the Houses choose and to provide escort across the Mids," Feng declared with all the haughty superiority to which he was, in truth, entitled. "The Dragon Horde will stand ready as reinforcements should they be required."

Shock rocked Bix. What had she and Tobek just said to that damned birdbrain up on the roof? No direct passing of data from the Houses to the Host. If the Host was in attendance, better believe there would be direct passage of data. It took everything she had not to reach across the pentagram to strangle Feng.

"The pantheons have called up the cavalry," the first male Fate argued. "Their numbers are vast."

"My offer is as good as you're going to get," Feng snapped. "Embrace the unknown. You are agents of chaos, after all."

All seven Fates looked to Bix. She made no assurances or promises. She couldn't. Musso-Koroni would be among the blended army of the gods. Getting the damaged servers to the Grove was as far as she could go with this mission. The goddess of discord had attacked her once and would do it again. Bix couldn't let that pass unchallenged, not with other gods there to witness it. That'd send the wrong message to the pantheons. And once Bix ended the goddess, her memories would take her out of commission, at least for a while.

"Chimera," Skuld drawled. "If you want us there, you *will* be there."

"The gods don't fear me, Skuld," Bix reminded. Skuld had been there when the Consortium had exiled Bix. She'd been there when Bix had returned to the Mids completely clueless. And Skuld had been there when Bix had learned she was the Chimera. As Fates went, Skuld had been an obvious presence in Bix's new life.

A flutter of tittering came from the other Fates.

"For eons and epochs, the mere mention of you made them cower." One of the female Fates chuckled. "Being off your game for a few centuries doesn't break that ingrained terror."

"Your actions at Zamarad are no secret, Chimera," the snotty male Fate harrumphed. "You ate an army. Ate them and then flung their entrails like an infant with smashed peas."

Drew snorffled.

"Word has spread throughout the pantheons that you are danger without discernment. That is who we demand," another female Fate insisted. "Not the Chimera of legend. Not the High Executioner of lore. We *want* the wild tempest to make the gods afraid."

"The only way to force bullies to heel is to import an even bigger bully, and that is you, Chimera, like it or not." Skuld took a long drag on her smoke.

"And if I am wild and tempestuous while the fragile Grove is present?" Bix challenged. "If they are damaged because of me?"

"Hot damn, total pandemonium." Another female Fate chortled. "Bring the Phoenix. He's got a few tricks he's been keeping from you."

Feng shrugged, more in admission than ignorance.

"Fine," Bix yielded. Eyes on the mission, and the mission was to get the build specs for Project Resen to the Angelic Host, with a pit stop through her team for a bug scrub. "The bogeyman will attend, though I cannot promise for how long."

"Tower Ballroom, Blackpool," Skuld announced, cutting through the crap and puffing on her blunt. "United Kingdom, Primary Mid World. Three days in the time of the Mids. We'll arrive as the sun sets. Dress appropriately."

Seven doors slamming echoed in the chamber as the Fates departed. The green glow of Other World magic abated, leaving only the bright blue lights of enraged Berserkers to illuminate the space. That and the dark green crackle and spark engulfing Tobek.

"Can, can we move now?" Cian wheezed into the heavy silence. "I need to check something."

Tobek visibly shook himself. The extra magic dissipated. "All right, men, you heard them. Three days and we move on Blackpool. Let's figure out what we're walking into. Runjit, move the survivors down to the barracks. Hywl, sync with base. Let's get on the same page."

Floodlights flicked on and men moved out. Cian bolted for the computers as the Berserkers helped the Sage servers and Nez into wheelchairs. Gurp turned his attention to directing the movement of supplies out of the main chamber into antechambers and sublevels.

"I'm going to visit the Host and brief them on the latest." Feng unfurled his wings. "I'll meet you in Blackpool."

Before Bix could throttle him or ask about those tricks he was keeping from her, he vanished.

Drew tweaked Bix's elbow. "You good?"

"Yeah, sure. How's the suit?" Bix shifted her attention to Tobek. Something was very off about him, she could feel it in the push and pull of his magic. What had once been rhythmic was frenzied and without a tempo. Was his heartbeat as erratic? Was he about to stroke out on her?

"Might actually live through this. The owner of it is as surprised as I am." Drew jerked her thumb over her shoulder. "I'm going to stay with the medics and be a familiar face for the survivors. Probably ought to get this broken bone properly set too. Ya know, leave the suit in better shape than I found it, yeah?"

"Yeah, okay. Sounds like a plan." Bix smiled with distraction.

"See you in Blackpool, bogeybaby." Drew kissed Bix's cheek, then raced up behind Runjit and goosed him.

Bix headed for Tobek. "What's going on?"

He tromped the pedal of a manual forklift, elevating a pallet of supplies. "Just an adjustment period. I'll be fine."

"Yeah, that means 'fine eventually.' You tend to omit the 'horrible near-term' parts," she chided quietly, laying her hand on his arm. Wild magic skittered over her fingers and raced up to prickle her ear. "Your netting is fraying. I saw it during the spell. Is that a good thing or a bad thing?"

He glanced around the room and leaned down to whisper against her temple, "Get that side of yours fixed before you tangle with the pantheons. Blackpool is a tourist town. There are going to be casualties. You need to be at the top of your game if you want your mission to succeed."

She started to argue with him, but Ashtad joined them. Tobek took the out, steering the forklift and supplies under an archway leading to who knew where.

"If it isn't the future Chair of the Consortium." Bix bumped her shoulder against Ashtad's. "You enjoy herding cats, don't you?"

"That's a long, long way away." Ashtad grinned, then sobered, sliding Tobek's athame into his belt. "I get the distinct impression there is something else going on with the Houses and Resen. Something we don't know but should."

"Agreed. It must have something to do with the convergence of superpowers. You know the Host is going to show up in full force, which will compel the gods to do the same." Bix stepped closer to her old mentor and murmured, "The Grove and the Host are going to be in the same room. Efforts will be made to bypass us in the data exchange. You and I need to review that data, preferably before it goes to the Host. If that's not possible, then we damn sure need a copy of it."

"Notice the way the Fates dismissed my bid to be the hard drive? They definitely have something else in mind." Ashtad kept his voice low and picked at the crud covering his jacket. "I'm going to chat up Nez. I think he knows more about this than he's telling. After that, I'm going to make some modifications to the tech setup we have. I noticed two of those Fates eyeballing the configuration a little too closely. I'll camp out here until we move on Blackpool."

"Need me to fetch your iron maiden?"

"Would you?" He thrust his chin at the wall of computers. "Stick it under the desk there. The case is keyed to me, so it should be safe enough."

Cian let loose a whoop, drawing all attention. "Blackpool. Three days. Magic convention preparties start. I knew it sounded familiar. Biggest illusionists' convention outside of Vegas. Takes over the town for a week. Well, two weeks what with the advance shenanigans happening."

"Did you say *parties*, as in plural?" Drew clasped her hands against her chest.

"Gaw, I haven't been in years." Hywl stroked his muttonchops. "What's the theme this go-around?"

"A salute to Vaudeville." Cian pretended to button a collar he didn't have. "The Fates are sending us to a costume ball. White tie."

"Gurp," the Berserkers called in unison.

"I do. I get. I know. I get." The goblin's chortle drifted from the recesses of an antechamber.

As everyone bent to their tasks, Bix quietly slipped away to see a god about making sure *she* wasn't the cause of mass casualties at Blackpool.

CHAPTER 18

O ther World magic welcomed Bix with a sultry embrace. She sauntered through dense fog scented with sandalwood, pepper, and musk with a hint of gardenia. Her dirty bare feet made no noise on the dark, polished floors built from compressed souls. Lamps housed within carvings of demonic caricatures blazed to life, casting ominous shadows. She followed the sound of lapping water, the low croon of a masculine voice, and the murmurs of obsequious minions past the master bedroom, past the closets, past the dressing rooms, past chambers of hooks and whips and sawhorses, past rooms she wasn't brave enough to inspect.

Sound and scent led her to her prey.

Clouds of steam parted, banking in the corners and lingering at the ceiling of a classic Grecian bath. Phobos stood with arms wide and stance wider as minions unbuckled his armor and reverently carried each bronze piece dripping with black, tarry blood to an antechamber. Where seams and gaps had left the god of fear exposed to his enemies, blisters and boils covered his skin. His dark hair adhered to the angles of his sharp features, framing his amber eyes and red pupils.

"Chimera," he purred. "Come to join me in a bath?"

"Looks like you've been busy." She crouched at the edge of

155

the Olympic-sized pool and trailed her fingers through the warm inky water, or rather what passed as water on a World wholly constructed from emptied souls to suit Phobos's whims and fancies. "I take it you convinced the pantheons to clear Bosch World of Devourers?"

"That would subvert the pantheons' political advantages within the Consortium," he tsked as his minions continued to strip him bare. "I merely had a night out with some old friends and rabble-rousers. That we happened to stumble upon a few of the old foes gave us a welcome reprieve from the doldrums of immortality. Freeing aggrieved angels from cages fashioned from the offal of their kin might have earned us favors to be spent at some future date."

"Thank you." She kept her inspection to his scarred torso and above, not that he cared. He was from a family for whom nudity was commonplace. "Was anyone hurt?"

He let out the most malevolent laugh. "Of course. What's the point otherwise? Once my comrades are satisfied with the reminder of pain and vulnerability, they'll get around to recovering. For now, they'll enjoy wallowing in temporary discomforts."

"And you? How are you doing, truly?"

"Join me in the bath. Find out for yourself," he taunted as he strode down the mosaic ramp into opaque water.

"Phobos, if I took you up on your offer, you'd run like hell the other way and we both know it." She wagged a finger at the beating heart inside the fob resting on a navy-blue velvet pillow upon an ornate stand at the edge of the bath and within his line of sight. That heart belonged to the woman he'd loved, the same woman who'd screwed him over Greek-tragedy style. "But if you're trying to politely tell me I stink, I'll make note of it."

"I wasn't going to bathe you. That's why I have them." He flicked his long elegant fingers at monstrous naiads waiting with trays and tubs of foods, oils, and soaps. Each of his attendants raked Bix with seductive regard. They'd had their hands on Bix's body before, so she knew how good they were at their jobs.

Bix winked at the naiads. "I'll have need of their ministrations soon enough."

"Ah, found another memory keeper, have you?" He took a pomegranate from the tray and broke it open, dumping the sticky pulpy seeds into the waiting hands of a naiad.

"Musso-Koroni, a goddess of discord." She sat on the lip of the pool and swung her legs into the scented water.

"Discord? *Discord?* Will that abominable lie never die?" Phobos opened his mouth as the naiad painted the seeds and pulp over his lips.

Bix thought about that for a moment. The goddess had introduced herself by name, as was custom. Bix and her team had been operating on the assumption that discord was the root of the goddess's magic because that was how Nez had described the fall of the research station. No one had proposed any other possibility.

"Obviously, you think I'm mistaken, so correct me."

"Musso-Koroni is the first goddess of the Bambara pantheon." Phobos tilted his head back as a different naiad poured a mix of oil and water over his hair while another gave him a scalp massage. "She, along with your Berserker, were part of the very first class of demigods to be tested in what became the Primary Mid World. This was back in the days when greater gods were still forming the World, molding continents and carving rivers, trying to lure the dragons and angels to their new creation to have them terraform it and make it part of the nascent collective of Mid Worlds."

"Wait, Tobek is *how old?*" Bix splashed her feet, then froze as webbed fingers rose from the ripples to massage her soles.

"Younger than you, older than I." Phobos paused for another mouthful of fruit. "Musso-Koroni married a dreadful twit on the promise that she and her new husband would rule other gods. A new pantheon for a new World. Unfortunately, her husband was like most men who are bestowed power. He got drunk on it and demanded more. She saw the way it warped him, was disgusted by it, and called him on it. He wanted her subservience. When she refused, he turned their people against her, so she left. Became a traveler goddess, untethered to any location. Her husband, in his futile fury, branded her a goddess of discord and formally banished her. His choice of derogative was better suited for himself than his wife."

"Yeah, well, I've seen her power at work. She pitted *Devourers* against each other. That's pretty impressive." Bix braced her hands behind her and groaned with contentment as the masseuse worked out the knots in her feet and calves.

"I don't doubt that, but discord is not what you witnessed." He leered at a naiad sinking underwater in front of him. "She is a goddess of truth. Not the truths we paint on our façades or the banners around which we hone our identities. No, she draws forth the facts of self that we bury, hide, and repress. Our private, personal, secret truths. She drags them to the surface and forces us to confront their very real existence. Devourers may be supreme soldiers, but even they have deep-seated ambition that leads to strife when exposed."

"Can she provoke the things we fear about ourselves? Trespass on your turf?" Bix vividly recalled her stark terror for Tobek and his well-being after her encounter with Musso-Koroni.

"If fear occurs, it is because we have certainty in the consequence of us acting on those repressed truths." A splash of water and Phobos appeared in front of her, his glistening wet body pressing against her extended feet. "She got to you. And you had more than fear. Terror? How delicious."

"Phobos…" she warned.

He bent forward and inhaled deeply. His eyes widened, the crimson pupils dilated, and he leaned back. "You're afraid *you're* going to kill him. Your Berserker, dead by your darkness."

"I was ordered to execute him," she admitted. "I clearly chose a different outcome."

"No, no, you didn't." Phobos pushed her feet down and stepped closer in the water to rest against her locked knees. "That's your repressed truth. That's what she plucked out of you. His order of execution still stands. You found him guilty of the crimes that brought him to your attention. You are the High Executioner, usually swift in your judgments and punishments, but not for him. He is an exception, and exceptions have so many unforeseen consequences."

"I don't know the whole story. I might once I get all my memories."

"Oh, there is a story there." He chuckled cruelly. His smile exposed his long canines. "But you already remember the most important bits. Tell me, when you're with him, is there a part of you that you hold back? There is. I can see it in your expression. And it is no small part. Interesting. So very interesting."

"Phobos, I didn't come here for relationship advice." She pulled her legs out of the water and regained her feet. "I came to warn you that I will be facing off with Musso-Koroni soon. That ends with me husking her and reclaiming my memories. It'll be the fourth installment, pushing me over the halfway mark."

"Yes, we witnessed how ruinous the third portion of your memories was for many Worlds," Phobos jibed. "At least endeavor to get clear of the Mids before you begin the draw. You're too dangerous to lose control in the Mids anymore. I will make the appropriate reinforcements to my home to support your recovery."

"Thank you." She mocked a bow and winced as the shard in her side made itself known. Again.

"This confrontation is due to that accursed Project Resen, isn't it?" He laid his hands atop the water and propelled himself out of the bath to stand before her. His studious gaze searched hers, then her face, then the whole of her body. "You didn't heed my advice to drop it. Why are you so committed when it will curb your freedom as much as ours?"

"Why are the pantheons wasting their time and effort quashing Resen before the Devourers are driven from the Mids? Why not wait to destroy Resen once it's served its purpose?" She countered his questions with questions, a typical intel evasion.

"Better to ask why we resist something that can fundamentally change our interminable lives when novelty is what we crave." He manifested loose pants for himself, ever dignified. "Some of us are too lazy to voice an opinion. Some of us are cowards. It is the cowards yielding to their fear of change who are blocking Resen. They fear change and they fear you, equally yet differently. If you want Resen to exist long enough to work in support of the Mids, then you must force the pantheons to hone their fear."

"Become worse than the High Executioner for all Worlds?" She huffed. "Like that isn't going to bite me in the ass?"

"The champion of the city is the enemy of those who want control of the city." He cupped his hand around her rib cage, the one still throbbing with pain. His brow furrowed. "Being a bigger bogeyman isn't your fear, however. You fear being responsible for harm befalling your friends."

"They've been harmed many times while on missions with me. It's part and parcel of what we do." She raised her arm on her festering side and placed her hand on her nape, giving him a better view of her injury.

"That's not the same as being irrevocably maimed due to an action *you* take or a decision *you* make." He waved his hand, and her dress dissolved, leaving her standing in her lingerie. There was nothing seductive in his touch; it was purely clinical as he poked and prodded her side.

"I decided to let Ashtad and Tobek clear the gods from Zamarad on their own. I could've saved more of those researchers. I could've saved the demis who fell to the gods and the Devourers. I could've saved the Berserkers who also died." She yelped when he pushed on the area that refused to heal. "But I didn't. It was my choice to let them run it without me. To wait for them to admit they needed me."

"You're right. You, the inarguably superior power, chose to allow lesser beings to wade into a situation you knew was going to end badly for them. Yet had you intervened as instinct demanded, you would have denied them the risk and the reward." His pinkie found the small hole between her fourth and fifth rib that hadn't completely closed.

Biting down on a cry, she pivoted to give him better access. "I'd have denied the demis their challenge and the Berserkers their pride in doing their duty. This work was so much easier when we were up against some upper-caste Chwed who had too much power and not enough sense."

"You're antagonizing a different class of enemy now, ones who can and will cause your loyalists lasting harm." He pulled her against his chest, one hand firmly on the back of her head, pressing it to his shoulder. "You've upgraded from honeybees to hornets. The former will die or flee. The latter never will. They'll keep stinging."

"Until you squish them," she muttered.

"Relationships with immortals don't fade away." He adjusted his hold on her and the way his body fit against hers. "They evolve and compound. Your faithful will always pay the consequences for your actions and your choices. That is part of being who you are. That is the reason the old Chimera never allowed anyone to befriend her."

Bix screamed as Phobos dug into her flesh. The soft round tip of his finger morphed into a claw, a scoop, a hellish scraper. She bit his scarred shoulder as he added a second finger to aid the first. The sound of tissue tearing echoed between her ears. Mist and midnight filled her throat as he searched for the chip of angel bone in her lung. He cursed repeatedly, foraging for the elusive fragment. Tears trickled over her cheeks to blend with the fragrant water clinging to his skin. Her shadows rippled along her spine, eager to stop the source of her pain. She willed them to abide until, with a grunt of triumph, he excavated the sliver. The moment it was free of her body, it disintegrated. She slumped against Phobos, still firmly pinned between his arm and body. A minion appeared with a bowl of water. Phobos rinsed his hand, then held her close while she juddered from the deep, deep breaths she could finally take while her body throbbed. The music of healing struck its opening chords.

"Having power is not the same as having control," he

murmured, not bothered by the mist and midnight spilling on his arm while her body began the process of mending itself. "Not over ourselves and not over others. It is a mistake made by many, deities most of all."

"I know I can't control what will happen when I reclaim my memories from Musso-Koroni," she whispered.

"My dear, you can't even control showing up to a costume gala underdressed." He pushed her out to arm's length and covered her in a cloud of navy and mulberry.

"How did you know about Blackpool?" Sure, time flowed differently outside the Mids, but even then… She gasped as a corset fitted to her form, covering and compressing her wound as the boning snugged up two notches past her usual comfort.

"Because the pantheons know about the Grove assembling in the human city. Rest assured, Musso-Koroni will not be the only god in attendance." Phobos curled a finger in her hair, drawing it to her crown as part of some elaborate updo. The cloud around her dissipated, revealing her evening gown of seafoam silks and ornate beadwork. "Make conscious choices, Chimera, and brace for the consequences. It is all any of us can reasonably do."

CHAPTER 19

The English coast in February saw tourists in puffer coats and snow slickers fighting to keep their hoods and hats in place as winter skipped along the Irish Sea, teasing whitecaps on the choppy currents and blowing the mist ashore. Two days ahead of the official start of the magicians' convention, the tourist town of Blackpool was already overrun with enthusiasts from around the Primary Mid World. Private parties had started days ago. The town had been preparing for it for weeks. The event had been sold out for months.

Fortunately, when superpowers wished to be in attendance, space was made available. No one knew how long it would take for the Grove to patch the Resen servers or if they'd transfer the data to Ashtad. The risk of having the Grove exposed to the gods meant the Grove wouldn't linger longer than it had to. Bix's team was operating on a week-long estimate based on the Fates' choice of venue. The magic convention would cover many inexplicable anomalies a human might perceive with the influx of very magical nonhumans, thus accommodating the Consortium's law of keeping humans in the dark about their magical neighbors.

Tobek and his men had descended on Blackpool earlier in the day to prep the Tower building and remove any wards from the city intended to keep the Angelic Host and Dragon Horde at bay. The Sage servers were safely ensconced at different hotels near the convention center under heavy guard. Bix would move them to the ballroom at the appointed hour. The Mid World Army had dispatched support troops from other branches to deal with crowd control if things got out of hand with the gods and the angels. That allowed the Berserkers to focus on the Grove and the Houses.

Runjit and his team of medics were manning first aid stations inside the Tower Ballroom. Hywl and his team of angel specialists were prowling the streets, breaking the angel-deterrent wards and keeping anyone from installing new ones. Tobek and Gurp were working with their peers from other MWA units to lay a variety of spells around town in hopes of minimizing the collateral damage from the anticipated clash of superpowers.

Security for the mortals was as good as it was going to get.

Defense Against the Dark Arts, or in this case the pantheons, was pretty much up to Consortium politics at this point.

Bix surveyed the scene from a World away. She'd layered gates to allow her to walk in Blackpool without actually being there to inspect the area and acquire mental images of potential relo sites should things go as expected. The moment she fully entered the Primary Mid World, the key players would know she'd arrived, including Musso-Koroni. Bix intended to delay that confrontation for as long as possible. She'd warned her team that they were going to have to carry the football into the end zone. She'd stay in the game as long as she could, but no one was to harbor the false expectation that she was anything more than a defensive tackle. She was the last resort, the final option if the gods got too close to the Grove. Once she made her first move against any god, all hell would break loose. Until then, she was overwatch. Again. With any luck, the Devourers would refrain from attending this time.

She took her near-World post in the crow's nest of the Blackpool Tower, a facsimile of the Eiffel Tower built atop a block-sized building of assorted attractions that included the ballroom where tonight's festivities with the Grove were scheduled to take place. Bright lights from the glass observation deck at the top of the Tower fought the lavender sunset to illuminate the beach, piers, and town some four hundred feet below.

"Big public events, especially in this neck of the woods, are a draw for all kinds of Chweds." Hywl spoke across the comm cuffed to Bix's ear. "The folklore of the isles is rich because much of it is true. The Chwed communities here are abundant and active. The annual magic convention is as much for them as it is the humans. We've got uppers, middles, and lowers in the mix tonight."

"They're going to be skittish and stupid with the influx of superpowers," Ashtad advised on the same channel. He and Cian were behind the scenes inside the Tower building, co-opting the town's surveillance and emergency systems. "The reckless ones will try to sneak their way into the ballroom tonight to curry favor with whichever superpower pays them attention."

"No one gets near those servers without proving they're a Fate or a Grove Sage," Tobek ordered. "Look for the shapeshifters and the illusionists. Take out any interloper quietly. We don't want to draw attention."

"I've tapped into the lighting and sound controls for the Tower," Cian interjected. "Fire and sprinkler systems too. Extending to the street cameras and city power grid now."

"Nez and I are in the ballroom, parking ourselves perpendicular to the stage and the main door," Drew piped up. "We're easy to spot. Clocking some mighty fine Berserkers but no superpowers or Chweds."

Bix kept half an ear to the chatter among the teams as she opened a second set of viewing gates behind her, overlooking the town instead of the beach. She drew in a sliver of ether to strip the view of Blackpool back to its sepia base tone and expose the presence of superpowers.

A lattice of variegated green caged the Tower building, starting beneath the sidewalk and rising to the tip of the Tower spire. It lacked the texture of Resen, being more translucent and having wider gaps. The Houses of Fate's magic, had to be. Were they taunting the pantheons with this reproduction, or did it serve a practical purpose?

At the edge of town, tiny red dots at each major transportation hub denoted lesser gods. The peppering of blue flecks throughout the city marked the advance teams of the Angelic Host.

"Angels are in town," Bix apprised. "Gods are at the transport depots. Fates in the Tower building."

"We have no eyes on the Fates, repeat no eyes," Ashtad said. "Rescanning the building now."

It would take less than a heartbeat for the armies of the Host and the pantheons to join their forward troops. The Fates didn't have that sort of mobility; they relied on third-party transportation.

The moment the sun dipped below the horizon, Bix turned her attention to the colorized viewing gate overlooking the beach. The wind picked up, shaking signs and causing people to lean into their stride. Rain fell, progressing to torrents as the whitecaps on the Irish Sea grew into waves that crashed as storm surges against the seawalls. The sudden deluge sent people running for cover.

"Instant storm," Feng drawled, materializing at Bix's side on the World adjacent in his tux with tails—suit tails that is. His own tail was tucked away. "The first section of the Grove is coming. Full escort as promised."

Flashes of lightning revealed angelic cloud riders escorting a four-masted sailing ship straight out of a high-seas adventure movie. The wooden keel cut through foaming surf, riding the crest and fall alongside…scaled spines? Bix slid gates to analyze the arrivals through the aid of ether. Six purple dots flanked the green ship, while seven blue dots circled the sails.

"Dragons?" Bix glanced at Feng. "I thought they were staying on the sidelines."

"The Dragon Horde and the Angelic Host have decided that enough is enough. Either the pantheons will live up to their obligations as members of the Consortium forthwith, or it is war."

Feng held up a hand to stop the diatribe welling inside Bix. "I know war among the superpowers is exactly what the traitorous faction inside the Consortium wants. They're going to get it if the gods don't rip their heads out of their asses. Tonight decides a lot more than Resen."

"Feng, we can't—"

"*We* have no say in this," Feng reminded, cutting her off. "The best we can do is minimize casualties. You look lovely, by the by."

"Thank you." She did a small curtsey. "I'm hoping the bogeyman only has to make an appearance and not go full tantrum. I don't want to be the excuse the faction uses to take the Consortium's focus off the Devourers, not again."

"The top echelon of the Consortium is convening as we speak. They will either hash out an agreement before the Grove concludes its business, or this isle and most of the Primary Mid World will cease to exist." Feng tugged his waistcoat. "We'll know where we stand before dawn."

"Did you tell the Host they're not allowed to get their mitts on the build specs until we run a bug scrub over the data?" Bix elbowed him.

"They scoffed at the notion," he admitted apologetically. "The damage was already done before you pointed out my error. It is up to the Houses of Fate as to whom the Grove will give Resen's data, and they have no reason not to hand it to the Host directly."

"Damn it, Feng." Bix glared at him and covered her comm. "Fuck me again on a mission and we're going to have real problems. Epic problems, you hear me?"

"I am here to do what I can to atone for my sin, or don't you believe people are allowed to make mistakes?" he challenged.

Two things kept her from losing it all over the Phoenix. One, being actively in the middle of a high-stakes op. Two, having served all those years under Ashtad's leadership and his insistence that she accept mistakes happen, and those who survive are made better for them. The trick was making sure everybody survived.

"When this is done, you find Ashtad Ba'al and you thank him for me not ripping you a new one tonight." She uncovered her comm and returned her focus to her job as overwatch while Tobek's voice rumbled through her earpiece.

"Nothing quite like the superpowers upping the ante," Tobek grumbled. "Status?"

"Ship coming from the northwest, full sails," Bix relayed to the Berserkers on the ground. "Angels are forcing everyone indoors to hide the nature of the Grove's arrival. Expect chaos inside as the distraction while they disembark."

"Roger that," Runjit confirmed over the noise of the orchestra tuning up.

"Roger," Ashtad echoed over plucking violins.

"Bix, over here," Feng beckoned from behind her. "I've got steam coils, looks like trains moving at the exact same speed. Odd, no?"

Bix swapped gates, the color for the sepia, as she shifted her attention inland. Sure enough, more blue and purple dots appeared on the map, and in their company brighter shades of green. Fates, angels, and dragons arriving in Blackpool together by land. Bix slid the sepia gate in a full circle around the crow's nest, taking in the three-sixty view.

"That's not the complete Grove on the ship," she said mostly to Tobek, though Hywl's team would benefit too. "They're arriving via the cardinal and ordinal compass points. Different transportation modes. Gods are waiting to intercept. The Grove might not make it to the Tower before things go to hell."

"Two more ships," Feng cut in, "true west and southwest."

"It's the three piers," Bix realized. "They'll dock at the piers."

"Ships that size will need the whole pier." Tobek cursed. "Pray the dragons dredged the area, or the Houses are going to beach the old gals. Those piers were built to be promenades, not docks. At low tide, those beaches extend past the footings."

Through the storm lights, Bix studied the beaches around

the piers. Sure enough, the sands cratered all along the coast. Posts of composite sea wreckages rose from the sea floor to reinforce the piers as the ships sailed closer.

"I didn't know the humans kept any of those galleons in operation," Bix whispered in awe as the ships neared. "They're a sight to behold."

"Not human-made galleons, my lady. Those are living ships birthed by the seas on certain Worlds," Hywl corrected. "You can tell by the way they crest. They'll dock themselves. No ropes or anchors required. The crew is there to tend to passengers and nurture the ship. Very different from the magic-forged trains they're bringing into the land-bound stations. Those require a collaborative effort to run, but they'll never break down or derail. Technically, they don't need rails."

Bix's heart hammered as the three huge galleons nimbly slotted themselves alongside piers that had never been meant to be more than pathways to the attractions at their bulbous tips.

Wild cheering blasted across the comms. Must have come from the general public in which Tobek, Hywl, and their men were embedded. The Fates might have intended to be discreet in their arrivals, but this was a country where a fictitious wizard boy was a national hero. Bix laughed and so did Feng.

"What? What's so funny out there?" Cian asked. "I've got access to CCTV, but I can't see much through the rain."

"The dragons just created a port in view of a bunch of humans celebrating magic," Feng harrumphed. "They're making it clear to the gods they are in attendance."

"Oh, like that isn't going to draw stupid people out to gawk," Cian snarked. "Jamming cell towers, emergency calls, and dispatches. Looping a broadcast message for all civilians and response teams to stay indoors."

"MWA confirming human and Chwed first responders are standing down," Tobek said. "Harbormasters along the coast are in blackout. Angels disrupting all radio. Full static. Ley line communications continue to be operational."

"Chweds can't help but feel the change in magic. No use hiding it from them." Feng adjusted his bow tie.

"How's it going at Platform Nine and Three-Quarters?" Bix asked.

"We've got eyes on the gods," Hywl murmured, his tension coming through the comm louder than his words. "They're surrounded by angels. One-to-five ratio, god to angels. So far, it's civil. A lot of posturing, but they're keeping to human form. Train is ninety seconds out."

Confirmations of similar standoffs came in from the other train stations.

"Holding to human form is a good sign," Feng noted. "Means both sides are adhering to the rules set down by the Consortium for being in the Primary Mid World."

"Train pulling in now," Hywl shouted over the piercing whistle and the screech of locomotive brakes.

"Decision point." Bix's heart quickened further, but she forced herself to draw steady breaths as she divided her attention among the piers and the stations.

"Hold," Tobek ordered. "We don't act until they do."

"Red dots are gods?" Feng put his back against hers despite the way their magics repelled each other. "This is an extremely useful tool you have."

"You show up blue, in case you're wondering." Bix had seven alternate locations for the Grove that would stymie the gods if she had to move the living library. Unfortunately, that was only a temporary solution, and it did nothing to stop any collateral damage to the human city should the gods get feisty.

"They're falling back," Feng said in surprise. "The gods are falling back. They're heading for us. Oh, here we go. Ring around the Tower. Looks like whatever the Fates did to the Tower building is keeping the gods at bay."

"The Fates waged a war against the pantheons and won their independence, so they're not helpless," Bix reminded.

"It's their crafty and unpredictable traits that worry me."

Feng pointed to the flares in the green netting around the Tower building. "How long do you think that'll hold?"

"That barrier will keep lesser gods at bay," Tobek answered in Bix's stead. "Same for minor angels and dragons."

Bix studied the lattice again. Was that Tobek's magic shielding the building? His personal mojo powered the coal plant's defenses. Post-ley-line encounter, he'd boosted the defenses of the Church of the Templars. Had he taken on the Tower building too? That would explain why Ashtad and Cian hadn't located the Fates during setup. Had Tobek always had this much magic in reserve, or was this a new side effect of the ley line? Was his evolution pushing him toward some new kind of Fate instead of a titan? Perhaps a titan of destiny? Was that why his magic glowed with the green typically associated with Fates?

"Packages disembarking from the trains, moving to buses. Should arrive in ten minutes," Hywl updated, drawing Bix's attention back to the mission. "Host rolling as cops to provide escort."

"Dragons swarming up from the sea, taking human form. MWA, pull back to the shelters," Tobek directed.

Through the full-color viewing window, Bix could see the Mid World Army in motion. Squads moved in sync to tourist attractions, hotels, and the amusement park. They gave the Tower and the loitering gods as wide a berth as a small town allowed.

Bix fixated on the galleons bobbing at the three piers where dragons in human form buddied up with angels to line the distance from gangplanks to the Tower building. Hundreds of them in the deluge provided safe passage. Natural nemeses, the dragons and the angels working together in close proximity was a miracle on its own. The watercolor beauty of their magics blending to form archways was something she never thought she'd witness.

"They're pretty when they work together, you know?" She nudged Feng, the lone dragon-angel hybrid entity.

"Almost heartwarming." He grunted. "Can you zoom in on the North Pier?"

On the North Pier, the rain held as a hard curtain of distortion to either side of the promenade while the passengers made their way down the gangplank unaffected by the weather. A parade of Sages in culturally appropriate variations of formal wear circa the early twentieth century were escorted by Fates, mostly women, though there were a few men pairing off with men. It was less about the perception of heterosexuality and more about the fact there were a heck of a lot more women than men who'd completed their trials to Fatehood. Amusingly, many of the female Fates weren't in dresses. Tuxedos abounded. So did formal pajamas. Some Fates walked with the assistance of canes. Some boldly showed their prosthetics. A notably smaller contingent had physical impairments that were obvious but did not inhibit mobility.

Nez had said every Fate had a deformity. Nothing quite like seeing them gathered to drive home the point.

"Now that is a wondrous sight." The awe in Feng's tone rivaled Bix's admiration of the galleons.

"Heads up, the buses are arriving," Bix warned, noting the ratio of gods to angels to dragons had shifted to 1:1:1 in the blocks surrounding the Tower building. "Gods are amassing in the streets and surrounding buildings. Dragons and angels holding the lines."

"Ballroom doors opening," Runjit announced.

A rat-tat-tat echoed, and Rimsky-Korsakov's *Procession of the Nobles* blossomed across multiple comms.

Cian's mumbled expletives declared the Fates and Sages had entered the ballroom. It must have been quite the moment for the kid, seeing two of the paths for his future gathering right before his eyes. A sight token few of his kind would ever see. What must it be like for him to behold the pomp and circumstance of the Houses assembled?

"Tower staff verification complete. Everyone is either a human or from a House," Ashtad noted. "Oracles are among the mix."

"They'd be here as additional security," Nez added. "No offense to the Berserkers leading the official effort."

A couple of overly confident snorts came across the comms.

"Get the impression Sparky and I are the only ones in this room who were never human." Drew's comment was muffled, as if she was speaking into her shoulder.

"That's all buses emptied and the first two ships through the door," Hywl reported. "Last group of special guests coming in now."

Bix studied the movements of the red, blue, and purple dots surrounding the Tower as the last of the green ones entered the building. The dragons and angels who'd provided escort to the Fates blended into the security formations on the streets, creating pixelized pictures through the filter of ether. Gods milled through the pictures, possibly moving below or above the dragons and angels. Gut instinct said the gods had shifted forms to inconspicuous beings—vermin, bats, reptiles, etcetera—to sneak past established protections.

"All entrances secured, final team of Berserkers inside," Tobek rasped. "Streets are lined with superpower foot soldiers. They're spinning enchantments to keep the lesser races indoors. Anyone feeling a bit odd, that's what's happening."

Sighs of relief bubbled across the comms as Tobek's explanation was repeated to those off comms. However, his account was a gross understatement of the invasion of Blackpool.

Rippling out from the Tower building in concentric circles of hostility waiting for the sign stood dragons, angels, and gods as far as the eye could see, including the newly made port. Thousands of superpowers crammed into thirteen square miles. One god. One angel. One dragon. That would have been more than enough to wipe the entire United Kingdom off the map. This many was a dick wag.

"Better hope the leadership of the Consortium reaches an agreement soon, or only the immortals are making it out of here alive." Feng ran his fingers through his hair.

"That they're allowing this standoff to happen, much less in the Primary Mid World, does not fill me with confidence." Bix monitored the movements of the gods. They were traveling with purpose around the dragons and angels, yet not advancing on the Tower building. What were they up to?

"This is all tinder begging to be lit, I agree." Feng chuckled nervously. "I can't shake the idea we're missing something right under our noses. Now might be a good time to consult with that observer friend of yours. The one who likes the cards?"

She covered her comm again and eyed Feng. "You're on edge tonight. You going to be okay in the thick?"

"Fates demanded we both attend, so I *will* be perfectly fine," he insisted, but his twitching belied that. "I am not a burden about whom you need to worry."

"Then shift your mind to mission mode," she said harshly, trying to snap him out of whatever mental spiral threatened his equilibrium. "If you think for one moment that you're going to lose your shit, even if it's a stray shiver, you get out, way out. Worlds away. Any stray spark will take everyone down, soldiers and innocents."

"PTSD doesn't render me a child," he snapped. Sniffed. Tugged on his lapels, then his shirt cuffs. "Stop assuming I'm inept."

She should bench him. It was her op, her call. He was too jittery. Yet the Fates had wanted him here. Plus, he was an authority to whom the angels and dragons would respond if the gods kicked off a war. Plus, plus, he'd sneak into the ballroom even if she grounded him. Better to keep him where she could see him...or at least feel his potent Mid World presence.

"The card?" Feng prompted. "Or are you opposed to leveraging that ally as well?"

Bix looked at the night sky and the clusters of red stars. The frequent requests for help were becoming a crutch on which she could easily be dependent; however, Feng was right. There was too much that was hinky on this op. Too much riding on its success. Too many changes at the eleventh hour. Too much she couldn't anticipate or control. Too many lives at stake.

A bit of guidance from an objective third party couldn't hurt, right?

She opened tiny gates and retrieved a blank Tarot card from home. Holding up the card, she formed the mental question. Something unexpected was bound to happen, especially with the Fates on scene. If she could get a heads-up, she and her team stood a chance of minimizing casualties.

"There's a gotcha lying in wait tonight. What is it?" she asked the überentity.

Arcane magic slipped along her arm and took the card from her. The expanding card whirled around her and Feng in a tornado of red lights, then came to an abrupt halt before them. Trepidation niggled at her nape as the card pivoted to show its face.

Feng slapped his hand over his mouth, muffling a curse.

The Ten of Swords. The card of defeat, betrayals, endings, and loss. The stabbed-in-the-back card, in meaning and rendering. It typically showed a corpse sprawled on a shoreline with ten swords rammed down its spine. In this card, the swords were praying angels with wings wide to represent the hilts. They'd sunk up to their knees in a tangle of colorful yarn spilling over gilded steps leading up to a grand stage. Instead of a sun rising beneath a midnight sky, the misty night was filled with shadowy eyes.

The impaled yarn ball had to represent threads of Fate, a Sage server most likely. If she interpreted the angels to be angel bones, well those bones would absolutely kill any member of the Grove…not to mention the doozy they'd do to her.

"Feng, if someone smuggles angel bones into the party—"

"I will be your shield," he assured gently. "They cannot hurt me. They only make me stronger."

Crackling comms interrupted as Nez whispered, "The Houses have assembled. The first dance is complete and now the Grove is ready. Time to bring the Sage servers and their very special guests to the stage."

"All right, gang." Bix returned the card to the stash at home and closed the viewing gates. "Be on alert for angel-bone weapons. Remember, they will turn anyone who isn't Feng or an immortal into ash."

Wicked masculine guffaws floated through the comms. Hywl's merry voice separated from the others. "Oh, my lady, what's a little skirmish without some ashes?"

Cheeky bastards. One of a hundred reasons she adored the Berserkers, yet she hoped with all hope ashes wouldn't be seen tonight.

Gates opened. The legendary Phoenix and Chimera crossed fully into Blackpool.

CHAPTER 20

The opening strains of Strauss's *Blue Danube Waltz* greeted Bix and Feng as they appeared on the steps leading down from the stage on which an orchestra had replaced the renowned Wurlitzer organ of the Blackpool Tower Ballroom.

Fates twirled with other Fates, Sages, Oracles, and Berserkers in a grand ring of formal dance around the sprung floor. Their costumes, the music, and this gilded ballroom made a fine tribute to the early twentieth century. A magical tribute to be sure, for a haze of green mist lay thick along the ground, releasing wisps to coat the red velvet conversation clusters surrounding the dance floor. Ghostly pastel green coils drifted up the double balconies to the reliefs framing the painted ceiling. Lacy webs of Kelly green cupped the globes of the ornate chandeliers. Laser-thin filaments of hunter green cut through every surface and entity as if none of them existed. Myriad shades of green throughout lent an ethereal dream state to the atmosphere.

The catatonic occupants of wheelchairs made from rattan to off-road chrome parked in the center of the dance floor were undeniably haunting. However, there was nothing as arresting as the original Berserker set upon a large throne of stiff green textiles in the heart of the stupefied.

Tobek's rage-bright gaze raked Bix from beaded hemline to the azurite tiara secure in her updo. Butterflies flitted in her stomach as he stood, never taking his eyes from her. Her Berserker. So tall. So proud. So elegant in his military dress uniform that was likely the actual one he'd worn over a century ago. His presence commanded the room.

Well, that and his unbalanced magics. The overcharged push and scrabbling pull. Tobek, not the Fates, was the source of the spells engulfing the Tower building. He was evolving, all right. Into what, how quickly, and with which side effects remained to be seen.

She took one step toward him, and he took one step toward her.

A deafening boom shook the building and silenced the music. The laser grid flashed red. Tobek's Berserker-blue eyes turned crimson. His body jerked sharply. He retreated one step; his calves pressed against the seat of the throne. The red faded from his gaze, bright blue returned. The grid resumed its hunter hue.

"The gods are assailing the wards," Tobek said, his tone sonorous, his words echoing as if traveling along the filaments of his protective spell. "The spell holds, for now."

The orchestra resumed its playing as if nothing was amiss.

As much as Bix wanted to race into Tobek's arms and dance the night away, there was the mission and the obvious wrinkles in their grand plan. Starting with Tobek. His posture was too rigid even for a military bearing. He stood too closely to the strange throne. A man of his mass maintained an excess of personal space to accommodate the movement of his bulk. If he sneezed, he'd buckle his knees on the lip of the seat. And when he'd dared to step away... He reminded her of the Sage servers trapped in their pods at Zamarad.

The green fog obscured everything from shins down. Odds were the tricky Fates had him tethered to the damn throne as if the combo was some amplifier for the spells keeping them safe from the gods. In a room full of soldiers under his command, men who very badly wanted to erase the Grove and probably the Fates, Tobek had been shackled. His choice or the Fates?

Hard to know when it came to Tobek and his weird woo.

Bix inhaled deeply and narrowed her eyes, searching out her team members. She found Runjit and his medics first. They formed an outer circle beneath the balconies, their supplies unpacked into red chair clusters behind them. They were all quite handsome in their retro finery. The Berserkers' security force had been divvied among the dancers twirling on the floor and the shadowy depths along the back pathways of the upper floors. The soldiers were far from inconspicuous in their dress uniforms, which appeared to have been the men's legit uniforms from Vaudeville's heyday. To a one, their eyes glowed with blue rage.

Ashtad sat in the first balcony with one of the male Fates from the Luz spell. They were positioned nearest the stage with a view of the main doors. Ashtad caught Bix's eye and brushed the tip of his nose.

She took another deep breath and caught it, the scent of patchouli and menthol made of ingredients hailing from Other Worlds.

"They've drugged the air," Bix murmured to Feng. "Depressants, downers. They're forcing the room to be chill."

"A bit more than a depressant." Feng descended two steps to her side and offered her his arm…then apparently thought twice about how their magics naturally repelled each other and clasped his hands behind his back. "They're flirting with airborne anesthesia. My entire body is tingling with the onset of numbness, yet I can't seem to care."

"Make sure you maintain enough fucks to not catch the building on fire, yeah?" She inclined her head at Ashtad, then sought out Drew and Nez. They were exactly where they'd said they'd be, parked in the velvet seating halfway between the door and the stage. They weren't alone. Skuld clutched Drew's shoulder, wreathing Drew in a dense cloud of smoky runes. Skuld was mostly blind, so her use of Drew as a seeing-eye draugr wasn't a total surprise. Plus, those two knew each other. Both had roots in the Norse pantheon. Roots, not hearts.

Skuld tugged Drew closer and spoke into the comm cuffed to Drew's ear. "Welcome to the party, Chimera and Phoenix. You can fetch the broken servers now too. Put them in the middle there with the others."

"Fifty-nine," Feng murmured at Bix's side. "I count fifty-nine men in wheelchairs surrounding your familiar, and that does not include those on the perimeter who appear infinitely livelier."

"Others, Skuld? What's going on? What's with the involuntary relaxation when gods are banging on the doors?" Bix used gates to bring the Resen Sage servers in their wheelchairs to the ballroom. She placed them at the foot of the stage steps outside the ring of dance. "This isn't exactly the time for a party."

All the dancers stopped, and the music rested. Oracles Bix didn't recognize swept forward and collected the Resen Sages, pushing the wheelchairs into the center of the dance floor. The rest of the dancers retreated to the edges.

"Time is such a fickle thing." The second male Fate from the Luz spell crossed his arms atop the curved lip in the uppermost balcony two-thirds of the way to the main doors. "You and the Phoenix are quite familiar with that, aren't you?"

"It's a spell." Feng cursed under his breath. "The Sages in the middle of the floor are arranged in the pattern of a spell the likes of which I have seen replicated only in the archives of the Angelic Host. It is a variant of a time-travel spell."

Both Bix and Feng knew a thing or two about time spells. Being key ingredients to the spells made that knowledge a matter of self-preservation. Tobek, however, was not a customary part.

"Very good, Phoenix." The voice of one of the female Fates from the Luz spell carried over the speakers in the ballroom. "The Host is wont to run off with information they are not capable of applying. They sit on it until it's forgotten. Gods are the same way. Dragons too. It's a waste of wisdom. A crime, really, so good on you for finding forgotten archives."

"That sounds suspiciously like you don't want the Host to have the Resen build specs." Bix held a hand up against the glow of the chandeliers. Lo, at the opposite end of the ballroom, up in the lighting booth, someone waved. Two someones. Cian and the Fate on the PA system. "Was this your plan all along? To have us deliver your own research to *you*, to the Houses? The Host is just a foil?"

Again, the building shook. Again, the protection spell flashed red. Again, Tobek reacted, a little less Berserker and a little more ancient demigod.

"Yes and no," answered the male Fate keeping Ashtad company. He leaned against the side of Ashtad's chair. His long, tattooed fingers curled over Ashtad's shoulder. "It was obvious we couldn't retrieve the servers ourselves without the damn gods interfering. For that, we needed the Chimera and her allies."

"Bix, I didn't—" Feng growled as the tips of his hair sparked.

"I know you didn't," she interjected. No, Feng hadn't known dragging her and her team into salvaging Resen was a setup. The Fates were so many steps ahead of every player in the greater game that Feng couldn't have known he was a pawn. Hell, she hadn't known either. Nez, on the other hand, Nez who had reached out to Ashtad as the fail-safe in case she'd refused Feng because she would never refuse Ashtad anything. She pinned the elder Sage with a gimlet glare.

Nez smirked and toyed with his mangled ear. The ear in which he'd worn the anger cube prior to Musso-Koroni's interrogation. Was he angry now, or was he trying to warn her… What had he said about mastering the anger cube?

There's a reason Fates don't congregate.

"Fates don't congregate," she announced, guessing at Nez's intention. "The Grove assembles, not the Houses, yet here you all are. The original seven Houses and the Grove. Tonight isn't about Resen, not to you, at least."

Nez blinked slowly.

Her gaze connected with Tobek's, and he nodded subtly. The

Berserkers had warned her summoning the Grove would be rife with chicanery. She hadn't imagined twisting time would be the nature of the deceit. Darkness rippled under Bix's skin, but she willed it to wait. Ripping apart the Houses wouldn't patch the Resen servers. End of the day, it didn't matter who had the build specs as long as the data was complete. She could steal them from whichever owner, have her team review them, then mass-distribute them. That was the mission; that hadn't been blown...yet.

Yes, her friends were being passively threatened by the Fates, but that risk came with the job. It was nothing they weren't expecting and nothing she couldn't undo as long as the Fates didn't snip Cian's threads. Drew and Ashtad didn't have threads, so they were immune to a direct attack. Cian, not so much. Nez either, for that matter. Technically, for this op, Nez was part of her team, so she couldn't hang him out to dry despite the temptation.

However, it was a wholly suicidal misstep for the Fates to exploit Tobek as their guard dog while they used Feng and her as parts in a time spell. They should've known better. Of all the superpowers, she expected more from the Fates.

Unless she was missing something?

"What, exactly, are you hoping to retrieve from the annals of time?" Bix allowed her darkness to slither from her spine, one part displeasure, one part distraction, one part discovery. "What is the blood of the Phoenix and the Chimera worth to the vaunted Houses?"

"Calm down, Chimera," cooed one of the two male Fates from the Luz spell. "We're not neophytes."

"Your drugs don't affect me, you contemptuous prick," she hissed as her shadows seeped into the haze of Other World magic thickening along the stage, steps, and floor. Every shadow was an extension of her senses, feeding her information and telling her of the new threads being woven through the bodies of the broken servers, linking the men in the wheelchairs to each other and to Tobek's throne. "Your choice of words, however, connotes your utter lack of respect for every woman in this room. Calm down, indeed. A platitude of the patriarchy, a legacy of the pantheons you went to war to escape. Don't you dare echo their drivel to *me*."

The Chimera was infamous for her temper, and Bix wasn't above using it to buy time for her darkness to inspect every inch of the ballroom, the lighting booth, the catwalk, backstage, and beyond. Her shadows fed her images of Cian trying to wriggle free from the prosthetic hand gripping his nape, the hand of the Fate holding him captive. Darkness told her the male Fate with Ashtad had a prosthetic foot and customized shoe that hid a blade like a gadget from an old spy movie. She knew Hywl's men were outside the ballroom in black tactical gear, weapons aimed at the ballroom and at the building's main doors, waiting for the signal. Most importantly, every thread binding Tobek to his throne had been mapped and registered.

Tobek, as the Fates' prized punching bag, had already been stitched into the time spell, which made his men the hostages the Fates had used to force his and each other's compliance. Every Berserker had threads of destiny that a Fate could cut on a whim, thus ending the Berserker's life. There was no relocation, no gate Bix could deploy that would save the Berserkers from that.

Shit.

"I recognize that look on your face, but hurting them doesn't hand us the build specs," Feng said quietly. "Perhaps they need us to go back in time to retrieve the servers before the goddess of discord ruins them. I am willing to pay that price if it results in saving the Mids from the Devourers."

"Sixty-four broken servers, Feng." She gestured to the collective of men in wheelchairs. "Can't you see? It's not just the Resen servers they want fixed. It's not just one trip through time they're after. They expect us to bleed for them. They expect us—willingly or not—to erase their failures for them. I'm not volunteering to exsanguinate simply because the Fates failed to protect their own and the Mids, repeatedly."

The Fates planned to work a spell that required her contribution without her consent? Oh hell no. That went triple for

Feng and Tobek who'd both been tortured by magic. A lot of the Fates' magic dealt in denying informed consent, and that was a big red button issue for Bix.

"Everybody deserves a chance to fix their mistakes, Bix, even the Fates." Feng tipped his head to the side and studied her with sadness. "Perhaps, most especially the Fates *because* they should have known better."

"I am tired of sacrificing my all and my everything to compensate for their ineptitude," she shouted as the ugly truth reared its head. A hidden truth. A buried secret. One she didn't recall ever putting into words, much less admitting to herself, which meant Musso-Koroni had to be near.

The building shook with enough force to dislodge fixtures. Feng reacted first, obliterating falling chandeliers before they took out Berserkers, Sages, Oracles, and Fates alike. The security grid lit up a darker shade of red. Tobek's twitches became a full seizure. He collapsed in his chair, flailing as his eyes shone red.

"It's Musso-Koroni." Bix took one step through gates to reach Tobek's side while her darkness went in search of the goddess, diving below floorboards and slithering up walls to follow the lines of Tobek's protection spell. "She's close, but she's using the magic of the dragons and angels as cover."

Beyond the ballroom, Hywl and his team shifted their aim toward the obvious entrances. Bix knew in her gut that whichever way the goddess of hidden truths accessed the ballroom, it wouldn't be via a conventional path. If she were the goddess, she'd have recruited the kind of gods who could give her access with minimum discovery. Gods of the seas would be high on her list for a meeting on an island. To a midrange elemental god, the United Kingdom was little more than a cornflake.

Concussive blasts shook the building again, yet this time the red lines of the security grid changed to purple and blue. Tobek ceased his spasms, but the red of divinity was slow to leave his eyes. Whether his pupils had returned to black or were simply a dark red was hard to discern without overhead lighting. Emergency lights worked; so did puck lights in the observation areas. Cian turned on a few spotlights and angled them at the dance floor.

"The angels and the dragons are responding, as promised," Feng assured. "Gods may have created this World, but it is the dragons and the angels who made it evolve. This is *our* turf. That said, time is finite. We either repair the servers now or not at all."

"Take a good look at the faces of some of those servers," Cian muttered into the comms. "I recognize one Greek mathematician from his bust in a museum and a Chinese botanist from a book report I did in the third grade. You've got some old, old, ooold dudes down there."

"I'm not fixing a damn thing while Tobek is in this condition and the gods are breathing down our necks." Bix helped Tobek sit upright. A bit of blood dribbled from the corner of his mouth. He'd likely bitten his tongue during his seizure. "Now is not the time. We retreat and reassemble somewhere else."

"Now is the only time we have." Skuld flicked the ash from her blunt. "Once Resen goes live, the peace you're fighting to preserve will cease to exist. There are many options for a different type of peace, but it'll be a bumpy ride to get there."

"Bullshit. This is about him." Bix smoothed Tobek's hair from his sweat-slicked brow as he clenched the armrests of the throne until the knuckles of his natural hand whitened and the security grid stabilized. Wherever his attention was, it was not in this room. "This is about you losing control over your prized guardian. You need him in the role of your lackey for the time spell to work, don't you? That's why now."

Touching Tobek, she could feel the threads suppressing his divinity continuing to unravel. His efforts to protect the Tower building were hastening his freedom from his contract with the Fates. She wasn't sure if that was a good thing. After all, the original Chimera could have broken his bonds and hadn't. She still didn't know why.

"He is the general who led our armies against the pantheons in our war of independence," the Fate in the light booth revealed.

"When he is no longer under our protection, what do you think the gods will do to him? Thank him or introduce him to tortures the likes of which you cannot remember? The only solution for all of us to get precisely what we want is to work together right now, this evening, for as long as our allies can hold off the gods."

Bix swore in every language she knew. A demi leading a revolt against the pantheons? A demi *succeeding* and living to tell about it? That was a festering wound shared by all the pantheons. Tobek would pray for death every moment he was alive, and she might not be able to protect him from the gods' revenge.

Tobek's hand clamped on hers. His unfocused gaze drifted her direction. "The mission matters most. Save the Mids. Restore the Grove."

Bix looked to Ashtad, to the mentor who'd taught her that people mattered more than the mission.

"Your call," Ashtad said through the comms. "I'll back whatever choice you make."

"Ditto," Drew added.

"Threes," Cian declared.

"Bix, no one has to be sacrificed for the spell. Neither you nor the Phoenix have to bleed for it to work," Nez piped up. "You're not pushing the present into the past or dragging the past to the future. You're not reshaping history either. All the spell does is open a hole that allows the Fates to retrieve the data threads from a time before the servers were corrupted. Once returned to this timeline, the Fates will swap out the broken threads with the undamaged ones. No one has to be hurt, but the whole of the Mids can be helped."

Bix reassessed the broken Sage servers. Data stores from across the ages possessed intel the other superpowers had known and had forgotten. It wasn't that the Fates were singularly privy to every occurrence and truth; however, they went to great lengths not to forget the past. By not forgetting, they were better equipped and more agreeable to learning from the past to shape the future. Foresight and strategy kept the Fates as powers of reckoning.

Something about Resen required the Houses of Fate to forfeit a piece of their existing power. Had to be related to the secret the gods were trying to quash. The Fates needed access to their old troves to backfill before a vacuum dislodged their place among the Consortium. Fixing the servers wasn't about getting a leg up on the other superpowers, it was about maintaining their spot. Screwing over their peers would come *after* Resen went live. It was the gap in the meantime that had the Houses worried.

As wily as the Fates were, anything that had them legit worried was enough to concern Bix too. But she still didn't like them twisting tonight's situation or their abysmal timing.

"I agree to fix your broken servers." Feng sauntered down the steps into the mix of broken servers. "Though I prefer you make a direct request in the future. I do not appreciate being manipulated. Deception is wholly unnecessary when we are after the same end. Show me where I am to stand for this spell."

The tiny fires at the tips of Feng's hair grew to candle flames as the Phoenix followed a pair of dancers to a spot behind Tobek's throne yet facing the main doors. Being used as part of a spell… Feng had done all right at Luz, but he didn't look so steady now. If Feng lost his marbles, the dragons and the angels outside the building would sense his distress and everything would go south fast.

Tobek wasn't exactly a bastion of stability either. His mind *might* be fine, but his magic was dorked the hell up. As for Bix, well, she had loyalty in spades, but no one would accuse her of being a rock, not with her temper.

So many, many ways this could go badly.

"How long will it take to fix the servers? In the time of the Mids, while the gods are beating against our defenses, how long will this take?" Drew asked the Fates. "How long are you planning on leaving us vulnerable while our MVPs are offline?"

"Once the Chimera rends a hole in the continuum, the speed of recovery depends entirely on the Phoenix's ability to slide through time," the flippant male Fate answered. "Don't worry, we'll guide him through the process. It's relatively painless."

"If it was painless, you wouldn't have drugged the air." Feng unfurled his wings and tail as he widened his stance and crossed his arms. "Come on, Bix, you and I are the ones who kicked off this mission. It is appropriate that we shoulder this cost. Apex entities, remember?"

"What's Tobek's role in this?" Bix skimmed her hand along Tobek's arm, over the rigid muscles that often held her close when she was most vulnerable. Oh, how she wished she could offer the same kind of sanctuary to him right now. "Clearly more than security what with the fancy chair and the complex weaving connecting him to the broken servers."

"He is a hub of many magics, a translator, a converter," one of the female Fates divulged. "Once we power up the servers, they will pass him the information on when and where to locate their healthy past selves. Through his unique connection to Mids' magic, he will relay that information to the Phoenix, who will then travel with one of us to that precise moment where we will retrieve the necessary threads."

"So you expect him not only to hold the line against the gods, but also to provide cosmic directions while he's at it? That's a hell of a demand even for a guy like Chief." Ashtad straightened his bum leg with a wince.

"As long as the dragons and angels do what they promised, he'll be fine." One of the female Fates tweaked a purple line of the security grid. It pulsed a brighter shade of plum, then dulled.

Bix pressed her lips to Tobek's temple and whispered, "I'm sorry to put you through this. I hate that you suffer because you chose to support me."

Tobek squeezed her hand again. It was the only indication that he was aware of her presence.

"We start with the Resen servers," Bix demanded of the Fates, recalling her darkness to her body. "The moment they're patched, my team gets the build specs and all related files from personnel and trial results to how to interpret the data from the live system."

"The draugr can't receive the download. Not built to be

compatible." Skuld slapped Drew on the back. "Then there's the small matter of leverage that'll keep you two engaged in the spell even if we're interrupted, so we'll patch one Resen guy for every dozen of the backlog. Call it motivation, inspiration, or us being assholes. Doesn't change anything."

"Fine. Let's get on with it." Bix sighed, reluctantly letting go of Tobek's hand.

"Bring your confidants down here, Chimera." Another female Fate motioned to the seats around Skuld. "Plop them in a chair, let them get comfortable right where you can see them. We're not total dicks, you know."

Bix brought Cian and Ashtad down to Drew and Nez. She gathered up the other Fates from the Luz spell and set them at the bottom of the stage steps.

"We'll need you on the stage, Chimera, center on the conductor's podium." The irritating male Fate swept a mocking bow, directing her to the orchestra, who readied their instruments. "Your proximity to the original Berserker affects his magics. Frankly, you're a distraction he can ill afford."

"Oh, for fuck's sake," Bix muttered and used gates to take her place on the stage as the seven Fates from the seven original Houses arranged themselves on the dance floor with the assistance of canes, prosthetics, or Oracles. Their positions were deliberate but their formation unfamiliar to Bix.

Another volley from the gods made the walls tremble, but this time, the security grid held to purple and blue. The allies were standing fast. However, the building continued to crumble.

Tobek's red-and-blue gaze caught Bix's eye. For the briefest moment, clarity returned to the evolving demigod. A slow smile surfaced on his furry face as more threads laced him to the throne; arms and legs, chest and head.

She was beginning to hate that particular smile. She much preferred his wicked or playful ones. This smile, this calm reassurance, this reconciled confidence appeared right before formidable magic left him charred to a crisp, exfoliated to the bone, or something equally dreadful. Her big blond bear had known he'd be fodder and fuel, but he'd deliberately neglected to mention it.

And here she'd been most concerned about his evolution. Silly girl.

"All right, Chimera, you and the Phoenix are up." Skuld extinguished her smoke in her hand. A twist of colorful threads leapt from her palm and from those of her peers, writhing like angry vipers as the orchestra struck their opening notes. "We're ready to get all kinds of holey up in here."

CHAPTER 21

Khachaturian's *Masquerade Waltz* set the tempo for Feng to slide back and forth through time carrying Fates. Fates plucked the necessary threads from the past and wove them into the servers in the present. Tobek acted as the anchor to the now and as the conduit that dictated the Phoenix's destinations. Bix existed as the eternal constant, the connection to linear time, and Feng's guidepost. She was the slide rule, Feng was the cursor, and Tobek was the hash marks telling everyone the answers.

The work was exhausting, and the attacks by the gods increasing in frequency didn't help alleviate the strain. Fortunately, the dragons and angels were true to their commitment to protect the Grove and the Resen data. The building continued to shake, weakening the structure with each volley. Bix could only imagine what the town of Blackpool looked like beyond the ballroom, caught in the middle of a superpower spat. So much for the rule about keeping humans ignorant of magic. There was no way "natural disaster" would cover up this conflict.

The peace talks the ranking members of the Consortium were supposedly having clearly weren't progressing. Yet in the ballroom, misfits and agents of mayhem pushed themselves to their limits trying to save the Mids.

Godsdamned politics.

By the time the orchestra struck up Shostakovich's *Waltz Number Two*, sixty-three Sage servers had been restored and rolled to the rubble-littered edges of the dance floor. The servers were reawakening and reorienting under the watch of the Berserker medics and Nez.

Cian and Ashtad sat with four of the fully functional Resen servers, having dragged their chairs to a corner of the dance floor. The servers had arranged their wheelchairs to flank the young Sage and not-ancient demigod. Two of the Resen servers clasped Cian's shoulders. The kid's slack-jawed rapture was the same expression the kid donned when in the throes of a virtual-reality RPG. Drew occasionally paused her pacing to dab away Cian's drool. Ashtad fared little better than Cian. Two of the other Resen servers gripped Ashtad's knees. His eyes twitched as though in REM sleep, but the electricity arcing around his fingers proved he was very much alert. The Resen servers were either splitting the data or delivering multiple copies.

Touch was the method of transference. It wasn't the telepathy the gods loved to employ, nor was it the mental hijacking the archangels preferred. No, it went back to the roots of the Fates, to their human roots. The human touch. Peaceful, passive, and a necessary component of the human condition, touch explained why the Fates had chosen to assemble in a ballroom under the guise of an era when formal dances required bodily contact. It explained why, when Feng had tried to heal the servers at Luz, they'd responded by grabbing him. They'd tried to tell him things, but he either couldn't listen or hadn't deigned to share what they'd said with the team.

The fifth Zamarad server was the last of the Grove backlog to receive his patch. Feng emerged aflame from the gate piercing time that Bix held open. Mids' magic shielded a haggard female Fate from Feng's fire and delivered her to the center of the ballroom floor. The Fate knelt at the server's feet and laid her hands upon the server's thighs. The server inhaled sharply, blinked rapidly, and beamed at the Fate. His hands cupped her cheeks, and tears filled her eyes.

"That's it, that's done. Never, ever ask for that boon again. I don't care which of my reincarnations is in existence at the time. Don't. Painless my ass," Feng snarled, calming his fire. He stumbled a bit. Stopped. Swayed. His eyes were wild and haunted, his skin too pale, and his attire stained from his journeys. "Close the damn gate, Bix. Close it and never reopen it."

Bix shut the gate and gripped her head. Fighting the insistence of time's forward motion had required a constant restacking of gates so she didn't trap Feng in whatever period he'd visited. The relentless reimagining had been like a woodpecker hammering at the back of her skull. Her teeth still throbbed with the ghosting ricochet. Her senses were shot to hell. Her concept of existing in the present was skewed somewhere between an out-of-body hallucination and a bad case of the bed spins.

One concern existed in her bruised brain. One and one only. The concern bordered on stark raving panic.

"Tobek," she rasped, staggering from the podium and down the stage steps.

Tobek, upon his woven throne, convulsed against the threads holding him in place. Blood, dried and fresh, streaked his blond beard. His eyes were closed but fluttering. At some point, his prosthetic had detached from his arm, tearing the sleeve of his uniform and singeing it around the edges. The myriad threads that had spun from the throne were neither red nor blue. They were gone. Every line severed.

That couldn't be good.

"Bixie." Drew ran to Bix's side and grabbed Bix's arm, draping it across her suit's shoulders. The draugr easily bore Bix's weight as they shuffled across the dance floor. "Take deep breaths, Bixie. Steady yourself. Come fully back to the moment. Follow the sound of my voice, the solidity of my suit, that's it. Breathe. Rejoin us. We need you entirely here in Blackpool. Right now. Breathe."

Bix's brain registered Drew's soothing tone, then Drew's firm body. Bix inhaled a long, deep, steadying breath, let it go, and repeated. The room became more real as her mind reacclimated to the moment. She stubbed her toe on a cluster of rubble and stared at the water sloshing around her ankles, still not fully comprehending anything beyond Tobek's distress.

"Tobek," Bix repeated with a quaver in her voice.

"Yeah, Bixie. That's the goddess messing with you. Chief is shielding the others in the room from her, but you're too much of a big shot to fall under his warranty package." Drew gave half a laugh, then sobered. "The gods are too close. They're flooding the town. The security net is gone. Chief is trying to help the dragons and the angels defend the ballroom. The rest of the building has fallen. The town is in shambles."

Confused, Bix dropped her head back and gawked at the ceiling. The once flawless reliefs were fractured, parts dangling precariously. Red stars in a night sky appeared through the missing chunks of damaged paintings. The balconies had collapsed upon each other, and walls looked as though they'd taken cannon fire.

When…? How had she…?

Soft fingers, uncalloused, laced with Bix's twitching at her side. Deep russet skin and the wealth of leaves inked upon it contrasted with her pallor. The fifth Resen server laid his other hand over hers and offered a knowing smile. He was an older man, Southeast Asian perhaps, late fifties with thinning hair and hazel eyes regarding her with warmth and compassion. Bix stared at him blankly while her brain struggled to fathom a reason the Sage server would want her company.

Information came first as a tickle through their clasped hands. It shoved aside the cloud of panic and tamped down the hidden truths trying to overwhelm her as it scampered through the midnight of her composition, setting off tiny sparks of recognition and depositing intel within her essence. The ripple and rush of data tripled in speed and content, flowing inside her arm as if a kitchen hose had hollowed out her veins. It wasn't the crippling deluge of a memory assimilation. It didn't demand her attention and focus forthwith, nor did it override her senses. Data didn't come as words, images, or any form of common communication. It was streams and rivers, creeks and babbling brooks. It was familiar and foreign without instruction manuals, blueprints, or how-to videos. It was more than knowledge and bordered on wisdom. It was everything at her fingertips, waiting for her to take hold.

The Resen server's eyes twinkled as if they were sharing the best joke. He drew her hand to his lips and kissed the air above her knuckles before letting her go. He wheeled himself to the other Resen servers where Ashtad and Cian shook off their stupors. Ashtad leapt up from his seat and fell back with a curse, his bad leg locked straight. Cian kneaded his shoulders and winced.

"Bixie?" Drew elbowed Bix sharply. "Bixie, you with us yet? We really need you to be present."

Bix's brain reengaged with all the subtlety of a swift kick in the ass. She gasped as she finally saw, truly saw, the circumstances around her.

Berserkers weren't the only soldiers in the room. Human in body only, dragons and angels formed an outward-facing circle along the perimeter of the dance floor. Their blended magics aimed at the holey walls, repelling the encroaching onslaught of Other World magic.

The pressure. Bix could feel it. The might of gods bearing down on the ballroom. The weakening of native magic. Feng linked with his kith, giving them everything he had left.

It wouldn't last. None of this could last. Not the clash of magics. Not the safety of the Grove. Not the safety of the people beyond these walls. Not the defense Tobek was doing his damnedest to provide.

The male Fate had said her proximity skewed Tobek's magics, so Bix backed away from her Berserker. As long as she had eyes on him, Musso-Koroni's magic lost its ability to overwhelm her. She couldn't afford to let the goddess derail her. Too many people were relying on her to finish the mission so they could all GTFO.

"The ships and trains that brought the Grove, where are they now?" Bix stood straighter, lightly resting one hand on Drew's shoulder as she pulled herself together.

"Long gone," Runjit answered, adjusting his earpiece. "They couldn't withstand the worsening weather. They were outside the protect—"

The floor heaved. Boards groaned, then splintered. Geysers burst. Thirteen gods rode jets of seawater into the heart of the ballroom. At their center rose Musso-Koroni.

"Kill them. Kill them all. If they can't die, take their heads. Resen ends here and now," Musso-Koroni commanded her troop, brandishing two short swords of angel bones. "Start with the godling."

Two gods rushed Ashtad, dragging him from the room in a torrent of waves.

"Ashtad!" Bix screamed as darkness burst from her spine.

"On it." Drew tackled a god falling from a tower of water courtesy of a dragon's well-aimed blast. Drew landed two blows to disorient the deity long enough to jump into the god's body. With a cackle and a howl, the god thrashed, flailed, then vanished with Drew inside.

"I have had enough of you and your rabid posse, Musso-Koroni," Bix shouted above the din of thundering water filling the ballroom faster than the broken doors and holey walls allowed it to escape.

Musso-Koroni spun on Bix. Pure delight animated her flawless features as she leapt from the tower of spewing water and waded toward Bix. "Auntie, orders are orders. The Consortium committee rejects the petitions of the Houses, the Host, and the Horde."

"There is no *committee* decision when three out of four powers insist Resen move forward. The pantheons are alone and in breach of the peace accords on which the Consortium is built. Tell me, Musso-Koroni, whose job is it to bring the defiant gods to heel?" Bix's shadows danced around her, a sinister peacock in full plume as gates deployed, removing what allied teams she could see amid the blinding deluge. Starting with Cian and the Resen servers, she grabbed mortal and superpower alike in mixed clusters, then dumped them in literal godforsaken places across the Mids to complicate the gods' pursuit. She hadn't ripped a hole in time to lose the fully restored Grove to the egos of the gods now.

"You stripped yourself of your authority when you divested your might and memories." Musso-Koroni circled Bix, casually swiping blades at her without earnest intent, testing Bix's reactions.

"Bix, ten and one, bunched and ready to roll," Nez barked through the comm still functioning on her ear.

At her ten o'clock, Bix caught a glimpse of a dragon and an angel latching wings over a huddle of Oracles and Sages. Gates moved them a beat before a god with a spear of angel bone landed on the spot. A second gate chucked the god into the ether, where his weapon would disintegrate.

Musso-Koroni laughed derisively. "This island is teeming with gods itching to rip you apart. It is out of respect for *me* that they wait, so go ahead, keep up your futile attempts at thinning my ranks. We are thousands, and we will not be reduced to prey by technology exploited under the name of Mid World defense."

"Coward," Bix taunted, buying time even though the water swirled around her thighs and showered her with brutal torrents. "All of you. Fearful, lazy cowards."

"Bix, duck," Feng bellowed.

Fire of pure native magic engulfed a blue-and-white arrow flying at Bix's throat. Feng soared above the waters, every bit the legendary Phoenix fully aflame and furious. He released a war cry that made Bix's bones vibrate. The night sky brightened with the armies of the Host and Horde answering his call.

"Take your friends and go, Chimera," Feng directed, his voice as punishing as the heat he exuded drying up the tides. "This is our World, our home, and we will fight any foe to defend it."

Bix's blood ran cold.

This was the war the traitorous faction inside the Consortium craved. This was the war that would lay open the Mids to the armies of the Devourers. This was the war that would start the irrevocable demise of everything her friends and fellow operatives had died to prevent.

"Feng, no. Do not stoop to grant the enemy this war. Resist being a pawn. Do not let them win," Bix pleaded as her shadows sought every echo of null space exuded by a human and every twang of Fate-branded Other World magic still in the ballroom. "The Grove is gone. The need for conflict is over. Order your armies to retreat. Deny the gods their war."

"They had a chance to stop this. Now they leave us no choice." Feng set nine gods on fire with a flick of his tail. That fire spread to the building as the gods thrashed, then winked out of the Mids, screeching their agonies.

Bix stared, stunned. Yes, she'd known Feng was powerful. He was the apex entity of native magic, but he'd just flame-broiled immortals. Deities. They weren't dead, but boy, they weren't going to be recognizable either.

"You shouldn't leave your heart unprotected, Auntie," Musso-Koroni crowed, leaping from the evaporating water with weapons high.

Bix pivoted sharply.

Twin blades of angel bone sank into Tobek's chest.

CHAPTER 22

Horror and disbelief merged with a scream that never made it past Bix's lips. Instinct wedded with unholy wrath that fed the thicket of malice residing within her, obliterating all other emotion. Shadows and tentacles morphed into brambles and thorns. Barbed vines lashed around Musso-Koroni and flung her against the ceiling, the floor, and the crumbling walls. Thorns dug into the goddess stronger than the iron spikes of the cruelest iron maiden. Every thrash Musso-Koroni attempted, the darkness turned back on her threefold. Every pulse of magic the goddess exuded returned to the goddess with greater ferocity.

Without hesitation, Bix drained Musso-Koroni of eons of living, of experiences, of emotions. Where Bix normally let the memories of those she husked flow past her unnoticed, Musso-Koroni had memories Bix wanted to inspect. Memories of Resen, of the Consortium committee who'd given the orders, of Tobek as a brash demigod fresh from the halls of his parents, green with naïveté and unearned bravado. Bix had never sought someone else's memories, only her own, but this time, she dared to take more than was hers. It wasn't easy. There were a lot of surrounding stories about which Bix did not care. Those moments she dismissed with the refuse of the goddess's emotions. She didn't care how Musso-

Koroni felt about Tobek or the Consortium committee. Bix only cared about the facts as perceived by a goddess of truth. Once Bix caught the image of Tobek in the goddess's memories, Bix followed that stream and its many branches as Musso-Koroni and Tobek flowed in and out of each other's lives. Bix culled those interactions all the way back to the headwater. Eventually, there was nothing more Bix could learn about Tobek from his old friend, so she repeated the process with the Consortium committee, starting with the Consortium's chambers and following the paths from there. Once there was no more knowledge to be gleaned, Bix removed everything except Musso-Koroni's seed of divinity and Bix's own debilitating memories. The latter she left as teeny specks of starlight with the translucent husk of what had once been the Consortium's finest cleaner.

The time to claim that which belonged to her was later. The time to face her buried truth was now.

Bix kept hold of the shell containing her memories and approached Tobek with her heart in her throat. The prison of a textile throne dissolved to ash around the highly destructive angel-bone blades piercing Tobek's torso. Mortal blood and divine essence swirled in the puddle surrounding him. She yanked the damn swords from his body and flung them into the observant night. The weapons exploded with a deafening boom and rained red sparks over the battling superpowers.

Bix left the superpowers to their chaos. Her only care in all the Worlds was for her Berserker. Even in the same room, she'd failed to protect him. She'd chosen to save the Grove, the Fates, her friends, Resen, and everyone else instead of him. She'd made the decision, and he suffered for it.

He wasn't alone in that.

Ashtad's life was in Drew's hands right now, and that assumed Drew could win a battle of wills against the god she'd hijacked. If not, both of Bix's best friends were dead. Yet as much as she loved her friends, she couldn't abandon Tobek. Not again.

The thing Tobek would never do to her, she'd done to him.

She knelt beside her Berserker as tears of shame and heartbreak fell. The threads of the Fates that had bound him to the chair were nothing more than streaks upon his bloodstained and sea-soaked uniform. What had once been a complex webbing suppressing the demigod inside the soldier had dwindled to a handful of frayed threads lighting up his body in patches. The Eternal Knot that contained the piece of her within him shimmered in dark teal and starlight amid the layers of tattoos alive and moving over his torso.

Whatever magic lay in those inked images had to have prevented the angel-bone blades from incinerating him, because Fates' threads sure didn't look up to the task.

"You can't die on me," Bix whispered, drawing Tobek into her lap. "You're supposed to be immortal, so why does it look like you're trying to die on me?"

Tobek focused on her, a hint of blue amid the red overtaking his eyes. His cheek twitched as though trying to grin.

"Reset," he gasped, spewing blood on his breath.

He meant his contract with the Fates, the contract that required them to restore his body to the state it had been on the day he'd signed over his divinity. The contract that had kept him alive and in his prime long after the gods had wiped their hands of him. The contract older than epochs.

One problem…

"Tobek, your evolution, the threads, your eyes." She forced her voice to come out evenly. "It doesn't look like the contract is still in place."

"Reset," he repeated. "Gurp."

The goblin had remained with the troops at Luz, holding down the fort. If Gurp was Tobek's familiar in a way similar to Tobek being hers, then, sure, she understood why he'd asked for Gurp.

"I'll send you to Gurp." She kissed his brow and inhaled his scent, committing the feel of him in this moment to her memories. "But if there's a loophole in your immortality clause you conveniently neglected to mention…"

The Eternal Knot upon her chest glowed faintly. His reassurance.

Gates dropped him in the center of the chamber at Luz and closed as Gurp let out a distressed wail.

Pushing to her feet, Bix wiped her sodden hair out of her eyes and smoothed her bloodied dress. There was nothing she could do for Tobek; she wasn't a healer of any stripe. His recuperation was out of her hands. He couldn't die; logically, she knew that. But he might not come through his recovery as her Berserker. He might not survive it as anything she'd recognize. If the Fates' failing bonds finally set him free, what would he become? Would he be a terror the original Chimera had kept locked down for cause? Would he be a titan hungry for revenge upon the numerous pantheons who had rejected him? What about the Houses, Host, and Horde who'd tortured him throughout his time in the Mids? Would he still be the confidant and friend she trusted with eighty-five percent of her being?

What a mess. What a disastrophy.

Bix took in the war raging around her. Gods versus angels and dragons. Feng, in his fiery glory, laid waste to a town that had done nothing more than host a magic convention for average, everyday mortals. The town no longer had Tobek to power its protections. Had anyone else stepped up? Could anyone else?

Pfft. Superpowers and their flagrant disregard for the lives they had sworn to protect. The Consortium and its political imbroglio that robbed the citizens of the Mids of faith in their leadership. The traitorous faction inside the Consortium who sought short-term power while obliterating long-term survival.

They thought the Chimera wouldn't rise to the occasion. They thought she *couldn't*. So they'd threatened, attacked, abducted, and harmed her friends.

Idiots.

A smile of malevolent delight spread across her face as Bix gave in to instinct, gave in to malice, gave in to the wild tempestuous Chimera the Fates had insisted show up tonight. Thorny vines unraveled from her body faster than the fires spreading from Feng's wings.

Gates removed Feng from the fray, burying him deep in muck on a far-flung Mid World. He meant well, but she couldn't let him be the tool the faction used to destroy the Mids. Next, she thinned the ranks of the dragons and the angels, tossing them to foreign shores to buy herself some time alone with the gods.

The deities were so jacked up on battle lust and ego, they didn't see her coming.

Her thorny brambles surged beyond the confines of the ballroom to the city streets on fire. Thickening night extinguished blazes and swallowed smoke as darkness crept up on its prey.

Gods feared *Resen* would make them vulnerable? They feared a defense system more than the High Executioner for All Worlds? Phobos had been right. It was time she honed the fears of the pantheons. It was time she demonstrated how Devourers were not the only deities on which she could gorge herself.

Her shadows pierced the gods preening boldly and those who slunk through hiding places, impaling them upon the tangible pikes of the Chimera's cold malice. Lesser lackey, foot soldier, midlevel shot-caller, she didn't care. She feasted upon divine essence, draining the gods until they were translucent casings hanging limply from her thorns in the aftermath of their arrogance.

Still she hunted.

Nothing less than a complete purge would do. Nothing less would arrest a war after its opening gambit. Nothing less would allow Resen to be built, to be tested, to be launched, and to exist until every last Devourer had been flushed from these Worlds.

Nothing less would deter the gods from fucking with her inner circle.

Every molecule of darkness in Blackpool became an extension of her body, of her senses, of her wrath. She was not confined to the form of flesh, she *was* the night. Gods noticed, shrieked their fears, and abandoned their posts. Most weren't fast enough. She took them down before they could fight back. No quarter. No mercy.

Not a single mortal did she touch as she expanded her territory, racing for the far corners of the isle, spreading over Ireland and the many islands off Scotland. Not a human or a Chwed suffered a single brush of midnight.

Surgical in her strikes, Bix allowed speed and precision to amplify her hunger. Gods were her fuel. Street urchin, feline sentry, or avian cavalry, whatever their guise, the gods fell to her gluttony. Once she'd cleared the isles, she turned toward the Continent.

Native magic pushed against her approach. Other World magic pulled. Pushed...Pulled... Pushed her darkness. Pulled the stars of her essence. Pushed then pulled. Pushed then pulled. Pushed then pulled.

It was a rhythm. It was a song. It was Tobek calling her back from the extremes. Even in his lassitude, he maintained their connection. Even dancing with death, he protected the Mids from her excess. She fought his demand, yet he persisted, ever patient, ever sure. She was just as sure she couldn't come back. Not now. Not yet.

There would be repercussions for tonight, and she needed to be ready for them. The Consortium would blame her for their failure to reach a peaceful resolution before Blackpool was sacrificed, purely because making her their scapegoat was politically convenient. Feng wouldn't be happy with her for booting him from the battle. Neither would the Horde or the Host. She wanted to find Ashtad, but his abduction had "demi challenge" written all over it. He'd be furious with her for intervening, so Drew would have to be his covert backup. Bix trusted Drew to fill that role, assuming Drew hadn't been extinguished by the god she'd occupied. Cian and Nez she'd relocated with a passel of Fates, so their futures were in the hands of those who decided that stuff anyway. Then there was Tobek and his evolution. Not a thing she could do but wait and see. To top all that off, there was the flood of information she'd received from the Grove. Part, all, or none of Resen? How many bugs and viruses had been included? Could the code be tweaked not to detect her? She needed a higher level of understanding to decipher what she'd been given. With any luck, that would come as part of having half of her wits back where they belonged.

The sad truth was, she couldn't finish the mission without the fourth installment of her memories. Whether the Fates had intended to take her offline by giving her intel she couldn't decrypt or it was a coinkidink didn't matter. Her team had known memory assimilation was part of her plan going into the Blackpool mission. She had to trust her team to fight their own battles in her absence. It was ridiculous and egotistical to assume they couldn't survive without her.

Right? Sure. It'd have to be.

Hurtling skyward with the trophies of her hunt, Bix opened gates to the vast ether.

The ether that had, at various points, been both prison and sanctuary welcomed Bix as she cast off the husks of useless gods and let them drift on the constant currents of nothingness. She kept the husk of Musso-Koroni, examining the tiny dots of gold, silver, and bronze lingering inside the emptied goddess. Memories. Bix's. The fourth segment. The portion that would push her past reclaiming half of her life for the small price of leaving the Mids and the Consortium to suffer the consequences of their follies.

Relaxing into her state of sentient night allowed filaments of herself to flow in and out of the husk, summoning her lost bits of starlit memories. They came home to her like lint to static, sparking the fragments of sound and taste, of touch and smell, of series and stories.

This was the moment Bix's corporeal body would fail her—had failed her every previous reclamation—trembling and juddering, senses diminishing, orifices bleeding. Not this time, though. She'd blossomed from that fragile humanoid form. She was the night and the stars, and her memories the auroras winding their way home. Winding their way into the chaos of a troubled mind replete with power, yet lacking all control.

Still, it was too much, the assimilation. Fragments searched for mates amid the halfway point; half her life, half her feelings, half her knowledge, half her relationships, half her everything. Too much to stay in the present moment. Too much to stay lucid. Too much to stay self-possessed. Too much to stay brave.

She cried out in terrified surrender.

A darkness larger than herself swaddled her in shimmers of red and whisked her from the ether.

CHAPTER 23

S leipnir. Bix's head felt as if Sleipnir was playing footy with her skull. An eight-legged horse birthed by a chaos god was an asshole. For the record. Bix attempted to sit up…and immediately regretted it. Her world spun, and her stomach went with it. She scrunched her eyes and put out her hands to stabilize her swaying body. What she wouldn't give for a cold cloth.

One was immediately pressed over her face like a diving mask. Snorfling, she batted at the hand holding the cloth in place.

"Phobos, you big dork, what are you doing?"

The cloth vanished. Bright eyes of red flames peered into hers. She yelped and scrambled back, her hands shooting off the edge of a hard slab. A creature, decidedly *not* Phobos, tilted his head to the side. His nose was broad and flat like a bull's. His ears were large and pointed, their tips resting against thick black horns veined in garnet. One set of horns curled tightly against the sides of his head. The other set twisted up to cage a wild mane of cherry hair. Three black tails whipped behind him, the plumes of red fur at the tips catching the slivers of light. His skin was darker than jet and glittered with the deepest crimson. He was massive, like a minotaur, but not threatening. If anything, he exuded curious amusement.

"Hello, sister." He chuckled, revealing long marbled canines.

Bix stuck her finger in her ear and wiggled it. Surely she hadn't heard him correctly. "I'm sorry, did you call me 'sister'? Is that a cultural thing?"

His thick brows furrowed, and his head tipped to the other side until his ear touched his bulky naked shoulder. "No. It is the proper relationship description for two individuals who have the same parents when the individual being addressed is one who has chosen the feminine gender."

Family. This was her family. She'd long wondered...she'd wished...she'd been warned...she...she didn't know what to do. She stared at him as her emotions flitted, fluttered, and conflicted.

Her brother extended the cold cloth to her on three fingers. He didn't have five. He had three. The hand didn't look like he was missing any; he just had three fingers. Big, huge fingers. How those fingers managed to lace up his buckskin pants had to be a feat of dexterity. Speaking of feats, his feet were like an elephant's only with talons instead of toenails. Three talons. Three toes. Matter of fact, three seemed quite the theme here. Three stained glass windows depicted nebulas. Three stars in a distant ceiling provided gentle light. Three legs on the large chair at the foot of the slab on which she rested. Three doors that opened to three corridors, none of which were the same. The air smelled of nothing, nothing bad, nothing good, nothing distinct, just nothing. She was grateful it didn't smell like her personal funk, but it was weird that it didn't smell like him either.

"The cloth, do you need it again? You look pained." He wagged the cloth at her.

She took the cloth that was tiny in his hand but more like a king-size blanket for her. It was blissfully cold as she buried her face in a corner of it. "Thank you...brother?"

"Yes. I am your first brother, the third child." He patted his chest. "You are the seventh child, the only one without a twin. The youngest and the last of our generation. We are the first children of the Chaos and the Cosmos."

The origins of existence, the first sentient entities. When energy evolved and became self-aware, it diverged into two states: the Chaos and the Cosmos. The Chaos was the primordial darkness, the feminine existence, the eternal welcome. The Cosmos was the masculine, the light, the order, the extemporaneous exclusion. Every pantheon traced their origins through the titans who descended from the Chaos and the Cosmos. The names of the originators varied as names always did for immortals, but their existence was undisputed across all Worlds, all faiths, all entities. Details about the original entities and their first children were sparse. There were allusions aplenty, but nothing concrete.

Yet niggling in the back of her aching mind there was a memory, of…scrapping? No. Yes? Young men arguing. Words of which she understood one or two, a language partially remembered. The tones, though, the tones of the short-lived clip trying to surface through the fog of an incomplete mind were definitely men arguing.

"There's a mark on your back," she blurted as the vocal memory matched to a visual and an emotional. The man in front of her now had his back to her in the memory. She was frightened, but not of him. She was holding on to his tails, trying to hide behind them, but she was staring at his back. "It's big, a very large scar? It's important, yes? I can't…I can't remember why."

"Yes, yes, that is correct." Chortling, he presented his bare back to her. Sure enough, there was a starburst scar, deep red like his hair, but veined in black. The inverse of his coloration. "It is where my twin and I separated from each other. You used to try to cover it up because you didn't want my twin to find you. You did not like the lessons you had to learn from him. You much preferred to stay with me."

"Your twin," she echoed, draping the cold blanket across her nape and shoulders, welcoming the way it calmed her erratic pulse. "Fraternal?"

"Depends on his mood." Her brother rolled his eyes. "I am

knowledge innate. Sometimes known as instinct or talent. My twin is knowledge amassed, learning and experience."

"You're the überentity who has been helping me through the Tarot cards," she said as her brain tried to function, but it was struggling with the new memory pieces, trying to make them fit, trying to create linear story lines. "My brother. Who likes cartomancy?"

"Yes, that is I, though the cards were of your choosing. When you were young and Father had forced you into isolation as part of your training, you would sneak messages to our siblings by rearranging our creations. Father, for whom order is paramount, noticed. I made you blank cards to use because they were so small, they existed beneath his awareness. Ever since, when you have wished to reach out to me, you have used a card written in whatever language you believed would intrigue me. I like the imagery of Tarot, and I like that it is new and evolving. You chose well." He held a finger out to her the way a lepidopterist would to a butterfly. Considering their size differential, she felt like an insect. Almost. More like a hawk to a falconer. "You should walk. Test your form. You've had difficulties maintaining this tiny human shape you wear so often."

That wasn't a normal side effect of memory assimilation. Then again, she hadn't known she *could* be less than corporeal until Blackpool.

"What am I when I am not me?" She set the blanket on the slab and wrapped her arms around her brother's finger, letting him place her on what appeared to be red granite tiles cut in triangular shapes. She also noticed she was wearing a fur-kini. Nothing immodest, just a little prehistoric for her taste, not that she was complaining. She was cleaned, clothed, and semicoherent. All in all, she was grateful to be well cared for by a brother she didn't know she had.

"What a peculiar question. You are always you, equal parts Chaos and Cosmos. You are the two-in-one, the embodiment of balance." He shuffled along, taking small steps while she scampered beside him into the leftmost corridor, where water flowed around three-sided picture frames that stretched from gabled black ceilings to black baseboards.

She paused in front of a picture oozing unique magics that set her hair on end. Seven circles of different colors and size rotated in 4D animation. Inside each circle was a symbol. She recognized the seven-sided pyramid inside the dark teal circle. "I know that one. That's me, right?"

"Each circle represents one of the first children. Go ahead and touch it, sister. Nothing here will break." He clasped his hands behind his back and tipped a horn at the picture.

"The first children are our siblings who are twins. All boys?" She poked the lavender circle with a trapezoid in the middle. Her finger slid through the circle into a gelatinous goo. It clenched her finger, wrapping it in a variant of Mids' magic, but purer and more concentrated than touching the baby ley line. Faint strains of music filled the hallway.

"Music always was your *second* favorite sibling," he harrumphed and gestured to the purple and blue circles parallel on the frame. "A pair of sisters. My brother and I. A brother and sister. Then you, the Chimera."

"I wasn't named for a monster? Good to know." She used gates to free her finger, then held her finger to her ear. A familiar song of nothingness in motion played ever so softly before fading away.

"No, no, the monster was named after you. A tribute. Though it should've been named after me, the three. After all, the monster is three creatures in one, not two."

"Your name is Three?" Bix hoped she hadn't sneered when she said that. For cosmic entities, Three wasn't exactly original. Except that maybe it was because he predated counting and math and most everything else.

And she was his sister.

Holy hell, she was ancient. No wonder Tobek thought it funny every time she called him an old fart.

"Three?" Her brother puckered his lips and hummed. "Yes, I would accept that as an endearment from you. In most languages of many Worlds, three refers to me. Third born. Third to manifest. Third try. Three is a lucky number, yes?"

"For a lot of people," she admitted with a grin. "If we're the first children of the Chaos and the Cosmos, does that make us older than the titans?"

"We created the titans as toys to learn, to expand, to understand." He pouted at her as he resumed their walk. "But not you. You're not allowed to create. Your attempts at creation are always extinguished. To have something you create be allowed to exist would cause a bias, a point of exploitation."

"That explains why I can't manifest a wardrobe," she joked, kind of, still confused as she deployed gates to keep up with him. "But I am a cocreator of the ether that surrounds the Mids."

He winced and shook his head. "It is better stated that you riddled out the puzzle, crafted a plan, and recruited assistance. It is not dissimilar to actions I have witnessed you take with your fragile toys. It intrigues me, how you interact with such microscopic beings."

"From the macro perspective of a cosmic creationist, I suppose the Mids seem small and trifling." Bix glanced over her shoulder at shadows slithering along the walls and ceiling, following them. They weren't her shadows. Her brother's perhaps? "But, I assure you, when you befriend residents of those Worlds and allow their lives to be the focus of yours, they are far from insignificant. Relationships have value."

"Interesting, this concept of value. It is different from purpose, for you have always known your purpose and excelled at it." He led her past archways that opened to galaxies in various stages of growth and death, breathtaking in their life cycles. "I think I might explore this theory of yours once you free me from this prison."

"*After* the Devourers are permanently expelled from the Mids," she insisted. Her brains might be scrambled, but she vividly recalled the terms of her agreement with her brother. "Plus, you will have to be careful if you visit the Mids. Your presence—much like mine—is a threat to their stability, and you know how I feel about threats to the Mids."

He threw back his head and laughed. "So fierce, little sister."

"I mean it, Three."

"Our father made his wisest mistake when he decided *you* would be the High Executioner for All Worlds." Sobering, Three lifted her hand on his finger and nudged it palm up. The Tarot card of the Emperor appeared. The king upon the throne. The embodiment of influence and control, the overseer of convention and society. "You are empowered to destroy but denied the ability to create in order to cultivate envy within you. That envy was meant to shape you into a ruthless killer. Isolating you from everyone should've rendered you compliant to his bidding. But you are the two-in-one, equal parts Chaos and Cosmos. Our mother's presence within you fostered an appreciation of the creations. The more Father separated you from us and from everything, the more you craved connections. That is why you fight so hard to protect what our siblings make."

"What our siblings make?" Her head hurt again. Distant shouting and clamoring sliced through her awareness, likely soundtracks of memories looking for their mates.

"Our sisters, Movement and Music, created the Mid Worlds you so zealously protect. It is Movement's push you mistake as rejection and Music's pull that draws you back. It is a dance of which you are very much a part." Three cupped her head. Instantly, the noises quieted and the discomfort dissipated. "I have done what I can to sort your mind. To keep the old with the old, the new with the new, and the stolen in a pocket of its own. We have explored many places together since you sought to repair yourself."

"You're referring to my memory assimilation?" She leaned into his soothing touch as it tickled another memory, one tied to giggles and being carefree. "My body goes where the images in my mind take me. If you're a prisoner, how did you come with me?"

"The same as I came for you." Shadows blossomed from him, from horns and shoulders, a veritable headdress of darkness. Her tentacles responded, slithering from her spine to wend with his. He guffawed. "Just like when you were a child. We played these games, you and I. You are closer to recapturing the might of what we inherited from our mother. When the gods tried to destroy that which you love, you rose up at last and *became* the night. You ceased to wield it as a tool and allowed yourself to embrace it as your native state. There is no place we cannot go when we are the darkness and the night."

"So your prison isn't a physical trapping. It's a...?" Bix waited for him to fill in the blank as her attention drifted to dimly lit chambers filled with instruments of science and make-believe. Things moved in those rooms, things she didn't want to inspect too closely.

"This place is a tether. I cannot be gone for long from it, and I can only depart it in my native state. This body you see before you, my preferred form, it cannot manifest beyond these confines." He scowled and huffed, the fires of his eyes blazing.

Okay, time to change the subject before this family reunion went south.

"Who created the Devourers? Was that you?"

"Devourers exist as a control to the gods. Otherwise, gods run amok without fear, without hesitation, and without respect for other creations." He manifested a card of the Five of Wands. It was a Too Many Cooks in the Kitchen card. Everybody shouting, clamoring, demanding attention, and creating conflict to gain that attention. "In the greater scheme, gods are nothing more than storage vessels for the Chaos. Each god holds a piece of something Mother didn't want to lose, something she may forget she owned but still needed it to play its part in the vastness of existence. That's why gods are immortal and, sadly, bountiful. Devourers give them something other than themselves to fight, something that reminds them of their vulnerabilities. The messy deaths of Devourers are glorious mockeries of gods' longevity."

"But isn't that my purpose? To terrorize the gods into good behavior?"

"You are the last fail-safe before the disruptions in cosmic order draw the ire of our father." Three gestured to her with grand formality and a twinkle in his eye. "There was a time when you accepted only his instructions. Then you rebelled, you stopped killing and husking at his whim. That's when you started considering petitions from our siblings and their creations. Father allows you this liberty because you continue to enforce order, even if it isn't the order he envisioned. Your behavior, your decisions, they intrigue him. Parents inevitably learn from their children in as much as the children learn from them."

"Did the Cosmos send the Devourers to the Mids to test me?"

"You could have erased the entire population of Devourers at any time, but you didn't because you understood their reason for existence. However, your attempt to maintain balance by rebuffing them has failed." Three handed her the Tarot cards, yet again evading a direct question. The moment she touched the cards, they shrank to an appropriate size for her.

"Was it sabotaged? Is that what you're avoiding saying plainly?" She lingered in the doorway of a room that tickled her mind. A memory that felt more like a dream. The chamber walls were dark, moist, and roughly hewn. The furnishings were upended and smashed, slivers scattered everywhere. It reeked of anguish.

From the far corner of the room, a groan. A rather humanlike groan.

"While you were healing, you babbled often about the netting of the gods," Three said, proving himself a master of evasions and redirects. "I believe you were attempting translations, so I was able to help you work it out."

"Project Resen," she sighed. "Most of the Consortium is finally getting their asses in gear to defend the Mids, but the gods are being cowardly and subversive."

"It must be frustrating not understanding what is already in your head. The robust vocabularies you once held now are remedial, if you're aware of the language's existence at all. On the one hand, you know more than you realize you do. On the other, your mind is too busy trying to construct linear memories rather than relational ones." He laid a new Tarot card atop the others she held.

The Four of Swords. It usually showed a knight in repose upon a tomb under stained glass windows. Three swords were mounted to the wall above him, positioned to strike in the throat, the heart, and the abdomen. All fatal shots if they fell. The locations also referenced three of the seven Chakras: communication, compassion, and connection. The fourth sword lay beside the knight, ready to be taken to hand in defense. Despite its initially ominous allusion, it was, in fact, the card of recovery and reflection. The knight after the battle. The knight divided in darkness and light. The mind at rest. However, in this iteration of the card, it wasn't a knight upon the slab, it was her in her chosen body of flesh, and the slab was her darkness. The swords upon the wall? Marbled white and blue. The sword at hand, forest green.

"Angel bones." She tapped the swords in the card. "They're my weakness."

"The bones aren't your weakness," Three scoffed. "Your love for your siblings is. Angel bones are nothing more than the concentrated essence of our sister Movement. Dragon bones are made from our sister Music. Only those we love can truly cause us pain because we allow them to. The moment you stop allowing our family to hurt you, the bones lose their efficacy."

"You mean if I no longer care for anyone or anything, then I will be impervious to everything." Bix laid her hand over the Eternal Knot glowing faintly beneath her skin, the piece of Tobek the original Chimera had used as a link to Tobek's empathy to rediscover her own. Right now, the knot was pulsating in an odd pattern, almost as if it was rolling a warm ball along the complex track. It told her Tobek was alive but not in what state. "I think I've been there, done that already. Not keen to repeat past mistakes. I'll take the pain because it means I'm living, which is so much better than merely existing."

"Then you have your answer to Project Resen." Three resumed walking, but this time, Bix didn't follow. Something in the chamber called to her, needed her. "You must make the gods care again, and the only way to make them care is to make them vulnerable to more than the likes of you and me."

Bix massaged her temple as memories fit together, memories and more… "The data from the Grove, you unlocked it for me?"

"I didn't need to." Three stopped and turned, confusion fleeting in his expression until he glanced at the doorway in which she loitered, then he appeared fascinated as he slowly returned to her. "You are the one who taught them how to render gods vulnerable. You are the one who armed the Fates in their war of independence from the pantheons. They were simply reminding you of what you already knew. I think they threw in a little extra information, though. I placed it near the surface, but not too near. It will take intention for you to find it. I believe that is what you would want as it frees you to contend with all that you must once you return to our sisters' Worlds."

A frisson of anger scampered up her spine. The whole monkeying with her mind thing…even if Three really was acting from a place of benevolence, she didn't trust anyone enough to let them fiddle around in her head. Yes, she ought to be grateful for his aid; and a part of her was, it really, really was; however, a big chunk of her couldn't get there. She felt violated. Conflicted. Maybe her infamous temper was to blame. She wanted to lash out, but for what? Having her questions answered? Being sheltered at her most vulnerable? For processing half her memories without blowing up whole sectors of multiple universes? Her brother had helped her. Truly he had. Just as he said he would.

Yeah, but.

"The consequences of dining on a lot of gods," she griped instead, picking a different and far more justifiable target for her anger. "How badly are they going to make me regret that?"

Three grunted indecisively. "It brought you closer to balance after your excessive consumption of Devourers, so there is one bright side."

"Only *one* bright side, though, right?" Bix stared at the image of her in repose on the Tarot card. "How long have I been gone from the Mids?"

"If my assessments are correct, it has been four months in their time." He tsked. "Four is my twin. You should've awakened after three to honor me, not him."

"It takes as long as it takes, dear brother," she countered with a half smile that matched his.

A scream echoed from the recesses of the chamber. This time, she knew with confidence it wasn't in her head.

"Three, who is that?" She marched into the chamber, her darkness sweeping ahead of her, clearing a path through the destruction. It was a huge chamber with angles and nooks…and what appeared to be the remnants of a bed hacked into a thousand pieces.

"A toy."

She spun around and narrowed her eyes. "*My* toy?"

He shrugged.

"Three," she scolded, drawing out his name. "Give me back my toy."

He rolled his eyes and flicked his wrist, lighting the way to a darkened corner of the room. The *whump* of a fleshy form hitting the floor sent her running toward a wan naked muscular body. The torso wasn't inked and he wasn't a blond, but she recognized the resonance, feeble though it was. His back was badly lacerated and replete with weeping punctures. She pushed one heavily scarred shoulder to roll the man to his slightly less mangled side. Amber eyes fraught with agony blinked up at her as red pupils dilated. His chest was a map of damage wrought by assorted instruments and none of them soft. Bruises, cuts, gouges, blisters … It was horrifying.

"Phobos," she gasped. "Damn it, Three. This one is important to me."

Three joined her in the corner, looming over her. "He appeared when your pangs of broken memories became too much for your preferred form. I could see he was special. I wanted to know why."

"So you tortured him?" She cradled Phobos's face in her hands, listening to his wet, labored breath.

"I tested him and, in so doing, tested you." Three twitched his tails along floor. "You leashed his primordial essence to force him to respond to you. But it is one-way only. You do not respond to him. You responded to the other one, but not this one. He is different from the other one, from the rotten godling."

He was referring to Tobek, and yes, her bond with Tobek was unique. Phobos was a provider, dinner, to be crass, whom Three apparently didn't need to consume to sustain himself. Maybe Three didn't need to eat at all. Or maybe he ate stardust. Or methane. Or who knew what. At the moment, she didn't care. As much as she wanted to learn more about her family, she needed to get out of Three's prison, get Phobos to sanctuary, and get back to her life in the Mids.

She also needed not to be an ungrateful brat, but boundaries had to be established.

"I don't share well, Three." She sighed as her darkness flowed around Phobos, bundling him up in a cloak of dignity. "This is the second of my favorite toys you've tortured. Please don't do it again."

"But I'm bored and I'm curious and I'm trapped," her brother growled.

Since he could make his own toys, she wasn't sure where the disconnect was, unless his creation abilities had been severely curtailed as part of his punishment...for crimes she had yet to remember.

"How about I send you more appropriate toys? Would that be okay?" She eyeballed her brother over her shoulder. "This one would've arrived with his swords and a special trinket that he kept in his vest pocket. May I please have those back as well?"

A reluctant mewl came from Three, but Phobos's xiphoi

and the fob holding the beating heart appeared beside her. She placed the fob in Phobos's hand and closed his fingers around it. Whatever Phobos's reasons, that heart meant a lot to him. The least she could do was ensure he didn't lose it. The swords she held with her shadows. He was in no condition to wield them and wouldn't be for some time.

"Thank you, Three," she said as she stood. She came up to her brother's waist. Dude was colossal but sweet in his special way. "Thank you for taking care of me and for helping my mind through the assimilation of memories."

"I would fix you all at once if you'd let me," he grumbled.

Nope. Nope. Nope. Her mind. Her turf. Hers. However, there were three segments still missing, which were three opportunities to go through this again with her brother. She wasn't going to burn a bridge that couldn't die. Besides, family. She wanted to come back and chat with him. Wasn't that what siblings did? The ones who got along? They talked, right? Even when one was in cosmic prison. Right. Sure. Normal. Totally normal.

"Part of the joy of living is the journey of fixing yourself when you're broken." She hugged Three, or the best approximation of a hug she could manage, which was like a fly against a skyscraper. "That's what guides me to wonderful brothers like you."

Three manifested one more Tarot card and handed it to her. This one was the Seven of Wands, showing six staves aggressively aimed at a lone soldier keeping the foes at bay with his lone stave. In this case, her lone stave. She, in her corporeal form, looking ever so winded and bedraggled.

"The Stand Your Ground card?" she asked.

"I have faith in you." Three patted her head. "Take your toy, little sister, and send me one of my own."

"You got it." With a smile and a wave, she opened gates, moving Phobos with her.

CHAPTER 24

Phobos's minions didn't have to be summoned. Like a squadron awaiting orders, they lined the decking around the pool when Bix arrived at the top of the ramp with their injured master. Two gnarled demonic henchmen lumbered forward to take ownership of the xiphoi. Another prostrated itself beside the bundle of shadows enveloping Phobos, the blue velvet pillow raised above the minion's head, waiting to accept the placement of Phobos's prized possession. A quartet of a lyre, psaltery, reed pipe, and double flute struck up a dirge at the back of the gathering. Large bronze braziers muted the light from musk-scented fires anchoring the four corners of the dimly lit bath.

Phobos extended one trembling, bloodied hand from the darkness cocooning him and placed the heart on the pillow. Apparently, he was conscious enough to know he was home. Bix took that as a favorable sign.

"Where do you want me to put him?" she asked the room.

Naiads surfaced in the pool. "Bring him to us, Chimera. There are fresh souls here in the water awaiting his pleasure."

Bix understood that pleasure was not of the carnal sense but the consumable. Any smart god kept stashes of lush souls since politics made you favored one moment and screwed the next. The pool wasn't as consistently deep blue as it had been during her last visit. Now, bright undrained souls marbled the water, swimming to and fro but never free.

She waded into the inky depths, towing Phobos behind her. She didn't want to be too far from him in his utterly vulnerable state. He hadn't abandoned her when she was defenseless; she wouldn't do it to him. The blowback the pantheons were likely itching to unleash on her for her actions in Blackpool could start with the one god who had no choice but to be allied with her. As Three had said, by feeding from Phobos's essence, she'd leashed him to her. Unintentionally or not, it wouldn't matter to his peers. Unfortunately, when she and Phobos had begun this parasitic relationship, they hadn't been discreet. It'd started in a bar full of gods and Chweds because neither she nor he had known what they were doing. Oops.

Shadows peeled back from the god of fear, allowing Phobos to float out of Bix's hold. Naiads flipped him to his belly in a move that would drown any mortal, yet for Phobos, it allowed him to catch bright souls with his long canines and drain the experience from the souls until they were emptied shells transformed into drops of water by his will.

Phobos shuddered. Spasmed. Convulsed. Seizures racked his body. The naiads swam in circles around him, creating a whirlpool of gentle pressure to stabilize him.

"Is that normal?" Bix whispered, backing up and recalling her darkness to her form so as not to impede the naiads in any way.

"It is not," cooed a red-eyed naiad surfacing in front of Bix. The naiad's webbed fingers pulled at the water, forming a liquid bowl. Within the curves of the bowl were gruesome implants that radiated Three's arcane magic. "His body expelled these. We are unable to touch them without pain. Perhaps they are better kept by you?"

"Thank you," Bix murmured as she scooped up her brother's gadgets. Three had probably left them inside Phobos as part of his continuing experiment. Gah, she didn't want to dwell on how her brother had tortured her provider.

Do not take them away, Phobos said, speaking in her mind. *I wish to study them.*

"Well, you certainly earned the right to do so," she drawled, a little too happy to hear his sardonic voice between her ears. "I'll leave them on the side table in your study, but you know he can track you with these, right? That's one of the reasons he left them in you."

The naiads exchanged curious glances.

Now that your brother is aware of my existence, he can find me anytime without assistance. Those implements were used to monitor and measure how you and I interacted. How your needs manifested in my essence. How your unconscious mind demanded my attendance. How each time you ripped apart your corporeal body with your shadows, you forced me to share your anguish. I found their results as enlightening as he did.

"If I'd been tearing myself apart, that chamber would've been coated in mist and midni—Oh, ew. The moisture on the walls? Was that me?" She grimaced as the naiads' expressions lit. Either Phobos was chattering in their heads too, or they'd figured out she wasn't having a one-sided conversation.

That room started off as opulent as a princess-theme-park penthouse suite. Then you began shredding your own flesh and crying out your agonies while cursing your family. Phobos floated his arms out from his sides and wiggled his fingers.

"Cursed my family?" Bix echoed, trying to remember harming herself, trying to locate the well of agony he mentioned. There was a flutter of anguish from a place buried but accessible. Now was not the time to go digging. "All of them, or just my brother?"

All, though most especially your parents. Phobos caught a soul in his teeth and sucked it dry. *While I am unfamiliar with the language of the Original Family, the purity of your vehemence exposed the great hate within you. A violent hate.*

"Malice," she admitted.

Too mild a description, he purred. *The strength of what you emoted hewed the walls of our prison chamber into a different shape as you vacillated between your native state and your preferred. You don't bleed in your native state, in case you wondered. It is an affectation you adopt when you wear a body of flesh.*

"Good to know," she mumbled. "How did my brother react to my tantrum?"

I have many siblings. I care for most of them, and it is mutual. I would place your brother's reactions on par with theirs should our places have been reversed.

That made her feel a little bit better about her ease with Three, and about her resistance to his meddling with her memories. The most similar relationship with which she could identify was with Ashtad, and she adored him, but there were definite boundaries.

"The damage to your body, did I inflict some of that?" she dared to ask.

No, you raged around me but never upon me. I can thank your brother for his close inspections of my person. Phobos stretched his arms in front of him, then fanned them down to his sides, a languid stroke that propelled him into a fresh cluster of undrained souls. *The last time you absorbed memories, you did not inflict damage upon yourself. Your behavior this time was different. Distressing, one might be inclined to say.*

"This is the second time you've incurred significant damage because of our bond." She bit her lip. "Do you want out of our arrangement?"

The only way out is for you to husk me. I'm not anywhere near ready for that, not by a long shot.

"There has to be another way."

No. There isn't, or did you never wonder where your previous meals were hiding? Did you never wonder why, if I cannot resist your distress due to our bond, none of the hundreds of thousands of other gods from whom you must have fed over your ageless existence came rushing to your aid when you sacrificed yourself? Where were they when you drifted, hollow in the ether? The only reason those who sustained you since your return were able to ignore your plea is because you were too weak to insist they appear. You are no longer weak, and I am no longer able to ignore you. That last bit is the only regrettable part, I assure you.

Eh, it was a fair point. She didn't know the consequences of bonding with Phobos because she'd assumed her last consistent provider had been an obsessed control freak. He had been, and she could never excuse his behavior, but maybe she understood it a little bit now.

"Then I will count myself fortunate that you have siblings who have conditioned you to be perpetually annoyed," she teased. "However, I do apologize for exposing you to a danger from which you had no defense."

Come now, Chimera, Phobos chastised, rolling to his back and floating. *Your pity is unwelcomed. I believe I am the only one of my pantheon to make your brother's acquaintance. The first children are to gods as gods are to fruit flies. You were the exception, the one who cared about the little lives.*

She wasn't sure about that. Her sisters had made the Mids. Music and Movement were the pure source. The fact that ley lines continued to be born, and with them dragon queens and archangels, meant her sisters cared, still, after all these eons. But now wasn't the time to hold philosophic debates.

"Torture's not so bad as long as it comes with novelty?" she joked instead.

Precisely. Now you're thinking like an immortal. You know you'll survive. The tricky part is hanging on to your wits. The pain and the unpleasantry passes, leaving you with a unique knowledge about your torturer. He snapped his fingers, and trays of bath oils and foods manifested atop the water. The naiads immediately set about tending to his slightly less mauled person. Their adoration was plain in their care of him.

"Since you are well enough to feed yourself, and I suspect your twin is waiting for me to depart before he assumes guard duty, I will leave you to the ministrations of your faithful." Bix waded up the ramp with a slight waddle due to the clumping of her unfortunate attire. "There is the small matter of the consequences of my actions in the four months we've been gone from the Mids."

I cannot undo that which your brother created. You will have to remove that primitive getup yourself, Phobos said with patent disgust as two minions approached her. One offered a plush towel; the other carried a lovely summery floral dress and appropriate underpinnings. The Cthulhu-patterned pumps confirmed Phobos truly didn't harbor ill will toward her since he was indulging her humor.

"What? You don't like my *One Million Years, B.C.* look?" She dried herself, then wrapped the towel around her.

You're no Raquel Welch.

"Doubt anyone can compare to the original." She smiled at the minion as she scooped her new clothes from its arms.

It took you quite some time after your previous memory assimilations to relearn your basic skills. Before you return to the Mids to deal with the fallout of your actions, I strongly suggest you conduct a thorough self-assessment.

In the past, she'd done those under Phobos's scrutiny, but the poor guy needed a break from her crazy. She could run a basic review out of her home at Vuornis, which was part of the reason she lived on an otherwise uninhabited World. Frankly, she didn't feel as discombobulated as those previous times. Whatever Three had done to sort her mind had so far squelched the uncontrollable echoes and hallucinations. The ghosting sensations came and went, but not with such ferocity that she couldn't discern memory from reality. All in all, she actually felt better than she had in a while. Of course, going full Ziggy Piggy on a bunch of gods might have something to do with it too.

"Thank you, again," she said as she opened gates. "While we were out of pocket, my team should've been working on Project Resen. With any luck, the Host has the specs by now. Keep that in mind when you return to the Mids."

Do not be so sure of progress in our absence. He sighed. *Cowards will go to great lengths to hide their fear behind a show of strength.*

"A passably wise god once told me power was not control," she reminded him, using his words. "If they didn't understand my demonstration before we left, I'm happy to clarify."

CHAPTER 25

Bix despised these prolonged periods of being so far out of the loop she wasn't sure who was safe, who was in jeopardy, and who might not have survived at all. Worse, she had no concept of what additional damage she'd wrought while in the fugue state brought on by her memories attempting to string themselves together. The best she could do was get back into the game with all haste and check in with her team.

Ashtad, Drew, and Cian had not been at their respective homes and she hadn't been able to raise them on comms, which was worrisome. On the upside, the Berserkers at the coal plant had confirmed the MWA troops not only made it out of Blackpool, but that Blackpool still existed. According to the guys, Luz remained an active base camp at which they'd quarantined Tobek. Yes, Tobek was alive. No, the Fates hadn't reset him to his robust demigod state. Yes, she had visited him quite often during her blackouts over the last four months. No, she hadn't harmed anyone in the process. No, as far as anyone knew, there was nothing to be done but wait until Tobek came through the other side of his evolution. Yes, Gurp kept constant vigilance. Yes, they would contact her the moment an issue arose.

Unable to do anything more than stare at her Prince Charming,

Bix chalked up the weird rippling of her Eternal Knot to Tobek's evolution and focused on her friends. The ones who didn't have an army at their disposal.

Thus, while Bug downloaded its latest update, she loitered under the late-June sun in Blackpool, United Kingdom, Primary Mid World. The sea spray roared over North Pier, where centuries-old planking now gleamed with new boards. The kitschy theater long in need of an upgrade had finally received one. The carousel was larger and the animals replaced with mythical beasts.

The beach under the piers had been restored as if the dragons had never gutted the shore. Back on land, the new metal girders of the Tower gleamed in the sunlight. The red bricks of the Tower Building were a bit lighter, as if they'd undergone a good power wash. The buildings damaged by fire had new roofs, walls, and windows. The dinge that had once lurked at the edges of the sea-side tourist trap had been eradicated. The whole town, as far as she could see, had undergone a community refresh.

The crowds, wow, the crowds were plentiful, cordial, and nattering.

Bix leaned against the new railings of the pier, picking out bits of conversations here and there.

A stack of newspapers thumped her in her chest.

"One day's worth of boots-on-the-ground reporting from cross-World news organizations." A rather sunburned, Rubenesque, middle-aged woman of flushed cheeks and mouse-brown hair unraveling from a bun slapped the papers against Bix's bosom twice more.

It was the lack of neutralizing space a living human would've projected combined with the resonance of the Under World entity inside the woman that made Bix grin as she accepted the newspapers.

"Drew," Bix greeted with a chuckle. "I should never have doubted you'd bring a god to heel."

"Gurl, the things you've missed." Drew adjusted her pink rhinestone sunglasses. "Reporters are *still* here. Humans continue to flood this place, swearing they feel the hand of God press upon their person the moment they disembark from the tour bus. There's a rash of Chweds professing to be angel divinators, and human mediums claiming to speak to the dead who've bought up a whole block on the outskirts. That tour group coming our way? Dragon spotters."

Bix snorted. "You can't blame me for any part of that. I did not touch a single mortal outside the ballroom."

"Oh, Bixie, this ain't blame. This is props." Drew put her head on Bix's shoulder. "The magic convention is booked for the next fifty years. The town is so flush with revenue, they're funding social care for the entire county, human and not. The local Chwed guilds are buying influence they haven't had since the fifteenth century."

"But?" Bix held her breath, waiting for the shoe to drop.

"For Blackpool, there is no but. The Host and the Horde stepped up. They did exactly what Feng promised they'd do. They protected the lesser races. After the town went to hell during the skirmish, they came back and repaired it." Drew mindlessly toyed with the narrow belt Bix wore. "As much as you know it pains me to admit it, they did not suck as partners in our Hail Mary."

"Speaking of Feng…?" Bix draped her arm along Drew's sunburned shoulders and set the pace of meander down the promenade.

Drew wrinkled her nose and moaned, falling into step with Bix. "A bit annoyed that you put him in time-out, but it was likely for the best. The events of that night triggered his PTSD. He's been in therapy camp whenever he's not helping Cian at the Host's homestead."

"The Host has Cian? Not the Houses? The Fates turned Cian over to the angels? Are we talking about our favorite blackballed angels or the high-and-mighty ones?" Bix didn't like the way Drew kept distracting herself by playing with the belt on Bix's dress. They knew each other too well for her to let that tic pass unchallenged.

"After you scattered the Houses and the Grove like glitter across the Mids, it took a concerted effort for anyone to find Cian,"

Drew hedged. "A lot of that was his doing, but the Host found him anyway. It didn't escape the angels' notice that the Grove only interacted with Cian, Sparky, and you. The assumption is Resen's build specs are divided among the three of you."

"They're not entirely wrong." Bix hip-bumped Drew. "Are you telling me Cian is a hostage of the Host?"

Drew nodded, her bottom lip trembling. "Our fallen-angel friends are unwilling to mount a rescue without your go-ahead."

A chill raced down Bix's spine. "Any idea if he's been hurt?"

"Not as far as I can tell, but we both know angels have no regard for human life. Once the kid serves his purpose, they could accelerate his expiration." Drew clenched her fists in front of her stomach. "I'm worried, Bixie. The kid's grown on me. I don't even mind the smelly foods he leaves on the counters for days anymore. I almost did his laundry once just because he had the sniffles. I don't like Sages on principle, but damn it, he's *my* little herb nerd."

"Aww." Bix tugged Drew closer and put her head atop Drew's. "I'll go break down some doors right now, okay? Get you your roomie back."

"Find Sparky first," Drew muttered on a whine. "The Host isn't going to give up Cian without downloading the build specs from you and Sparky. I tracked our godling for a month before the gods gave me the shake. They're playing hot potato with him. Remember when we had high-risk VIP protection duty?"

"In our Dark Ops days? Of course. SOP was to move the package every six hours to keep the bad guys from getting a bead."

"They're running the divine version of that with Sparky as the package. They're moving him across Worlds, Uppers, Unders, and Others, without a pattern I could detect. The only place they haven't come back to is the Mids. Possibly because the pantheons have recalled all the gods from here."

"The political tit for tat after the siege of this town. If the gods aren't here, that means no one is exterminating Devourer nests where angels are being held captive. The pantheons are making one more concerted effort to bully the other superpowers into dropping Resen." Bix returned a head-high salutation from a pair of women walking hand in hand past them. "The gods didn't kill Ashtad on the spot, and they're going to great inconvenience to keep him alive, so they want him for something."

"They don't need the build specs for Resen, and his family isn't influential enough to stop a Consortium kill order." Drew shrugged. "I've been working my pantheonic contacts trying to get a hint as to who decided he was worth keeping alive and why. Anyone who might know something is too scared to speak up. Word that Resen is going to happen has everyone not of the Mids chasing their tails or burrowing under rocks. It's full pandemonium on the other side of the ether."

"So why are *you* hanging out here, in Blackpool?" Bix jostled Drew. "If your contacts are going to reach out, this isn't your usual turf."

"Bixie, babe, if you think the lesser races didn't notice what the mighty Chimera did that night, you're straight-up delusional." Drew elbowed Bix right back. "This place is ground zero for the anti-divinity community. You have a legit fan club now, and it's thousands strong. If any of my contacts grow a pair, this is where they'll come."

"I'm sorry I've left you alone to cope with all this." Bix steered Drew away from a yapping dog curling a lip at the draugr inside the woman.

"Psht." Drew rolled her eyes. "I knew you weren't coming out of the ballroom with us. You had a hot date with your marbles, and your well-being is not only important to me personally, but to the defense of the Mids. Honest talk here? Even if Resen launches and is as glorious as the hype makes it out to be, it's just a detection system. It doesn't stop the Devourers' army from invading. It only tells us who is already here. Babe, you can't retire yet. Sorry, hate to burst your bubble."

Bix snickered. "I'm not abandoning the Mids, I simply take inconvenient vacations in the middle of active operations. I'm a very bad soldier, ask Nez. Where is Nez, by the way?"

"Fuck if I know. Could be with the Fates, the Grove, or at the bottom of the sea. Really hard to tell." Drew puckered her features. "There is something definitely off about that guy. I'd hoped to find him hanging around here so I could take him for a spin and finally learn what it is he's been lying to us about this whole time."

"Noticed that, did you?" Bix smirked. "I thought I was reading into it due to the fact I can't stand him."

"Sha," Drew harrumphed with a head snap. "Whatever it is has to do with Resen or Zamarad. Those topics make his body language scream 'liar.' Now, I know he's an elder Sage and lying is part of what they learn in their trials. But…"

"Don't waste your energy on Nez. He's on the cusp of ascension, which means he's the Fates' problem." Bix pressed a finger into Drew's crispy shoulder to distract Drew from the topic of Nez. Bix was fairly sure what it was Nez was hiding, particularly from her, the evil Chimera. However, on the list of her immediate priorities, Nez and his secret didn't rank. "You consider applying sunscreen to this suit? Before you sizzle and attract a hangry Chwed?"

"How do you think she died? Reaching for the sunscreen in her fanny pack on the roller coaster, asthma inhaler falls through the tracks, has an attack before the coaster hits the top of the first hill, and is welcomed by psychopomp by the time the car rolls back into the station. When Fates weave the endings of mortal stories, I'm pretty sure they're laughing their asses off." Drew hiked her leggings up and tugged her tunic down. "Go find Sparky. I need my antagonist available to be antagonized. Then I want my herb nerd. In that order. Shoo. Fetch. Be gone."

Bix kissed Drew's temple and handed her the newspapers. "I'll ping when we're back."

CHAPTER 26

The diffuser filled Bix's cistern home with the soothing scent of vanilla and star anise. Her hot-pink comforter covered the cluster of illuminating quartz, leaving bioluminescence in certain paintings and shadow boxes to hint at details. Bix set her earwig and smartwatch on the side table and settled into her pink-and-white rocking chair. Her shadows slithered from her back and set to rocking her in time to the tune playing from the music box.

There were a few things she knew about the gods who'd taken Ashtad. They'd worked for Musso-Koroni. Musso-Koroni had worked for a committee within the Consortium. Before Bix had husked Musso-Koroni, she'd scraped the goddess's memories for the names, faces, and hidden truths of the committee members. Musso-Koroni had known which members of the committee were part of the traitorous faction and which members were the spineless toads easily manipulated. The committee member exerting the greatest influence on behalf of the faction had a hidden truth of having been husked twice by the Chimera and would've been husked a third time had the Chimera not gone off to fight the Devourers single-handedly. That same committee member took orders from the faction out of fear of being husked, but not by Bix. Not this time.

Gods could only husk other gods of lesser power. The faction's mouthpiece had been a midlevel god, which meant whoever was going to husk him was a greater god. Greater gods didn't sit on Consortium committees; not only was it beneath them, they were barred from attending Consortium sessions since those sessions happened in the Primary Mid World. Greater gods weren't allowed in the Mids because the power they exuded jeopardized the stability of native magic.

Intel amassed and analyzed said the Consortium committee who'd authorized the eradication of all Resen knowledge had the political backing of a greater god. That greater god had extensive political influence, as demonstrated by the complete lack of censure from the Consortium despite the obvious affronts to the other superpowers who'd tried to pursue Project Resen. That greater god had the influence to rescind a Consortium kill order to keep Ashtad alive.

The biggest reason to abduct the seneschal of the demigods was to see if the Chimera would come for him. Sure, a thorough interrogation to unearth the Chimera's weaknesses would be underway as well, but they didn't have to keep him alive after that unless their real goal was testing his usefulness long-term. Could Ashtad be turned? Could he be used against her as a spy inside her operations? If the greater god calling the shots could guarantee Ashtad's ascension to godhood, would Ashtad sell out the Chimera? As long as the greater god felt Ashtad would betray Bix, then Ashtad was not only alive, but he wouldn't be too hard for the Chimera to find.

After all, a mole was only useful if he remained a beloved confidant inside the operation.

Drew hadn't been able to discern the pattern of the abductors' relocations because Drew had come at it from a peer perspective. Looking at it from a top-down point of view, every bounce-house operation used locations maintained by the organization. Now that she knew it was a greater god running the organization, all she had to do was hunt the greater god.

The more power a god had, the more they radiated with it, and the easier it was for her to find them. Basic hunter-in-search-of-prey strategy. While there were a lot of greater gods, not as many were affiliated with the politics of the pantheons. Most had done time as leaders of their god gaggles. Those who'd left due to boredom had drifted away from politics altogether in search of something new and invigorating. However, those leaders who'd been overthrown? They were a different story. They were seething, festering egos pulling strings and building puppet empires in preparation for their return to the top of the heap. Those greater gods might be barred from the Mids, but they weren't far removed from those Worlds.

She didn't have to search limitless universes to find Ashtad; she only had to search Worlds existing at the outer edges of the ether. Three had said there was nowhere she couldn't go when she became the very night.

Why not give it a whirl?

There was a picture on the wall, one Tobek had drawn of her in both her states, corporeal flesh and feminine starry night. She'd achieved the latter due to a surfeit of sentiment. Right now, however, she wasn't in a pocket of excess emotion. No, she was clearheaded and mission ready. Eyes on the prize.

She wanted to become the night, and she wanted to do it intentionally this time.

Half her wits were back in her head now, half her knowledge, half her self-awareness. Shifting states of existence was bound to be something she'd done with regularity. It couldn't be *that* hard as long as she didn't overthink it. She was, after all, made of mist and midnight.

Chuckling with anticipation, Bix unraveled her darkness from her body, tentacle by tendril, thread by thorn, ribbon by rivulet, until her corporeal body gave way to stars and night. Her body freed itself long before her mind let go of functioning within the habitual limitations of a confined self. Once she consciously acclimated…she laughed. No lungs, no vocal box, yet joy audibly poured from her.

The sounds and the sensations were odd, and they were awesome.

She auditioned the gamut of noises she was accustomed to making as a person. In some sounds, she could recognize her corporeal self. Some, no. Not even close. Some sounds, she should probably never make again while in this state. Lessons learned. Good to know.

She itched to move, not actually itched, more like she really wanted to test the freedom of formlessness, to feel that limitless state of being. So, disembodied, she raced everywhere and through everything on Vuornis. It was almost like remote recon, existing in a World adjacent while walking through the neighboring World. But this time, she didn't need images or visions to create gates, she didn't need gates at all. Wherever there was a particle of darkness, so was she. Connecting was akin to acknowledging an outstretched hand. That uncomplicated. That effortless.

The space she occupied could be vast or it could be a mote. Size was irrelevant. She didn't need room to exist; she simply existed.

Free from the haze of rage that had held her focus in Blackpool, she savored the moments, the sensations, and the novelty that was simultaneously familiar. Much like a rehabilitated bird testing its wings, she flowed away from her home and banked toward territories she knew better than well.

The convergence of the Under Worlds marked the starting point. This was where she'd first dragged her feral corporeal self out of the ether after having sacrificed her all to defend the Mids. Back then, the convergence had been an overwhelming labyrinthine warren of lost souls, hungry gods, and slavering beasts. Now, from the perspective of being everywhere and somewhere, it was like looking at a piece of coral in the palm of one's hand. The onslaught of stimulation that had once upon a time crippled her could be turned down or tuned up to suit her needs. All these months of learning how to perceive and process the deluge of information her multitudinous tentacles provided her had inadvertently trained her for this moment, for this state of existence. Despite the clamor and pandemonium inherent to the convergence, she suffered no disorientation, no confusion. She tested all her senses, even the tactile ones. Nothing was out of whack.

She could not recall being this...composed? Complete? Functional for sure. Perhaps some of that was her brother's doing. Perhaps some of that was due to her halfway status. Perhaps all of it was her coming into herself. Whatever it was, it was glorious and liberating.

Inordinately pleased with herself, she set off through the maze of passages that connected countless Under Worlds. This was her stomping ground. Her home away from home. Here were gods she knew, some she liked, one or two who liked her, and a whole lot more she'd happily husk the next time she needed to balance out her gluttony.

Swifter than a fleeting thought, she swept through domains, testing her predatory skills. The cold blue glaciers of Helheim welcomed her as she homed in on the beacon of a greater god in the penthouse of the glass tower belonging to the Norse pantheon-cum-corporation functioning at its peak. The pantheon's present-day leader, Hel, glanced up from a conference table covered in maps of the Mid Worlds with tacks marking Devourer sightings. Hel's hounds lifted their shaggy heads from the polished floor as the pale eyes of the goddess tracked Bix's movement. A smirk, a two-finger salute, and the goddess bent back to her studies. Hel had been the goddess to bring Bix back from exile, to defy the Consortium, and to set Bix on the path of reclaiming her identity. They would never be friends, but Bix held a wealth of respect for Hel, enough respect that she didn't linger for a mutually unwelcome chat.

Good manners wouldn't allow her to pass through the Under Worlds without visiting Hades, the god who'd taken her in as a savage creature and had taught her how to do more than survive. Her first teacher, at least in this iteration of her life, Hades had shown her what compassion was and the confidence it imbued in those who gave it and received it. Finding him wasn't hard; his presence was a lighthouse in the immensity of the Greek Under World. He sat on a weathered bench in her old training ground, reading poetry to a single white flower. She tousled his shaggy locks, then raced for Cerberus to pet the pup. The Greek god set aside his book and blew a kiss to Bix as his faithful hound rolled on his back and showed his belly.

Next, she visited the lovers Ereshkigal and Nergal. The god of plagues turned from his laboratory with a look of surprise. His queen—herself an entity of limitless night—cast up her fine filaments of shadows to run with Bix through the Mesopotamian cities of the dead. Ereshkigal had patiently guided Bix through her reacquaintance with her darkness. This visit was as much a thank-you as it was a wee bit of showing off, all of which the goddess indulged and encouraged.

Her test run a success, Bix left behind her allies, more confident in her ability to stalk her prey in this rediscovered state of starlit night. Now she hunted in earnest. Now she tapped that thicket of malice, that violent hate that had perplexed Phobos. Now she let it infuse her essence. Now she embraced her reputation as the bogeyman of the gods.

It didn't take her long to leave the unfriendly denizens of the Under Worlds quaking and cowering. They all knew what she'd done in Blackpool, and she exploited their unease. The four months she'd been gone was less than a blink in the timeline of a god; her need for recovery didn't occur as a concept in their hushed whispers. Neither did Resen. The Mids defense system was no longer their topic of disquiet—she was. Good. She'd intended to shift their fears, and it seemed to have worked. Alas, none of the greater gods in the Under Worlds had Ashtad, so she moved on.

From the Unders, she coasted to the Other Worlds abutting the ether. The Other Worlds nearest the ether weren't connected like the Unders had been. They were their own little scattered havens, creations of the gods who didn't want to deal with their peers and had somehow been spared obligations to the greater community of their pantheons. Many midlevel gods lived on the fringe of the ether, transforming the area into a cosmic suburbia for the divine; close enough to mingle in the Uppers or the Unders without the inconvenience of neighbors being up in one's business. Without the ether, these gods would've had a nice view of the Mids.

As Bix pinballed through the Other Worlds, one thing became readily apparent: Devourers had been here. Too many of the Worlds were shriveling from decay. Pockets of toxic vapors lingered in places Worlds had once occupied. The gods who'd owned these Worlds were either prisoners of the Devourers or they were refugees to the Uppers or the Unders. Some were probably hiding in the Mids unbeknownst to the Consortium and their pantheons. It was as good a reason as any not to want Resen operational since Resen could easily find them and track their movements. Perhaps that was how the Consortium's committee had found so many recruits to show up at Blackpool.

Still, Bix wasn't looking for midlevel gods. Her mission was to get Ashtad, then transfer Resen's build specs to the Angelic Host, which should free Cian from the angels. After that, she had a date with the greater god who was politically derailing the Mids' defenses. Once that was done, she'd come back to map the path of destruction. Maybe she'd invite Phobos, get his insight as a strategist who'd led troops against the Devourers. Later. Eyes on the prize.

Girding her impalpable loins, she headed for the canopy of the Upper Worlds. Unpleasantly bright and overly shiny, the convergence of the Uppers sat like the ferrule of an umbrella above the connective ribs arching out to the assorted heavens. The last time she'd been here, she'd been starving, begging for help. Every god dwelling in the Upper Worlds had violently rejected her, as in with armies of gods to beat her back. The gods of the Uppers owned every superlative in the categories of arrogance and assholery. In contrast, the gods of the Unders could be considered kind.

Here in the Uppers, greater gods abounded, living shoulder to shoulder in a false fraternity, a breath away from ripping out each other's spines. Here, the boot of oppression held extra weight, but sycophants kissed the soles and begged for more, terrified of being deprived the favors of the greaters. Here, the only thing that scared these gods more than the original Chimera was being banished.

Time to shift their fears.

Bix started by expanding her footprint, by spawning darkness to smother the light. Alarms sounded, and gods rallied as she fed her disdain for their existence into the malice already rolling off her. Troops of the vain and the spoiled lashed out like the pitiful inconsequential entities they knew in their heart of hearts they would always be. They weren't titans, first children, the Cosmos, or the Chaos. No, they were glorified Tupperware, and only because the greaters called them back from their saber rattling did she leave their lids intact.

Why were the greaters ordering their lessers to stand down? Consistently. Upper World by Upper World, the reigning gods commanded weapons sheathed and magics held in check. Curious. The lessers glowered and glared, shuffled and spit, all typical passive-aggressive behaviors, but to a one, they ceased openly antagonizing her. Interesting, but not enough to dissuade her from taking closer looks at their domains. False peace hid all sorts of things, and she couldn't afford for one of them to be—

There. Irregular electrical currents. So subtle and barely perceptible amid the fully evolved magics of the gods. If she'd been hunting using ether as a filter in viewing gates, she wouldn't have caught it. She was fully on World, nothing between her and the sporadic bursts. Not sporadic. Morse code. Three short bursts. Three long bursts. Three short bursts. Break. Ah, the beauty of living among humans was learning from them.

Ashtad.

Bix's heart swelled with relief, or, well, what passed as her heart in this state. Ashtad was alive, and he was calling for her. Praise to the powers that be.

Circling the World, Bix condensed her darkness to engulf it, to study it, to search it. It was a water World under the umbrella of the Lithuanian heavens. She'd already scoped the homes of titans' heirs, but this place echoed with power earned *and* inherited. Feminine power. The greater goddess who'd created this World was a child of a titan's spawn. Yes, that felt accurate. Alas, the goddess wasn't home. Disappointing, but not fruitless. There were other gods here, midlevel and lesser. The Consortium committee members, perhaps. Faction lackeys more likely.

Bix committed the sensation of the goddess's resonance to memory, so she'd recognize the goddess no matter the disguise. Water goddesses liked to be…fishy in form and behavior. Next, Bix narrowed her attention to the details of what stood between her and Ashtad. Water. Water was a conduit, even water made from drained souls instead of oxygen and hydrogen. It was also a barrier, a shield, and a curtain that hid many tricks.

Nothing on this World could physically hurt her, not in a significant manner. Oh, but the gods knew that; they were in the same boat. No, they'd hurt Ashtad to hurt her. He'd had four months in the hands of this greater goddess and her toadies. With notable effort, Bix braced herself for what she was likely to find. She couldn't let her temper get out of control, not while on mission. She was trying to stop a war, not feed one.

There was a time to be a dervish and a time to be deliberate.

Like a massive stingray, Bix rippled the edges of her incorporeal existence and dove into the water of souls.

CHAPTER 27

The water was a net. Woven from assorted divine magics, it was nonetheless a shameful simulation of Resen lacking the crucial components that would make the real thing part of an effective defense system. If this was yet another attempt by the gods to get her to table Resen, they were nuts.

Laughter bubbled up from the tips of her being. It wasn't joyous laughter. It didn't classify as manic. Malevolent better suited Phobos. No, this laughter was nothing less than contemptuous. It carried through every withered soul, vibrating the translucent shells until they disintegrated out of existence. Souls formed the building blocks of all Worlds, and Bix had no qualms about eroding this World back to its very core until the greater goddess had nothing larger on which to stand than a shoebox. Bix knew she could do it. She had memories of doing it many times before. Real memories. Memories where images matched sounds and sensations. The absence of emotions didn't concern her. The original Chimera had buried them so deeply, she'd needed Tobek to help her access them.

"Fools," Bix whispered as water vanished from the World's surface, exposing the cabal of gods running for the north pole. Men, mostly. She wished she could be surprised by that, but mortal

242

patriarchy had its roots in the pantheons. "You hide beneath the tides in darkness and think I who am the night could not find you? You entangle me in concentrated energy, yet fail to consider I consume that which makes your energy possible? Do you not know who I am? Have you forgotten, or have your egos overrun your better sense?"

"You speak as though we should fear you." A bold god, lean, virile, and eternally stuck in his twenties, flipped his frosted caramel locks away from his face and surveyed his surrounds with a haughty flamboyance. "You who couldn't protect the Mids as promised? You who slunk back to the eternal abyss after your abject failure? You hid for centuries, hoping we would forget. Forgive. We've done neither. We've watched, and we've learned. The stories of the vaunted Chimera were nothing more than exaggerations to subjugate us to your whimsy."

"Whimsy? *Whimsy?*" She gasped then purred, mulling over the notion. "I suppose I could begin acting on *whimsy*."

She swallowed the pompous god in a coil of darkness and drained him of all but the seed of his divinity, swiftly, silently. First, however, she combed through his recent memories looking for Ashtad's location, the name of the goddess who created this World, whether that goddess was aware her home had been co-opted, and… Oh. Oh my. Oh, how delicious, delightful, and unexpected.

These gods weren't from the Consortium committee; the committee had made the mistake of attending Blackpool. She'd husked every divine member of the committee. The only survivors were Ashtad's abductors, and they stood before her now, in the back of the gathering. She noted who they were before digging deeper into the framework of secrets held by this glorified Mason jar.

These gods, every single one of them, belonged to the faction of traitors, the ones selling out the Mids to the Devourers. These were the resentful and the disenfranchised. These fellas were hungry for power yet lacked the drive to acquire it. Their stagnant or declining status was someone else's fault, anyone else's, but decidedly not theirs. These were the exceptionally entitled who'd been smacked down by someone higher up their chain of authority. They were covetous, envious, and everything that had made them ripe pickings for the greater goddess who ruled this World.

Indraja. A planetary goddess, one whose early believers had forsaken her after she'd been stood up at the altar. Indraja hadn't been a mopey miscreant like these petulant whelps. No, she'd been busy amassing copious quantities of power to become a greater goddess. Who, what, how, when, why, all good questions to be answered later.

Bix filed the name Indraja away for future research. She'd gotten what she needed from this gaggle of gods. Now the fun could start.

"Traitors, traitors, one and all," she cooed, continuing to erode the World. Ashtad was here, but he wasn't visible. They'd buried him alive and kept moving his location to thwart her. Any of these gods could end him before she got to him, so let the game of chicken begin.

"Now, now, Chimera, no need to be disrespectful. After all, you're hardly the same omnipotent power you used to be," one of the gods asserted. This one had white hair and black skin. He was attractive as gods inevitably wanted to be perceived, though he'd chosen to appear slightly older than his husked counterpart. No one among this cabal dared to display a wrinkle or a character line. Hell, they didn't even show their scars from their demigod trials. They were all too polished and too pretty, which meant their actions and their politics were all about optics.

The optics of thirty-seven gods against one demigod weren't good, but thirty-seven against one Chimera could be considered hors d'oeuvres.

"I don't have to know everything, not when I can simply pluck what I want from *you*." She dragged the husked god through the ranks of his associates as though a child trapped at the dinner table with a slice of liver.

The strident unity of the cabal faltered. Gods leapt away from the shell of their compatriot, horrified or disgusted.

"We are willing to trade." One of Ashtad's abductors stomped his foot twice. A large clam burst from the muddy ground that had once been an ocean floor. "The son of Ba'al for your agreement to stay out of our business with the Consortium."

They'd needed thirty-seven, no, thirty-eight gods to make that demand? That really would've worked better as a one-on-one, which a goddess like Indraja would know. A greater goddess would also know this many gods weren't necessary to complete the illusion of a rescue for a newly minted asset. Something else was going on. Bix was a spy at heart, and spies were all about the intel. Ashtad would be mad at her if she didn't take the extra beat to get the scoop.

"Your business isn't with the Consortium, it's with the Devourers," she jeered. "They get the Mids, you get to rule a gutted pantheon. It's a false power exchange, and you traitors are too stupid to realize you've been conned."

She didn't snatch the clam because she wasn't certain Ashtad was inside. Plus, this gaggle of goons made her question whether their game was about spycraft at all. None of them seemed to have the wits and patience intel gathering and analysis required.

"You've no idea where we stand," the second of Ashtad's abductors blurted.

Could Ashtad's abductors have gone double rogue? Could they have chosen to save him from Musso-Koroni despite—not because of—the faction's orders? The skittering desires inside the mind of the god she'd just husked, the excessive delusions of grandeur, had she misread them? Had they been his hopes?

"Don't tell me the faction of traitors inside the Consortium has fractured." She gasped as the obvious finally hit her. "Are you the new rebels? Operating on your own side? Seeking out new alliances?"

"We don't need to ally with you. As long as we have him, you'll do exactly what we say." The black god snapped his fingers, and the clamshell popped open.

Ashtad, emaciated, bald, bruised, bearded, and shackled in god-forged irons, sprawled upon a gritty bed. The scars from his old battles lay in thick ropes along his leg, obscuring his knee completely.

It wasn't whimsy that impaled the gods. It wasn't a lack of control that delivered the idiots to a cosmic prison where a very bored creator of titans abided. It was, however, training that kept Ashtad's abductors with her as Bix carefully folded Ashtad into her existence. His heart beat, feeble, but it beat, and that was all she really needed to know.

"There's a saying," she whispered. "Something about conquests and no quarter."

The kidnappers cowered, raising their hands above their heads. One of them had sparks dancing all over his body. A storm god, calling energy to himself.

"Leave one alive as the messenger," Ashtad wheezed into her darkness.

Before she could act, the storm god blasted the bejesus out of his peer, sending the other god into convulsions.

"I will be your messenger, Chimera. I will return to Indraja and the others to deliver your message." The storm god prostrated himself before her.

Even if Indraja hadn't set all this in motion to convert Ashtad into a mole within Bix's operations, there was no reason Bix couldn't turn this storm god into a mole inside Indraja's.

"You will be more than my messenger, snack bag," Bix snarled. "You will be my spy inside their organization. I want every name of the decision makers. Not the lackeys, not midlevel management, I want the top of the food chain. I want the gods, the Fates, the dragons, the angels, every single shot caller in bed with the Devourers. And then? And then I want the names of the Devourers with whom they're working. That is the price of your life."

"Done," the god answered without hesitation.

"It's not an easy job," she challenged. "Perhaps your fried friend here would be better equipped."

"Ashtad is my nephew," he blurted. "He is alive because I convinced the others he had value beyond Resen. I convinced them he had sway over you."

"Extortion was your plan? Since Blackpool?" Bix wasn't convinced this storm god and his cronies were sly enough to fool the faction.

"Since Zamarad, since the Devourers attacked." He shuddered and sneered. "You were right, we'd bought into the false power exchange. We'd never seen them in action before. We'd never seen the damage they could do to us with minimal effort. We were more fragile than mortals in the face of their troops. That is not what we were told about them. That is not an ally who lifts you to rule a pantheon. That is an enemy who uses you as a weapon, then imprisons you when they're done."

"Ashtad, what say you?" Bix wasn't sure how this family dynamic would play out. She knew Ashtad and his dad weren't buddies, but he was close to his grandmother. Plus, Ashtad would know if his uncle was qualified.

"Let him try. You can always husk him later," Ashtad slurred, the effort of consciousness apparent.

"Very well. Because Ashtad lives, you get to live. The faction comes after him again, you'll pay the price." Bix husked the fried god, scraped his memories, and pushed the husk beside Ashtad's uncle. "Be useful."

Leaving the World of Indraja significantly smaller than when she found it, Bix took Ashtad home.

CHAPTER 28

Ashtad's penthouse reeked of chicken soup and funky tea. House brownies had come regularly throughout his recovery to clear away the tower of takeout containers and wash the mountain of teacups. All fabric had been laundered, from bedding to briefs. The brownies had steam-cleaned every inch of the condo, from the blackout curtains in his bedroom to the tiles in the foyer. Every window had been shined and opened to admit fresh air. Heck, they'd even polished the hairpins Bix had amassed on his desk. She played with one of those hairpins now as she paced the balcony, listening to the sound of Ashtad in the shower. It was his first without her darkness holding him upright. His dignity was hella bruised, but she preferred that over his frail body incurring any more damage. She'd stayed by his side throughout the convulsions and delirium as nurses had weaned him away from the brink. Each time she'd fallen asleep and her mind had compelled her body to wander, her subconscious had taken him with her.

She could only imagine Tobek's surprise when she'd shown up—as she inevitably did when she slept—with Ashtad in tow.

"Bug, any word from the coal plant or Luz?" she asked her tech. The Eternal Knot on her chest twitched like a pup chasing rabbits in its sleep. It would randomly glow brightly, then fade to barely a shimmer. Its activity told her Tobek was still in the throes of evolution. Beyond that, she had to rely on Gurp or the guys to tell her if something was wrong. They hadn't sent up a flare, so she'd stayed where she was needed. Mostly stayed.

No new messages. Place a call?

"No, thank you." Bix paused in the doorway to the living room when the sound of water shutting off created a tense quiet inside the condo. Muttering. The whump and thump of the cane's rubber tip. Creak of the laundry hamper. More cane thumping. This time moving across the hall to the enormous dressing room.

"I'm fine," Ashtad groused loudly.

"You're lying, but you're standing, so I'll let you continue your struggle."

Hey, she'd stood back while he'd warred with gods, antagonized Fates, and barreled through his demi challenges. A slip and fall in the bath was not a trial toward godhood, so she was allowed to hover. Friendship parameter. Staked. Right there.

"We need to have a real talk about Resen," he said amid grumbles, mumbles, sounds of hangers spinning, and fabric being tossed.

"But our fake ones were so much fun?" She let heavy sarcasm imbue her tone as she ambled into the condo and perched on the arm of the couch.

He emerged from the closet dressed in very loose cotton pants and a white undershirt that had once been fitted. He was mostly bulbous joints and slack skin, but the green tint was gone from his flesh. His lips were more rose than mauve, and his eyes were no longer yellowed. The fuzzy brown regrowth along his pate was still more nectarine than peach. He was running at maybe forty percent, on the extremely generous side. He sank into his desk chair slightly breathless, his scarred leg straight as a board. No mauling boot until he was at least eighty percent. Nurse's orders.

"Don't overdo it," she chided. "You'll only regress."

"I'm a demi, I heal faster than average mortals." He spun his cane...and dropped it. He stared at Bix as though waiting for her to say, *Told you so.*

She didn't. She didn't pick up his cane either. Grown-ass man in need of proving something to himself. If he fainted, she'd put him back to bed. More than that, as long as it didn't involve sharp edges and his skull, no. He was too prickly from being feeble for longer than he found personally acceptable.

"So, Resen?" she prompted.

He stared at his fallen cane. "The gods are hell-bent on keeping Resen a secret because it can do more than detect them, it can trap them. It's built from the same netting basics as the Fates used on Chief to bind his magic and tether him to the Mids."

By Chief, he meant Tobek, and by the netting, he meant the weapon she, the original Chimera, had taught the Fates how to create during their war of independence against the pantheons. She had the bulk of those memories, and what she lacked, the Sage server had supplied. Her brother had highlighted the more egregious gotchas for her, and he'd pushed up the memories of how to ensure Resen didn't burn itself out by trying to detect a first child. She'd have to stop using gates to move around if she wanted to pass unnoticed, which she didn't like. With any luck, Ashtad and Cian could figure out how to get Resen to ignore her.

"It can confine the lessers, inhibit the midrange, but only detect the greater," she clarified. "Greater gods are banned from the Mids anyway, so the issue for the pantheons is how they farm the Mids within these new parameters."

Ashtad huffed and blinked up at her as if she'd lost her mind. "Resen bestows incarceration powers to whoever builds and maintains the netting. Think about how many ways that's going to be exploited. How many weapons are suddenly going to appear in the Crimson Market that are specifically built to target gods once the build specs are leaked, and we know they will be, and we know by whom."

Bix hummed her agreement. "Unlikely to outnumber the weapons built to hunt dragons and angels, though."

"Bix, I'm serious," he admonished. "Do you have any idea what this tech will do to the demigod challenges? How many of us will end up exactly like Chief? Trapped, tethered, confined, unable to continue our trials? We will be stagnant mortals forever."

Oh. Wow. She'd long known Ashtad's greatest flaw was his disdain for lesser races. It wasn't that he disliked them; he just believed he was better than they by dint of birth. Unlike the gods who'd taken him hostage, he didn't resent others' success, nor did he begrudge them that achievement. He did, however, judge himself as lacking if he hadn't or couldn't achieve that same milestone. Proving to himself that he was worthy of the status into which he'd been born was his motivation. That motivation didn't come entirely from a pure place. It also came from racial arrogance.

"You still feel it, don't you? Musso-Koroni's influence?" Bix tilted her head.

"This argument isn't a matter of discord, it's a matter of survival and strategy, not only for me but for all demigods and the future demis." He thrust his jaw forward and focused on curling his toes around his cane, trying to retrieve it.

"Musso-Koroni was, is, a goddess of hidden truths, our private motivations, the dirty secrets about ourselves that we bury." Bix drew her hair over one shoulder. "Ashtad, your hidden truth, the thing you don't like to admit to even yourself, is that you're a racist. You know you're an elitist, and you work on trying to be better about it, but it's the racist bit that taints your leadership aspirations. If you want to head the Consortium and guide it into a new and noble era, you're going to have to confront that part of you."

He didn't speak for a long time, simply kept struggling with his cane. Finally, he got it between the toes attached to his fully functional leg and brought the cane within his reach.

"Gods *are* the superior race. We *are* better than anything created by the Mids. It is why gods are immortal and everyone else can be erased," he confessed softly, laying the cane across his lap. "The current chair of the Consortium is an archangel. Look at how broken that organization is. The leadership is to blame."

"Politics is to blame. Greed is to blame. Ego and fear are in there too, right alongside racism. The pantheons are as guilty as the other races. Just because a god can't die doesn't make them better."

"We are not going to agree on this topic, and I accept that. What I cannot abide are the inevitable abuses of Resen." He crossed his wrists atop his cane. "I happily assumed the role of seneschal for the demis. I cannot and will not enable something that will ruin the unguarded progeny of the gods. Less than fifteen percent of demis pass their trials. Less than ten percent survive the ascension. Resen will cut those numbers in half."

"Probably," she said bluntly. "This class of demis and the next will have a hell of a grisly time. No doubt about it. But the class after that? And after that? Imagine what sort of gods will ascend coming from a series of trials where their divinity is their weakness? Where hubris can be met at the hands of a gnome instead of the almighty Chimera?"

"Quality over quantity, is that really your best argument?"

"Ashtad, your class of demis is fucked regardless. Your class gets the Devourer education up close and extremely personally. Devourers have and will continue to gut this generation of demis. If we don't stop them, they'll be here waiting for the next class, and the next, until there are no more Mids. Those gods who aren't imprisoned by the Devourers and the ones who have survived the infighting of their pantheon as scarcity takes hold? They might have enough wherewithal to procreate and eventually birth a new generation of demis who will go through trials in some other collective of Worlds. But the single-digit graduation numbers will not be percentages, they will be full body counts."

"Resen doesn't stop the Devourers," he argued.

"It can contain, it can inhibit, and it can detect," she countered, repeating her stance, giving voice to the knowledge lived and amassed. "For each rank of god, there is a corresponding rank of Devourer. There is every possibility that Resen can act as a cosmic sieve, so that when the full armies of the Devourers finally charge the Mids, Resen will cage the foot soldier, weaken the troop leader, and point us to the commanders."

"It's not a stand-alone solution," he insisted.

"Agreed. The Consortium still has to get their shit together and cooperate with each other." Bix rapped her knuckles on the top of his desk. "Only with Resen, the pantheons can't refuse to participate until their price is met."

That snapped his chin up. His eyes narrowed as they scanned the back wall of the adjacent kitchen.

"Resen shifts all power inside the Consortium, more so than any of the cyclical wars, which amount to nothing more than a shuffling of players." He focused on her again. "There will be turbulent times once it goes live, once the Devourers are punted to far-off galaxies. So many contracts among the superpowers will have to be revised."

"Oh, that is a gross understatement. Throughout all these discussions and power plays, a few critical components have been excluded that will force changes inside the Consortium." She nodded vigorously. This mission had taught her quite a bit about Resen. While she lacked the data about the minutiae, she was abundantly clear on the big-picture gotchas.

Skuld had warned them back in the ballroom that the road to a new peace would be rough, but the Fate had neglected to mention peace would come at the price of humans being actively involved in the defense of the Mids. Resen couldn't work without humanity's stabilizing presence at every point of data transference. Wherever there was a Resen operations center, there would have to be a large human population. Gone were the days of keeping the grounding race in the dark. Once humans figured out their value, they'd demand a seat at the Consortium table.

There was also the small matter of compatibility with the Mids' current defense system; aka the ether, to which Bix had given *everything* to reinforce. Getting rid of the ether was going to cost the superpowers so much more than they could fathom.

There was no way the Consortium would ever be the same again, and Bix couldn't wait to watch them writhe in the consequences of their high-handedness.

"Those components must be in pieces of the build specs I don't have," Ashtad said warily.

"One chunk lies with the heart of native magic, and another is probably in the piece Cian has."

If Cian hadn't told Feng or the Angelic Host about humanity's involvement yet, the kid was sitting on a doozy of a surprise. It would be just like Cian to pull a stunt like that, to withhold critical data to keep himself alive. His mother hadn't a raised a fool.

"Then we need to sync with Cian, get the specs offloaded, reviewed, and ready for delivery." Ashtad heaved himself upright with the aid of his cane. "I'm going to take a nap while you guys set up the meet."

CHAPTER 29

The baby ley line emulated the overgrown plants on Zamarad, morphing from fruit to blossom, to reed, to stalk, to leaf, to full tree, then back down to seed to repeat as though learning the stages of development along with the differences in flora. The line had grown in Bix's absence and broken ground right in the heart of the mess left by the Devourer skirmish. The ley line dipped into the taint and twirled, then straightened as if playing with black paint. The toxin left slight stains in the blue-and-purple glow of the ley line but didn't poison it, at least not visibly.

"We have the master station set up at Luz. We have a second set up at the Host's stronghold. I have replication stations on thirteen Worlds with teams of angels building more on every Mid World as we speak. Now you're telling me we don't need them?" Cian's plaintive bleating was distorted by the comm baked into his full-face mask.

The kid and Ashtad wore the necessary respirator gear. Drew, Feng, and Bix had opted for the pure-pollen experience. At Bix's insistence, the Angelic Host had not been invited to this confab. Feng, for once, had listened. More importantly, he'd pulled rank on the archangels and laid down some heinous threats to spring Cian from their clutches. Of course, letting the kid go and setting the kid free were not the same thing. Cian was probably on an angelic watchlist for all eternity. Regardless, Bix had her core team with her now, sans Berserkers, and they were finally going to put a bow on this messy-ass mission.

The MWA had cleared out of Zamarad, leaving the World unoccupied by the pawns of the superpowers. It was just the ley line, the plants, the insects, and probably the Nabaziix to keep Bix and her team company.

"Four hundred facilities, thirty years, thousands of Sages and Oracles, yet the only functional prototype happened here." Bix gestured to their surrounds. "Care to guess why?"

Cian adjusted his respirator gear for the umpteenth time. "They weren't bumped off by the gods super fast and had time to do the research?"

"Okay, herb nerd, how smart do you think you'll be in forty years?" Drew wore the suit of a train conductor from London. Her dark blue pants matched her dark blue hijab. The starched creases in her light blue shirt peeked from the orange zipper on her open dark blue vest. "You got the cheat codes from the Grove as a newb. How long would it take a middle-aged Sage to figure it out? Thirty years? Twenty?"

"Pfft, psht, phfft," Cian huffed and rolled his eyes. "Probably twenty if we started from nothing, but a compound of Sages should've gotten through full product lifecycle in ten."

"Should've, didn't, though," Feng pushed the kid to think. "Come on, why?"

"Uh, sabotage?" Cian floundered for an answer that ended with a shrug. "Seems to be a theme."

"Start with 'why Nez?' That was a question I couldn't answer for a long time." Bix pointed to the emptied research station sitting like a silent sentry amid the resurging plant life. "Why did the Fates recruit a behaviorist to a group building a tech-based defense system? His skills didn't fit the mission."

"Nez's specialty is why people do what they do and how to get them to do what you want them to do," Ashtad explained to Cian.

"That made him invaluable to the CWIG and to our Dark Ops team. He excelled without equal, not even among mind readers."

"Sounds like they brought him in to be the team shrink." Cian twirled his finger by his temple.

"Or management." Feng brushed his sleeve and examined the pollen sticking to his fingers.

"Nutty Nez was nowhere near the authority food chain," Drew scoffed. "That Oracle I wore? She was not a fan, nor was anyone else on security detail. They didn't really get his deal."

"Exactly." Bix snickered as the ley line mimicked Ashtad's hunched form, from air tanks to cane. "They needed someone who understood mortal behavior better than anyone else because they needed him to teach it to the one thing that made this facility different from all the others."

"The ley line." Ashtad stood straighter, leaning less on his cane. The ley line mirrored him. Ashtad managed to locate his inner child long enough to play a few rounds with the line.

"And it is to the ley line that the three of us will consign our portion of the build specs," Bix announced.

The chorus of disbelief from all but Cian was a little annoying.

"I must strongly advise against that," Feng asserted. "Do you not recall what happened in the bedrock with your Berserker?"

"The ley line holds the fourth component of the build specs. The line is physically part of the build. We agreed at the beginning of all this the only way Resen was going to survive the gods' interference—"

"Was to disseminate the data widely yet encrypted to prevent Tom, Dick, and Harry from getting their hands on it," Feng said, interrupting Bix. "When I suggested we bake the data into the line, I meant a fully functional line. This line isn't connected to the others yet. We give it the data, and it doesn't go anywhere."

"Ergo, this is how we force the Angelic Host and the Dragon Horde to begin this initiative on equal footing." Bix held out a hand to the line, but it was more interested in Cian. "Every archangel and dragon queen is intertwined with a line, right?"

Feng nodded.

"So they bring their ley lines to meet this one." Bix grinned as Cian played with the line. "If they don't work together, they don't get Resen. Period."

"We've lost archangels and dragon queens over the epochs. Not every line has a proper pairing." Feng rubbed the back of his neck. "Though, I suppose once the archangels and the queens understand how the foundation of Resen must be laid, then they would own the responsibility for incorporating all lines into the data flow."

"We know from Blackpool they are willing to work together on this," Drew reminded.

"I understand the necessity now." Feng nodded, then shook his head. "But there is still the danger to your team. We don't know how direct contact with the line will affect them or the line. Again, what happened with your Berserker? He barely survived it, and no disrespect to Ashtad and Cian, but…"

"There was an entire team of Berserkers it touched and did not harm. As for Tobek, it took him because it tasted my sadness and got scared by it." Bix laughed as the ley line shifted from playing with Cian to inspecting Drew, spiraling around her, poking and mimicking.

"Tobek the Teddy Bear." Drew looked up and around with feigned innocence as she held out her arms, allowing the ley line its curiosity.

"He *is* hairy enough," Ashtad concurred with a mutter. Volume didn't really matter when they were all on comms, but Ashtad cleared his throat and tipped his head at the ley line. "I'm a demi, and while I gain a lot from being in the Mids during my trials, I have no desire to become a Mid World guardian. A direct infusion of native magic could very well lock me into that destiny. No thanks. What's Plan B?"

"Mr. Ba'al, I was hoping you'd have one since you know more about cyborg tech than I do." Cian winced as he adjusted the straps holding his air tanks. "While you guys spent months getting your asses kicked, I spent that time trying to download everything the Grove gave me. There is no direct transfer method. When the angels tried to pull it from me, they got Mom's jalebi recipe instead. I've spent months of straight transcribing what I know, and I'm barely past chapter one. So much of it is hard to put into words."

Ashtad looked expectantly at Feng.

Feng raised his hands in surrender. "I too tried to acquire the information from Cian. It is locked in his threads, not in the tissue of his mind. It's similar to what I encountered when trying to heal the Grove Sages back at Luz."

"If they'd put the data in the kid's soul, I could help, but since it's in his threads, there's not a lot I can do." Drew chuckled as the ley line tapped her nose, then ruffled her hijab. "What about you, Bixie? Can you extract it from him? Like you do with the gods?"

Bix shook her head. "I'll shred his threads if I try it."

"That'll kill me, so pass." Cian grimaced.

"If the Grove baked it into the kid's threads, where'd they stuff your data, Sparky?" Drew sucked her cheeks into hollows and waggled her brows at Ashtad.

"Knotted it around my unevolved divine essence." Ashtad eyed Bix, then the ley line. Then Bix, then the ley line.

"If I take the data from you, Ashtad, it comes as part of your memories," Bix cautioned. "Memories aren't linear, they're relational. You will remember nothing connected to the Grove. That includes me and, by extension, every intersection I've had in your life. Same for Nez. Cian. Feng. Tobek. Drew. All of us. You will have huge gaping holes in what you recall of your life."

"So my options are addlepated fool who fails his demi trials, or a future as a Mid World guardian." Ashtad hunched over his cane. "Guess that answers that, then. I can grow up and be just like Chief."

Feng looked to Bix with red brows rising.

Whatever Ashtad's issue with Tobek, it went deeper than his elitism. Ashtad and Phobos regularly warned her away from her

Berserker, but that was neither here nor there at the moment.

"Ashtad, I would very much like it if you would dance with me." Bix held out a hand and bowed in front of him.

"Um, not at the top of my—ah, touch, like the Sage servers, I get it." Ashtad waved her into his arms, his cane clasped between their hands.

"Feng, the ley line is one part music and one part movement," Bix prompted, waiting for the big bird to catch the drift.

"Oh yes, yes, of course." Feng unfurled his wings and beat the air. Native magic rolled with each gust. His barbed tail thumped the ground. The song of nature amplified and modified to fit the tempo he set. He extended one hand to Drew. "May I have the pleasure?"

Drew giggle-snorted and damn near leapt into Feng's hold. The ley line surged in height, formed a flower, then shed its petals. A beautiful rain of morphing color and shape. Ashtad held Bix as though they were teenagers at the middle school dance, mostly rocking back and forth while Feng swept Drew around the grounds in a grand formal waltz.

"Nice. Always a wallflow—"

Before Cian could complete his whine, the ley line took the shape of Drew and wrapped one shimmering tendril around Cian's hand. It made a claw with another tendril and hooked it over the strap of Cian's gear. It hovered. Waiting.

"One, two, three, boy. One, two, three," Feng coached. "Move, two, three. Now, two, three."

Cian stumbled and fumbled, but the ley line stuck with him as he figured out how to dance with the pure essence of native magic. The kid's awkward guffaw brought a smile to every adult. Cian followed Feng's impromptu ring of dance, and as the kid grew more comfortable, his posture mimicked Feng's. His green eyes glowed behind his mask as the ley line learned from him.

Eventually, it peeled away from Cian and inserted itself between Bix and Ashtad.

Bix happily gave the ley line room to take her place. "It'll be okay, Ashtad. It doesn't want to hurt you. It wants to learn from you, like I did all those years ago."

"You didn't try to get *inside* my business," he drawled, attempting his best locked-leg waltz with a semicorporeal entity.

"It's okay to show it your fear," Bix encouraged. "It doesn't have bias. It can't judge you, but you can show it that not all gods, even the unevolved ones, are monsters trying to hurt the Mids. You're not Musso-Koroni, you're not the cleaners, you're not Tobek either. You're just a guy with aspirations doing the best he can to protect those he loves. Project that to the line."

A light tap on Bix's arm turned her to face Cian.

"May I?" the kid asked with eyes aglow. "Partner swap, right?"

"It would be my pleasure." Bix stepped into his hold, setting her hand lightly in his and the other above his bicep.

"It, um, takes a minute for me to get the count," Cian offered with chagrin.

"Take your time. Let yourself feel it."

With a lurch, he yanked her into the movement. Laughing together as they synced with the music, they followed the others around the basin of native magic still raining petals as part of the line danced with Ashtad. Bix adjusted her hand on Cian's arm and detected an odd solidity cupping his shoulder.

"Cian, what is that? Beneath your jacket?"

His smile was a little sad. "It's what happens when magic hits my body, remember? My allergy, as we're calling it."

Her heart sank. The crystallization that surrounded a leaf marking one of his Fate trials had replicated where the Grove Sages had clasped his shoulders when they'd transferred the data to him.

"I am sorry," she whispered in earnest.

"Why? You didn't make me sick with this stuff." He shrugged, and both his truly solid shoulders crunched against the metal buckles on his air-tank straps. "I choose to look at it like the start of a Gundam suit."

"A sci-fi cartoon about ginormous robots operated by human

pilots inside the robot? Nice choice." She grunted her approval. "Did your dance with the ley line trigger more crystal growth?"

"Not yet." The kid missed a step and tromped her toes, but she didn't mind. "It felt like an acute case of the butterflies, you know? Mids' magic inspecting me from the inside. Cool and a little creepy, but mostly cool. Definitely memorable."

"How was your time with the Host?" She changed the subject, not wanting to further ruin a moment.

He rolled his eyes. "They're as snooty as the academics at school, so it wasn't really all that different."

She slapped his arm. "School. Oh shit. Your thesis. Your paper. Your defense. It's June. Did it happen? Did the angels let you finish school? Did working this mission completely screw up your human education?"

The kid was a Sage, so book smarts weren't ever going to be his problem. The importance of school wasn't about him ticking boxes of human normalcy either; there was no going back to a human's version of normal for him. It had everything to do with a promise he'd made his mom before she'd died: he had to stay in school until he turned eighteen. Graduation was important because delivering on the promise demonstrated his honor, his integrity, and his pride in himself. The kid had been kicked in the dirt way too often, so that core belief in himself was critical to his survival as a decent and compassionate person.

"There's a funny thing about working with a bunch of angels and the Phoenix. The human committee at university turned out to be overly agreeable to allowing a video chat defense," Cian joked.

"So you did it? It's official? You graduated?"

Cian nodded. "Feng and Drew made sure I walked. Pretty sure Drew recorded the whole ceremony. There was a phalanx of angels there as security too. It was awesome in an I'm-a-hostage-and-I-know-it way."

Bix squealed and hugged the kid, completely screwing up the dance. "Congratulations. We'll celebrate as soon as we wrap this. Total party of your choosing."

"Honestly? Getting to sleep in my own bed would be amazing. Doubles if I could not be stared at all day too."

"Once we're done here today, the Host could be convinced to let you reside in your hovel," Feng intruded over the comms. "However, you will be under constant surveillance indefinitely."

"They'll thumb-wrestle over whether it's the noble or the ignoble angels who get watcher duty," Drew cracked wise. "As Cian's roommate, I vote for the dirty rotten bastards we already know and tolerate."

"Okay, that's it for me," Ashtad panted, staggering away from the ley line as it returned to its greater form. "I think it got what it needed, and now I very much need to go home."

Bix and Cian rushed to Ashtad's side. Bix stabilized him while Cian caught the cane before it hit the ground.

"You okay?" Bix asked as Feng and Drew joined them.

"Winded, woozy, and in desperate need of alone time, if you don't mind," Ashtad said, barely hanging on to his dignity as his body trembled and his skin paled.

"You got it. I'll be along as soon as I'm done here." Bix opened gates but stilled as Ashtad grabbed her arm with curious strength.

"No, Bix. I need time apart from *you* for a while. The nurses will be around to make sure I'm alive, but beyond that, I need space. Got it?" His gaze burned with a fever she hadn't seen before, and they'd been through a whole lot together.

Wounded, she nodded. "Sure. If that's what you need. I'll keep my distance."

Ashtad released her and claimed his cane. "I think my part in this mission is done. It's been an adventure, all."

With that odd farewell, he hobbled through the gates to his penthouse. Gates closed, leaving the others in the group baffled. Ashtad's comm dropped its connection.

"Well, that was unpleasant, even for him," Drew drawled.

"He, an entity not of native magic, just connected directly with it," Feng reminded. "That he walked away from the encounter is a remarkable feat, and that does not take into account his poor health."

"It tells you things, the ley line," Cian added quietly. "Maybe it told him things he didn't want to know."

"What kind of things?" Drew clenched her hands in front of her chest and cringed.

"Things," Cian evaded and looked at Bix. "I wouldn't mind going home now too, Bix, back to my apartment. I'm thinking of ordering two of everything on the Afghan takeout menu, playing video games until I fall asleep at the controller, then waking up tomorrow afternoon with my face glued to a couch cushion. After that, I'll be happy to see you and anyone else in need of my expertise."

"I'll go with him." Feng held up his hand as Cian readied an objection. "Long enough to sweep the apartment for unwanted guests and to settle any dustups between the Host and the renounced angels already living on your block."

"Yeah, sure, whatever." Cian hitched his tanks. "Mostly I really want to get out of this gear. Talk about oppressive. I don't know how the Berserkers do it."

"Drew, what about you?" Bix asked.

"I'm all for giving the kid some breathing room as long as he responds to the check-ins." Drew tore her gaze from the continually changing ley line and stared at Cian until the kid rolled his eyes but nodded. "I think you and the baby here need to bond on your own, Bixie, so I'll take a ticket to Blackpool. Keep my ear to the ground on the pantheons' scuttlebutt."

"I'll also talk to the archangels and the queens about connecting with this ley line after I finish with the kid." Feng tucked his wings into his body as Bix opened gates to the respective destinations. "That should give you plenty of time to do your thing."

"Thank you." Bix inclined her head. "Thank you, everyone. I know this mission was harder than we expected, so you have my gratitude for stepping up and sticking with it all the way through."

"Somebody has to save the Mids, right?" Cian waved goodbye and crossed through the gate to his apartment with Feng right behind him.

"Don't take Sparky's grump personally. He's realizing how small a god is in the greater scheme." Drew kissed Bix's cheek. "I am never more than a ping away. Love ya, Bixie."

Bix shut the gates behind Drew and Feng, then turned to the ley line.

"Oh, little spawn of my dear sisters, do not be afraid of me. I have wondrous stories to share. Perhaps, if they are so inclined, perhaps, my sisters will deign to share a waltz or two with us."

Bix opened her arms and gave up her form of flesh to become the night. Bodiless, she wended with the offshoots of Movement and Music to dance to the song of galaxies in motion.

CHAPTER 30

There were many stories exchanged between Bix and the ley line. For moments that had been far too brief, Movement and Music had joined them. Bix had apologized for not understanding her sisters had always been with her, their touch in every push and pull of native magic. They'd laughed and shushed her, promising there was so much more to their shared story than she remembered. Before they'd left, they'd made her an offer, one they weren't sure she'd accept. One that involved Tobek.

She'd been mulling it over when the ley line had requested something odd of her. It held an urgency concerning Waylon Nez. While Bix would've been far more content to leave Nez to the Fates, the fear of a childlike entity merited consideration, especially when that entity was the backbone of the Mids' defense system. It wouldn't do to have it be skittish and worrisome.

Thus, corporeal, clothed, and mildly annoyed, Bix ambled the grounds of the Church of the Templars in Luz. Her heels clicked and clacked against worn cobblestone passages as the setting summer sun wrapped the church and towers in sultry orange that highlighted the dark green glow in the glass of the windows, in the stones of the walls, and in the soil beneath the small garden. Tobek's magic was very much present and frenetic. However, his resonance wasn't the trail she was following through the chapel and out to the shady archway of one of the crenelated towers. Not that she needed to hunt by magical signature. The wheelchair tracks in the dirt leading to the tower were obvious.

In a narrow ray of tangerine sunlight, surrounded by shadows thrown by the winding staircase lining the tower, sat Waylon Nez. Chin high. Eyes closed. "It's done, then? The Resen mission?"

"Our part," Bix conceded. "It's up to the Host and the Horde now."

He grunted. "We did it. The old gang. One last hellfire mission. Those were always our strength. The worst odds. The impossible outcomes."

"Is it really the last one, Nez?" She paused in the shadows, welcoming the cool embrace of darkness.

He chuckled. "Sense it, can you?"

"You ascended," she confirmed, perceiving his Other World resonance. "Full Fate. You didn't stop at Grove server, you signed with the big leagues. You get threads of destinies to weave. Congratulations."

"I don't think I would've made it without you." He glanced at her, then at his lap.

"There was a time that, had it been my say, you wouldn't have made it at all," she admitted. "However, at the start of this mission, someone reminded me I needed to change my perspective and adopt a new point of view. Perhaps, I needed to give the Hanged Spy a second chance."

"The Hanged Spy, eh?" He nodded. "Not exactly the way I'd imagined reintroducing myself to you, but I'm not quibbling with the outcome. I learned a lot from you all those years ago. Even without realizing what you were doing, you gave me a course correction. A well-needed one. Thank you for that."

"Should you ever require another, keep in mind Fates aren't truly immortal." She inspected her nails, lacquered and shimmering. "You're hard to kill, but not impossible."

He barked with wry amusement. "Why do you think the

Houses are working so damn hard to evict the Devourers from this one little haven in all the multiple universes? It was the only place free of the things that could kill us. Humans are scattered across existence, but the Mids is where we grow stronger, smarter, and more mentally resilient. The souls the gods inflict upon us? The weaknesses the dragons and angels insist on baking into our bodies? All of it makes Mids-grown Fates exceptional."

"You going to tell them it's safe to come out, or do you want me to be the bad guy?" she asked, getting around to the real reason the ley line had sent her.

"Coming into your power finally?" Nez looked at her fully this time. It wasn't anger in his heavily scarred expression. It was wonder.

"Basic intel analysis. First, there was your recruitment to the Zamarad station. Then, Ashtad said it felt like something else had evac'd from Zamarad with you. And down in the bedrock, I found the prison your peers had fashioned. I also found the wards broken by small claws that did not belong to the Nabaziix." She stepped into the light. "I know you're here, children. I have come from your ley line, and it feels your fear and indecision. It requested I help you find your paths."

Rustling in the rafters. Wisps through shadows. Flutters. Whispers as two teens alighted to either side of Nez in his wheelchair. A large plum serpent and a scrawny youth with black eyes far too large for his face. The dragon queen and the archangel.

"You are the Chimera, High Executioner for All Worlds," the boy accused, his voice cracking with the indicator of his age.

"You are an entity of terror and ruthlessness, a punisher," the queen hissed, her violet wings drawing high and back.

"When it is necessary, yes," Bix acknowledged without shame. "Of greater relevance is that I am an entity of balance. There is a pendulum of progress and regress. Both are necessary."

"Let me guess, your job is to knock it out of darkness when it gets stuck," the angel boy snarked, clearly not buying her spiel.

"No, no, I'm here for when a big bad picks up that pendulum and wields it as a battle-ax." Bix smiled with all teeth and no charm.

Nez snorted. His snort protracted into a guffaw that devolved into chair-shaking laughter. "It's all right, children. Bix is, for all her complex reputation, a good egg."

"But she's here to take us away from you," the dragon whispered loudly.

"We've been through this." Nez cradled the paw of the dragon queen in his scarred hands. "There is a journey of lessons and life that you must walk before you take your places among the Dragon Horde and the Angelic Host. Your families are forbidden by their traditions to interfere in your growth, but make no mistake, they are very much aware of your existence. That is equal parts challenge and promise."

"Lessons like you had to learn?" The angel rested his hand on the frame of Nez's chair.

"Possibly less disfiguring," Nez quipped. "Now, Bix, where is it you have in mind to set our fair youths on their journey?"

"You guys have been here for months. I assume you've not only met but befriended Gurp?" Bix smirked as the kids swapped looks that screamed *busted*. "Good, because there is no one in all the Worlds with a keener understanding of needs than that goblin. I'm going to solicit advice from him and Nez. Meanwhile, take another week, hang with Nez, get your heads in the space of tackling your pending adventure. We'll meet back here, and I will provide you with an express pass to your respective next steps. Sound like a plan?"

The angel looked to the dragon and scrunched his face. The dragon gave the angel silent encouragement. This went back and forth like a tennis match.

"Can we make it two weeks?" the angel finally asked. "There's a festival coming up and…"

"And he met a giiiiirl," the dragon finished, rolling her eyes.

"Oh, okay, then, yeah, sure, two weeks to the day, back here at sunset," Bix agreed, never the one to stand in the way of twue wuv. Besides, she had a few players to put on overwatch for these kids. With the Devourers running around, she wasn't going to leave two morsels of pure native magic unprotected. Screw the no-interference rules. "One thing, kiddos, this bond you two have going right now? Try to keep it no matter the crap storms that come your way. Dare to be better than the other dragon queens and archangels. Dare to be lifelong friends. That's way harder than falling out and giving up on each other. Got it? Good. See you guys in two weeks."

Bix turned and headed out of the tower.

"Bix, wait," Nez called after her. The sound of his wheels crunched over the dirt and cobblestones. "You and Ba'al hit a rough patch?"

She gave him a flat stare. She might not despise him anymore, but he sure as shit wasn't her confidant. "Nez, dragons and angels are natural nemeses. Goth Queen and Lover Boy in there are the first I've seen get along, truly get along. I don't care if it's an anomaly, something fostered by their ley line, or if you were the one who taught them the value of a teammate who would always have your back. Whatever it is, if they can hold on to that friendship, then I have high, high hopes for the future of the Mids."

Nez nodded and adjusted his grip on the hand rims of his chair. "Speaking of teammates who always have your back, you should really check on the original Berserker. Trust me on that."

Bix slapped her hand over her Eternal Knot and looked to the main church, under which the battalion was still running operations.

"What happened to him, Nez?" she demanded.

"Not past tense, present." He wheeled his chair back to the tower and his charges waiting in the shadows. "I'm a Fate of the Present, and I suggest you get your butt in gear. You have fifteen minutes before his evolution erases something the two of you have been working toward for eons."

CHAPTER 31

Angry growling. Bestial braying. The scent of electronically purified air over millennia of old magic and older earth. Those things welcomed Bix as a few Berserkers turned from the banks of monitoring equipment beeping and flashing in a rotunda three levels below the chamber used as the makeshift clinic beneath the Church of the Templars. The lighting was dim, mostly button-sized task lights at the workstations. The bleak dungeon strobe light effect came from behind thick panels of tempered glass as Tobek flung himself against the walls.

Shifting forms.

Her big blond bear held half his human body, while the other half, the half missing a chunk of his arm, stretched and distorted trying to contain a sea monster oozing dark green fog. The ink of his layered tattoos shone brighter than stars as they strained over the flesh trying to contain the creature. One leg of Tobek's tactical pants had blown out to accommodate a thick, corded amalgam of an octopus and a man. Tobek's once-easy smile had yielded to a mouth half warped by multiple rows of pointy teeth; his strong jaw distended with half a sharklike snout. One blue eye blazed. The other gleamed red, iris and pupil. The damage inflicted by the angel-bone swords had been erased. He wasn't injured. He was evolving.

271

And fighting it.

On this side of the glass, hands and face pressed to the surface, unflinching as Tobek bounced off the panel in front of him, stood Gurp. He kept up a banter, his voice unfaltering as he babbled in that special language only Tobek seemed to understand. Tobek howled responses that contained no words.

Bix's heart stopped. Broke. Broke into smaller pieces. Then gathered itself up with cosmic duct tape to resume beating.

"Thank the greater powers you're here," Runjit murmured, coming to her side, tech tablet in hand. "It's getting worse. Time spent in fully human form is down to fifteen minutes for every three hours. He hasn't rested since you left this morning."

Bix glanced at the Berserkers' lead medic and tried not to look surprised. When she'd returned from her brother's, the guys had told her she'd been a regular visitor throughout her recovery. They'd told her they'd put Tobek in quarantine. They'd told her he wasn't done evolving. However, there was knowing...and there was *knowing*. Despite always locating Tobek in her sleep, whether she meant to or not, she never remembered the visit unless she was awakened. Hard to believe she'd slept through this Jekyll and Hyde battle.

"Has he eaten?" She opted for the most normal question she could think of. Tobek was probably famished, burning all that energy trying to stop the new...or maybe even the old and repressed version of himself from escaping. Whatever the green creature was, it wasn't holding to a single beast. It changed with each impact of Tobek smashing that half of himself into a wall. The sounds coming from him ran the gamut from confusion, pain, and anger, to dogged determination.

It crushed her to hear him in such agony. Her shadows rippled underneath her flesh, eager to escape and console him.

"Not since yesterday morning." Runjit scratched his thumb along the edge of his turban. "He only calms when you're here, but he doesn't sleep."

"You guys record my last visit?" she asked with distraction.

"Yes." Runjit tapped his screen and handed her his tablet.

As she'd suspected. Ashtad had been with her. She'd brought him inside the cell with her and Tobek. The moment he'd awakened and had spotted Tobek, Ashtad had scrambled to the glass, his back against it, eyes wide, hands trembling, like a man facing a starving tiger. Tobek had acted every bit the feral monster until she'd pierced her Berserker with darkness and enveloped him in night. There they'd all stayed. Ashtad wide awake and frozen in place, staring at what looked like nothing but was Bix in her state of starlit midnight. Gurp had brought Ashtad food, a blanket, and a pillow, but no one had let him out of the cell.

If nothing else, that scene provided a damn good reason for Ashtad's extreme resistance to turning into Tobek. Also, a good reason Ashtad wanted to get away from her for a while. Yeah. Suddenly she did not blame him.

She handed Runjit his tech. "I'm going to take Tobek away from here. Let Xipil and the others know your fearless leader has been abducted by a friendly for an indeterminate amount of time."

"Probably best for all." Runjit clasped his tablet to his chest and frowned. "Can you fix him?"

"Don't know," she admitted. "Can tell you he has some big decisions to make and about eleven minutes in which to make them. He wouldn't want a body count tied to this."

"Yes, of course. Right. I'll write it up as a medical sabbatical. If it's not too much to ask, let us know if we're ever going to get him back," Runjit said with the first hint of despondency she'd heard from the perpetually dour medic. He cleared his throat and shuffled to a workstation.

Bix approached Gurp and laid one hand on the goblin's shoulder. "You know what's happening, don't you?"

Gurp looked at her with tear-filled eyes and nodded. "He grow."

"I'm going to take him, and while we're gone, I need you to plot the next steps for the kids Nez hid away here. It's time for them to grow too. There is no one I trust more than you with the future leadership of the Mids."

Gurp blushed, wiped his eyes, and rubbed his hands together. "Yes. I help. I think. I plan. Good kids. Strong. Smart."

"Thank you." She beamed at him. "Two weeks, I'll be back for the kids. I don't know if Tobek will be ready to come back then or not, but if not, I will bring you to him."

"You help Chief. Chief and you home." The goblin snuffled. "Then we family again, yes?"

"Always family." She kissed the top of his bald head, then used gates to enter Tobek's cell.

Tobek spun on her and whimpered. She opened her arms and fought a tear. "We got all dressed up for a ball but never had the chance to dance. Will you dance with me now?"

He lurched toward her, unbalanced, unable to work the body of the sea monster and the body of the man as one being. His hand of flesh with knuckles torn, nails ripped to the quick, and palm punctured closed gently over hers. The stump of a fin flailed at her side, unable to remain in a consistent state. Didn't matter. She set her hand upon the shoulder of uncontrolled magic and hummed the tune of Worlds in motion. He shuffled to the rhythm, no grand movements, no fluid poses, just a shuffle and a hum an octave below hers.

At the third strain, she moved them out of the Mids.

CHAPTER 32

Her cheek upon Tobek's amorphous shoulder, Bix cozied up to his body. The weightlessness of nothingness allowed them to drift in the ether. Away from the Mids, away from the magic native to any World, she could finally get a clean read on his condition.

The last palm-sized patches of netting the Fates had woven around him all those eons ago clung to the side of the man. The side of the sea creature was completely unfettered. His recent confrontations with excessive Mids' magic had accelerated the erosion of Fates' threads. The baby ley line had told her it had tried to fix him because it wanted to keep him as part of the Mids, as part of native magic. Instead, it had made his condition worse. It was sad, like she had been sad. It had broken something important and couldn't put it to rights.

Her sisters had offered to fix Tobek for her. But it wasn't her place to accept. His life was his choice.

"You have a decision to make," Bix murmured against the tingle of Tobek's frenetic magic. "Complete your evolution now or be restrained by stronger bonds than those the Fates inflicted upon you."

"I'm not done evolving, I can't be, not yet," he slurred through his mutation. "It's too soon."

"Too soon for what?" She looked up at him, bemused. "Don't you want to be greater than a god or a titan?"

"I don't want to be your *food*," he snarled, flinched, then whimpered. "My tone. Harsher than I meant. I apologize."

"I've never freed you from your bonds because I…I wanted more for you?" She paused, searching for the partial memory, finding many, but none that held the whole story. "Your evolutionary target is to become a new type of creation, one that supersedes the titans? First children too?"

"Never your better," he rumbled through distorted teeth. "Only nearer your peer, righteous daughter of the Chaos and the Cosmos. Hard to do. First children are their own class. Nothing similar exists, nothing comes close."

"Yet that hasn't stopped you from trying."

"All you've wanted, all you've ever needed, was a partner who could balance you. That I couldn't fill that role drove me mad in a very literal way." He moaned sadly. "My ignorance, frustration, and misplaced ego caused far too much heartache for you and far too many fights between us for far too long. I floundered for epochs before I understood the answer to our happiness lay in your uniqueness. Because you are the two-in-one, your balance would be something as yet undefined. Something Other. So I set off to figure out how to become Other."

"One of your many encounters with the Grove?"

He growled. "By then, you'd taught me to listen for what they didn't say. The truth hid between the omission and the evasion."

"To become Other, you needed the piece of me within you to absorb not only my magic but also *all* World magic." She laid her hand over his Eternal Knot, glowing bright teal amid the dark green monster he couldn't contain. "In return, you anchor me emotionally and physically."

"That is the nature of our relationship, to be supportive where the other is vulnerable." He drew their laced fingers along her cheek. "It didn't happen quickly or smoothly. There were times when kindness could not be found in either of us, just as there were times when passion fully consumed us."

"Those passionate times must be what my brother buried when he was futzing with my memories." She snickered, tracing his Eternal Knot. "Musso-Koroni told me how you used to feel about me. That you hated me, that I was the reason you failed your god challenge. Got the impression I'm your white whale."

He groaned in combination of mirth and pain. "Ah, the foibles of youth. What an ignorant ass I was. I despised you for ages. Every failure, every setback, I blamed on you. Even after we met, I still wanted to end you in the most gruesome ways possible."

She lifted her head and pouted. "No love at first sight?"

"No." He winced and clutched her hand tighter as half his face suffered another transformation. "Not on either of our parts."

"So much for that fairy tale." She sighed. "When you became my anchor to the Mids, did I force you or did you volunteer?"

"You gave me a choice," he rasped through a cringe as half his body followed the changes of his face. "I could be executed as my abominable actions had merited, or I could accept the punishment of not only having to endure your presence but also to have it flow inside me, forever binding me to you."

"An eternity with a woman you hated or death...and you picked misery. You really are a very twisted man," she teased then sobered. "How do you not hate me now?"

"What we are reminiscing over was only our beginning. The things we have done to, with, and for each other since have made us something I never ever want to lose. Again." He tugged her closer, pressing the cheek of the man against her hair. "The centuries you were alone in the ether were the worst torture for me. I couldn't feel you, I couldn't find you, I couldn't help you. It drove me insane. The moment you returned to the Mids, it echoed in every cell of my body. I tore up Worlds looking for you. I diverted all my resources to your hunt. The men of my battalion volunteered their free time to the search because the MWA refused to sanction it as an official mission. The army deployed us with increasing frequency to keep our downtime minimized. Gurp located you first. He's the one who found you in the coal plant basement before the renovation. I got there mere moments after you'd left for the op that ended in your exile. The candle wax was still warm, the sheets still damp, perfume that wasn't yours still in the air."

She wasn't going to discuss her sex life of the last thirty years with him. They weren't quite there yet, not in this version of their relationship. And even then, some things didn't need to be shared. "Your bosses knew where I was the whole time. The Consortium, they knew."

"They did, and it was imperative to them I not find you because I would remind their worst nightmare of who she really was," he grumbled. "I was unaware of the state of your memories until you crashed into my home and looked at me without a flicker of recognition. In that moment I died and rejoiced, and scrambled, oh, sweetheart, you have no idea how badly I fumbled through that first encounter with you. I felt like a sweaty-palmed youth all over again."

"You poked me with your broadsword, and I don't mean that euphemistically," she retorted indignantly, then chuckled and tapped his Eternal Knot. "This is the first time you've been able to talk about our past without the curse driving you to your knees."

"Because your curse is tied to the magic I siphon from whatever environment I'm in," he confessed. "This half-baked entity you see struggling before you now doesn't consume magic, therefore it is immune."

"This will probably be the last chance I have to share memories with you," she whispered, her voice catching. "Alas, we have only ninety seconds left in the time of the Mids before your evolution is complete. If you are positive you want to be shackled and your powers forcibly restrained for eons longer so your development can continue, then we ought to get to getting."

"Sweetheart, when it comes to our memories, they don't need words to be shared." He held their hands against his glowing chest. "A look. A touch. A smile, even the way you clutch my leg between yours when you sleep. What we have lives in the everyday little comforts of coexistence."

She wrapped her arms around his neck and kissed him as fully and awkwardly as the mangled mouth of a man-monster allowed. She let him go and wiped her tears.

She'd known something was off with Tobek's netting before the events at Blackpool. The Grove Sage had shared the intel warning of Tobek's worsening condition as Tobek continued to filter and blend her magic with that of the Mids. So, after Music and Movement had made their offer to fix him, she'd reached out to Three. To bind Tobek so that he could continue evolving into something Other required an imbalance. It required Three plus her sisters. Her brother had taken some convincing, but her gift of many petulant gods had swayed him almost as much as his innate curiosity.

Now, she had to make sure this was what Tobek really wanted. She had to give him the choice. Informed consent. It seemed the basis of their relationship from the very beginning.

"Although I'm one of the first children, I am unable to create something from nothing; therefore, I have asked my sisters and my brother to fashion new restraints for you that will allow your evolution to continue." She fought to keep an even tone. Failed. Miserably. She warbled worse than Drew that time at drunk karaoke. "When all is done, they will bring you back to me as a man once again of flesh and blood. You will have challenges adapting to bindings far more potent than those inflicted by the Fates. The magics you've so freely wielded will be altered by the absence of the Other World bonds you are shedding and by the primeval bonds you are gaining. The foundations on which you have relied for so long will be gone, thus requiring you to change your methods and means. You will enter a period of reeducation and rediscovery. Most importantly, you will have to negotiate a new contract with the Fates should you wish to remain a Berserker. Do you still want to continue?"

He nodded. "I do."

"Okay, then." She tried to smile but wasn't at all certain it didn't look as pained as she felt. "I'll be waiting for you."

Before she could bid him a weepy farewell, Music and Movement swept through as a gust and a song, whisking Tobek away. Bix laced her hands over her Eternal Knot and drew an unsteady breath. Three's primordial magic blossomed around her in shimmering red starlight. It tickled her palms, then vanished. Card stock of eternal night lay cool against her heart. She stared at the card, bemused as her brain took a few beats to shift gears.

She hadn't asked her brother a question this time, nor was the card one from her deck. However, the back of this card echoed the pattern of the red-and-black box in which she kept her deck. Curious as to what her brother wanted so desperately for her to know, she flipped the card.

The Tarot card of Death.

It was the card of endings and new beginnings. It heralded transformation and transition. Death was usually a skeleton knight upon a pale horse tromping through a battlefield of corpses, carrying the black-and-white banner of thirteen or sometimes a sickle. This Death was her blond bear with his silver arm and a sword of light dripping with black tar astride a beast of green magic trampling a field of Devourers.

She snorted. Snotted. Laughed. First with ruefulness, then with joy. All hail evolution and the surprises that came with it. She couldn't wait to see what this new chapter held for Tobek and for her. One thing was for certain, the Mids were getting a new and improved champion. Things were not going to go well for the Devourers and their invasion.

Other Books
by K.A. Krantz

<u>Urban Fantasy</u>
The Immortal Spy Series:
THE BURNED SPY
THE PLAGUED SPY
THE CAPTURED SPY
The Hanged Spy

<u>High Fantasy</u>
Fire Born, Blood Blessed Series:
LARCOUT

The Exposed Spy
Available Spring 2019

Want to be notified when a new book is released?
Subscribe to K. A. Krantz's email newsletter at
kakrantz.com

If you enjoyed this book, please spread the word and
leave a review with the retailer of your choice.

Acknowledgments

To my family, for their unfailing enthusiasm and support…even when things take longer than anticipated. To Jenn Stark, for reminding me there is a time to dance and a time to pick up a stave. To Linda Ingmanson, my development editor, for insisting emotion live side by side with action. To Toni Lee, my copy editor and fact checker, for reining in my ellipses, em-dashes, and hyphens so this book no longer appears to be written in Morse code. To the team at Gene Mollica Studios for the amazing cover and formatting.

About the Author

KAK splits her time between Cincinnati and the DC 'burbs with her faithful hairy beast. When not writing, she indulges in a shoe obsession, conducts a love/hate affair with paint, and makes epic messes in the kitchen.

Visit her website at kakrantz.com for free flash fiction, blog posts about her latest fancies, and more. If you're on Twitter, she'd love to hear from you. Tweet @KAKrantz.